THE FUTURE OF LONDON

(L-2011, MR APOCALYPSE, GHOSTS OF LONDON)

MARK GILLESPIE

This is a work of speculative fiction, some of it inspired by real people. All of the events and dialogue depicted within are a product of the author's overactive imagination. None of this stuff happened. Except maybe in a parallel universe.

www.markgillespieauthor.com

Cover Art by Vincent Sammy

JOIN THE READER LIST

Keep up to date with Mark Gillespie's new book release news. Join the Official Reader List.

www.markgillespieauthor.com

You can also follow him on ***Bookbub****.*

ALSO BY MARK GILLESPIE

Sleeping Giants (Future of London #4)

Kojiro vs. The Vampire People (Future of London #5)

Black Storm (Exterminators Trilogy #1)

Black Fever (Exterminators Trilogy #2)

Black Earth (Exterminators Trilogy #3)

The Complete FAB Trilogy

For more info on the books

www.markgillespieauthor.com/books

L-2011

For Íde, who always believes.

PHASE ONE: RIOTS

CHAPTER 1

6th August 2011
London, England.

These people weren't his people. Mack Walker knew this much. He certainly didn't know the dead man whose death had brought all these faces – mostly black ones – outside Tottenham Police Station to protest on a Saturday night.

Not for the first time that evening, his shoulder bumped into a young woman standing behind him. Mack glanced over his shoulder, intending to apologise, but the woman didn't bat an eyelid.

The lanky black teenager standing next to him giggled.

"It's no' that funny, eh?" Mack said. His Scottish accent – so mild and inoffensive back in Edinburgh - sounded so alien in London.

"That's four times I've seen you bump into her mate," said the teenager, dressed in a plain black hoodie and baggy navy jeans. "Just ask her for her number, why don't ya? Maybe she likes pasty-faced Scottish lads."

The lanky teenager tipped the visor of his black baseball cap upwards. He turned around and was about to say something to the woman, but Mack forcefully turned him back around with a deft push.

"Aye right Sumo," Mack said. "Don't be a dick, eh?"

Sumo Dave - the only name that Mack had for the lanky teenager - turned back to the front, still giggling away to himself.

"Is that why you asked me to come here anyway?" Mack asked. "To be the half-time entertainment?"

Sumo Dave shrugged. He kept his eyes on the door of the police station as he spoke.

"Felt sorry for you, didn't I?" he said. "You being the new boy in London and all that."

At that moment, a male voice - a booming baritone - yelled out from the front of the crowd:

"We want answers!"

Other voices scattered throughout the crowd, followed his lead.

"We want answers!"

Scattered voices quickly grew into a collective chant. Sumo Dave joined in. Mack stood beside him, mumbling the words only because he felt he had to.

But the door to the police station remained closed.

"Must be at least four hundred people out here, eh?" Sumo Dave said, glancing around.

"Aye," Mack said. "At least."

The light was fading on Tottenham High Road but Sumo Dave's eyes were bright and alert. Of course *he* was excited. He came from that Broadwater Farm Estate shithole like most of the other people gathered here. Sumo Dave might have known the dead man, Mark Duggan, or at least spoken to him at some point in passing. If he had, he hadn't mentioned it to Mack so far, but then why would he? They'd only met a couple of days ago in McDonalds – the same day that Mark Duggan had been shot dead by the police. The same day that Mack and his family had arrived in London.

"We want answers. Somebody come out and speak to us!"

The two lads standing on the other side of Sumo Dave made a valiant but unsuccessful effort to start their own chant.

"Get out here you bastards! Get out here you bastards!"

Sumo Dave had introduced Mack to these two teenagers earlier that evening. They were Sumo's best mates from the estate - Tegz and Hatchet. They were both sixteen, the same age as Mack and Sumo Dave. Tegz was the little one, dressed in baggy jeans and a red t-shirt that was at least two sizes too big. He also wore a matching red baseball cap, which he kept pointed to the side, reminding Mack of Flavor Flav, that old rapper from Public Enemy.

Hatchet - dressed in camouflage jeans and a grey hoodie - was short too, but with massive Herculean shoulders that were somehow unnatural on such a young lad. Indeed, Hatchet already possessed the thick, muscular build of a grown man despite his lack of height. And with his short hair, shaved completely at the sides, Hatchet resembled a young Mike Tyson, back when the boxer was at his most vicious, when he could win a fight just by looking at his opponent.

"Oh fuck this," Tegz said, giving up the chant. He kept turning back and forth, to see if something – anything – was going to happen.

From the front line of protestors, a banner was held aloft.

BLACK LIVES MATTER TOO.

Mack looked around. For the first time, he noticed that the crowd gathered outside the police station consisted of predominantly black women. They were young women too, most of them, many who had brought their children with them to Tottenham High Road, where the police station was located.

"Shame on you!" somebody shouted.

"Fucking police," Tegz said, throwing his hands up in frustration. "Where are they? Why don't they show their faces? Eh?"

"Hang on Tegz," Sumo Dave said. He was standing on his tiptoes now, looking over the crowd and towards the entrance of the police station.

"I think this could be it," he said. "Somebody's coming out."

At that moment, a chorus of jeers emanated from the crowd.

"Can't see fuck all," Hatchet said, standing on his tiptoes, trying to find a chink in the crowd.

"What's happening Sumo?" Tegz asked. "Who is it? I'm too much of a short-arse for this."

Sumo Dave was too busy watching to answer.

Mack jostled for position and managed to find a gap in between the heads of those standing in front of him. He looked down towards the police station, trying to keep up with the action.

A tall, middle-aged man was making his way out of the police station and walking towards the crowd. He was wearing a uniform, but given the elaborate design of the outfit, he was clearly more than just an ordinary police officer. As he walked towards the front line, the policeman looked at the crowd apprehensively. Boos were still coming his way. With a cautious step, he approached a small group of people in the front line.

"So who's that then?" Tegz asked, jumping up and down, trying to keep up.

"Big boss man, innit?" Hatchet said.

"Fucking hope so," Sumo Dave said. "They're hardly gonna send out the cleaner, eh?"

Mack wasn't so sure.

"The big boss man doesn't work in Tottenham Police Station," he said. Again, as he spoke out loud, he heard his accent and was aware of how different he sounded to North Londoners. "This is probably some poor bastard who drew the short straw."

Hatchet looked at Mack like he was a cockroach crawling over the dinner table.

"D'fuck do you know about it Scottish?"

Mack didn't answer.

"That's gotta be the big boss man," Tegz said. "They've snuck him in the back door or something."

"Gotta be someone important," Sumo Dave said. "This is going to be on the news, innit? The police don't want to look like a bunch of cold-hearted tits."

Mack positioned himself a little to the right, in between the heads of another two people. He'd momentarily forgotten his own awkwardness. Now he wanted to see what was going to happen. Would this satisfy the crowd? Would they speak to the man and then walk back home, fall into their armchairs and catch up with Saturday night TV and a drink or two?

The policeman and those standing in the front line, who Mack assumed were Mark Duggan's family, were talking. But the signs weren't good. The policeman kept shaking his head, apologetically and yet stubbornly. Mack heard raised voices. In turn, the Duggan family were shaking their heads and pointing back towards the police station.

"What's happening?" Hatchet said.

"Looks like they're having a barney," Sumo Dave said, grinning. The lanky teenager pulled out his iPhone and turned the video on. He raised it aloft, pointing it towards the action at the front.

"You think it's a sob story?" Tegz asked.

"He'll tell 'em whatever it takes to make us piss off home," Hatchet said. "Last thing he and his mates want are hundreds of black people hanging about outside the station all night, eh?"

"I don't think so," Mack said.

Hatchet didn't look at him. "Fuck off white boy."

"His name's Mack," Sumo Dave said, looking at Hatchet. "And I invited him here so don't be a dick Hatch. Yeah?"

Hatchet shrugged. "Whatever mate."

Sumo Dave was checking out the clips he'd just recorded on his phone. "These are all shit," he said. "It's too dark out here."

Mack pointed to the front. "They're sending him back. They're sending the old boy back."

Sumo Dave looked up, instinctively thrusting his phone into the air. "What? What's going on?"

"He's going back into the station," Mack said. "The family don't look happy down there, do they? I don't think he was important enough to satisfy them."

Sumo Dave grinned. "Big boss man, eh? Bollocks."

"Nice one," Tegz said. "Be a shame if it all ended here, eh?"

The crowd resumed the chanting, unsatisfied by the police response to their presence.

"We want answers! We want answers!"

As time passed, the crowd seemed to be moving closer to the police station. And they continued to chant, calling over and over for a high-ranking officer to come out and speak to the Duggan family about the controversial shooting, which had taken place two nights earlier in nearby Ferry Lane.

"Murderers!"

Soon the last dregs of daylight faded. The police station, a massive red brick Georgian structure with elegant paned windows, became a towering black shadow framed within the dark. From inside the building, office lights poured through windows and onto the High Road, like eyes looking down from above.

Mack took a deep breath. He was thinking about calling it a day. He'd done his bit, hadn't he? Surely he wasn't expected to stand out here all night with these people. After all, he hadn't even known Mark Duggan - jeez, he'd only just moved here. Whatever this was, it wasn't his fight. And then there were his parents to think about. Holy shit. They'd go loopy if they knew he was out here on the street protesting outside the local police station.

His thoughts of leaving were interrupted when the crowd burst into a sudden frenzy of boos and jeers. Mack looked around, trying to see what was going on. Was this yet another low-ranking police officer walking onto the scene? At first, due to the growing darkness, he wasn't sure what was going on.

Then he saw them.

It was the riot police. They were making their way down the

High Road, positioning themselves in between the police station and the crowd.

"Shit," Mack said. "Who called them in?"

There wasn't that many of them – Mack guessed about twenty or thirty at first – but with their protective equipment on, the helmets, the shields, the batons, they looked as if they were expecting - or bringing - trouble.

"This is a peaceful protest," somebody shouted. "What are the riot police doing here?"

"MURDERERS!"

The chants resumed, turning the High Road into a football stadium on a Saturday afternoon.

Sumo Dave tapped furiously at his iPhone. Once he'd found the video camera and pressed record, he hoisted it aloft yet again, pointing it at the riot police.

"I'm filming this," he yelled above the din. "You're going to be on the Internet first thing in the morning!"

Mack watched as some of the crowd, particularly those with young children in tow, backed off, putting distance between themselves and the police station. At the same time, Tegz and Hatchet, like a lot of other young men in the vicinity, pushed their way forward through the crowd. Sumo Dave did likewise, his iPhone still raised over his head.

But Mack held back. The atmosphere had taken a nasty turn, which meant this was as good a time as any to do a runner.

These people weren't his people.

He turned around and squeezed past the protestors standing behind him. And behind those protestors were more people standing on the sidelines, those who had gathered for the sake of having something to do. Too many people, not enough air. Too loud, too much. For a second, Mack almost missed Edinburgh - a place that he couldn't have gotten away from any faster if he tried. But at least there was something comforting in the old familiar, unlike the streets of Tottenham, which were at that moment as unfamiliar and as dangerous to him as the deepest, darkest jungle.

His thoughts turned to Princes Street Gardens on a Saturday afternoon. To standing in the shadow of Edinburgh Castle, near the Gothic Spire of the Scott Monument. The maroon and white buses, driving past The Old Waverley Hotel.

Christ, you sound like a Tour Guide.

Behind him, a furious roar erupted within the crowd. Mack's heart was beating furiously as he turned around slowly, not sure he wanted to see what was going on behind him.

What he saw was the riot police trying to push the crowd further back from the police station. In turn, the crowd were letting them know what they thought about their roughhouse tactics. There was furious hollering of obscenities and much posturing on the part of the younger males in particular. Others continued with the endless booing and jeering.

Mack watched from a distance. Real fucking riots, holy shit. He wanted out of there, but at the same time something kept him from running away. It was like nothing he'd ever seen before. Fascinating and horrifying all at once – the sudden loss of control, like looking through the tiny gaps of civilisation into a gaping black hole.

As the riot police pushed back the crowd, Mack stood perfectly still, feeling the hatred around him growing, as if fuelled by the aggression of the authorities.

The first missile was a rock.

It was hurled at police lines with tremendous force. And then came the second and the third in quick succession.

A bloodcurdling scream.

The riot police thrust their shields out and pushed forwards, moving away from the police station and into the crowd. The protestors did their best to stand their ground, refusing to be pushed back.

Mack watched as more people fled the scene, realising that the peaceful protest was now over. They grabbed hold of their children and held them close, pulling them away from the police station and further along Tottenham High Road.

Mostly, it was crowds of young men facing off against the police now. More missiles were hurled, but these were no longer aimed solely at the riot police themselves. The police station itself had become a target, as were police cars that had the misfortune to be parked nearby.

Mack heard a high-pitched crack, like the sound of glass being smashed. He looked around but couldn't see where it had come from. At the same time, several police vans were pulling up at the side of the police station. Reinforcements. Side doors were flung open and police in riot gear, both to the north and south of the police station, jumped out and quickly went to work. Instructions were yelled out. The voices of the police and protestors were now intermingled in one guttural roar.

Mack looked at his phone. It was 8.44pm. Time to get the hell out of here.

As he turned to run, a hideous wailing sound cut through him. Mack turned to his right, where the scream had come from, and saw a wall of riot police moving towards a section of protestors who were bouncing about furiously like caged animals at feeding time. But as the police closed in on them, many protestors ran away. In fact, nearly all of them did except one young woman – the screamer – who was perhaps no more than a teenage girl. Despite the onslaught of the riot police, this girl alone stood her ground and didn't back off, even when they ploughed into her at full force.

"Fucking hell!" Mack said.

Other witnesses started hurling obscenities at the police.

"It's a girl," someone said. "It's a fucking girl, look how you're dealing with her, it's a fucking girl you cunts!"

One angry young black man pumped a clenched fist in the air. He was lifted up onto the shoulders of his friends and yelled a battle cry into the night.

"GET DEM!"

Mack's head swirled. Where were the others? Sumo Dave, Hatchet and Tegz? Were they in that tangled mess of protestors and police up ahead?

He turned around, looking for a way out. Further ahead on the High Road, about one hundred and fifty metres from the police station, he saw a large crowd descending upon the scene. Where were all these people coming from? More than likely, the trouble had drawn most of them out of their holes, like a predator hearing the cries of a wounded animal. This was their Saturday night action. And they were ready.

As Mack looked on, two parked police cars came under attack from the crowd. Several youths with cloths or bandanas covering their faces, ran up to the vehicles, smashed the windows, and threw at least two Molotov cocktails inside. In a matter of seconds, the streets were drenched in a thick orange glow as the cars were engulfed in flames. But it didn't end there. Mack watched, his mouth hanging open, as the crowds began to push both the blazing vehicles onto the High Road, establishing a barrier between themselves and the riot police who were trying to force them back.

Mack took temporary refuge in a bus shelter on the other side of the street. There were about ten other people crammed under the shelter, watching events unfold from a distance. Mack tucked himself in at the edge of the shelter, still watching as the crowd numbers, swelling with every passing minute, advanced towards the police lines.

Suddenly a police helicopter appeared, circling above the scene. It hovered for a while, before shining a spotlight down onto the crowds on the High Road. Somebody tried to speak through a loud-speaker, but the muffled voice was lost in the racket that was being made on the ground.

Mack watched as a gang of masked figures broke away from the main crowd and started kicking in the front windows of a solicitor's office close to the police station. Behind them, others waited, their hands ready to launch Molotov cocktails through the broken glass.

Moments later, the building was up in flames, just as the two police cars were on the road.

At the sight of the solicitor's office in flames, the crowd roared its approval and encouraged by this success, they pushed back against the oncoming riot police.

The flames in the solicitor's office spread quickly to nearby flats and shops. This must have taken even the protestors by surprise because Mack noticed that people in masks were screaming at the top of their voices to anyone still inside those buildings to get out.

"GET OUT! GET OUT OF YOUR FUCKING HOUSE!"

More police vans arrived, swelling their numbers in response to the energy of the crowd. The police cordon moved forward, a blur of helmets and shields, intent on reclaiming the streets. With a hard push, they forced the crowd back further down the High Road, away from the besieged police station. Now they were winning. But even as the crowd were being forced onto the back foot, missiles - stones, rocks, Molotov cocktails – whatever was available, continued to be thrown at the police lines. And more fires were appearing on the High Road at every second. One nasty looking blaze was lit in a rubbish pile outside a nearby community centre and it caught on quickly to its surroundings.

Mack heard the sound of sirens blaring, coming closer, and the screech of tyres on the road. The first fire engines were arriving on the scene. Mack watched as the firemen leapt out of the vehicle, quickly unrolled their hoses and set about extinguishing the flames.

Nobody on the streets tried to stop them.

Mack remained in the bus shelter throughout, but he didn't feel in any danger. Civilians were under no threat from either the crowd or police. But that didn't mean they could ignore the rapid spread of fire and the roaming missiles, which were still flying overhead.

He looked around.

There was no sign of Sumo Dave, Tegz and Hatchet. Either they'd gotten out or they were in there, mixing it up with the protestors and police.

Not long after the first fire engines had arrived, came the TV news crews. The large vans raced along the High Road and from a distance, Mack saw the huge letters printed on the side of the vans: CBC NEWS. SKAM NEWS. These were the big boys and amongst the first on the scene. Many more would follow.

The police continued to push the protestors further back. And even though the crowds were being overwhelmed in the battle for position on the High Road, they cheered all the way throughout, as if this was one giant carnival or celebration. Amongst the faces of the young men - black, white and brown - there was a look of sheer rapture on their faces. There was no fear of recriminations. No fear of what the law could do to them. In fact, the law couldn't touch them - not tonight, not ever or so it felt in that moment. This alone made it the greatest night of their lives.

Mack left the bus shelter and walked quickly north along the High Road, where there was little sign of trouble. On his way, he turned back for one last look at the action behind him. The riot police were getting the better of the crowd. At last, they were pushing the defiant mob backwards, seemingly at will.

Mack turned away. The noise in his ears faded.

It was over now. The crowd would disperse and a few arrests would be made and at best, the story would merit a day or two in the news headlines.

And in the aftermath, everyone would forget about Mark Duggan.

CHAPTER 2

7th August 2011

www.NewsLeak.com

Riots have broken out after a man was shot dead three days ago in Tottenham, London.

Mark Duggan, 29, was shot by police on Thursday as he travelled in a minicab over the Ferry Lane Bridge. Police had been pursuing Mr Duggan as part of a covert operation and after the minicab was pulled over, officers approached the car intent on making an arrest. For reasons that have not yet been confirmed, marksmen opened fire and Duggan was shot dead. The shooting enraged the local community and two days later, several hundred people from Duggan's home on the Broadwater Farm Estate, marched tc Tottenham Police Station seeking an explanation for the controversial circumstances surrounding his death.

A vigil outside the police station began peacefully but trouble has since escalated and violent outbreaks have been reported across the city. The outbreaks have seen buildings and vehicles set alight, including a double-decker bus, one police van and at least two patrol cars. Shops were also being looted as police in riot gear arrived on the scene.

One local, who declined to give her name said: "The man they shot – he dropped his gun, but they shot him anyway. That's why we're out here tonight. We're not going anywhere. Not until we have justice."

CHAPTER 3

8th August 2011

The CBC News at Six

TV VOICEOVER: It's six o'clock and now it's time for the news with Sophie Wallace.

Cue the staple news theme. As the music blares out of millions of TV screens across the country, we are shown multiple images of inner-city riots and this is followed by an aerial view of a large building on fire.

SOPHIE WALLACE: (*Reading over intro*). Tonight, London is burning. In scenes reminiscent of the Blitz, multiple buildings across the capital are set alight. Rioters have attacked police in Hackney, East London, and the violence has also spread south to Lewisham and Peckham where shops and cars have been set on fire. And these were the scenes in Birmingham today (*the images cut to a gang of masked youths smashing local shop windows with baseball bats*) as the violence spread outside the capital for the first time.

(*Cuts to a stern looking image of the Home Secretary at a press conference. Cameras flash incessantly as she addresses a flock of reporters*)

HOME SECRETARY: Make no mistake about it. There is no excuse for this kind of behaviour. There is no excuse for violence and no excuse for thuggery. And I assure you that those responsible for the looting in London and elsewhere will be made to face the consequences of their actions.

(*Cuts back to scenes of rioting*)

SOPHIE WALLACE: (*Voiceover continued*) And in the last hour it has been confirmed that the Prime Minister will be cutting short his Mediterranean holiday and flying home to attend to the crisis.

The camera cuts to Sophie Wallace sitting at the news desk. Wallace – in her early forties - is the CBC's most popular anchor. Today her shoulder length blonde hair is loose, resting on the shoulders of a light brown jacket. The expression on her face is grim.

SOPHIE WALLACE: Good evening and welcome to the CBC News. It's six o'clock and I'm Sophie Wallace. Serious violence has broken out on the streets of the capital for the third night in a row.

The latest trouble broke out late this afternoon on the streets of Hackney in East London, before spreading further south to Lewisham, Peckham and more recently, Croydon. In Peckham, clothes stores were being looted while others looked on, many filming events as they happened on their mobile phones. In Croydon, at least two double decker buses have been burned and a large furniture store has been ablaze for at least an hour now, as emergency services struggle to cope with the crisis. For our first report this evening, we go to Dick Ronson in Hackney, where the latest wave of violence began this afternoon when police were attacked by rioters with rocks and missiles.

The camera cuts to Dick Ronson. Dick – a longstanding CBC *reporter - is bald-headed except for two thick shocks of black hair on the sides. He's standing in a narrow inner city street, staring at the camera through a pair of thick-framed spectacles. Fresh disturbances are visible in the background – youths running amok, smoke, and the sound of sirens.*

DICK RONSON: Yes Sophie, I'm standing here in the danger zone, amidst a level of crisis not seen in the capital since the days of World War Two. Yes, not since 1945 has the great city of London seemed so vulnerable. Here in Hackney, the disturbances started in the late afternoon as police - who promised to have more officers on the streets after last night - faced off against a massive gathering of rioters who proceeded to throw missiles and bricks into police lines. The Acting Commissioner of the Police, Nigel Whitburn, has tonight made a heartfelt appeal to the public asking for help.

Cuts to a shot of Acting Commissioner of the Met Police standing on podium. Camera lights flashing.

ACTING COMMISSIONER: We have thousands of police officers on duty but we must request the public's help on this matter. I urge parents to contact their children and ask them where they've been and what they're doing. And I would also say that there are far too many spectators out there getting in the way of police operations, many of them filming on mobile phones. This is a nuisance and an obstacle to important police business. Please, parents, spectators and anyone else who can, help us to clear the streets so that my police officers can best deal with the criminality that we're witnessing today. We can fix this. But we need your help.

The camera cuts back to Dick Ronson. Standing beside him now is a twenty-something Asian man, smiling happily into the camera - in stark contrast to Ronson's grim countenance.

DICK RONSON: I'm here now with a young man, Sayaar Laham, a young international student living here in London. Sayaar, you've been on the streets like many amateur filmmakers today, filming some of these shocking scenes.

SAYAAR LAHAM: (*Smiling*) I was, yes.

From behind Ronson and Sayaar, shouts of 'alcohol, let's get alcohol' can be heard in the background where a gang of youths sit atop a white transit van.

DICK RONSON: Tell me Sayaar, with all these random acts of

violence and the looting of people's businesses going on, have you ever seen such a shocking disregard for human life?

SAYAAR LAHAM: Yes. Actually I have.

DICK RONSON: I'm sorry Sayaar, you said yes? Do you understand what I'm saying?

SAYAAR LAHAM: Yes I do. I come from Pakistan. I'm used to this.

DICK RONSON: You're used to this? To *this*?

SAYAAR LAHAM: (*Smiling*) Oh yes. Ahh my beloved Karachi. I'm quite used to this - gunshots, rioting, cars burning and the smell of fear. How can I not be reminded of my beloved Pakistan?

DICK RONSON: But Sayaar, this is London. This is not Karachi – with all due respect – or the West Bank or Syria.

SAYAAR LAHAM: It is surreal, I admit. But I am not afraid for London.

DICK RONSON: But it's a *crisis* Sayaar.

SAYAAR LAHAM: No, no, no. It is not. I read on the Internet today that almost two thousand police officers have been deployed. Plenty of arrests have already been made. People will eventually be prosecuted for these crimes. And London will move on. You are lucky because you have the resources to heal, unlike so many other countries.

DICK RONSON: Clearly you're not shocked Sayaar.

SAYAAR LAHAM: You should be relieved that you *are* shocked Mr Ronson. Pray to Allah that you never become accustomed to such things. In Pakistan, we have no choice but to inoculate ourselves against fear and violence.

DICK RONSON: I understand, but this -

SAYAAR LAHAM: This is London, yes. And it's a crisis. Buildings will burn, but they burn in other parts of the world too. This is no more disturbing than when it happens in Baghdad or Karachi.

DICK RONSON: Sayaar, you're taking this very well. You almost look happy.

SAYAAR LAHAM: Oh I'm very relieved today. That's the right word – relieved.

Ronson's face turns an angry shade of pink.

DICK RONSON: Relieved? How can you be relieved with all this going on?

SAYAAR LAHAM: Because for once it isn't the Muslim community being demonised. We're always the villains – but not today.

DICK RONSON: Uhhh...thank you Sayaar. I think we'd better leave it there.

SAYAAR LAHAM: (*Smiling again*) Thank you Dick.

Dick Ronson turns back to the camera.

DICK RONSON: Now in a development that will alarm both politicians and police, today the trouble has spread outside the capital for the first time. In Birmingham, vandals and looters were out in force in the city centre. It's believed that as with here in London, social media has played a massive part in the spread of information and police are warning that anyone inciting violence through social networking sites will face prosecution.

Sayaar can be heard giggling off-camera.

DICK RONSON: This is Dick Ronson, CBC News, on the war-torn streets of Hackney.

CHAPTER 4

8th August 2011

Mack Walker sat on the edge of the armchair. He stared blankly at the flat screen TV in the corner of the living room, not so much listening to words of the reporters, but instead being pulled in by the images.

Endless rows of shop windows had been smashed in - people's homes and businesses - and plumes of smoke billowing out of cars and buildings. It was everywhere. And to think he'd been there at the start of it. It was enough to make him feel like an accomplice to the rest of it.

Hard to believe that was London on the TV, and not somewhere in the Middle East.

On the other side of the living room, Mack's parents sat on the black leather couch, seemingly as transfixed as he was by what they were seeing on the CBC News.

"For God's sake," Archie Walker said. He ran a hand slowly

through his thinning brown hair. "Mindless bloody thuggery, that's all it is."

Isabella Walker sat on the opposite end of the couch from her husband.

"Oh my God," she said, shaking her head. "All those poor people and their livelihoods ruined and because of what?"

"They're protesting," Mack said. He regretted saying it immediately.

Isabella turned towards her son. A moment ago she'd looked tired and on the verge of falling asleep after making dinner for the family. Now her eyes were wide open and her tawny hair – the colour that she'd passed onto her only son – was tied back behind her head.

"Protesting?" she said. "By hurting innocent people?"

Archie Walker sat forward, reaching for his cup of coffee on the living room table. He brought it to his lips and blew into the steaming cup.

Isabella kept her eyes on Mack. "What are they protesting then?"

Mack shook his head. "A young guy got killed last week Mum. The police are trying to cover it up, I think."

Isabella started to laugh, but stopped almost immediately.

"And what exactly does running out of a shop with a box of trainers, or a mobile phone, or a flat screen TV, what does robbing from ordinary working people do to help that situation?"

Mack didn't answer. But what he wanted to say was – *okay so they may not give a flying fuck about why the police shot Mark Duggan. I know that –we all know that, right? But look at them! Mum? It's exciting, isn't it? It's not just another boring day in the land of Normal. That's got to be worth something.*

"Isn't that absolutely ridiculous?" Archie bellowed. He was pointing at the TV.

Mack and Isabella both turned back to the news. Aerial shots of the city and the damage done were being broadcast to maximum effect. Mack felt the chicken and peppercorn sauce he'd just eaten doing somersaults in his stomach. From the air, it looked as if London was under attack. Scattered across the city, several prominent buildings - including the huge Carpetright furniture building in Tottenham - burned as if this was another Blitzkrieg. Clouds of thick black smoke climbed out of the wreckage and made towards the sky.

"What will you tell people at work tomorrow?" Isabella asked Archie.

Archie shook his head as he took a sip of coffee. "They can work at home," he said. "We're too close to the High Road to risk people travelling into the office. They can work at home till this is sorted."

"That's a shame," Isabella said, reaching for her own cup of coffee.

Archie shrugged. "It's a graphic design company. Graphic designers can work at home too. Better that than risking getting hurt, isn't it?"

Isabella nodded. "This wouldn't have happened in Edinburgh, would it?" she said.

"No," Archie said.

Mack sighed. Loud enough so that they could hear him. "We didn't *have* to move here," he said.

Isabella looked at him. "Oh Mack," she said. "Of course we had to move. You know very well we couldn't have stayed up there, not after what happened."

Mack shrugged. "But why Tottenham? It's a shithole."

Isabella raised her eyebrows. "*Language.*"

Archie put the coffee cup back down the table and fell into the black leather couch, putting a hand over his contented stomach.

"This was the best transfer the company could get me," Archie said. "That's all there is to it. Tottenham was the quickest way out of Edinburgh. And besides, I never knew the bloody place was going to riot, did I?"

Isabella poked her husband on the leg. "You mind your language too," she said, smiling.

Archie Walker grinned. He pulled the sleeves of his sweatshirt back and then reached out for his wife's hand.

"At least you're not out there Mack," Isabella said, taking her husband's hand. "There's that to be thankful for."

Mack nodded, inhaling the pungent aroma of coffee in the air.

Archie looked over at his son. "What about that friend of yours?" he said. "The Sumo wrestler guy. Or whatever his name is."

"Sumo Dave," Mack said. "What about him?"

Archie pointed at the TV. "You think he's out there?"

"Dave?" Mack said.

"That's the one."

Mack shook his head. "Why? Because he's black?"

Isabella shook her head. "That's not what your father meant."

"You said he was from the Broadwater Farm Estate, that's all," Archie said. "I was just wondering if he knew Mark Duggan."

"I don't know," Mack said. "I've only known him a few days."

"Fair enough," Archie said.

"You'll need to bring him round for dinner one night," Isabella said. "It'd be nice to meet your new friends down here."

Mack nodded and smiled.

Sure Mum. I'm not stupid you know. You want to meet my friends, don't you? To see who I'm hanging around with. Can't blame you for that.

"Okay," Mack said. But he knew it would never happen.

Mack sat back, and like his father, put a hand over his full stomach. He hadn't seen or heard from Sumo Dave since Saturday night. Maybe Sumo Dave hadn't taken the new boy under his wing after all. Maybe it was just for a couple of days, or maybe that grumpy fuckwit Hatchet had persuaded Sumo to drop him.

Not that Mack needed friends. But it would be easier to know people before school started in September. He didn't want to be *that* boy – the one that got picked last for every group project.

"Jesus Christ!"

Archie Walker was shouting at the TV again. The news had finished and now - in place of scheduled programming - a CBC documentary on the riots was showing. Archie's reaction had coincided with a scene in which seven or eight masked youths could be seen smashing their way through the window of a newsagent in Croydon. Once they'd made the opening, the looters stormed inside, emptying the premises of its stock, mostly cigarettes and fizzy drinks.

"That's a great advert for the London Olympics next year," Isabella said. She was shaking her head again.

"Ach don't worry," Archie said. "It'll blow over in a couple of days. A week or two from now, it'll all be forgotten."

Isabella shivered and buttoned up the pink cardigan that she had on. She leaned towards her husband, resting her head on his shoulder.

"It's time the Government did something about this," she said.

Archie's gaze never left the TV. The documentary was now cutting between various shots of masked gangs running rampant across the city – looting and starting fires.

"Look at them," he said. "They're like a pack of wild dogs chasing a car. They've no idea what they're doing."

Isabella nodded.

On the other side of the room, Mack leaned forward in the armchair, his eyes never leaving the TV screen. It was as if something was pulling him, beckoning him forwards into the violent images. And it had little to do with Mark Duggan and the desire for revenge or justice or anything like that. Mark Duggan was a good excuse, but he wasn't the reason.

'On every street in every city of this country there's a nobody who dreams of being a somebody.'

Mack recalled the tagline of his favourite movie. Martin Scorsese's *Taxi Driver*, a film he'd seen more times than he could count.

He sat there, half-watching the TV, half-thinking about a way to get back out there onto the streets. As he did so, he caught sight of his mother watching him over the rim of her coffee cup.

CHAPTER 5

8th August 2011

FIXX News Channel

After a brief commercial, the camera cuts back to the FIXX News studios, where veteran anchor Dan Cunningham is behind the desk. Cunningham smiles into the camera, flashing the pearly white teeth and clean-cut good looks that have made him such a housewives favourite over the years.

DAN CUNNINGHAM: Going back to the London riots now and joining me in the studio is our very own FIXX National Security Analyst, Kit McAdam. Kit, thanks for coming in.

The camera cuts to a handsome middle-aged woman, sitting alongside Dan at the desk. She's dressed in a sleek red business suit and her hair is jet black with a blue sheen.

KIT MCADAM: My pleasure Dan.

DAN CUNNINGHAM: Now Kit, I think we're all struggling to understand how this kind of thing can happen in a civilised city like London. I believe you have some interesting insights for us - particularly into how the rioters are communicating with one another?

KIT MCADAM: Yes. There are a couple of things going on here Dan. First of all, we've got a bunch of out of control kids. They're high-school age. Some of them are even primary school age – as young as ten years old. They're a mob – it's called a flash mob and they're communicating with each other with cellphones.

DAN CUNNINGHAM: They're using cellphones to keep each other informed of hotspots and where to go?

KIT MCADAM: Right. They're using Blackberry Messenger, as well as Facebook and Twitter to a lesser extent. They're coming from a lot of different places and they meet up somewhere - a store or whatever - and there's just so many of them that the police are overwhelmed. They break into stores and steal flat screen TV's, trainers, mobile phones and whatever else they can get their hands on.

DAN CUNNINGHAM: But what about the arson attacks? Why are they burning everything down?

KIT MCADAM: Yes, well that's the next step. It's getting out of control, it's escalating to a new level – there's no social order in these communities and it's spreading because there's no consequence to their actions. These kids don't think they're going to get in trouble.

DAN CUNNINGHAM: What I want to know is – the parents?? Where are they? If your twelve-year-old child comes home with a flat screen TV one day, don't you say – *hey where'd you get that son?*

KIT MCADAM: You'd think so, wouldn't you?

DAN CUNNINGHAM: And you mention the role of social media and technology in general. Could you talk a little more about that?

KIT MCADAM: Yes Dan. Blackberry Messenger is the popular choice here when it comes to coordinating action. This is a closed system and much less of a public forum than say Twitter and Facebook, where it's easier for authorities to access information. The thing about BBM is that it's extremely efficient and secure. BBMs are private and encrypted during transmissions and I'm sure many of the rioters are aware of this. That's not to say it's completely beyond law enforcement, but it's tough to do anything about it in the heat of the moment.

DAN CUNNINGHAM: Are Blackberry at fault here Kit?

KIT MCADAM: Well, I think it's important to remember that Blackberry didn't design BBM with teenagers in mind. Blackberry's original target was business people, not teenagers. And it's important for these business people - while sending confidential information - to have security. Nobody really thought that young people would have taken to Blackberry like this, but it's not surprising because compared to other forms of technology, it's a cheap way to communicate.

DAN CUNNINGHAM: But you mentioned that it's not beyond law enforcement? The authorities could still get access to these encrypted messages?

KIT MCADAM: (*Sighs*) It's very complex Dan. The manufacturers of Blackberry will find it difficult to do anything here because BBM users are entitled to privacy and in order to identify criminal activity - that would involve searching messages. To do that without the proper authorisation is unlawful and could get the manufacturers into trouble.

DAN CUNNINGHAM: And what about Twitter and Facebook? Are they coordinating these riots too?

KIT MCADAM: No, I don't think they're as important here. Some people have tried to use Facebook to coordinate and publicise riots in various cities and towns across the UK. But it's much easier for the authorities to clamp down on social media activities. That's the difference between the likes of Facebook and BBM.

DAN CUNNINGHAM: And of course, we want to say that it's not all bad. People are using Twitter and Facebook for good purposes too, aren't they?

KIT MCADAM: That's right Dan. Social media is also being used to coordinate and publicise for the sake of good. There are sites calling for the public to back the police and we mustn't forget those who are trying to help the situation by organising clean-ups in their local communities.

DAN CUNNINGHAM: And even the police can use social media to their advantage, can't they?

KIT MCADAM: That's right. Particularly on image-based sites such as Flickr. The police can distribute CCTV images on these sites in the hope that members of the public can identify suspects.

DAN CUNNINGHAM: I guess the message here is that we're not blaming technology for the riots.

KIT MCADAM: (*Shaking her head*) Of course not. It's wrong to simply demonise technology and social media because of their ability to spread the riots. That's not the problem. Social media is not the root cause of these riots. Technology is always neutral and unfortunately, that makes it all about people.

DAN CUNNINGHAM: Kit, as always, thank you very much. It's nice to see you.

KIT MCADAM: Nice to see you too Dan.

CHAPTER 6

9th August 2011

Must have been a skinny fucking King.

That was Mack's first impression as he set foot onto the grand-sounding Kings Road. With a name like that, he'd been expecting to find something a bit special - at the very least a main road with some posh houses and flash cars parked on either side of the street. In other words, the kind of place you wouldn't expect to see in Tottenham.

It sure wasn't up to much.

Kings Road - the actual road itself - looked as if it had been squeezed in between both sides of the pavement. Such a narrow road and at best, it was a mere afterthought or balls-up in the construction process. One side of Kings Road was covered in parked cars for as far as the eye could see, taking up more space, and only contributing to the inherent claustrophobia of the place.

Kings Road. Good joke.

Mack walked further down the narrow street. He passed a quaint row of brown brick houses, walked under a bridge, and saw something up ahead that might have been the building he was looking for. He passed some more parked cars, his route shadowed all the way by a short stretch of wood panel fencing to the left. A couple of minutes later, he found himself standing outside the austere red brick of Lancasterian Primary School.

It was a grim looking building – an uncertain combination of flat and gable roofs, paned windows and the ubiquitous red bricks. It was like something out of a Charles Dickens novel, somewhere he could envision orphaned children being sent into a life of toil and premature misery.

School was closed for summer and there were no signs of life behind the tall black fence that guarded the building. Mack took a look around, his eyes wandering the immediate surroundings. He could see the backs of houses from neighbouring streets. If anyone was standing at their windows, they could see him too. What would prying eyes think if they saw a teenager climbing over the fence and jumping down into the school grounds? How long until the police sirens came his way?

Mack turned back to face the school and put his foot on the horizontal strip of metal that ran along the base of the fence. He looked to the sky and pushed his body upwards. On the first attempt, his outstretched hand missed the tip of the fence and he fell backwards onto the pavement.

God, I hope nobody was watching that.

Mack tried again. All he had to do was reach the tip of the fence and pull his legs over, but gaining enough distance from the ground to grab onto the top was proving difficult. He tried again. Each time he fell back onto the concrete.

"Fuck sake!"

With each new failure, he was convinced that the surrounding neighbours were gathering at their windows, on the brink of calling the police to report the 'rioter' who was trying to set fire to the primary school next door.

Mack felt beads of sweat gathering on his forehead. He stared at the black fence.

The fucker. It wasn't going to beat him.

He was about to try again, but stopped.

There *were* sirens coming. Somebody had called the police after all.

That was all the motivation he needed. This time, he gave it everything and hurled his lean frame up and hooked a hand over the tip of the metal fence. With his feet dangling about a foot off the ground, he thrust a leg over the side. He got the second leg over and with his backside resting atop the fence, jumped down into the school grounds, close to where the staff car parking spaces were.

His heart was pounding. How long did he have?

The sirens were already fading into the distance.

Mack looked towards the windows of nearby houses. There was no one there - no neighbourhood watchman of the year rubbing his hands together. No smug grin on his face, waiting for the police to come and catch the bloody little yobbo.

Wherever the police were going in a hurry, it wasn't to Lancasterian Primary School.

"Idiot," Mack said in a low voice. Still, he'd conquered the fence. Turned out all he'd needed was a little kick-start.

Next up, the world.

He walked past the parking bay, taking a left turn at the rear of the school. At last he was out of sight of Kings Road.

At the narrow edge of the building, he saw the place where Sumo Dave, Tegz, and Hatchet were sitting. Sumo and Tegz had their backs propped up against the red brick wall. Hatchet sat across from them. Mack saw the three teenagers before they saw him. As he approached, they were pulling various items out of their rucksacks, passing them back and forth, and examining them. At the sound of Mack's footsteps, the three teenagers looked up at the same time, their eyes wide, almost fearful.

"It's cool," Mack said. "Only me."

Sumo Dave grinned as the other two made themselves comfortable again. "Found it then?" he said.

Mack nodded. "Piece of piss."

He noticed that Sumo Dave was wearing a fresh-looking dark hoodie with a Nike Jordan baseball cap on the top, its visor pulled up over his forehead.

"Been shopping?" Mack said.

Sumo Dave smiled. "Nice bit of new gear, eh?"

Tegz was grinning beside Sumo. His new hoodie had horizontal black and white stripes. On his head, he wore a plaid beige and black Burberry cap – turned to the side. In terms of fashion it was a car crash, but it made the little man happy.

"It's like you say mate," Tegz said, his voice cracking with excitement. "Shopping. Retail therapy. Does wonders for the poor black man's soul."

Hatchet laughed. It was the first time Mack had heard Little Tyson laugh. It sounded like a little kid chuckling with delight while stomping bugs on the street. Hatchet wore a brand new navy blue puffa jacket over his black hoodie. His buzz cut, which was shaved to the bone at the sides, was the only head - apart from Mack's - not buried underneath a baseball cap. Mack had already heard Hatchet say a couple of times that he didn't like wearing caps because he liked people to look him in the eyes when he was talking.

Tough guy.

Mack slid his back down the wall, sitting next to Sumo Dave. The others continued pulling items out of the bin bags, which had been stashed in their rucksacks.

Mack thrust his hands into his pockets. "What you lads had been up to then?" It was a stupid question, but he said it anyway. "Haven't heard much lately."

Sumo Dave gave him a friendly nudge. "Oh yeah sorry about that mate," he said. "It's just that, well, we'd only just met you, eh? Didn't know if you'd be cool with all this."

Mack nodded. "It's cool. I get it."

Sumo gestured at the assembled goodie bags. "Yeah? You're cool?"

"Aye," Mack said. "Totally. So you boys were in on the fun then? Lucky bastards."

Sumo Dave gave him the thumbs up. "Oh we're knee-deep in crazy shit mate." He went back to rummaging through the bin bags. "Been inside every bloody shop on the High Road, eh? Bargain hunters, that's us mate."

Tegz pulled out a bag of Rizla from his back pocket, followed by a small plastic bag, which Mack saw was nearly half-full with weed.

"What a buzz," he said to Mack, pulling the skins of out the Rizla packet. "It's like the coppers don't exist anymore mate. Take what you want and run."

At that moment, Hatchet pulled out a pair of pink and white Reeboks from one of the bin-bags. Going by the look on his face, he might as well have pulled out a bloated rat corpse.

"What the fuck is this?" he said. "Fucking women's shoes. Who lifted these?"

Sumo Dave burst out laughing. "That's your bag, innit precious!"

Hatchet threw the box to the side. "Shut it, fat fuck," he said. Mack had heard Tegz and Hatchet insult Sumo Dave - who was anything but fat – by calling him a fat fuck a few times now.

Must be a London thing.

Hatchet pulled a flick knife from the back pocket of his jeans and cut into the pink fabric, slicing through like it was a slab of soft butter. An unpleasant tearing sound ripped the air as the shoes were slowly massacred.

Hatchet grinned. "Fucking useless things anyway," he said. He threw the shoe corpse away and went looking inside another bag.

Mack wanted to tell Hatchet that he could have sold the shoes. That he could have made some money instead of slicing them up and throwing them away. But it was too late now and he decided against saying anything.

Sumo Dave and Tegz ignored Hatchet's tantrum. Tegz had abandoned the half-built joint he'd been working on and was now rummaging through another bin bag. He pulled out several small packages and spread them out in front of Sumo Dave. Mack leaned in for a closer look.

"You got phones?" he said.

Tegz didn't look up. "Yeah," he said. "Didn't you hear? There was a sale on at Currys."

Sumo Dave looked at the assembled haul. "We got four iPhones and three Blackberry Bolds."

"Not bad," Mack said.

"Better than a pair of pink trainers," Tegz said. "Innit Hatch?"

Hatchet scowled. "Fuck off dickhead."

"There's a spare iPhone if you want it Mack?" Sumo Dave said. He pushed one of the boxes towards Mack.

"What?" Hatchet said. He jumped to his feet and grabbed the box before Mack could touch it.

"Fuck that," Hatchet said, stepping back. "He's already got one. We took all the risks and you're giving our loot away to a fucking rich kid?"

Sumo Dave didn't blink. "Got a problem with that Hatch?" he said. "I lifted these, remember?"

Sumo Dave reached over and grabbed the phone out of Hatchet's hand. Once again, he offered it to Mack.

"Want it?" he said.

Hatchet sat back down, shaking his head in disgust. "Fuck me," he mumbled.

Mack stared at the package in Sumo's hand. It was a brand new iPhone 4. But even as he looked at the box, feeling the desire to take it, he was well aware that he was already carrying the same phone in his pocket.

He shook his head. "I've already got one mate," he said. "Thanks anyway though."

"So what?" Sumo Dave said, still offering him the slim package. "Take this one and sell it. Get yourself a few quid for that."

Mack hesitated.

"He doesn't want it," Hatchet said.

Tegz looked at Mack. "Take it," he said.

Mack shook his head and stared at the rest of the loot. "Tell you what though Sumo," he said. "I wouldn't mind a Blackberry. Got one of those spare?"

Sumo Dave laughed. "No can do mate," he said. "There's only three of those and we need 'em to keep in the loop with what's happening. You know? This is how we found out where the action is."

Mack nodded. "Aye sure. No bother mate."

Sumo Dave looked at Mack. He scratched at his top lip, where a hint of dark fluff was trying to grow.

"Hey. Why don't you come with us tonight?"

Mack felt his muscles twitch nervously and he sat bolt upright. "Me?" he said. "But I thought you said - "

Sumo Dave grinned. "I trust ya mate. You're a good sort."

"Cheers Sumo," Mack said.

Sumo Dave shrugged. "Yeah we're thinking about going south of the river later. According to Blackberry, it's kicking off big time in Croydon again tonight."

Mack smiled. "Aye?"

"Oh yeah," Sumo Dave said, rubbing his hands together. "You up for a little excitement? Grab yourself a nice Blackberry while everything's going free."

Tegz leaned in closer. "Police ain't doing nothing mate," he said. "If that's what you're worried about it. On the streets, we outnumber them ten to one. At least, eh Hatch?"

"Easy money," Hatchet said.

Sumo Dave nudged Mack in the ribs. "So what do you say mate?"

Mack smiled. It was a challenge.

Are you one of us?

"Aye," he said. "I'm in."

Sumo Dave leaned over and put an arm on Mack's shoulder. "Didn't doubt you for a minute mate," he said.

"Cool," Mack said. Archie and Isabella need never know what he was up to.

"Oh yeah, I nearly forgot," Sumo Dave said. He was scrolling on his other iPhone now, the one he already had up and running. "Did you see this bloke who's turned up on the Internet?"

"What bloke?" Mack said.

Above the school, a flicker of sunlight crept through the clouds.

"Chester George," Sumo Dave said.

"Chester George?"

Sumo Dave was nodding as he swiped the phone screen. "You should see this mate," he said. "This guy is off the fucking wall, off the planet. He's like a poet or something - a spokesman for the rioters. At last."

"He posted a video on YouTube last night," Tegz said. "He's already got over half a million hits."

"Chester George?" Mack said again.

Tegz pointed at the iPhone in Sumo Dave's hand. "Not his real name, is it?" he said. "What does it matter? Go on, watch it."

Sumo Dave handed the phone to Mack. A video clip was ready to play.

CHAPTER 7

Transcript of a video uploaded to YouTube.com (posted on 8th *August 2011*)

The video begins with a message displayed in bold black letters on a white screen. Music is playing in the background – 'Anarchy in the UK' by The Sex Pistols.

"all is creation, all is change, all is flux, all is metamorphosis."

The message fades and the film cuts to a dark figure standing in an empty room - empty except for the sprawling walls, which are smothered in music posters celebrating the classic punk rock era - The Sex Pistols, The Clash, The Slits, The Damned, and more. The dark figure steps into the light and the broad shoulders suggest a male with a stocky build. He's wearing a short black zipper skull hoodie. It's a hoodie that zips all the way to the tip of his forehead, so that his face is covered by a luminous yellow skull design. Dark eyes look out through a gap in the fabric - two small circles of black netting, which reveal only a hint of the man underneath the mask.

He stares into the camera for almost a full minute before speaking. And when he does, his voice is low and raspy, and the words are staggered. He talks like a man struggling for breath.

"Ladies and Gentleman of London town.

My name is Chester George.

What's been happening in this city over the last couple of days - this is the rain that's long overdue. And not just a gentle downpour either - no what's coming to London town is a flood of Biblical proportions. It's the same downpour that Travis Bickle once fantasised about - the 'real rain' that would come and wash the scum off the New York sidewalk.

It's here, right now, today. Human rain.

You've watched the news. You've heard the lies and how they're calling it a 'riot.'

You and I call this an opportunity.

It's an opportunity to get rid of the parasites that for so long, we have let run and ruin our country. You all know who these parasites are - you see them everyday wearing a suit and tie and a mask of a different kind. They call themselves 'good and honest citizens'. And they talk about making our country a better place to live, but all they really want is to hurt the poor and to frighten people into thinking that we need them.

But listen to this.

The British government are a gang of lying bastards. You know this, don't you?"

Chester George takes a step closer. In the background, Anarchy in the UK starts over again, as if playing on a loop.

"But knowing isn't enough anymore.

You've tried political campaigning, haven't you? You've tried online petitioning and marching down the street in hundreds and thousands on protest marches. You've done everything to avoid bloodshed, haven't you? Because there has to be a realistic alternative to violence.

Not for the likes of us.

You know it isn't working. You're sick of this constant stream of everyday disappointments because the system doesn't work for the likes of you and I.

Slowly - very slowly, a profound truth has come to you.

Change. You have to take it.

These are your 'riots'. This is something that deep down in your heart, you've always dreamed of, but never thought you'd live to see. This is the great antidote to the sick times you live in - this, your age of anxiety and productivity-obsessiveness. Think about it. What do they teach you when you're young? To Work. Produce. Work. Produce. *They* want you to integrate into *their* society and work the machines.

They crush your dreams.

You are taught to worry about the future. About careers, about money – you *must* have them. You must have a car – two cars and children, because that's what everyone else is doing.

God help you brothers and sisters.

All across this city, people are waking up. Take to the streets and join them. Oh yes, some people will call you names – thug, vandal, criminal, looter, and all kinds of petty narrow-minded insults. Because that's what happens when you refuse to be a cog in their twisted machine. YOU become the problem.

I want to read you a quote by the philosopher, Alan Watts.

'The working inhabitants of a modern city are people who live inside a machine to be batted around by its wheels. They spend their days in activities which largely boil down to counting and measuring, living in a world of rationalised abstraction which has little or no

relation to or harmony with the great biological rhythms and processes.'

It's time to wake up.

But be careful, because when you wake up, they'll want to kill you. Waking up is a threat to their big fat bank accounts, to their three holidays a year and to their luxury cars and chubby bejewelled fingers.

They will portray *us* as devils. Because as devils themselves, they can't let anyone know the truth. There is nothing more deadly than the devil in a sharp suit.

But you and I know better. *We*, not them, are the real good and honest citizens.

And so I say this to you – the good and honest citizens of London Town.

Here is something we can do to change the world. Let there be no fear and no going back.

If dying is the only way to save your soul, then choose to die."

Clip ends.

CHAPTER 8

9th August 2011

Sumo Dave, Tegz, and Hatchet stood on the platform, waiting for the Tube to take them on the first leg of their journey from Tottenham Hale to Croydon in South London.

Mack held back a little, keeping his distance until he was done talking on the phone.

"I'd prefer you at home Mack," Isabella Walker said on the other end of the line. "Your dad and I would feel a lot better."

Mack pushed the phone against his ear.

"Mum, I'm just hanging out at Sumo Dave's place," he said. "I won't be out on the streets or anything like that."

He could just picture the scene back home. His mum sitting at the kitchen table, looking at the television on the kitchen counter as it showed more scenes from the riots. Biting her fingernails. Looking at the clock.

"But they're burning half the city down Mack," Isabella said. "You should be here. With us."

"Mum, I'm trying to make friends. Don't make it any harder."

He heard his mother sigh down the line. "Oh. I'm not sure Mack."

"Mum, I'm going to be playing video games and having dinner with his mum. Indoors."

Bullshit.

Isabella Walker was silent. But not completely so – Mack could hear the steady, rhythmic breathing of his mother. He could hear the worry in her heart. As his dad delighted in pointing at every opportunity, that breathing noise was the sound Isabella made when she was thinking.

"Phone me in a couple of hours," she said. "And don't you dare try walking home. Let us know when you're ready and we'll come and get you. Okay?"

"Okay Mum. Thanks."

Mack heard a faint rumble in the distance. The train was coming.

"I'd better go," he said, before she heard this for herself. 'I'll speak to you later, okay?"

"Take care son. Have a good night and don't forget to phone me."

"Right. Bye Mum."

And with that, Mack hung up the phone and ran towards the platform. The train was just pulling in at the station as he reached the others. Sumo Dave gave him a curt nod.

"All set?" Sumo asked.

Mack nodded. "Aye."

Sumo Dave rubbed his hands together in anticipation. "Good. 'Cos this is going to blow your fucking mind."

They were on their way. They were going to Croydon, a place that only the previous evening had been described on the news as a 'war-zone'.

The four boys sat in pairs directly opposite one another. Mack and Tegz on one side and Sumo Dave and Hatchet on the other. The three boys from 'The Farm' were still wearing the clothes they'd looted from Tottenham High Road on the night before. And they were all carrying a rucksack each, empty now that the previous evening's loot had been stashed in Sumo Dave's flat.

Mack wasn't exactly dressed for rioting. He was wearing a pair of cream chinos and a plain black t-shirt that exposed his pale forearms, one of which displayed a striking two-inch scar near the wrist. He didn't have a jacket or a hoodie or anything to cover his face with.

Who goes out looting in a pair of chinos?

He'd expressed his concern to Sumo Dave about a lack of disguise on his part. Sumo Dave told him that he'd sort it and not to worry. That was good enough for Mack.

Sumo Dave leaned forward in his seat.

"Where'd you tell your folks you were going?" he asked.

Hatchet sniggered. "What a pussy," he said.

Sumo Dave jabbed an elbow into Hatchet's ribs. "Shut it Hatch," he said. "Just because your mum don't give a shit."

Hatchet fell back into his seat.

"I told them I was at your place," Mack said to Sumo Dave. "Sampling some of your old dear's Jamaican home cooking."

Sumo Dave let out a high-pitched shriek of laughter. At this, some of the other people sitting in the carriage looked their way.

"What the fuck mate?" Sumo Dave said in between giggles. "My mum can't even do a slice of toast without setting the room on fire. You might as well jump in front of a train and have done with it. Be a quicker death than eating something that woman made."

Tegz was laughing as he scrolled down the screen of his new iPhone.

"Nice one Sumo," he said.

"I'm serious Dave," Mack said. His face was like stone. "If you ever talk to my parents - "

Sumo Dave let out another shriek-laugh, bouncing up and down as if he was having a seizure.

"Sumo," Mack said, edging forward on his seat. "Fuck sake mate."

Sumo Dave held up his hands. Gradually, he pulled himself together. "Alright Mack," he said. "It's cool. It's just the thought of my mum in the kitchen making a civilised meal. Before he left, my dad used to say she'd need a map to find the bloody kitchen."

He wiped a tear from his eyes.

Mack leaned back in his seat. He looked around the rest of the train. Despite the fact that it was almost rush hour, the train was practically empty. There were a few bodies scattered throughout the carriage, but not what you'd expect at this time on a working weekday.

"Can we stop talking about his fucking parents?" Hatchet said. "Bunch of fucking babies."

Mack shook his head. But he said nothing.

Sumo Dave gave Hatchet another nudge. "Ooooh! Somebody's grumpy, eh? Time of the month is it love?"

Tegz grinned. "He's got a sore vagina, bless him."

"Fuck off," Hatchet said.

The journey took longer than Mack expected. All in all, it was just short of an hour from Tottenham to Croydon. From Tottenham Hale, they travelled on the Victoria line for about twenty minutes to Victoria Station. And after a brief wait on the Victoria platform above ground, it was another twenty minutes on the East Grinstead route to East Croydon.

Outside East Croydon station, the first thing Mack noticed was the number of young men loitering on the streets.

The four teenagers from Tottenham walked in a westerly direction along George Street. Considering the trouble that had occurred in Croydon on the night before, the streets were surprisingly calm.

The shadowy figures hovering on the sidelines however, suggested that this mood wouldn't last. But at that moment, as the boys walked towards the town centre, there were no visible plumes of smoke on the horizon and cars still filled the roads.

Darkness bled slowly over Croydon. A thick blanket of grey settled in the skies above the town. The road gradually emptied of car headlights and the surrounding buildings seemed to have switched off entirely, perhaps trying to make themselves invisible in the night.

As the boys walked towards the town centre, Sumo Dave, Tegz, and Hatchet, began wrapping bandanas around their faces. And when that was done, they pulled up the hoods of their tops over their head, finishing the job.

Now they were ready.

Mack felt exposed under the orange glare of the streetlights. Not only was he about to go looting in the most intense area of London, but he was letting the world get a good look at his face while doing it. He envisioned watching the news with his parents later that week - Archie and Isabella tut-tutting at the masked men and women running riot and the destruction they were heaping upon the great city. And then it would happen - Mack would pop up on the CCTV. Perhaps he'd be walking out of a burning building with a couple of boxes under his arm. No mask, no hood, no nothing. Just him, waving at the camera like the gormless idiot he was.

But Sumo Dave was on the case. He turned towards Mack, while pulling open the rucksack he was carrying on his shoulder. He tugged at the zip, reached in and dragged out a spare black baseball cap.

"It's my old one," he said, handing it to Mack. "It's all I've got mate. Just pull it down over your face. You'll be alright, eh?"

Mack grabbed the hat, put it on and pulled it over his face. He couldn't see too well past the visor and some of his tawny hair still poked out at the sides and back. But it was better than nothing.

Deep breaths.

"I know some of these faces over there," Hatchet said. He was pointing to some of the people who'd gathered on the other side of the street. "All from different parts of London and look at 'em standing side by side. No gang beefs today. It's everyone against the law."

Hatchet nodded his approval.

"Keep moving," Sumo Dave said.

They walked towards the town centre. With every step, it felt to Mack like Croydon was getting darker. And that something was waiting for them in that darkness.

The closer they got to the town centre, the more people in hoods and masks they saw filling up the streets. Many hadn't bothered to cover their faces. White face, black faces, brown faces – different accents, male and female.

Truly it was a multicultural riot.

Sumo Dave led the way towards the town centre. Mack remained constantly alert. This was like nothing he'd ever encountered before – it had all the appearance of a street carnival, and one organised by the lowest members of society.

To their left, a small crowd of masked youths had gathered outside an electronics store. They were attempting to break the windows and kick in the doors. Ear-piercing screams contested with the sound of feet slamming against the door. There was a dull thud as the windows repeatedly came under attack.

Sumo Dave kept them moving. Like so many others, the four teenagers from Tottenham pulled over bins and attacked cars that had been abandoned on the street - several of which were already burned out wrecks. There was a contagious violence in the air and Mack succumbed willingly to its advances.

Soon after, they encountered a single decker bus on George

Road, which had been abandoned at some point. The automatic loudspeaker on the bus was still playing:

'This bus is under attack. Please dial 999.'

In the distance somebody laughed. Or screamed.

They followed the tramlines on George Street and onto Church Street. The road veered off to the left, but the boys continued in a straight line towards the shops and town centre. Dark shapes surrounded them - clusters of people and loud voices yelling back and forth at each other.

Sirens blared in the distance.

Mack stole a glance at the flats located above the shops. He hoped that there was nobody still in there, no families cowering in the dark while the world went mad for another night. Mack recalled the picture that had been on the front page of most of the newspapers that day: a woman jumping out of her first-floor window to escape the flames of the shops below.

Hadn't that been in Croydon?

He quickly caught up with the others.

Hatchet pointed at something up ahead. "Is that Reeves Corner?" he said.

"Yeah," Sumo Dave said. "That was on TV. C'mon, I want to see that."

They picked up the pace, running further west along Church Road. Mack felt a surge of adrenaline pushing him forwards. His arms felt like wings, lifting him off the crude earth and into the night sky.

The area up ahead, known as Reeves Corner, was cordoned off with tape. Suddenly Mack recognised where they were. Up ahead was the historic House of Reeves furniture store, which had been all over the news last night. It was a burned out shell. He recalled the words of the newsreader – about how the building had stood there for over a hundred and fifty years old. And how it had survived Hitler's bombs.

"Shit," he said.

It was just a wreck on the street corner now. That great building - whatever its history – was a forgotten corpse on the battleground. And like a dead body strewn across a field alongside countless others, there was nothing left to do but look briefly and move on.

Hatchet looked at the building for some time, his eyes gleaming in the dark. Mack couldn't see the rest of Hatchet's face under the mask, but somehow he knew, he just knew, the other boy was grinning.

Countless shops had already been set on fire. The fires spread quickly, latching onto other buildings, which themselves were soon engulfed in flames. Yelps of delight filled the night as the inferno spread across Croydon town centre.

Sirens continued to blare up ahead. Fire crews or the police – it was hard to tell who it was.

Tegz and Hatchet stopped in every shop along the way. Most places had already been emptied the night before, but that didn't stop them from running in and having a look. Sumo Dave was more selective in his choice of looting. Mack followed Sumo into a pawnbroker, which after a quick check, they realised had already been stripped of cash and jewellery. But Sumo Dave took whatever he could find lying around – old CDs, DVDs, computer games, anything that hadn't already been taken.

Mack went further into the shop and underneath an upturned chair at the rear of the building, found a small stash of Xbox games. With his heart pumping furiously, he pulled the zip on Sumo Dave's rucksack and put them in. As he did so, he anticipated a large hand upon his shoulder.

"You're under arrest son..."

But it didn't happen.

The two boys ran out of the shop. Nobody else on the streets gave them a second glance.

Mack's legs felt as light as feathers. His hands were visibly shaking and for a second or two, as the smoky air infested his lungs, he was convinced that he was on the brink of passing out.

But he stayed on his feet, following Sumo Dave over to where Tegz and Hatchet were waiting. With their masks on and bulging rucksacks thrown over their shoulders, the pair looked like bank robbers making off with fresh loot.

"You'll get us lifted!" Sumo Dave said. He was pointing at their rucksacks. "We've got to get back on the train with these bags. Look at 'em. They're about to burst!"

Hatchet shook his head. "Cops have got enough on their plates," he said. "I'm just a bloke carrying a rucksack. On my way home from the gym, eh?"

"You could stash them somewhere," Mack said. "Then come back for it when the heat dies down. It's probably safer than travelling back with them."

"Listen to the man," Sumo Dave said.

"You could hide them somewhere nobody would think to look," Mack said. "Like a graveyard or something. Every town's got one of those and nobody's going looting in there, are they?"

"Fucking graveyard?" Hatchet said. He was looking at Mack as if he'd just sprouted another head.

"Listen boys," Tegz said. He was looking around, his limbs flailing and full of nervous energy. "This bag's coming home with me. If I leave it somewhere - anywhere - it ain't going to be there when I get back. Yeah?"

"Me too," Hatchet said. "Fucking graveyard."

"Well you'll be sitting on the other side of the train from me," Sumo Dave said. "That's for sure. Right pair of dodgy looking fuckers you are."

The town centre was under siege.

Mobs of youths smashed their way through shop windows. Mack lifted the visor of his cap for a better look at what was unfolding around him. It was like watching a school of piranhas in the midst of a feeding frenzy, tearing the flesh off a large animal in a matter of minutes. It was something terrible, something fascinating, but something you couldn't help but watch. The looters moved fast, fuelled by adrenaline and bravado. And there were no consequences to their actions.

"Let's show these rich cunts!" somebody yelled.

A gang of about eight people hurled a barrage of bricks at a shop window. Mack watched as the four boys were passing by. It was a butcher's shop, one that billed itself as providing 'Fresh Meat For All The Family'. The bricks smashed through the glass at the first attempt.

Sumo Dave cheered the gang on as they stormed inside. Tegz and Hatchet did likewise. Mack found himself cheering too, despite the fact that to most people there, he probably was one of those 'rich cunts'.

Mack gave up on the idea of finding a Blackberry. The town centre had already been looted the night before and most of the good stuff was gone.

But still, just to be there - to see this.

It was surreal. Seeing it on TV was one thing, but there's always crazy shit going on inside a TV. And usually crazy shit happens somewhere else. But seeing it for real – knowing that it was actually happening outside the safety of the living room window – it was a wake-up call like no other.

He saw a gang of looters storming into a bike shop, dragging an assortment of bikes out onto the street and pushing them or cycling them away down the road.

He turned to his right and saw a trio of teenage female rioters. They were dressed in hoodies or jackets with hoods, but none of them had bothered to pull the actual hood up over their head. They were running out of a newsagent with plastic carrier bags, bulging with soft drinks, sweets and crisps. Mack watched them as they ran past him, taking off down the street in the direction of the train station. All the while, they were laughing and screaming with joy, as if they'd just looted Fort Knox.

The random beatings were the worst thing Mack saw that night. He watched, a sick feeling rising in the pit of his stomach, as three men kicked another man who was covering up on the ground in the doorway of a restaurant. The victim had rolled into the foetal position, his hands over his head as he tried to protect himself from the constant blows from above. The victim - a young man in his twenties who was well dressed in a dark suit - screamed and begged for his attackers to stop.

The police had gathered mostly in the town centre. A huge crowd of rioters stood opposite them, taunting and jeering, while others ignored the police altogether and continued with the looting elsewhere. Mack and the others held back and looked at the standoff from a safe distance.

The police stood bravely against the rioters, but they were hopelessly outnumbered.

The boys watched as several masked rioters approached an overturned vehicle lying at the side of the road, in between the police lines and the crowd facing off against them. Two of the rioters threw something at the car before sprinting back to their own lines. There were screams of delight as a spark lit. Seconds later, the car was ablaze.

Several times, the police tried to march forward but they were met with a constant barrage of bricks and bottles. The police cordons were fragile in the face of such overwhelming numbers. Mack could sense a shift in the power scheme happening. The authorities were losing control and in a couple of hours from now, he guessed that Croydon town centre would have fallen completely into the hands of the rioters.

The noise was deafening.

Mack turned away from the standoff. He didn't say anything but slowly he started walking back towards the train station. And in that moment, he didn't care whether Sumo Dave and the others were following him or not.

But they were. Apparently, they'd seen enough too.

"Fuck me, that was intense," Mack said to the others. They were back on George Street, having put some distance between themselves and the standoff.

He pulled the visor of the baseball cap up off his face.

Sumo Dave nodded. Tegz and Hatchet hovered in the background.

"I'm going back Sumo," Mack said. "We should probably catch the train, eh? Before it gets any worse around here."

Sumo Dave nodded. "I'm up for that," he said. "Knowing when to leave the party is the sign of a considerate guest, eh?" He turned and called out to Tegz and Hatchet, who were still lagging behind.

"Time to clear out lads," he said. "Let's go home."

Tegz came forward. "You guys go," he said. We'll meet you at the station in a bit, yeah?"

Hatchet stood silent in the background.

"Where are you going?" Sumo Dave asked. "Ain't you seen enough already?"

"PC World," Tegz said. "It's not that far from here. Hasn't been hit yet and we just heard someone on the street say it's getting done now. There'll be nothing left if we don't go now."

Sumo Dave looked at Mack.

Mack shook his head.

Sumo Dave turned back to the others. "We'll wait for you at the station. But hurry the fuck up, yeah?"

Tegz nodded, turned around and he and Hatchet ran back towards the town.

Mack and Sumo Dave walked slowly towards the train station.

Sumo Dave said. "PC World. They're moving away from the town centre."

Mack nodded. "Aye. It's fucked."

Sumo Dave stopped dead. He thrust a hand on Mack's shoulder, as if holding him back.

"Holy shit!"

Mack's heart skipped a beat. "What?"

Then Sumo Dave started laughing. He let go of Mack's shoulder and pointed further along the road. A large van was coming their way, travelling at high speed. Mack instinctively thought about running, but much to his relief, he quickly realised that it wasn't the police approaching.

The van drove past the two boys. On the side, in large print, it read: 'SKAM NEWS'.

"Sheeeeeiiiittt," Sumo Dave said. "I thought we were done for a second there mate."

"The news crews," Mack said, watching the van lights fade into the night. "You know where they're going at that speed, don't you?"

"Where?"

"PC World."

Sumo Dave shrugged. "Yeah maybe."

Mack started to laugh. It was a deep belly laugh, seemingly out of nowhere.

Sumo Dave looked at him as if he'd just laid an egg. "What's so funny?" he said. "You lost the plot mate?"

Mack spoke in between the giggles. "Tegz and Hatchet," he said.

"Yeah?"

Mack pointed in the direction in which the van was travelling.

He smiled. "They're going to be on TV."

CHAPTER 9

9th August 2011

SKAM News Channel

A middle-aged male reporter and his cameraman are trying to keep up with two masked youths. The youths are running out of PC World carrying a brand new flat screen television between them. All around, dozens of other people - all with masks and hoods over their faces - are running out of the building, almost all of them with their hands full of oversized electronic goods.

REPORTER: (*Out of breath*) Can we have a quick word lads?

LOOTER (1) (*Still running*) How about two mate? Fuck and off.

REPORTER: (*Undeterred*): Can I ask why you're stealing that TV? I mean, aren't you supposed to be protesting the circumstances of Mark Duggan's death?

LOOTER (2): What do you think we're doing, eh?

REPORTER: But this is just plain old robbery, isn't it?

LOOTER (1): This is a 65-inch flat screen TV mate.

REPORTER: (*Falling behind the looters*) But what does that have to do with Mark Duggan? What does that have to do with justice?

Looter (2) *stops running and turns back to the reporter.*

LOOTER 2: Look mate, the coppers bent the rules first. Not us. There's no evidence that Mark Duggan shot at them. They just took him out, yeah? They started this, all of this. Look around ya. The good and honest citizens are making their voices heard, like Chester George told 'em to.

REPORTER: So you're stealing the TV to make a point?

LOOTER 1: Funny that, innit?

CHAPTER 10

Sadie Hobbs: Filthy Rich And Worth It!

(Blog post by Sadie Hobbs – 10th August 2011)

OH MY GOD!!! Did you see the news last night? Those two idiots running out of PC World with a flat screen TV stuck in between their grubby little, poverty-stricken fingers?

Is it *really* too early to call in the army? As somebody very nearly once said in a Bruce Willis film:

I see morons.

Besides, any excuse for the men in uniforms to come rushing to our rescue.

Hmmm...

Now let's get serious for a minute. I'm a proud London girl - Chelsea born and bred and I've lived here for every one of my forty years. Yes, I know I look much younger! But all I can say is this - what the bloody hell is going on London? What's happening to my beautiful city? Who are these feral rats wreaking havoc upon our streets? And where did they come from?

Oh yes, that's right. The SLUMS!!

And how stupid they are. So, so, so stupid! I mean, look at how they're using technology and social media to incite further violence. Seriously people?? If you're going to start a Facebook group called 'Let's Start A Riot In Brixton' and use your real name as an admin, then don't be surprised when the police come knocking on your door.

Duh!

I think it's safe to say we're not dealing with criminal masterminds.

Citizens of London – DO NOT WORRY! There's no need to fear these criminal geniuses who are at present, most probably looting the sweetie aisle in their local Tesco or Sainsburys. Local police departments are on top of things. As of today, they are tweeting that if you use social media to incite disorder you can expect a knock on the door very soon. (Any chance of a sledgehammer instead?) One police department also just tweeted that another looter has turned himself in after watching a clip of himself looting on a Facebook clip. Oh God!!! Give that man a hand. And then throw him into the bog of eternal stupidity!!

The point I'm making is this: we shouldn't just punish these people for inciting riots via social media. We should punish them for being stupid. No seriously, I mean it. Take a good look at yourselves scumbags. YES YOU!! You with the Poundstretcher bandana wrapped around your acne-ridden face. You're publishing highly illegal activity on a global platform like Facebook and guess what? A gazillion eyes are watching. The whole wide world can see you and what happens next?

Knock-knock.

Who's there?

(Sledgehammer!!)

Well hello Mr Policeman.

This is the kind of mentality we're dealing with. It's evolution in reverse.

I'll finish by saying this. Let there be no more talk about the underprivileged, underclasses, fighting to make their voices heard, standing up to the man, blah-blah-blah!! And I don't want to hear anyone saying that government cuts are the cause of these riots. What utter codswallop!! There is not a single shred of nobility or justification about these riots. Underprivileged? Don't make me laugh. Underworked, more like. Let's be honest. These rioters are the dregs of society and they're too lazy, thick, or both to work. You and I dear reader? We're different. We earn our money through hard work and thus earn the right to do a bit of shopping. But the feral rats? They've bypassed the whole hard work bit, right?

CHAPTER 11

10th August 2011

The door of Charlie's Cafe swung open. Tegz was the first to swagger in, followed closely behind by Hatchet.

Mack and Sumo Dave were already inside waiting for them. They were sitting at a table in the corner furthest from the door. Both boys had their backs to the wall, eagerly awaiting the arrival of the others.

"Look out everyone," Sumo Dave said, watching the newcomers arrive. 'Here they come! It's Batman and Robbing!"

Mack leaned back, propping his chair onto its two back legs. He tried to suppress the laughter swelling up inside him.

Tegz winked across the room, but his attention was fixed on the other customers. Both he and Hatchet looked around with the expectation of minor celebrities, hoping someone might recognise them.

Even Hatchet was grinning.

But if the two teenagers were expecting some kind of red carpet treatment, they were out of luck as the customers scattered around the compact interior of Charlie's paid them no attention whatsoever.

In the background, David Bowie sang on the radio: '*Ch-ch-ch-changes...*'

Undiscouraged by the lack of fanfare, Tegz and Hatchet swaggered over to the table at the back corner, where Mack and Sumo Dave were waiting.

Sumo Dave was fighting back tears of laughter. "Look at the state of 'em," he said. "What a couple of celebrity villains, eh? You had masks on lads. You do remember that, don't you? No-one's going to recognise you."

Hatchet leaned in closer.

"You saw it then?" he said in a low voice.

Tegz looked across the table at Mack. "Did you see us mate?" he said. "What about that bit where he asks us for a quick word, eh? And I said I'll give him two. Fuck and off. What a fat tosser, eh?"

Mack picked up his can of Coke on the table and drank a mouthful. "I saw it Tegz," he said. "You were amazing wee man. If you're not up for an Oscar next time around, I'll eat your hat."

Tegz grinned. "*Yeeeeeeaaah!*"

They laughed - all of them. With that, Tegz stood up and swaggered over to the narrow counter. A middle-aged woman came over and Tegz ordered something, while at the same time digging his hands into the pockets of his oversized jeans. He found some coins and threw them onto the counter.

Mack looked around the room. It was nothing special – a typical low-key greasy spoon cafe, located on Philip Lane, just off the High Road. Wooden tables, plastic seats, and salt and vinegar pots sat on tables, alongside ceramic sugar bowls and large blood red bottles of tomato sauce. The smell of sizzling bacon wafted throughout the air, teasing hungry noses. The sound of people slurping at mugs of tea and coffee was constant. Every now and then, a teaspoon clinked against a cup.

Charlie's had thus far remained untouched by the riots. Whether this was because it was something of a local institution or just an old shithole that wasn't worth looting, who could say?

Tegz brought two cans of Coke back to the table. He put one down in front of Hatchet.

"There you go my lovely," he said.

Hatchet pulled the metal tab back. "Cheers," he said, bringing the can to his mouth.

"So what happened after they interviewed you?" Mack said.

"Yeah," Sumo Dave said, leaning into the table. "And more to the point, where is it?"

Tegz slurped at his Coke, his blank eyes peering over the edge of the can.

"Where's what?" he said.

"Don't fuck with me Terence," Sumo Dave said. And then lowering his voice, he added – "Where's the TV? You didn't carry that thing back on the train, did you?"

Tegz nodded. "Oh right."

Hatchet sat stone-faced. He sat quietly, drinking his Coke and staring into space.

Tegz leaned across the table.

"We hid it," he said quietly.

Sumo Dave fell back in his chair, letting out one of his signature shriek-laughs.

Tegz tilted his head, like a confused puppy. "What? What's funny about that?"

"You hid it?" Sumo Dave said, quietening down again. "That's what Mack told you to do last night. You remember? You gave him an earful about it."

Sumo Dave did his best Tegz – an over-the-top impression delivered in a grotesque and squeaky voice: *"There's no fucking way I'm hiding anything. Fucking graveyard bollocks, eh?"*

"I never said that," Tegz said.

"Where'd you hide it?" Mack asked. "In the graveyard?"

Sumo Dave - in the middle of taking a sip of Coke - shriek-laughed all over again. Dark liquid came gushing out of his nose, but still he kept laughing.

Some of the other customers turned around. Their faces grim and disapproving.

Tegz and Hatchet exchanged sheepish glances.

"No we didn't hide it in the graveyard," Tegz said. "Smart arse."

Sumo Dave piped down. He wiped his face dry and took a moment to regain his composure. Too many people were looking at them.

"Alright," he whispered. "So where is it?"

"It's in Wandle Park," Hatchet said. "We hid it away in some thick bushes."

Sumo Dave's jaw dropped. "Bushes?"

Hatchet shrugged. "Yeah. Bushes. You know, like bushes in the park."

"We hid it somewhere near the bandstand," Tegz said.

Sumo Dave shook his head in disbelief. "Somewhere near the bandstand?"

Tegz nodded. "Yeah. Somewhere near the bandstand."

"You've thrown it away, haven't ya?" Sumo Dave said.

"It's near the bandstand!" Tegz said.

Hatchet leaned in. "It's safe Sumo. Nobody's going to find it."

Mack leaned in. "How are you going to get it back here?"

Tegz shrugged. "When things quieten down I suppose."

"And when's that going to be?" Sumo Dave said. "Your TV will be long gone mate. No, the only chance you had was to hide it properly, but not you two, no. You had to hide it in a fucking bush. A giant flat screen TV!"

Sumo Dave slid his empty can across the table. "Muppets," he said, looking at Hatchet and Tegz.

"Croydon's still kicking off," Mack said, looking at the news app on his iPhone. "It's the first time there's been serious rioting during the day."

Sumo Dave sat up straight. "It better not mess with the start of the Premiership season," he said. "I've got football to watch. How are Spurs supposed to get to White Hart Lane with all this going on?"

Hatchet looked at Sumo Dave. "Chester George would be proud," he said sarcastically.

"Chester George is big news," Tegz said. "That's what he is. Ever since that video went viral he keeps getting mentioned on SKAM, the CBC – all of 'em. They keep calling him our leader. Fuck, even Hatch mentioned him to that reporter last night."

Mack looked at Sumo Dave. "You think he'll do another video?" he said.

Sumo Dave nodded. "He ain't just gonna fuck off is he? He's famous now."

"Suppose so," Mack said.

"Anyway," Sumo Dave said. "Word is, another video will be on YouTube any day now."

"Who told you that?" Hatchet asked. "Was it that Michael King bloke?"

Sumo Dave smiled, as if to say yes.

"Who's Michael King?" Mack asked.

"Bloke who lives on our estate," Sumo said. "He's about twenty, but he's been a big player in the riots so far. He's doing a lot of the co-ordinating and all that bollocks."

Mack looked at Sumo. "Does he know who Chester George is?"

Sumo Dave shrugged. "No idea mate. *He* could be Chester George for all I know."

Hatchet leaned in. "As long as Chester George wants us to stay on the street, smash shit up, burn things down – he's the right man for the job. That's what I say."

Tegz was grinning at something on his phone.

"Bloody hell," he said, pulling his cap back to front.

"What?" Sumo Dave said.

"You been on Twitter lately?" Tegz said. "London's trending all over the world."

CHAPTER 12

#LondonRiots

Sample of Tweets - *posted 10th August 2011*

Ramsay Davison *@Rramjet75 · 10 Aug 2011*

Reports say that shops are shutting up in Soho and Shoreditch High Street. #londonriots

Louise Edgerton *@Lou_180 · 10 Aug 2011*

#Riots kicking off in Lewisham. Just saw a car jacking. Shops closing, trouble everywhere. Wish I didn't live alone.

Jason B *@JBVenom · 10 Aug 2011*

Just been sent a list of 'suggested targets'. Hammersmith is on for tonight - #londonriots

Michelle Rolland *@mickyhistory · 10 Aug 2011*

LA #riots in 1992 saw amazing acts of bravery. London 2011 – people mugging injured people while others film on their phones.

Mona *@monaUK_91 · 10 Aug 2011*

#londonriots prove that if any major city was to rebel, the law can't handle it. Not even the army if we had the numbers.

Maverick James *@Mav_Jam · 10 Aug 2011*

Anyone else get their Tesco vouchers thru the door? Oh shit, where am I going to spend them now? #LondonRiots

CHAPTER 13

10th August 2011

Footage taken from a documentary filmed on a mobile phone. The footage was recorded and narrated by Luke, a 19 year-old student, on the streets of Croydon. It was later uploaded to YouTube.

Luke is walking down a busy street in Croydon recording the events of the riots as they unfold. The shaky hand held footage switches back and forth between street scenes and the face of its narrator. When the camera is pointing towards the street, masked or hooded figures can be seen running along a main road surrounded by ruined shop fronts. Thick pillars of smoke rise in the distance. And every now and then, ear-piercing screams can be heard, both near and afar.

LUKE: Peckham, Lewisham, Hackney, Bethnal Green, Beckton, Walworth, Ilford, Kilburn, Clapham, Camden, Croydon. This is where we live. To see the fires across, you know, various places – it's the number one thing trending on Twitter. It's all over Facebook. Lewisham's getting hit. There's a bus on fire in Peckham. Shops getting looted in Brixton. And then suddenly I seen it on the news today – we're getting reports that Croydon was hit badly again last night. Like really bad. And now they're saying that the riots are taking place during the daytime. And I thought, well wait a minute, I live in Croydon – on the main road – and I couldn't hear any sirens or police or anything like that. So me and my mate, we got in the car and drove about. We've been driving past buildings that looked normal and then on our way back around they were on fire. The smoke, I think, attracted most of the people and that's when they started gathering there. It's unreal. I saw a double decker bus on fire. Cars on fire. I'm surrounded by it now. I see property, businesses on fire – that's somebody's livelihood and yet why is everyone smiling?

In the background somebody can be heard screaming:

"GET OUT OF YOUR FUCKING HOMES. GET OUT!"

"GET 'EM OUT."

A woman screams: "FIRE!"

LUKE: There are people trapped upstairs in their houses. What can they do? I don't get it. I just can't connect the dots. This is – oh God! People have had to leave their houses. Their houses are getting burned down. Oh my God! I've never seen anything like this in my life. Never.

CHAPTER 14

10th August 2011

The four teenagers - Sumo Dave, Mack, Tegz and Hatchet - left Charlie's Cafe and walked back towards Tottenham High Road. It was by then, early afternoon and dark rainclouds were gathering in the sky. Tegz and Hatchet led the way, with their hoods pulled up over their baseball caps, walking with their heads down and hands thrust into jeans pockets.

Sumo Dave and Mack kept up the rear. As they walked, Sumo Dave took off his cap and rubbed down his shaven skull with the palm of his hand. Both teenagers said little, busy as they were surveying the aftermath of the riots.

Most of the shops they saw had their shutters pulled down. By now the vast majority of small businesses along the High Road were closed. Handwritten signs had been put over either doorways or shutters to inform customers that business would re-open again once things had quietened down.

What struck Mack most of all were the amount of bricks that lay scattered across the road and pavement. It was like looking at a pile of debris from a fallen skyscraper – a pile that stretched beyond reach of the naked eye, trailing further down the High Road, which was almost entirely shut off to traffic. Many bricks and stones lay at the doors of ruined shop fronts. In some ways, it was like looking upon a fresh murder scene, in which gun and dead body lay together side by side. Mack was well aware in this instance, that when the light began to fade later that day, the murderer would return to his weapon, pick it up and strike again.

Further along, several fire engines were parked on the street outside a row of shops. The firefighters were busy at work; the long hoses attached to the vehicles spraying jets of water into the building that still, many hours after being set alight, still threw out furious columns of smoke. It was impossible to tell what sort of businesses had once existed there.

Mack wanted to look away, but found he couldn't. How many more people had woken up that morning and realised that their livelihoods had been reduced to smoke and rubble?

"Jesus," he said quietly.

They stopped next to the ruin of a small newsagent. It had been nothing fancy, just the sort of place that someone might nip in for a pack of cigarettes or a newspaper or a lottery ticket. Not anymore. The front window had been smashed in and the shelves stripped of merchandise. That was before they'd set fire to it, but only half the interior had been badly burned beyond recognition, while the other half remained untouched – a reminder of what the shop had once looked like.

Sumo Dave stared into the ruined shop. Mack noticed the other boy's eyes twitching, as if wrestling with his own thoughts, struggling to come to terms with the terrible sight before them.

"Poor bastards," Sumo Dave said. "I used to come in here, you know? The bloke who worked here, he was alright."

And there was something else nearby. A small crowd had gathered around something big – the wreckage of which had expired in the middle of the High Road at some point over the last few days. The people swarming around the dead object were thrusting their phones in the direction of the metal corpse, filming, taking pictures, while some of them huddled together in the foreground of the ruin, striving to achieve the perfect group selfie.

One teenage girl stood pointing at the wreckage, her body convulsing in a fit of high-pitched laughter.

"It's a bus," Hatchet said, moving closer. Tegz and Mack followed his lead. Sumo Dave stayed behind, still looking at the ruined newsagent.

Mack did a lap of what appeared to have once been a double-decker bus. He guessed that maybe the bus had been abandoned and then set on fire. Now its mangled and charred remains were glued to the street, almost like a grotesque work of modern art.

"It *was* a bus," Tegz said. He pulled out his iPhone, pointing it at the wreckage.

Hatchet shook his head, calling over to Tegz. "Don't waste your time. This thing's probably been on YouTube for days."

Tegz kept on filming.

Mack took a couple of photos himself. Then he walked away. As he did so, he could still hear the teenage girl laughing behind him – that terrible shrill laughter, so out of place at that moment. Some of the people standing around the bus were now filming her instead. Mack hurried his step, wondering if there was something wrong with her.

Sumo Dave was waiting for them outside the newsagent. He was scratching at his neck and bouncing on his toes, as if unable to keep still.

"Let's get out of here mate," he said to Mack. "This place is giving me the creeps."

"Aye," Mack said. "Me too."

They started walking away and Tegz and Hatchet soon followed behind them.

A few minutes later they passed the McDonalds on the High Road. Despite everything else, it was still open for business.

"Right," Tegz said. "I'm starving. Who's with me?"

Sumo Dave gave him a playful tap in the ribs. "You've just been sitting in Charlie's, surrounded by food for the last hour and a half."

Tegz wasn't listening. He was already crossing the street. "Yeah," he called back. "But Charlie don't have Quarter Pounders with Cheese, does he?"

Hatchet turned to Sumo Dave. "I'm in," he said. "You coming?"

Sumo Dave looked up at the McDonalds sign - the golden arches still intact and shook his head. "How come this place doesn't have a mark on it? And that newsagent back there...?"

Mack smiled. "They're not going to fuck with McDonalds are they?" he said. "Rioting works up an appetite and besides, look around you, they're running out of other places to eat."

Through the window of McDonalds, Mack spotted a young girl sitting next to an older woman – her mother probably. As the little girl chewed happily on a burger and picked at a carton of fries, her mother kept her eyes on the streets, watching, waiting for the first signs of something kicking off.

When the woman caught sight of Mack and the others standing across the street, she looked away quickly, avoiding their eyes.

Hatchet stood at the edge of the kerb. He was glaring at Sumo Dave. "You coming or what?"

"I'm not hungry," Sumo Dave said flatly. "Go on. We'll meet you later at the school and talk about tonight. What's happening and that."

Hatchet nodded. "We've gotta get back to Croydon mate," he said. "We need to check that the TV's still there and... " Hatchet looked at Mack. "Move it to a cemetery."

Sumo Dave grinned. "Yeah. We'll talk about it later."

Hatchet crossed the street and followed Tegz into McDonalds.

"You know something," Mack said, watching the little Mike

Tyson go. "Hatchet doesn't like me, does he? He didn't invite me in for a Mickey D, did he?"

Sumo Dave and Mack both burst out laughing.

"Hatchet doesn't like anyone," Sumo Dave said. "Don't worry about that. He's a miserable git, but be nice – you wouldn't want to cross him, would ya?"

Mack nodded. "Aye. He's built like a fucking tank. What's that all about?"

Sumo Dave shook his head. "It's not the muscles you want to be afraid of mate."

"What do you mean?"

"He keeps a gun in the flat," Sumo Dave said.

Mack lowered his voice. "A gun?"

Sumo Dave nodded. "Used to be his old man's, eh? Must have left it there when he took off and left Hatchet's mum holding the baby."

"Fucking hell," Mack said. "I don't want to think about Hatchet with a gun. Does he ever carry it outside?"

"Sometimes," Sumo Dave said, the hint of a smile forming on his lips. "Just don't piss him off too much mate. Hatchet's a bit of a psycho and yeah he don't like you, but I don't think he's quite ready to shoot you - yet."

Mack sighed. "Lucky me."

Sumo Dave gave him a playful tap on the arm.

"It's not your fault mate," he said. "You're white, your family's got a bit of cash. You've got a mum and dad who actually give a shit about you."

Sumo laughed softly. "Yeah, you're the good boy in our gang, ain't ya?"

Mack shook his head. "You don't know jack-shit about me mate. If you did, you wouldn't be calling me the good boy."

Mack pointed a finger across the street to the fast food place. "And neither would he."

Sumo Dave and Mack walked north along Tottenham High Road. The ongoing sideshow of burned out cars and buildings became a blur. Eventually they arrived at Lancasterian Primary School and after checking that the coast was clear, jumped the black fence and continued around to the back.

As they arrived, a steady rain began to fall. Seconds later, it had turned into a downpour of near-biblical proportions. The boys ran for cover, laughing to themselves as huge drops of water, like fists, came crashing down on their heads.

They eventually found an artificial shelter, which had been built on as an attachment to the building, facing the small playground.

They sat down, leaning their backs up against the brick wall. Sumo Dave let himself slide until he was almost lying flat out on the concrete.

"You alright?" Mack asked.

"I am now," Sumo Dave said. He had his eyes closed.

Mack knew what he meant. "It was pretty freaky back there, eh?"

Sumo Dave shook his head. "It was hard to see it like that mate. And you know what's even worse, I'm one of many who's out there doing it, aren't I? I'm rioting and looting with the rest of 'em."

"Aye," Mack said. "I suppose."

Sumo Dave took off his cap. He ran a hand over the tight buzz cut, sanding it down furiously.

"What about you?" he said to Mack. "Your folks still giving you grief about going out?"

Mack nodded.

"So what you been saying?"

"That I'm hanging around with you and your mates," Mack said. "I leave the details out though."

Sumo Dave put his cap back on, pulling it down over his eyes. "Smart lad."

Mack looked out at the rain, like falling seeds sprouting dozens of puddles in the playground; thousands of tiny drops of water, so insignificant on their own and yet together, capable of creating a flood.

"Oh yeah," Sumo said. "I've got some news."

"Oh aye?" Mack said.

Sumo Dave sat up straight, pulling the cap away from his face.

"There's a geezer from my estate who's going to be on TV tonight," he said. "He's going to be talking about the riots. It's that Michael King bloke we mentioned earlier."

Mack nodded. "I remember the name."

"Yeah," Sumo Dave said. "Michael's a good bloke. He's a real smart cookie, yeah? He reads a lot I think. Does a lot of protesting too – racial things, equality, anti-police brutality. He's into all of that marching stuff. He's like the Malcolm X of Tottenham, know what I mean?"

"What's he going to be on?" Mack asked. "The news?"

"*The Paxton Show*. You know it?"

Mack nodded. "*Paxton*? That's a big deal."

"Yeah, that's it," Sumo Dave said. "The political one with the mouthy twat presenter."

Mack grinned. "He's a clever mouthy twat though."

Sumo Dave shrugged. "Yeah. He's still a tosser. Loves the sound of his own voice, especially when it comes to winding up his guests."

Mack grinned. "So your mate's going to be on his show?"

Sumo Dave nodded. "He's more of an acquaintance than a mate. But yeah, he's on it."

"Just talking about the riots?"

"Talking about the police I think."

"He's actually going to be in the studio?"

"I dunno, do I?"

Mack laughed. "You don't know much, do you?"

Sumo Dave smiled. "Good thing I'm handsome, innit?"

"What's this Michael guy like?" Mack asked.

"He's alright," Sumo said. "About twenty or twenty-one. He's a bit intense but he's got some serious brain power man."

"He'll have his hands full with Paxton," Mack said.

"Trust me," Sumo Dave said. "Paxton's going to have *his* hands full. Michael's going to have a right go at the coppers. And the government. Be a right giggle."

"You watching it?"

The lanky teenager shook his head. "Nah sod that. We're going back to Croydon tonight to get that TV by the looks of it. I'll watch it online tomorrow or something."

Mack nodded. "Cool."

"I'm ready to get back in the saddle," Sumo Dave said. There was a huge grin on his face as he spoke, and he was rubbing his hands together enthusiastically in anticipation of the night ahead.

Mack smiled. But his thoughts drifted back to the fate of the little newsagent on the High Road. To the man who used to work behind the shell of a counter and what he was thinking about tonight. What about his family?

Mack thought about how Sumo Dave had seemed so troubled back there, standing outside the building, at least for a moment or two.

And how quickly it was forgotten.

CHAPTER 15

10th August 2011

'The Paxton Show'

The studio lights go up.

A well-dressed man in a slick navy suit is sitting in a leather chair. He gently spins the chair in a clockwise direction, turning to face the camera as it zooms in. When James Paxton smiles, the CBC's finest political commentator looks younger than his fifty-something years.

But Paxton never smiles.

PAXTON: Good evening. Now unless you've been in a coma for

these past few days you'll be aware that the streets of London are currently in a state of chaos. And no doubt you – like the rest of us - are wondering what the government is going to do about it. Well, today we tried to ask them but we were told that neither the Prime Minister, the Mayor of London, nor the Home Office Minister were available to speak to us. So tonight we're going to do something different and instead of speaking to the politicians, we're going to talk to one of the rioters instead.

My guest tonight identifies himself as Michael King.

The camera cuts to a shot of a young black man sitting perfectly still next to Paxton. Michael King is wearing a faded leather jacket, over a white T-shirt, and khaki combat trousers. He has a handsome face, but the features are undeniably gaunt and the cheeks hollow. The young man stares back at the camera, blinking slowly and deliberately, like a lizard.

PAXTON: Michael, thank you for coming in. Now, you know why these riots are happening, don't you?

MICHAEL KING: (*Nodding slowly*) Because of the police.

PAXTON: What do you mean by that exactly?

MICHAEL KING: First of all, they shot a man in controversial circumstances. And then last Saturday, along with a few hundred other peaceful protestors, I went to the police station in Tottenham looking for answers. But the police failed to produce a credible spokesman to meet us. It's just another example of police disrespecting their communities.

PAXTON: But Michael, that's no reason to burn down half of London, is it?

MICHAEL KING: None of this would have happened, not if there'd been better policing last Saturday.

PAXTON: But don't you think the police have a difficult job? That maybe they're doing their best under difficult circumstances?

MICHAEL KING: No I don't. And the government aren't helping either. Our local youth services budget was cut by seventy-five percent in January. Eight out of our thirteen youth centres closed in February and all the others are under threat. So yes, there's a lot of young people on the streets because they're bored. And the government - who breeds this kind of society - doesn't care.

PAXTON: Michael, let's go back to the police. Are you suggesting a catastrophic mismanagement of this situation? From the very start?

MICHAEL KING: As a peacekeeping force, they've failed us. They failed us when they shot Mark Duggan. And they failed us on Saturday night when they disrespected the wishes of the local community.

PAXTON: Can you elaborate?

MICHAEL KING: The riot police turned up before anybody was even rioting. They tried to push us back from the police station and a young girl was knocked over. The police struck this young girl repeatedly. I saw it happen - four officers hitting one girl just because she didn't back off. It's disgusting.

Paxton turns to the camera.

PAXTON: Let's go now to Jack Coren, who's waiting to join us over in our East London studio. Jack is the Deputy Chair for the Metropolitan Police Federation.

A heavyset, bearded man appears on a large screen behind Paxton. He stares blankly at the camera, dusting down the jacket of his brown suit as he waits for the link-up to start.

PAXTON: Jack Coren, thank you for joining us.

JACK COREN: It's my pleasure James.

PAXTON: Jack, you've been listening to Michael here - do you accept that relations between the police and young people are somewhat lacking?

JACK COREN: Well, what I will say is this - there's been an enormous improvement since the late eighties when the relationship between ourselves and the -

PAXTON: An improvement? (*Laughs*) It doesn't look like it, does it? In fact, it looks like the police haven't got a clue how to deal with this situation.

JACK COREN: I disagree James. I think that, since the eighties, an enormous amount of effort has been put in by our local police services to engage with their communities and that they're working hard to keep those relationships going.

PAXTON: (*Leaning closer to the screen*) Well it's not working, is it Mr Coren? The streets are overrun with rioters and everyone's asking the same question: where are the police?

Coren's face slightly reddens.

JACK COREN: The police *are* doing their best to contain the situation James. We are dedicated to putting a stop to all of this, but the reality is that there are finite resources and -

PAXTON: How does this affect police morale? You've got more cuts looming, three commissioners have resigned in a relatively short period of time, and then there's the Olympics next year. Are you worried Jack? I'd be worried if I was you.

JACK COREN: I think the government can support us better than they are currently doing. Cuts aren't going to help ahead of the Olympics. But despite this, the dedication of the officers on the streets tonight is absolutely without question.

PAXTON: Thank you very much Jack Coren.

Paxton turns back to Michael King.

PAXTON: Michael, you say that your grievance is with the police. But tell me this - how does looting the local convenience store or newsagent - how does ruining some poor guy's business, raise awareness about the police?

MICHAEL KING: You're wrong. We're not mindless criminals. I was there and initially, no private homes were targeted and no local businesses either. The targets were big corporate entities and any buildings associated with the corrupt police and law system.

PAXTON: But what about the furniture store that was burned down in Tottenham? There were twenty-six flats above that building. These were people's homes and families occupied them - families with small children. I mean, what do you have to say about that?

MICHAEL KING: It was getting too big to control. But people checked that building out and others too before they were torched. We're not looking to kill people. We're trying to make a point and the point is this - if the police keep treating us like shit, we're going to fight back.

PAXTON: So it was a show of power?

MICHAEL KING: It was many things. Unfortunately for you lot - the media - these riots can't be defined by one simple explanation.

PAXTON: What do you mean by that?

MICHAEL KING: The London riots are a complex issue with deep roots. People aren't necessarily rioting for the same reasons. In Tottenham, the riots are anti-police. But in Croydon and Ealing, it's more about class because the targets down there are cars, posh cafés, properties and businesses in the middle class areas. And yes, in other areas it's about sheer opportunism. The point is that the media just bundle it all together and call it mindless criminality.

PAXTON: So what's the answer? How do we fix it?

MICHAEL KING: (*Shrugs*) I'm just telling you why. I don't have all the answers.

PAXTON: Let me ask you about Chester George. He's released one clip on YouTube and already he's something of a Messiah figure amongst the rioters. Who is he?

MICHAEL KING: Chester George speaks for us. We are the 'Good and Honest Citizens'. That's all you need to know.

Paxton reaches down to his notes and pulls out a photo tucked in between the pages. He hands it to Michael

PAXTON: Look at this Michael. This is a picture of Robert Hart, a forty-year-old man who was punched by rioters as he tried to stamp out a fire in west London yesterday.

MICHAEL KING: I know what happened.

PAXTON: Well for those who don't, let me finish please. Mr Hart's head hit the ground when he fell and suffered what doctors described as 'catastrophic' brain injuries. He is not expected to recover. Now this is a husband and a father of three young children. There he was, not getting in anyone's way, but simply trying to prevent a fire spreading – and one that had been started in a wheelie bin by rioters. What would Chester George have to say about that?

MICHAEL KING: I'm sorry for the man and his family. And to all those who don't want to be a part of this, I'd say this - leave the city now. Because this thing is far from over.

PAXTON: You're sorry? Is that supposed to be good enough? Mr Hart had nothing to do with the police or the government or even the media. Would you be willing to sit down with his family and tell them why you feel his death is justifiable?

MICHAEL KING: If they'd like to, yes I would be willing.

PAXTON: You would?

MICHAEL KING: The objective is not to kill. It is to teach the police and government a lesson about people power.

PAXTON: And you think you're winning, do you?

Michael King leans forward, a half-smile on his lips.

MICHAEL KING: Tell me something James. Would I be sitting here tonight if we weren't?

CHAPTER 16

10th August 2011

Croydon was falling.

A massive crowd had amassed on the fringes of the town centre. They were at that moment, in the midst of running battles with the riot police who, although outnumbered, were desperately standing their ground, trying to seal off the central areas of town from the masked invaders intent on breaking through.

"Jesus Christ," Mack said. He lifted the peak of Sumo Dave's baseball cap from his eyes. Then he pulled the hood of his light grey hoodie over his head, leaving enough room for his eyes to take in the action up ahead.

The four teenagers from Tottenham stood on the outskirts of the standoff, watching the action unfold up ahead.

The signs had been there from the start - that things were getting worse in Croydon, something that hadn't seemed possible to those who were there the night before.

How could things get worse?

Mack, Sumo Dave, Tegz, and Hatchet had arrived at East Croydon train station at just after six in the evening, only to be welcomed by a recurring tannoy announcement informing passengers that trains wouldn't be running past nine o'clock, which was less than three hours away.

Due to the 'disturbances' the man said.

Outside the station, George Street had been packed with people – almost all of them with their faces covered by hoods and masks. The smell of stale smoke hung in the air. Like something big had burned down.

The vast majority of people outside the station were on the move, making their way towards Church Street and the town centre. Others stayed put, lingering in the doorways of ruined shops, watching and waiting.

Mack noticed that some of these people on the sidelines were injured. Several had even sat down on the pavement while their friends tended to their wounds. Amongst those who had taken off their masks, Mack saw some nasty looking head wounds. One young lad, who couldn't have been much more than fifteen, appeared to have a massive haematoma forming on the side of his head. Just above his left ear. When Mack saw it, he grimaced and turned away. *Shit.* It looked like the guy's head was about to explode.

He had to forget these things. Otherwise, he wouldn't make it anywhere near the town centre.

Might as well go home now boy.

On Church Street, the rioters were throwing police helmets into the wall of riot police. Those who hadn't managed to steal a helmet during the running battles had to make do with the usual, bricks as well as other improvised missiles, such as burning bottles stuffed with paper.

At the same time, four masked figures carrying baseball bats were clambering onto the roof of a white Transit van. The van must have been abandoned there recently, as the only vehicles left on the streets that weren't police cars or vans - were burned out wrecks.

Once on top of the roof of the van, the rioters started jumping up and down, screaming with delight, much like overexcited children on a bouncy castle. They pummelled the roof with their feet and taunted the watching police with one and two fingered salutes. About a minute later, the four masked figures started smashing at the windscreen with their baseball bats.

"Right, let's get our TV back," Tegz said. He was pointing at the standoff that stood between them and their prize. "How are we going to get past that lot?"

"Wandle Park is down that way," Hatchet said. "That means we've gotta get through that mess. Somehow."

Mack shook his head. "Forget the TV lads," he said. "Just forget about it, eh?" He pointed at the rioters up ahead. "Look at all those people. Some of them have been here for days, probably been sleeping in Wandle Park too. The TV's gone."

"Fuck do you know?" Hatchet said.

Little Mike Tyson took a step forward, assessing the obstacle up ahead. "That TV's still there," he said. "I can feel it in me bones." He turned to Tegz and grinned. "We've just gotta find another way through little man."

"Take the long route," Sumo Dave said.

"What's the long route?" Tegz asked.

Sumo Dave pointed away from the crowds. "Through the back streets," he said. "Shortcuts through gardens and private property. Ain't nobody at home, not with all this going on. But no slipping yeah? If the old bill see you, they'll nick you just like that. You're black and you're out on the street in the middle of a riot – thank you very much says the old bill."

Tegz shook his head. "I need a spliff," he said, pulling out a bag of Rizla from his back pocket. "We need to think about this."

Hatchet snatched the packet out his hand.

"There's no time for that shit," he snapped. "Or thinking. We gotta get that TV out of the park. Now!"

Ahead of them, the rioters were picking up steam. The four teenagers looked on as the crowds rushed forward in a clumsy unison, repeatedly charging at the ranks of the more organised, yet outnumbered police.

Mack saw the police lines wobbling, shifting further back.

Tegz let out a whoop of delight. "Holy shit!"

Sumo Dave tapped him on the arm. "Quit standing around here wasting time," he said to Tegz. "If you're going to get that TV - go and get it now. And hide it somewhere good this time, like a fucking cemetery."

"You ain't coming with us?" Hatchet said.

Sumo Dave shook his head. "Nope. It's your buried treasure. You deal with it."

Tegz and Hatchet tried pulling up a map of the area on their phones, but found the signals jammed. Finally they decided to head south on Old Palace Road. From there, they said they would cut off and try and veer left towards the park without being seen by anyone in a uniform.

"Good luck," Mack called out, watching them set off.

Tegz turned back, giving them the thumbs up.

A little later, Sumo Dave and Mack were standing outside the ruin that used to be *Shoe Zone*. Although the shop hadn't been burned to the ground, its front window had been smashed in and the shelves plundered and toppled to the ground. Looking through the rectangular gap where the window used to be, it was clear that there was nothing left but wreckage in there.

"We'll give this a miss then," Sumo Dave said. "Who needs a new pair of shoes anyway?"

"Aye," Mack said. "There's not much left worth grabbing in this town, is there?"

The two teenagers started walking back towards the centre. The rucksacks over their shoulders were still empty.

"I'm getting fed up with this," Sumo Dave said.

Mack nodded. "Aye, this is a bit shite mate. What's the point of going looting when there's fuck all left to loot?"

They could hear the rioters chanting in the distance.

"Bloody hell," Sumo Dave said. "I've been to a lot of Spurs games at White Hart Lane mate. But I don't think I've ever heard us chant as loud as that. And I'm talking about thirty-five thousand people."

Mack looked towards the noise.

"They're going to send in the army," he said. "The police

Sumo Dave nodded. "Yeah," he said. "But what are the army going to do different, eh? They can't shoot us all. That's genocide or whatever it's called."

Mack pulled his phone out of his back pocket and checked the time. It was 7.51pm.

He looked over at Sumo Dave. "They've been gone for over an hour now."

"I know," Sumo said. "I don't know what they're doing mate. Probably still looking around every corner of Wandle Park for that TV."

All of a sudden, Sumo Dave burst out laughing. It was one of his usual, high-pitched, almost feminine shrieks.

"I can just picture 'em running around the park," he said. "Looking under every fucking bush for that TV."

Mack quickly put a hand to his mouth, but he couldn't hold it in either. He doubled over at the thought of Tegz and Hatchet, prancing around the park in distress over a flat screen TV, while all around the rest of Croydon fell apart.

Sumo Dave wiped the tears from his eyes. "Hey we shouldn't

laugh," he said. "Maybe the cops have got them. They've been gone for - "

Something cut him off in mid-sentence. It was the sound of a man screaming.

The two teenagers turned around. Up ahead, they saw five or six dark shapes bundling something down the street. Mack took a closer look and as his eyes adjusted to what was coming their way, he saw that the 'something' being bundled was wearing a police uniform.

"Oh shit," he said. "Dave, that's..."

"I know."

The police officer's assailants had covered his head with a T-shirt. They were kicking him repeatedly to the body as they dragged him towards the alley. Others in the gang picked up random objects on their way and struck the helpless victim on the ground. As the two boys watched from a distance, one of the dark shapes grabbed a plank of wood from the other side of the road. He ran over to the gang and started hitting the helpless policeman with it. Mack heard the man's muffled cries for help, loud at first, but getting weaker with each strike.

The rioters dragged the man towards a nearby alley. As they disappeared out of sight, the policeman's cries for help faded.

Moments later, everything went silent.

Sumo Dave took a step forward.

"That's it," he said. His voice was low, calm, and deadly serious. Mack had never heard Sumo Dave talk like that before. "Let's go Mack," he said. "This is getting real nasty. People are going to die and no one gives a fuck."

Mack struggled to find his voice. A hoarse whisper barely came out.

"Sumo," he said. "They're going to kill him. Shouldn't we...do something?"

Sumo Dave locked his hand around Mack's forearm. It felt like a vice squeezing down on Mack's bones. "Yeah," Sumo Dave said. "We should. But if we do, we're dead too. You know that, eh? Don't you? Now let's go Mack."

At that moment, an explosion – which sounded like an earthquake or a giant clap of thunder – ripped through the night. Sumo Dave and Mack both jumped back in fright, uncertain of where it had come from. Instinctively, they put their hands over their heads, shielding themselves from the inevitable shower of bricks that would come crashing down from above.

But nothing fell near them. The teenagers, realising that they were safe, straightened up and looked around.

Over the tips of the surrounding buildings, they watched as a yellowy-orange ball of flame lit up the dark sky.

As the sound of the explosion faded, a deafening chorus of voices could be heard in the distance. Cheering. Howling. Celebrating. It sounded like a vast and ancient army, rejoicing in the aftermath of victory on the battlefield.

"What the fuck was that?" Mack said.

"We need to go mate," Sumo Dave said, his voice trembling. "Now! Mack. C'mon let's get the fuck out of here mate. They're going to stop the trains after that."

Mack took one last look down the alley where they'd dragged the policeman.

Black smoke was rising over Croydon.

"Mack – let's go!"

Sumo Dave pulled him back. Slowly, as if waking up from a nightmare, Mack returned to his senses.

"I'm alright Dave," he said.

Sumo Dave let go of his arm. The two teenagers ran back towards George Street at a furious pace, stopping only occasionally to catch their breath.

"What about Tegz and Hatchet?" Mack said, during one stop.

"Fuck knows," Sumo Dave said. He reached into the pocket of his hoodie and took out his phone. After looking at the screen, he shook his head. "No messages. No missed calls. I don't know where the fuck they are."

"So what do we do?"

Sumo Dave didn't hesitate. "We go."

Back on George Street, the rioters were doing the only thing left to do after looting the town - burn it to the ground. The supermarkets, fast food restaurants, pubs, betting shops, fishmongers, pharmacies, butchers – whatever was still standing was in the process of being torched as Sumo Dave and Mack hurried past, making their way back to the train station.

In all likelihood, there wouldn't be much left of Croydon in the morning.

Nobody paid any attention to the tall skinny youth and his companion. They were just two more rioters on the move, their faces hidden behind hoods and masks, as they trawled through the streets.

Mack could feel the heat of the flames pinching at his skin as he ran past the burning shops. The stench of smoke was overpowering, and his lungs fought for clean air to breathe.

Things were a little quieter as they got closer to East Croydon station. As they walked, Mack glanced at the flats above the shops, trying to convince himself that these homes would have been evacuated by now. There were no lights on at least.

Likewise, he was still trying to convince himself that the policeman who'd been dragged down that alley was alive.

"SUMO! HOLD UP!"

It came from behind them.

Sumo Dave and Mack turned around to see Tegz running up the street towards them. Mack was surprised to see that Tegz had taken his mask off, and that as a result, he'd probably breathed in too much smoke.

The cocky smirk that was always on Tegz's face was gone. Now he was someone in a daze, somebody not quite there.

Hatchet walked slowly into view behind him. Strolling with casual indifference, as if detached from the surrounding chaos.

"Where the fuck have you two been?" Sumo Dave said. "The fucking town's burning down and you're out there fucking around, looking for a 65-inch TV?"

Tegz didn't respond.

"You alright Tegz?" Mack asked. "You're looking a bit green around the gills mate. You should put your mask on, you're breathing in too much smoke."

Tegz looked at Mack. For a moment, Mack thought that the little joker was about to resurface. That he would burst out laughing and go back to his normal self, cracking jokes in 3-2-1.

But he didn't.

"I'm alright," Tegz said quietly. "Let's just go yeah? I want out of here."

Hatchet caught up with them.

"Hatch?" Sumo Dave said. "Did you find the TV or what?"

Hatchet looked at Sumo, his eyes like blank holes behind the mask.

"Nah it's gone," Hatchet said. "You were right, it wasn't there. Fuck it anyway."

Sumo Dave shook his head, but neither he nor Mack felt the need to gloat.

"What happened to you two?" Sumo Dave said. "Earlier on getting that TV back was the most important thing in the world. Now it's like – *fuck the TV*. What happened?"

Hatchet shrugged.

"Please," Tegz said, looking around as if someone was about to catch up with them. "Can we just get the fuck out of here?"

As the four teenagers boarded the train, an announcement reminded passengers that all services were about to end. The speaker made no mention of when normal service would resume.

The train itself was practically deserted. A few people sat scattered here and there, but as the four boys walked down the aisle of the first carriage, they had their pick of seats and sat down at a small table with two seats on either side.

Mack glanced over at Tegz, who'd sat at the window seat. He had propped his head up against the glass and was staring out into the darkness, saying nothing.

Mack had never seen Tegz so quiet. He wasn't even looking at his phone or talking about the next spliff. He was just sitting, staring into the glass at his own reflection.

As the train pulled away from the station, Sumo Dave took out his phone. Mack did the same – he wanted to see what they were saying on the news about Croydon. The army had to be coming now. How could they not be?

Hatchet, sitting beside Tegz at the aisle, turned and looked back towards the toilet sign at the rear of the carriage.

"I need to piss," he said to no one in particular.

Hatchet stood up and as he did so, he put both hands on the table to support himself. That's when Mack saw the blood.

His heart skipped a beat. The blood on Hatchet's hands had dried in, but there was still enough of it, coating the palms and fingers to make it obvious.

There was a lot of blood.

Hatchet turned and walked down the aisle towards the toilet.

Mack looked at his own hands. He recalled the feeling of warmth, of somebody else's blood seeping into the pores of his skin.

Not so long ago.

CHAPTER 17

11th August 2011

Parliament has been recalled.

In a packed House of Commons, the Prime Minister - fresh from a Mediterranean holiday cut short - rises to make a statement. His boyish good looks glow in deep hues of brown and red. This, combined with the tailored blue suit that he's wearing, give the appearance of an overgrown public schoolboy.

SPEAKER: Brief Public Disorder Statement, the Prime Minister.

Cheers and grunts of approval from the backbenchers.

PRIME MINISTER: Thank you Mr Speaker. With permission, I would like to make a statement. Due to the fact that there is important work to be done, this will be brief. But once order has been restored, its finer details will be expanded further.

Cheers. Grunts.

PRIME MINISTER: First of all, let me thank you and Honourable and Right Honourable members for returning to Parliament today. In times of crisis such as these, it is crucial that we show a united front.

More cheers. More grunts.

PRIME MINISTER: What we have seen on our television screens over the past few days is sickening. We've seen people looting, vandalising, robbing, and attacking other people. Houses - HOMES - have been burned to the ground, as have countless offices and shops and private businesses. The livelihoods of many hard working citizens in this country have been ruined. We have also seen police officers being assaulted by missiles and fire crews attacked as they try to put out fires. There are even people robbing others as they lie injured and bleeding on the street. It is completely unacceptable and I am sure that the whole House joins me in condemning it.

Cheers. Grunts. Heads nod furiously in agreement.

PRIME MINISTER: First of all Mr Speaker, we must understand

the sequence of events that has led us here today. A week ago, a young man, Mark Duggan was shot and killed in Tottenham. There are obviously questions about this incident that must be answered. This - I can assure the House and Mr Duggan's family - is being thoroughly investigated by the IPCC. But what we are seeing now on the streets of London and elsewhere has no connection whatsoever to Mark Duggan's fate. It is an excuse, latched onto by opportunistic thugs.

BACKBENCHERS: (*Collectively*) Hear, hear!

PRIME MINISTER: These young people stealing flat screen televisions and burning shops and houses – this has nothing to do with politics or protest – it is simple theft. These riots are criminal and their behaviour is motivated not by a need for justice, but by simple criminality.

The Prime Minister turns towards the Speaker.

PRIME MINISTER: Mr Speaker, we will not put up with this. Not in our country. I want to assure the public that we will do whatever it takes to bring order to Britain's streets.

Cheers. Grunts.

The Prime Minister turns back to the rest of the House.

PRIME MINISTER: Yesterday, I held an Emergency Committee Meeting where we discussed the action that was needed to help the police combat the disorder that we've seen over the last few days. I've also previously met with the Home Secretary and the Metropolitan Police Commissioner for further discussion on the matter.

The Prime Minister pauses for breath.

PRIME MINISTER: We commend the bravery of our police officers. But it is clear that we need much more extreme and robust police action. So after speaking with the Commissioner, an additional ten thousand police have been deployed onto the streets of London this week. All leave for police officers has been cancelled and we are bringing in aid from other police departments around the country. There are now more police on the streets, more arrests being made, and more people being prosecuted.

Cheers. Grunts.

PRIME MINISTER: Whatever it takes to restore law and order to the streets and to rebuild our communities, we *will* do it. This includes existing measures such as baton rounds and contingency plans are in place for water cannons to be available at twenty-four hours notice. And should things get worse Mr Speaker, the armed forces are on stand by for emergency interventicn.

This rouses the backbenchers into life.

BACKBENCHERS: Hear, hear!

PRIME MINISTER: It is disturbing for decent people everywhere to realise the level of anarchy that exists in our society. And in particular, how social media can be used to inform, to encourage and to spread violence quicker than ever. As a result, we are working with the police, intelligence services and industry to ask whether it is right to stop these young people communicating via these means when we know for sure that they are plotting violence and anarchy. Of course, we're all aware by now of the video blogger going by the name of Chester George.

There is some muted laughter amidst the usual cheers and grunts.

PRIME MINISTER: Well this man, whoever he is, has been particularly effective at inciting hatred amongst young people. Attempts have been made to locate him, but of course there is very little evidence to go on. The YouTube account that originally posted the video has been shut down, but of course when so many others are distributing the clip online that doesn't matter. I'm afraid this is just the age we live in. But rest assured, we are looking for the perpetrator and we will find him. To Chester George and his followers I say this: we will track you down, we will find you, and we *will* punish you.

This last line gets a roar of approval.

PRIME MINISTER: Mr Speaker, more details will be revealed once we have restored order to our streets, particularly about victim compensation and dealing with gang culture. But right now, restoring order is our number one priority.

Cheers. Grunts. The Prime Minister sits down and is congratulated by his colleagues.

SPEAKER: The leader of the opposition.

The leader of the opposition stands up to address the House. Like the Prime Minister, he is boyish, dark and handsome, but in an equally bland and indistinguishable way.

LEADER OF THE OPPOSITION: Mr Speaker, I would like to thank the Prime Minister for his decision in asking you to recall Parliament today.

The Leader of the Opposition stares thoughtfully into space.

LEADER OF THE OPPOSITION: Yes, today we stand united. Let's put our political differences aside for the good of the country. Let's stand shoulder to shoulder in condemning the violence and vandalism we have seen on our streets.

Cheers. Grunts.

LEADER OF THE OPPOSITION: And I just want to say this to Chester George and his followers – the people out there on the streets.

His face contorts into a mask of grotesque sincerity.

LEADER OF THE OPPOSTITION: I know you're in pain Chester George. I know that you're disappointed and fed up with politics. I feel that. I get it. *Yeah?* But what you're doing - you're not just wrecking other people's lives, you're wrecking your own. We - the politicians - must try to understand you. Why are there so many young people who feel they have nothing to lose by looting? We cannot afford to let this situation calm down, to let it pass, only to find ourselves in the same position in the future. Especially with the Olympics just around the corner.

Cheers. Grunts.

LEADER OF THE OPPOSITION: Mr Speaker, I have to ask - is the Prime Minister really doing enough? Is he doing enough to ensure that CCTV can be used to identify the rioters and bring them to swift justice? Above all Mr Speaker, is the Prime Minister doing enough to make sure that the police have enough resources to deal with the rioters?

This gets a roar of approval from the opposition backbenchers.

LEADER OF THE OPPOSITION: Look, I'm not trying to score any political points - this is not the time for that - but given the absolute priority that the public attach to a visible and active police presences, does the Prime Minister understand that they will not be pleased if the proposed cuts to police numbers go ahead as planned?

More cheers. More grunts.

The leader of the opposition sits down.

The Prime Minister gets back to his feet.

PRIME MINISTER: Mr Speaker, these riots are not about government cuts. The violence is being directed at shops; it is not being directed at Parliament. It is the ordinary working man who is being made to suffer. Numbers and figures can be dealt with after this crisis has been abated, but public safety is our number one priority.

The Prime Minister sits down.

Cheers. Grunts.

The Leader of the Opposition stands up.

LEADER OF THE OPPOSITION: Will the Prime Minister then

accept the reality that is the sick culture that's inherent in our society? This is a culture that glorifies violence, shows disrespect to authority, and says everything about rights, but nothing about responsibility. How did the Tories let this happen?

The Leader of the Opposition sits down.

More cheers. Even more grunts.

The Prime Minister stands up.

PRIME MINISTER: Of course, there are inherent flaws within the rioting communities. But these have been festering for generations and can't just be blamed on the actions of one government. What we are concerned with Mr Speaker – instead of playing the blame game, which we shouldn't be doing today - is the breakdown of traditional family structures. In too many cases, the parents of these children – that's if they're even around – don't care where their children are, who they're with, let alone what they're doing.

Cheers. Grunts.

PRIME MINISTER: This situation needs to be addressed from the bottom up. We need a benefit system that rewards work and that is on the side of families. We need an education system that is more disciplined. This will breed a better, happier society. Above all Mr Speaker, we need to put our foot down and show some tough love.

The Prime Minister sits down to a roar of approval. When the cheers fade, a temporary silence sweeps across the House while outside, far beyond the walls of the Houses of Parliament, the sound of sirens can be heard.

CHAPTER 18

Transcript of a video uploaded to YouTube.com (posted on *11th August 2011*)

Chester George is wearing the same black skull hoodie, zipped up over his face with the luminous skull design leering back at the camera. At first he doesn't speak. He's just standing there in the same room as before, not moving, but biding his time in front of a large backdrop of classic punk rock posters.

'Straight to Hell' by The Clash, is playing quietly in the background.

When Chester George finally speaks, he does so in a quiet raspy voice - one that labours to be heard above the music, and that hints of exhaustion and world-weariness.

"Mr Prime Minister and all the politicians in the Houses of Parliament.

That was a poor pretence of unity yesterday. Yet you said everything that you were expected to say.

Which wasn't much.

I feel however, that I must add something on behalf of the people you are trying to understand – something you forgot to mention amidst your feeble efforts to put on such a united front.

You ask - why are so many of them quick to steal? It's criminality you say. It's the fault of our parents, you say. Or it's our sick culture.

Sssssick Culture.

It's quite simple to you and all the other MPs – we're simply rotten from within. Our communities have no morals. This is nothing you cannot comfortably classify as a revolt of the feral underclass – isn't that right Mr Prime Minister?

But YOU are too humble sir. You forgot to mention yesterday how much the greed and selfishness that we see in the city inspires us to be as rotten as we are.

You see, our conception of right and wrong comes from more than just our parents. Have you forgotten Mr Prime Minister? Just a few years back, the bankers publicly looted this country's fortune. When they did that, they showed us that the acquisition of individual wealth is clearly a measure of success. They took millions and destroyed people's life savings. They were caught red-handed, but very few were punished. And yet you criticise us - the Good and Honest Citizens - for taking a mobile phone or a pair of shoes?"

Chester George steps closer to the camera.

"And what about all the MPs who got caught fiddling their expenses? You must remember that one Mr Prime Minister? Or how about the phone-hacking scandals?"

He lets out a throaty laugh.

"If we are devils, then we learned from the very best. You - the suits and ties - are the original looters of this country. You are the original gangsters.

Now of course, I understand your reasoning for trying to label us as rotten. If there are no sociological, political or economic causes for the revolution that you call the riots, then no one in authority is to blame."

He wags a finger from side to side, like a parent telling off a naughty child.

"Such irresponsible behaviour from our so-called leaders.

Mr Prime Minister. The worst violence London has seen for decades is happening against the backdrop of a global economic meltdown. It's never pretty when society wakes up, is it? But society *is* waking up. That's what this is. We live in an uneven world of uneven wages and opportunities. Did you know Mr Prime Minister, that last year the combined wealth of the one thousand richest people in Britain went up by thirty per cent to over three hundred billion pounds?

Isn't that a remarkable number?

London is now one of the most unequal cities in the developed world. You and your kind have turned it into a gigantic shopping mall. And yet you expect our kind to be satisfied with window-shopping.

Mr Prime Minister. What you see now on the streets of London - and in other cities also waking up - is the result of a society that's been run on greed. For us - the Good and Honest Citizens - there has been little cause for optimism over the years and opportunities have been too few and far between.

Until now that is.

Mr Prime Minister, let me close by giving you a word of advice. You would do well to pay closer attention to the private activities of your

MPs and to the moral implications of the bankers involved in 'casino capitalism'. It was white-collar vandalism that brought the world to its knees – not us. Remember that, the next time you talk about 'criminality.'

Clip ends.

CHAPTER 19

12th August 2011

CBC News at Six

(Intro music)

A series of increasingly familiar images are broadcast. Thousands of rioters line the streets, throwing missiles at a wall of riot police. Dramatic aerial shots of buildings and cars that have been set alight. Angry and frightened citizens comment upon the 'atrocities'. All of these images are accompanied by one prolonged headline, which remains glued to the bottom of the screen:

LONDON IS UNDER ATTACK.

SOPHIE WALLACE: Tonight, the armed forces have been deployed onto the streets of London. It's a desperate move by the Prime Minister who has ordered this intervention to prevent yet another night of heavy rioting. Last night saw the worst violence yet as more fires continued to destroy businesses and homes in scenes that once again, can only be compared to the Blitz back in 1940 and 1941.

Cuts to daylight aerial scene. Huge billows of smoke rise into the air, pouring out off a massive apartment building that has been targeted by rioters.

SOPHIE WALLACE: And amidst the tangled wreckage of the city, there's been stinging criticism of the police as well as the parents whose children are causing such catastrophic damage.

Cuts to member of public - a young thirty-something blonde woman - taken from an earlier interview.

WOMAN: It's absolutely disgusting! They are feral rats. What are their parents doing about this? Their children should be at home. They shouldn't be out there on the streets causing mayhem.

Cuts to CCTV images of a gang of unmasked black youths. The gang are trying to break into an unknown building – kicking and pounding at the entrance, which refuses to yield under the assault.

SOPHIE WALLACE: Police have also released more images of suspected rioters wanted for questioning, but as of yet - are no closer to solving the identity of Chester George, the man the authorities now consider to be the leader of the rioters.

Cuts to an aerial shot of London – the camera panning left over Wembley Stadium with visible plumes of smoke in the distance.

SOPHIE WALLACE: Tonight's World Cup qualifier between England and the

Netherlands has also been cancelled due to sustained unrest in the capital. Other friendly matches scheduled for this evening have also been called off.

Cuts back to Sophie sitting at the news desk.

SOPHIE WALLACE: Good evening. At last, the military have been deployed onto the streets of London in an attempt to curb the wave of violence that has swept over the city for almost a week now. Thousands of people gathered in the streets today to cheer the arrival of various regiments, including 3rd battalion The Parachute Regiment.

Cuts to a scene of armoured vehicles making their way down the city streets. The vehicles are flanked by hundreds of troops, while large civilian crowds stand behind makeshift barriers on both sides, cheering the troops on, many of them waving tiny Union Jack flags in the air.

SOPHIE WALLACE: The Prime Minister - who this week cut short his holiday in the Mediterranean - has also reiterated his promise that those involved in the rioting will pay a heavy price.

Cuts back to Sophie in the studio.

SOPHIE WALLACE: But despite the threat of military intervention, last night saw the worst rioting on the streets of London in living memory. An old-age pensioner, Richard Coggins, was brutally murdered in Croydon on Wednesday night and at least a dozen more people - two more pensioners amongst them - have been killed this week. Let's go to a special report by our man on the spot - Dick Ronson - on last night's violence.

Cuts to aerial scenes of buildings on fire across the London skyline.

DICK RONSON (*Voiceover*): It began long before nightfall. All across London, the violence spread and it became clear that despite their best efforts, the police were not equal to the task of peacekeeping our streets. The escalation was rapid as violence increased throughout the day and into the night. It was on occasions alarming, but for the most part it was truly frightening. The valiant efforts of the firefighters were no match for the rapacious flames that feasted on buildings across London. A photographer caught this image of yet another person being forced to leap to safety from the first floor of a burning apartment building.

A young woman is seen jumping from a building into the arms of waiting firefighters – the backdrop is consumed by a thick yellow glow.

DICK RONSON: In the west, Ealing continues to be under siege, bringing terror to everyday suburban life. People are already evacuating their homes, terrified of what the rioters might do to them, or to the lives of their family members, if they don't.

Cuts to interview with local wine bar owner (identified as 'Suzie Rastovic').

SUZIE RASTOVIC: They broke the window of my bar, climbed

in and started looking for the till, the alcohol – everything. I escaped through the back, through the corridor. Then I locked myself into the kitchen and I thought they couldn't get in there because it's a fire escape. But I could hear them breaking everything. It was terrifying.

DICK RONSON: Suzie, would you like to see more being done by the police?

SUZIE RASTOVIC: (*Getting angry*) Yes I do, I want protection. That's what they're here for. Where are the police? (*Pointing straight ahead*) The police station is just up there. Why weren't they here to protect us?

Cuts to further scenes of looting - a gang of youths smashing into a designer clothes shop.

DICK RONSON: (*Voiceover*) In Clapham, hundreds of youths smashed shop windows and continued to loot at will. These pictures show how young some of them are, some of them barely out of childhood. And in one clip, which has since gone viral –

Cuts to a scene in which a group of youths are assisting a young boy who is lying on the pavement.

DICK RONSON: - a group of rioters pause to help a young boy who is lying on the street. They appear to be helping him at first, but what they're actually doing is distracting him while others help themselves to the contents of his rucksack.

Cuts to Dick Ronson - bald and bespectacled - standing on the streets of Brixton.

DICK RONSON: Sophie, I'm in in Brixton where last night, rioters ran amok until at least five o'clock in the morning. There is a real sense of insecurity out here on the streets. But there is also a quiet, underlying anger and not just at the rioters but with the police for their failure to control the situation. And many people are angry at the politicians too – for what they believe to be their part in the root causes of these disturbances.

Well with me now is Jamie Lee, a local equality campaigner, based here in Brixton.

The camera zooms out to reveal a short, bald-headed black man standing beside Ronson. A small crowd of mostly black people from the local community surround the two men. Behind them, a long row of buildings - once containing both shops and apartments - has been burned to the ground. The area is sealed off and firefighters can be seen in the background assessing the structural damage.

DICK RONSON: Jamie Lee, thank you for joining us. The violence shows no sign of ending. Would you agree with that?

JAMIE LEE: (*Nodding*) Of course. And let me say this - nobody here condones violence. But people don't wake up one morning and suddenly decide to burn down furniture shops. It's part of a long process of FRUSTRATION. But the police and the politicians had no idea this was coming. They had no idea that our inner cities are pressure cookers. That the steam is building up as unemployment rises and as inequality rises. And when that steam builds up? It has to be released. It's got to have *SOMEWHERE-TO-GO!*

Jamie hits the palm of one hand with the back of the other, tapping out the syllables of 'SOMEWHERE-TO-GO'.

JAMIE LEE: You ask the people standing around here Dick. These people have lived here for years and they'll tell you - something was always going to happen.

Several locals in the background nod their heads as he speaks.

DICK RONSON: Yes Jamie, but that doesn't condone what's happening now. Does it?

JAMIE LEE: I don't condone violence! I was out on the streets till three in the morning last night trying to encourage the rioters to stand down, to stop what they were doing. But we can't be blind to the root cause of this sickness. Poor communities like this one in Brixton and throughout inner city London are in pain. There are cuts to public services; there is a lack of opportunities; there is little to no hope. They are stopping and searching black people for -

NO-GOOD-REASON!

JAMIE LEE: We condemn the violence Dick. But Chester George is right - we must also condemn the government, the politicians, and the bankers - all of those who are guilty of economic violence.

This gets a round of applause from the onlookers.

JAMIE LEE: The bankers and politicians have done more damage to the world than these kids out here on the streets.

DICK RONSON: Isn't it true Jamie Lee, that you yourself have been involved in riots in the past? In the 1981 Brixton riots?

JAMIE LEE: (*Furious*) Have some respect! I have never been involved in riots. I have been involved in marches and demonstrations, but never riots.

DICK RONSON: Jamie, tell me. Are you disgusted by what you saw last night?

JAMIE LEE: You tell *me* Dick. Would you be here today - would the topic of social inequality have been raised at all had these people not taken to the streets? Answer me please.

DICK RONSON: (*Touching his earpiece*) Well it seems like we're running out of time. Jamie Lee, thank you very much.

Dick Ronson turns to the camera, showing his back to the crowd.

DICK RONSON: Well Sophie, that name - Chester George - is everywhere at the moment. A video blogger, with just two short clips to his name, has become an Internet sensation, not to mention the spearhead of the London riots. But who is he? Where is he? And what will he do next?

This is Dick Ronson, CBC News at Six, in Brixton.

CHAPTER 20

12th August 2011

Mack fell into the armchair, and the soft leather swallowed him up like quicksand.

He stared blankly at the CBC News. His eyes followed the pictures - the masked hordes, the journalists, the authority figures, and of course, the burning buildings - but his mind was reluctant to get involved.

He laid a hand over his full stomach. Isabella Walker's home-made lasagne was making a nest in there, forcing the rest of his body to shut down, and to declare a national state of food coma. Any second now, the front of his body would rip open and it would be John Hurt in *Alien* all over again.

Mack dabbed the back of his hand against his damp forehead.

The Walkers had gathered in the living room after dinner to watch the news. Mack's parents were as usual sitting on the leather couch next to the large flat screen TV. Mack was on the other side of the room, sitting in one of two black leather armchairs.

On TV, the newsreader Sophie Wallace was talking about the trial of former Ukrainian Prime Minister, Yulia Tymoshenko, who was facing charges of abuse of office. Mack raised a half-hearted eyebrow. *Finally.* He always knew there had to be something else going on in the world apart from the London riots.

And you did nothing to help that policeman.

Why haven't they mentioned him on the news? Maybe they haven't found the body yet? Maybe there isn't a body left to find? Maybe he didn't die? Maybe he got a few bumps and bruises and picked himself up and walked away?

You let them drag him down that alley. You did that, by doing nothing.

He's dead. Somewhere.

Mack shot a worried glance at his parents. They were still looking at the screen, listening to a CBC journalist talk about the events in Ukraine.

His mother – perhaps just as uninterested in the Ukraine story as he was - turned towards him.

Oh shit.

"It's terrible isn't it?" Isabella said. "I can't stop thinking about that poor old man who died in Croydon a couple of nights back."

Archie Walker - reclining in an old T-shirt and a pair of loose jogging pants - piped in.

"Aye, bloody scumbags," he said. "Beating a helpless old man to death in the street. Stick a rope around their necks. It's gone way too far now."

Mack's blood ran cold. *Richard Coggins. Croydon. Two nights ago.*

"Hmmm," he said. He rubbed at his belly, trying to soothe the angry monster swimming around in his digestive fluids. Any more talk about the riots and he'd puke for sure.

Don't think about that policeman then.

"A war veteran," Isabella said, shaking her head. "Richard

Coggins. He was a pilot. He fought for his country, defended us against the Nazis and look what they did to him."

Archie Walker nodded. "Let the army deal with it now."

Mack glanced across the room at his mother. She looked like she'd aged twenty years over the past week. There were bags under her eyes, little hammocks made out of loose hanging skin. His mother had always been a thin woman but Mack wondered now whether she'd been losing weight recently too. He'd watched her pick at her own dinner that evening, and not for the first time that week.

Isabella had been coming downstairs in the middle of the night too. Mack had lain in bed, listening to her run the tap in the kitchen, bringing a glass of water into the living room. What was she doing in there? Sitting by the window no doubt, watching and waiting. Waiting for the sound of glass breaking on Stanmore Road, and for the first whiff of smoke to come drifting across their neighbourhood.

Archie Walker put an arm around his wife and stroked the back of her tawny hair, which hung loose around the shoulders. Then he turned to his son. The grim expression on his face filled Mack with an immediate sense of dread.

"We've been thinking about moving back home Mack," he said.

Mack didn't blink. "To Edinburgh?"

His mother turned towards him. "We can't stay here," she said. "Not with all this going on."

She pointed at the TV, which was showing a department store building on fire. Several fire engines were parked outside, and the crews were working furiously to control the blaze. The caption below the images said the store was called Morleys and that it was an important location with historic value for the community.

"It won't be forever," Mack said.

"It's been six days son," Archie said. "Croydon's in ruins. Ealing – that's in trouble. And it looks like Brixton's next. It's only a matter of time before Tottenham goes down too – look at what's happening on the High Road every night. It's only going to get worse."

"But what about your job?" Mack said.

Archie smiled. "I'll work something out," he said. "I'm sure I can get the old one back in Edinburgh. And your mum can get back into teaching up there if she wants to."

"Nothing's certain yet," Isabella said. "We're just preparing for the worst."

Mack knew that wasn't the case. The decision had already been made and they were just softening him up.

"What worries me is that *we're* the targets," Archie said. "The middle-class. I don't want a brick crashing through the window in the middle of the night. Do you?"

Mack shook his head.

Isabella turned towards him.

"What do you think?" she said.

"I'm just beginning to make friends here," he said.

Isabella shook her head. "You're settling in *here*? Into this madness?" Once again, she pointed at the TV.

Mack nodded. "It's not as bad as they make it out to be."

"It's not bad?" she said, her eyes bulging. "Riots, burning buildings, supermarkets low on food, old-age pensioners getting beaten to death in the street - what else has to happen before you think it's bad Mack?"

Both his parents were staring at him now. They were steeling themselves for a fight about the pros and cons of the Walkers leaving London.

Mack knew he couldn't win.

"I just like it here," he said. "That's all. Can we drop it?"

But Isabella was just getting started.

"Where exactly have you been these past few nights young man?" Isabella asked. "All we ever get from you is 'out' or 'Sumo Dave's'. Well 'out' is no longer good enough. Where have you been spending your time? And if you don't tell us, you won't be setting foot outside that door until we're leaving for Edinburgh."

Mack's shoulders sagged in defeat. He wanted to crawl upstairs to his bedroom, to close the door, dim the lights and lie on the bed. To open a window and let the cool air float gently into his lungs.

To think about that policeman. And his wife and children who you let down so badly coward.

"Well?" Isabella said.

Mack felt sweat dripping down his forehead. Food coma, or was it?

"What do you want me to say?" he said. "I go down to Sumo Dave's flat. We play video games."

Isabella didn't blink. "And...?"

"And what?"

"Why do you never bring him back here?"

Mack threw his hands up in the air. "Just spit it out Mum," he said. "You think I'm one of them, don't you? You think I'm one of the rioters, out killing old men and setting police cars on fire."

Archie looked away. But his mother kept her eyes on him, like a hawk on its soon-to-be-prey.

"It must be tempting Mack," Isabella said. "All that free stuff lying around."

Archie Walker looked at his son.

"You know you can't be getting into any more trouble son," Archie said. "Not after what happened in Edinburgh."

Mack shook his head. "The same Edinburgh you want to take me back to."

Archie sighed. "Mack..."

"Let's not go there," Mack said. "I don't want to talk about it."

For a while, the three members of the Walker family stared at the TV in silence. They watched as the news finished and the next programme - *The Magazine Hour* - was introduced. Usually, this was a light-hearted show with interviews, celebrities, and so on. But it was filmed in Central London and Mack just knew - as the cheesy intro theme came on - that there'd be more about the riots coming up.

"We don't want you to fall in with a bad crowd," Isabella said.

Mack looked over at his mother.

"Just tell us son," she said. The anger seemed to have left her. "Please, just tell us - are you involved in the riots? Have you been doing a bit of looting with the rest of them? It's okay, you can tell us."

His parents looked across the room at him. Their eyes still hopeful that they'd got it wrong. That it was all a big mistake on their part.

Mack heard those muffled cries for help in his head. The policeman was calling on him, again and again.

He saw himself running away.

Would he ever stop running?

"No," he said. "I'm not involved."

His parents nodded, and then turned away quietly. Nothing more was said that night. Mack sunk deep into the folds of the leather armchair. He glanced at his parents, now leaning into one another for comfort.

Mack turned his attention back to the TV. On *The Magazine Hour*, somebody was talking about the Blitz.

CHAPTER 21

12th August 2011

The Magazine Hour

Kris Sayers, a lanky twenty-nine year old television presenter with a riot of ginger hair and a pair of horn-rimmed glasses, is standing on the steps beside the studio audience. The camera has just cut back to him following yet another montage of clips from the London riots.

KRIS SAYERS: I'm sure we're all agreed ladies and gentleman – shocking scenes there on the streets of London today.

Kris turns around and walks up a couple of steps.

KRIS SAYERS: Several of those buildings we saw on fire in the film actually survived Hitler's bombs during the Blitz in 1940. Seventy years later and tragically - they've fallen to a gang of thugs.

He stops beside two women sitting at the edge of the middle row.

KRIS SAYERS: Well a little earlier tonight, we found out that one of our audience members actually lived through the Blitz.

Kris squeezes past the two women and sits in a vacant seat next to the one furthest from the steps. She's an elderly lady, dressed in a white cardigan and pale blue skirt. A walking stick sits neatly between her legs.

KRIS SAYERS: Ladies and gentleman, how about a big round of applause for Joni Banks.

The crowd applauds while the presenter squeezes up tight next to Joni, who smiles politely.

KRIS SAYERS: (*Grinning*) Hello Joni my love!

JONI BANKS: Hi Kris.

KRIS SAYERS: Joni, thanks ever so much for making yourself known to us. Who are you here with tonight?

JONI BANKS: My daughter Michelle.

Joni touches the arm of the middle-aged woman to her left. The other woman smiles bashfully at Kris.

KRIS SAYERS: And if you don't mind my asking Joni – how old are you my darling?

JONI BANKS: I'm ninety-one.

This sparks another round of applause.

KRIS SAYERS: (*Standing up*) YES! YES! Ninety-one! You go girl!

Kris sits down again and holds his hand up for a high-five. Joni is quick to respond, slapping the palm of his hand gently.

KRIS SAYERS: Well it's a real honour for me to speak to you Joni, especially because you lived through the Blitz.

Kris gives Joni another round of applause – no one else joins in.

KRIS SAYERS: So Joni, how does it make you feel to see what's happening out there in London right now?

JONI BANKS: Well it brings back memories, that's for sure.

KRIS SAYERS: I'll bet. You probably remember those old buildings from way back in the day don't you my love? Look at them now!

JONI BANKS: (*Laughs*) Oh no. I wasn't talking about the buildings. I meant the looting. It's the looting that brings back memories.

KRIS SAYERS: (*Looking slightly confused*) Okay it sounds like you've got a story to tell my love. Who wants to hear Joni's story?

Kris stands up and frantically leads the audience into a cheering frenzy.

KRIS SAYERS: C'MON! You can do better than that. I said who wants to hear Joni's story? Let's hear you!

The audience responds with a little more oomph, and Kris sits back down beside Joni.

KRIS SAYERS: Go on Joni dear. Tell us about the Blitz.

JONI BANKS: (*nods*) Well, back in 1941, I was twenty-one. And like most twenty-one year olds I was on the lookout for a little excitement in my life. Especially during the war when everything was so serious. Anyway, that's how I ended up in the Café de Paris on the night of the 8th March.

KRIS SAYERS: The Café de Paris?

JONI BANKS: You're too young to remember dear, but I'm sure there are a few people out there who can still recall what happened that night.

KRIS: What did happen Joni?

JONI BANKS: A bomb hit us.

Momentarily at least, Kris Sayers is lost for words.

JONI BANKS: I loved going out back then. And I never gave a damn about the sirens either. Sometimes I'd find myself in the cinema watching a film when the sirens went off, warning us that a raid was imminent.

Kris is now listening intently, hanging onto every word.

JONI BANKS: No way, I used to say to myself. I want my sixpence worth. And so I stayed and watched the film all the way to the end. Hitler be damned.

Some of the audience members laugh softly.

JONI BANKS: Sometimes I had to walk home in the blackout, but even that didn't bother me. You had to point your torch down onto the pavement so that there wouldn't be any light for the planes above to see.

KRIS SAYERS: Wow. Isn't that incredible?

JONI BANKS: (*Sighs*) I was young and fearless back then. And that's how I ended up in the Café de Paris that night. We'd been warned that bad raids were coming, but I didn't care. Reg - my fiancée - was on a rare week's leave from the army and we were determined to go out and have a good time.

KRIS SAYERS: So this was a nightclub? I don't mean to be rude Joni my love, but are you going off on a tangent here? Does this little story of yours have something to do with what's going on in 2011, eh? The riots remember?

Kris laughs at his own joke – no one else does.

JONI BANKS: It used to be a real upmarket club. But after 1941 the prices lowered and it was a bit more accessible to the rest of us. The commoners. I remember it well. You had to walk down a long steep staircase, which seemed to go on and on forever. But once you were inside, it was actually quite a small place. The dance floor wasn't that big and it didn't take many couples to fill it up. But you were safe because you were underground, away from the bombs. Or so we thought.

Joni smiles, her eyes looking back into the past.

JONI BANKS: It was one of the best ways to forget about the war - to go out dancing. And if we were going to be blown to smithereens then wasn't it better to be out having a good time rather than cowering in a bomb shelter somewhere. That's what I always thought anyway.

Kris puts an arm around Joni.

KRIS SAYERS: Joni Banks, you're my kind of gal!

Kris removes his arm immediately.

JONI BANKS: It wasn't that late when the bomb hit. It was before ten o'clock. Lucky in a way I suppose, had it been an hour later there would have been more people in the club.

KRIS SAYERS: And do you remember my love? The moment when the bomb landed?

Joni nods.

JONI BANKS: They said it came through an airshaft. Through the skylight and that it landed on the dance floor, right in front of the band that was playing. I'd been up there dancing just minutes earlier, but Reg - he'd dragged me away because he wanted to go get a drink. He liked a drink, did my Reg.

KRIS SAYERS: Sounds terrifying Joni.

JONI BANKS: The band had only just started. Ken Johnson - that was the bandleader's name - I think he'd only just turned up at the club. 'Snakehips', they called him. I heard somebody say that the bomb took his head clean off. Then again, somebody else said that he was unmarked. But who knows? Either way he was dead.

KRIS SAYERS: What about you and Reg?

Joni grimaces at the recollection.

JONI BANKS: A tremendous force blew me back. It was as if all the glass in the club had been thrown at my face. There was a flash of blue light. I thought I was dead.

KRIS SAYERS: Good Lord!

JONI BANKS: But at some point I said to myself – quite calmly I recall, that no, this was a bomb. We've been hit.

KRIS SAYERS: And then what happened?

JONI BANKS: I heard Reg screaming my name. 'JONI, JONI'. I lifted my head off the floor and saw him clambering over a heap of bodies. We were lucky to be alive. Some people had their limbs ripped off and they were lying in different corners of the room from the rest of their body parts. And yet some of the other bodies hadn't moved an inch. I mean you'd expect to see people all over the place after a blast like that, wouldn't you? But I remember seeing this couple sitting at a table near the edge of the dance floor. The man had his hand outstretched like he'd been offering her something - a cigarette maybe? They looked completely undisturbed even though they were stone dead.

KRIS SAYERS: So you were unhurt?

JONI BANKS: (*Smiling*) Nothing more than cuts and bruises to worry about, both of us, although my right eye was badly sliced open by bits of glass and metal. Anyway, that should have been enough horror for one night.

Joni turns towards Kris.

JONI BANKS: But then the looters came.

KRIS SAYERS: Looters? That's hard to believe Joni.

JONI BANKS: (*Nods*) Oh yes. There were as many looters as there were people helping. In fact, it was impossible to tell who was who. There were civilians, wardens, police, and God knows what else. It was chaos but the looters were everywhere. *Nasty* people. Little devils they were, pouring in through the smoke, reaching and grabbing at the bodies. At one point, I watched a man pull a dead girl from the wreckage. I thought he was trying to help her or drag the body outside, but then he pulled a knife from inside his coat pocket and cut off her ring finger.

KRIS SAYERS: Good lord.

JONI BANKS: And I saw another wild-eyed character – in his thirties or forties probably, kneeling over a woman and cutting the necklace away from her neck. Taking everything he was. Jewellery, clothes, handbags, they went after it all.

Joni looks over towards the studio window, which offers a stunning view of Central London lit up at night. For a moment or two, her eyes are lost in the past.

KRIS SAYERS: Well, that's quite a revelation Joni my love. Who'd have thought it? Looting at such a time.

JONI BANKS: We kept Hitler out and that's all our children need to know in school.

KRIS SAYERS: Are you saying it was a cover up Joni?

JONI BANKS: It was the preservation of our morale. Looting threatened the whole idea that we were in the war together. Some of the newspapers called for the looters to be hanged, but most of them just ignored it. But the looting was so bad during the war – it really was. It was every bit as nasty as what we're seeing now – if not worse considering the fact that we were at war. I remember reading about a gang of teenage girls who were caught stripping the clothes from dead bodies. Oh yes, children looted back then too. I heard reports of them stealing coins from the gas meters of burned out houses. There were thousands of cases of juvenile looting back then, just like today.

KRIS SAYERS: And here we are - during these riots - lamenting the loss of the Blitz Spirit in Britain. Was the Blitz Spirit just a lie then?

JONI: (*Shakes her head*) The Blitz Spirit was real Kris. Nothing can ever take that away from us. But certain truths are conveniently forgotten, especially by the media who use the Blitz as a moral yardstick.

KRIS SAYERS: And what truths are those my love?

Joni looks into the camera.

JONI: That the world's full of bastards. It always has been.

CHAPTER 22

13th August 2011

Mack kept to the other side of the street as he walked past Tottenham Police Station. He didn't look over, but he could feel the thirty or so armed officers watching him as he walked past. He imagined their eyes, following his every move, their rifles primed and trigger fingers alert.

The station was now under guard twenty-four hours a day. It had been the target of constant attacks since the trouble first began and now the police and rioters had attached a certain symbolic importance upon the building.

Both its survival and destruction were crucial.

He continued walking south along the High Road, half expecting, half-hoping to see a tank, an armoured vehicle, or a squadron of soldiers marching to battle. But there was nothing, at least not today. Whatever armed forces had been deployed onto the streets of London, they were somewhere else that day, somewhere with more urgent needs than Tottenham.

A small gathering of people stood in the middle of the High Road, standing on the bricks and other fallen debris. It took Mack only a moment to realise that these weren't rioters - they were mothers and fathers. And with them were young children, clutching at their parents' hands or being cradled in their arms. Some of the children were crying and in their collective sobs, Mack heard an aching pain – a gnawing hunger that was unfamiliar to most children in a First World city.

The older kids didn't cry. They just stared blankly into space, their eyes unusually large within their sunken faces.

Some of them looked at Mack as he walked past. He quickly hurried along.

He was almost at Charlie's Cafe now. Just as he was about to turn right onto Philip Lane, Mack saw a small procession walking towards him in the middle of the street. A woman at the head of the procession was talking through a loudspeaker as the group came forward. Mack was tempted to ignore it, to hurry towards Charlie's, but something held him back. He stopped for a moment to watch. There were about ten or twelve of them, mostly black middle-aged women. They were moving slowly - like a funeral cortege - up the High Road, through the fallen bricks and debris. As the procession drew nearer, Mack listened to the elderly woman who was talking through the loudspeaker.

"Fresh food and water supplies are coming today. Listen carefully. FRESH. SUPPLIES. From one o'clock this afternoon, stock up on food, water, medicine and whatever else you need. Come to Tottenham Police Station! Queue outside for supplies. People of Tottenham – One o'clock. FRESH SUPPLIES! FRESH SUPPLIES!"

Mack thought about the people standing outside the police station. And he remembered the children with the hungry eyes.

One of the women in the procession noticed him and walked towards him. She was a small and portly black woman, forty or fifty-something years of age, and dressed in a faded denim jacket and dark jeans.

She looked at Mack with a kindly smile.

"Do you need food and supplies son?" she asked. Her accent had a hint of the Caribbean. She held out a small sheet of paper and offered it to him. "Here's some information about the supply drops outside the police station. There's one today at one o'clock." She thrust the slip of paper closer. "Go on. Take it."

Mack reached out, but quickly withdrew his hand again.

"I'm okay thanks," he said. "My dad's got a car and he's making a food run into Central London this morning. You should give this to somebody else."

The woman put the sheet back on top of the pile.

"I wish we were all so lucky," she said, smiling. "To have a car."

Mack nodded "No shops still open around here?" he said.

The woman shook her head. "No shops," she said. "Everything's been destroyed and if it hasn't, it's closed anyway. The buses aren't running around here either – the roads aren't up to much as you've probably noticed."

Mack couldn't remember the last time he'd seen a bus in Tottenham. Cars were becoming something of a rarity too.

"Charlie's *is* still open," the woman said, pointing down Philip Lane towards the cafe. "But not for much longer. It's overrun with people and there's no way Charlie will be able to keep up."

"People can still use the Tube can't they?" Mack asked.

She nodded. "Yes, but you can only imagine how crowded it is. All those people trying to get in and out of Central London. It's like rush hour every hour. And I'll tell you this – they're raising the prices in the city centre too. They don't care how many children are starving out here on the outskirts. Not when there's a chance to make money."

The woman looked over at the procession, slowly making its way north.

"Better catch up," she said. She smiled at Mack and her eyes lit up. "Goodbye son," she said. "And good luck."

"Thanks," Mack said, calling after her. And then in a whisper, he added:

"I'm sorry."

There was a massive queue outside Charlie's. The line began at the door and stretched further down Philip Lane. There was probably over a hundred people at that moment, tucked into the side of the pavement, all searching for a hot meal. To Mack, it looked like a group of bargain hunters standing outside a department store waiting for the Boxing Day sales to begin.

A small blackboard had been placed outside the door. Scribbled in white chalk were the words: *WAITING TIME – 1HR APPROX*

Shite.

Sumo Dave and the others were inside waiting for him.

Mack walked towards the door and glanced through the window but the place was jam-packed and it was impossible to see beyond the mass of bodies gathered by the window.

As he took a step back, he noticed dirty looks coming his way.

"Don't think about skipping the line sunshine," somebody called out. "I've got my eye on you."

Mack took a step away from the building. He pulled his phone out of his pocket and found a text waiting from Sumo Dave.

'Fckn rammed in here m8. Waited 45min to get in! Txt wen u get here.'

Mack sent a brief reply – *'Here. Stuck outside.'*

A few minutes passed. Nothing happened. Mack was thinking about leaving when the cafe door opened and Sumo Dave popped his head outside. He pointed at Mack.

"Hey," he said. "Are you the lad who hasn't eaten for two days?"

Mack looked behind him.

"What?" he said.

Sumo Dave beckoned him over. And this time he spoke louder so that the others in the queue could hear him too.

"Charlie sent me out," Sumo Dave said. "He told me there's a little white boy outside who hasn't eaten in two days. Is that you mate?"

Mack didn't answer.

Sumo Dave nodded. "Yeah that's you, innit? Remember?"

"Yeah," Mack said. "I suppose..."

He looked at the queue. Everyone was staring at him.

"But I didn't want to jump the queue," he said. "That's not fair on these people. We're all hungry."

"Of course," Sumo Dave said. "That's very noble of you, especially with your cancer n' all. You didn't want to jump the queue."

At the front of the queue, a tall black man, dressed in a slim leather jacket, turned to Mack. "Is that true?" he said. "You got cancer?"

Mack took a step forward. "I'm okay," he said. "I want to join the queue like everyone else. We've got to try and keep civilised, haven't we?"

"He was definitely acting a bit funny when he got here," somebody else said. "It was like he didn't know where he was."

Mack coughed.

"So pale and pasty," Sumo Dave said. "Poor lad."

"Get inside son," the man at the head of the queue said. He turned to Sumo Dave. "Get some hot food into the lad. He looks like he's about to pass out."

"C'mon mate," Sumo Dave said. He stepped onto the pavement and took Mack by the arm, guiding him towards the door. "Thanks everyone," he said.

Mack managed a feeble wave.

Once inside, Sumo Dave dropped Mack's arm. "You overdid it a bit there mate," he said. "You'll get us lynched if they find out."

Mack shrugged. "You started it ya prick."

"Yeah, whatever," Sumo Dave said. "C'mon, we don't have long in here. Charlie's rule is you eat, get out and make room for the next lot."

Mack looked around the cafe. All the tables were full, but that didn't mean they were turning back customers. There were people sitting in a huddle on the floor. Others were tucked up on the window-ledge. Some people were content simply to stand with a plate of food in their hand. For most people, it was enough just to be in there.

The room was full of chatter, and the scent of freshly cooked bacon hung in the air.

Sumo Dave led Mack past the counter where the staff were working at a ferocious pace – cooking fry-ups and making toasted sandwiches as if their lives depended on it.

Hatchet and Tegz were waiting in the far corner of the room. As Mack arrived, they were devouring a plate of toasted sandwiches between them.

Tegz acknowledged Mack's arrival with a curt nod.

Hatchet kept eating.

Behind them, fixed to the wall, a large TV was on. It was showing a chat show with a bunch of women sitting around a table drinking tea and talking. Of course, they were talking about the riots.

"Alright?" Mack said to the others.

"Fucking starving mate," Tegz said, through a mouthful of food.

Mack nodded. "You guys been out since Croydon?" he said.

"Yeah," Sumo Dave replied.

"Where?" Mack asked. "Back to Croydon?"

Sumo Dave shook his head. "No way mate," he said. "You saw it. It's a bloody war zone innit? Nah, we stayed here on the High Road."

"Any action?" Mack asked.

Sumo Dave shrugged. "It's alright."

"Yeah," Tegz said.

"Just the usual," Sumo Dave said. "You know, standing in a crowd squaring off with the riot police, that sort of thing."

"That it?" Mack said.

"A few running battles," Sumo Dave said. "Missiles and all that."

Sumo Dave lifted a can of Coke off the table and brought it to his lips. At the same time, Mack looked up at the TV in the corner. Sadie Hobbs, the reality TV star, was a guest on the talk show. They were still talking about the riots.

INTERVIEWER: Sadie, isn't it fair to say that there are genuine underlying reasons behind the riots? Social issues? Class issues? Government failings?

SADIE HOBBS: C'mon – these little rats are using anything to try and justify their actions. Are we really supposed to believe that they're targeting JD Sports because they think that JD Sports use child labour to produce their shoes? How do they know that then? They're desperately trying to justify their devious little criminal minds by telling us that the riots are noble. Yet they've still gone after small businesses and independent retailers, which means it's got nothing to do with major companies and exposing exploitation. They're reaching for explanations that will justify the greed and violence.

Sumo Dave looked up at the TV screen. "Talentless bitch," he said. "Everywhere I look it's Sadie fucking Hobbs this and that."

"Yeah," Tegz said.

"Seen the army yet?" Mack said.

"The army," Sumo Dave said. "What are the soldiers going to do, eh? Nah they're probably in Croydon or Brixton, standing around looking pretty in their uniforms."

Mack nodded. "There's a crowd outside the police station too," he said. "People waiting for food."

Sumo Dave sighed. "Yeah I saw it. Poor buggers."

"You hear that Hatch?" Tegz said, wiping the crumbs from his mouth with the back of his hand. "There's free grub outside the cop shop later."

Hatchet nodded. "Yeah, that'll do me," he said. "Can't see my mum getting off her arse to go shopping anytime soon. Not unless the vodka runs out in the flat."

"Fuck off," Mack said. "There's people starving out there and you're in here stuffing your fat fucking face with toasties. You don't need the supply vans anymore than I do."

Mack's heart began to race. He'd never spoken to Hatchet like that. Had anyone?

Hatchet straightened himself up. His broad shoulders expanded, like he'd just pushed a button, and his doll eyes glared across the table.

"What the fuck did you just say to me?" he said.

Mack felt the hormones surging through his body.

Fight or flight?

The easiest thing to do would be to look away. *Just back down.* But something bigger took a hold of Mack and in that moment, against all rational thinking, he forced himself to stand tall, staring back at Hatchet and meeting his eye.

"Fuck you *Harold*," he said. "I'm not scared of you."

Harold was Hatchet's real name. Sumo Dave had once told Mack how much Hatchet hated it and that nobody - nobody - was allowed to say it to him on the street. Not without serious consequences. Only Hatchet's mum called him Harold and nobody ever saw her anyway.

Hatchet's entire body twitched, as if on the brink of a spasm. "*What?*"

Tegz instinctively backed off. Sumo Dave hovered on the outskirts of the confrontation, like a boxing referee about to stop a fight.

"Easy boys," he said.

Mack kept his eyes on Hatchet. "You've got a problem with me man," he said to Hatchet. "You've had a problem with me since the start. Want to tell me something?"

Hatchet took a step forward. So did Mack. Now they were standing face-to-face. And even though Hatchet was built like a brick shithouse, Mack still saw the uncertainty lingering in his eyes.

Typical fucking bullyboy. Somebody stands up to you and you don't know what to do.

"Tough guy, eh?" Hatchet growled. His upper lip was raised, on the brink of forming a snarl.

Mack shook his head.

"You're right Hatchet," he said. "What do I know about being a tough guy? If I was a tough guy I'd have come back from Croydon with a pint of dried blood stuck to my hands."

Tegz flinched in the background.

"Did you guys hear about the old man who died in Croydon that night?" Mack said. "The war hero. What was his name? Coggins, wasn't it?"

Hatchet's face drained of all colour. He took a backwards step, as if some unseen force was getting him out of there.

"Aye," Mack said. "I heard all about it."

For a moment, nobody spoke. There was only the constant chatter of other customers, as well as the high-pitched scratching sound of steel forks on plates.

And from the TV above their heads, came the voice of Sadie Hobbs.

Sadie Hobbs: We need to get serious. And I am serious about this problem that's out there RIGHT NOW infesting our streets. The only way to deter these little crooks is to scare them out of their wits. And the good people of this country – and by that I mean the REAL good and honest citizens – do you hear that Chester George or whatever your name is? The real citizens need to get serious about fixing this mess. If our government are too soft to do it then let's do it ourselves. Let's DO IT. Let's rise up, take to the streets and make a stand against these vermin. There are more of us than there are of them. It's either that or we watch our city fall into the hands of a minority of degenerates. And here's another solution that no one else will bring up. What about lynch mobs? If lynch mobs were to make an appearance on the streets of London and target these criminals, then I guarantee you we'd see the back of this problem in a matter of hours. HOURS! But we're too soft for that. Aren't we Britain?

"FUCK YOU!"

Hatchet barged past Mack on his way towards the door. The impact of one of those thick shoulders was enough to send Mack staggering back a step or two.

Tegz turned around, watching Hatchet storm out the door. Then he turned back to the others.

"I'd better go after him," he said quietly. "Somebody better calm him down, eh?"

"Yeah," Sumo Dave said. "You do that. Text me later, alright?"

Tegz nodded. He turned and walked slowly towards the door. As he left, another person who'd been waiting in the queue outside entered the cafe.

"You alright?" Sumo Dave said to Mack. "You're looking a bit white mate. And I don't mean that in a racist way or nothing."

Mack tried to speak but no words came out. The adrenaline dump was over and his brain was trying to re-establish a connection with the rest of his body. He could feel his entire body shaking from head to toe, just as it had done the last time he'd had a much worse confrontation back in Edinburgh. Different city, different bully, but thank God, this time a different outcome.

"That was close," Sumo Dave said. He lowered his voice. "Listen mate, Hatchet is NOT a bloke you want to piss off. Remember the gun thing, yeah? And he's a nutter."

Mack nodded.

"And he won't forget something like that in a hurry," Sumo Dave said. "You embarrassed him. So just watch out, yeah? Even if he acts cool next time you see him, he'll still be looking for a way to hurt you mate."

Mack shrugged. "He's hardly going to shoot me, is he?"

"Probably not, but Hatchet's a pyscho. Worth bearing in mind."

"Hatchet's a dick," Mack said. "We both know what he did the other night, don't we?"

Sumo Dave sighed. "He's just a fucked up kid mate. I've known Hatch all me life. I remember his dad - he was a nutcase too, a proper bloody gangster."

"The old boy bugger off did he?"

"Yeah," Sumo Dave said. "His dad wasn't half as violent as his mum though, the crazy old witch."

"They sound like a nice family," Mack said. "So where's his dad now?"

Sumo Dave shrugged. "I dunno. He disappeared when Hatchet was a little kid. Dead probably. Lying at the bottom of the river or buried in cement somewhere. That messed his mum up proper good that did. When he left. She hit the bottle big time but at least she's too drunk most of the time to be violent, eh? Silver linings and all that."

"So that's why he hates me?" Mack said. "Cos I don't have shitty parents?"

"Cos you had a chance. You weren't born in this shithole. You probably won't stay here forever, like the rest of us. You've got a chance mate."

Mack sighed. "Chance of a good life?"

"Yeah," Sumo Dave said, looking around. "Something better than this. You're a smart lad. You'll finish school, go to uni and travel the world and all that stuff. Things that are beyond the likes of us."

Mack looked at Sumo Dave. "I'm not the angel you think I am mate. In fact, come to think of it, I'm a lot like Hatchet."

Sumo Dave raised his eyebrows. "Eh?"

"I fucked up once."

"What do you mean?"

"Back in Edinburgh. I hurt someone."

"What like, hurt their feelings?"

Mack shook his head impatiently. "I *hurt* somebody Sumo."

"Like...?"

Mack hesitated. "I stabbed a boy."

Sumo Dave's jaw dropped.

"*You*?" he said.

Mack nodded. "I'm no better than Hatchet. Or anyone."

Sumo Dave urged him on. "Don't just stand there. What happened?"

Mack sighed. "I ran with a bad crowd," he said. "Ever since I started secondary school, I ran with the wrong people."

"Story of my life," Sumo Dave said, smiling.

"It was the usual things at first - smoking, drinking and then a bit of weed."

Sumo Dave nodded. "Sounds normal."

"Like you say," Mack said. "I do have a good home and good parents. And these kids, they weren't the type of people that someone like me - with my background - should have been hanging around with, eh? That's what made them the cool kids I suppose."

Sumo Dave nodded. "Just like you're doing now, eh? Hanging with the cool kids."

Mack smiled. "Aye," he said. "But they only liked me because I could afford to buy them things. Know what I mean? I was never really one of them. I was always the one stumping up cash for fags and booze every weekend."

"So what happened?" Sumo Dave asked.

"I was always trying to prove myself to them," Mack said. "It's so fucking stupid. Trying to prove that I wasn't this nice middle-class boy. I'm doing the same thing with you lads I guess - going out to Croydon and all that."

Sumo Dave shrugged. "I like ya mate. Haven't asked you to buy anything for me, have I?"

Mack grinned. "Not yet"

Sumo Dave winked at Mack. "Although if I hadn't been nicking everything I need for the past week, then who knows? Eh?"

"Aye."

"Anyway, go on," Sumo Dave said.

"We were always getting into scraps with other gangs," Mack said. "Just fistfights you know. I was coming home with cuts and bruises – my parents knew something was wrong. I said it was nothing. They worried anyway. Anyway, one Saturday we were all hanging about in Leith and this guy from another gang walks past and he starts having a right pop at me."

"Yeah?"

"Aye," Mack said. "Calling me a rich cunt, a spoilt wee bastard and all that good stuff. Fuck off back to mummy rich boy."

Sumo Dave smiled. "Sounds like a real charmer."

Mack nodded. "We used to carry knives on us," he said. "I don't know why - we never used them. They were just there in our back pockets. All the scraps we used to get into – it was always skin. Punches and kicks, you know? But we carried these knives anyway."

"Yeah," Sumo Dave said.

"Well this guy," Mack said. "He was a few years older than me. Rossi, his name was. His family was probably more fucked up than Hatchet's. *Heroin*."

"Oh shit."

"Well he starts in on *my* family," Mack said. "Calling my mum all sorts of things and telling me what he'd like to do to her, you know?"

"Nasty," Sumo Dave said.

"I flipped," Mack said. "It wasn't just what he was saying, it was all sorts of shit I'd been burying inside for years. It all bubbled to the surface in that one moment. I pulled the knife, hoping he'd back down. Guess what?"

Sumo Dave leaned in closer. "What?"

"He had a knife too."

"What a bastard," Sumo Dave said.

"It got serious in a hurry," Mack said. "The chants started up - *Fight, fight, fight.* I don't mind telling you mate - I've never been so shit scared in all my life. He kept jabbing at me with the knife and I found myself thinking about all those old films from the fifties, know the ones?"

"Yeah," Sumo Dave said. "James Dean."

"Aye," Mack said. "So this Rossi – he charges at me. With his arm out, steaming in and I thought – I swear to God – I thought he was going to kill me. I actually thought I was about to die. And so fuck it, I thrust the knife out at him, more out survival instinct than anything. And I was faster than him. The knife went into his stomach."

Sumo Dave grimaced. "*Sheeeeeeeeit!*"

Mack closed his eyes. "All that blood and screaming."

"What age were you?"

Mack opened his eyes again and looked at Sumo Dave. "Sixteen," he said. "Same age as I am now. Why do you think we moved to London?"

"Holy shit," Sumo Dave said. "This just happened? "I thought it was because of your old man's job that you came to London?"

Mack shook his head. "Nah. That's just what we tell people down here," he said.

"Is Rossi, is he...?"

"Dead? No. He pulled through."

"And you didn't go down for it?"

Mack shook his head. "I'm a rich kid, remember? We had a better lawyer than he did. And it was self-defence."

Sumo Dave grinned. "You are *the* original rebel without a cause mate. Bloody hell, I never would have guessed it. Not a chance."

Some of the kitchen staff were looking their way, and then looking at the queue piling up outside the door.

"Rossi had a record and I was clean," Mack said. "Who would you believe? I was cleared."

"You see," Sumo Dave said. "There are advantages to being a rich tosser."

Mack smiled.

"Bloody hell," Sumo Dave said. "And here's me telling you to worry about Hatchet," Sumo Dave said. "I'll need to tell *him* to watch out, eh? Don't mess with Mack the Knife."

Mack looked down at his hands. "That's what the local kids called me after it happened."

His palms were warm and sweaty.

"Did you see the blood on Hatchet's hands the other night Sumo?"

Sumo Dave spoke quietly. "Yeah, I saw. He's a crazy fucker. But he's a mate."

"That's what my hands looked like that day."

"LADS," someone at the counter shouted over to them. "If you're not eating can you make room for the others outside please?"

Without another word, Mack and Sumo Dave started walking towards the door. As they squeezed in between the bodies that filled the cafe, voices came down from the TV above their heads.

INTERVIEWER: Are you seriously suggesting Sadie, that we should become vigilantes? That we should be hanging people on the streets of London?

SADIE HOBBS: We need to stop being so soft in this country. This would NEVER have been allowed to happen in America.

INTERVIEWER: But it did happen. It happened in 1992 in Los Angeles. And before that, it happened in 1967 in Detroit.

SADIE HOBBS: Whatever! Look, these are desperate times and this is not the time for political correctness. There are rats running riot out there. Feral rats! And it's about time they were exterminated.

PHASE TWO: CIVIL DISOBEDIENCE

CHAPTER 23

Transcript of a video uploaded to YouTube.com (posted on *14th August 2011*)

(*Mobile Phone Footage*)

A shower of electric light pours down from above, illuminating a vast and abandoned supermarket. Within every aisle, the steel shelves have been stripped bare and in some cases, overturned. The floor is covered in empty boxes, tins, and the carcasses of rotten fruit.

There are flies everywhere, attached to the supermarket like it's a giant decomposing corpse.

In the distance, a small crowd - their faces hidden behind masks – explore the ruins. Scavenging each aisle, one by one, looking for scraps.

As all this is happening, 'London Calling' by The Clash, is playing through the speakers.

The cameraman flips the phone around. It's pointing directly at his face – a face covered by a skull hoodie, zipped over the top of his head. Dark brown eyes glare through the peepholes, while the camera-

man's breathing is heavy and laboured. When he talks, the quiet, raspy voice is a familiar one.

CHESTER GEORGE: This is London Calling. This is London Calling. Welcome one and all – welcome to the unofficial Olympics, brought to you by us, The Good and Honest Citizens of London.

He turns the camera back on the supermarket.

CHESTER GEORGE: Mr Prime Minister of the Dis-United Kingdom. Today, I want to do you a favour – I want to save you some money. I want you to forget about pumping billions of pounds into the 2012 Olympic Games next year. What about helping the Londoners – the real Londoners who live in the shadow of the Olympic Village? I'm talking about the people who will still live there and pay taxes long after the athletes have gone home. Okay? So this is the plan - you take care of them. I'll take care of the Olympics. Right here, Right now.

Chester George approaches a couple of masked figures - one short, one tall - with the hoods of their jackets pulled over their heads. Various bits and pieces of food – rotten fruit mostly, are scattered about the floor at their feet.

CHESTER GEORGE: So let's get the 2011 Supermarket Olympics underway, shall we?

The two masked youths giggle.

Chester George positions himself in the middle of the others, turning the camera on all three of them.

CHESTER GEORGE: Up first is the Four Hundred Metres. Or as close to four hundred as we can get. You know the drill, don't you lads?

The other two nod their heads, still giggling excitedly. They get into their starting positions - feet shoulder width apart, one foot forward and pointing towards the imaginary track.

CHESTER GEORGE: Are you ready? Set. GO!

The two runners take off at high-speed along the front of the supermarket, next to the checkouts. They shrink into the distance while the others cheer them on and shout words of encouragement.

The runners take a left at a ransacked alcohol aisle and disappear out of sight. Less than a minute later however, they both appear at the opposite end of the fruit and veg aisle where the race began, and it's neck and neck as they run towards Chester George.

CHESTER GEORGE: Ooooh! It's going to be a photo finish Mr Prime Minister. It's going to be soooooo close.

The shorter of the two runners prevails. He celebrates by picking up his baseball bat, lying at Chester George's feet, and proceeding to destroy Checkout Number 14.

Chester George walks over to the next aisle, where a gang of masked youths are messing around in what used to be the bakery.

CHESTER GEORGE: Now, after all that excitement – are you ready for the next event in the Supermarket Olympics?

Somebody calls out from afar – 'WHAT IS THE NEXT EVENT?'

CHESTER GEORGE: I thought you'd never ask. Time for the javelin, what do you say?

The Good and Honest Citizens cheer.

CHESTER GEORGE: There's only one problem. We don't have a javelin.

More cheers.

CHESTER GEORGE: (*Pointing the camera towards the youths*) Which one of you lads is the skinniest?

Instantly, a lanky individual, wearing a baseball cap, a blue mask and a black hoodie is pushed forward.

CHESTER GEORGE: Perfect. Perfect. Our javelin has volunteered willingly. Let's get on with the Olympics, shall we?

While Chester George films, several of the others pick up the skinny youth - despite his high-pitched squeals of protest - and with little restraint, they proceed to throw him over the bakery counter as if they were tossing a caber between them. The human javelin crashes onto the hard floor with a thud and cries out in pain upon landing. Slowly however, he gets up and seemingly without any serious damage. He jumps over the counter and returns to the fold, where the others cheer and pat him on the back like a conquering hero returned.

Chester George points the camera towards his face - close up - and laughs.

CHESTER GEORGE: Let's take a break from all this sporting excitement, shall we? How about something a little bit more intellectual?

He looks at something out of shot.

CHESTER GEORGE: Now this is interesting.

Chester George turns the camera towards the front of the building. There's a masked figure sitting at one of the checkouts. The body shape is clearly that of a female: large hips, pert breasts, and thin shoulders. Chester George keeps the camera pointed at her as he speaks.

CHESTER GEORGE: Hello there.

GIRL: (*Waving*) Hi.

CHESTER GEORGE: Now my dear, I'd like you to talk to the camera for a little while. You're a representative of The Good and Honest Citizens after all.

GIRL: What am I supposed to say?

CHESTER GEORGE: Well, for a start – tell us how old you are love.

GIRL: Eighteen.

CHESTER GEORGE: And where are you from?

GIRL: The East End.

CHESTER GEORGE: And isn't it true my dear, that you're an athlete?

GIRL: Yeah.

CHESTER GEORGE: What kind of athlete are you?

GIRL: I run. Look I don't really want to go into too much detail about it.

She points at her mask.

CHESTER GEORGE: Sorry my dear. It's just that I want the people watching this to know something about the Good and Honest Citizens. You see for some reason, they think we're all mindless thugs.

GIRL: Alright then.

CHESTER GEORGE: Now - you've never been arrested before have you?

GIRL: Never.

CHESTER GEORGE: You've never been in any sort of trouble with the police, have you?

She shakes her head.

CHESTER GEORGE: And isn't it true my dear, that one day you might run in that other Olympics – the boring one that everyone gets so worked up about every four years.

GIRL: I *will* run in the Olympics.

CHESTER GEORGE: And tell me. Why aren't you at home with your mum and dad tonight?

The girl takes a quick glance around the supermarket.

GIRL: 'Cos this is fun. This is probably the best time of my life.

CHESTER GEORGE: (*Laughs*) Me too love. And your mate who's somewhere in here, the one you're running around with. Tell me about her.

GIRL: She's a nurse. She's a bit older than me - twenty, she is.

CHESTER GEORGE: A nurse? A nurse and an athlete. That's interesting isn't it Mr Prime Minister. You got any other mates who run with The Good and Honest Citizens?

GIRL: Yeah. I know of one girl who's a social worker and she's been out every night since it started. I've met law students, riding instructors, and even a ballerina on the streets. My mate's a lifeguard and he's having it large big time.

CHESTER GEORGE: Thanks love. You can go back to the rest of the Olympics now. And remember - this is your time to shine.

The girl gets up and walks towards the aisles where the others are holding impromptu Olympic events. Chester George stays put and turns the camera back on himself.

CHESTER GEORGE: Now I can guess what you're going to say. All you academics, crawling out from underneath your little universities and chasing after us with your psychological and sociological theories. Desperately seeking understanding.

Chester George sits down on the supermarket floor. Nearby, the sound of breaking glass can be heard.

CHESTER GEORGE: Now let me save you academics a job. This is what you're going to say about the likes of that girl and all her friends in their well-to-do jobs – out on the streets rioting with the likes of me.

He scratches his chin carefully.

CHESTER GEORGE: Contagion theory. That's it. It's ordinary people getting carried away in crowds and losing themselves in the mob. Ordinary people doing things they wouldn't normally do in their everyday lives.

He pauses to catch breath. The camera remains steady in his hand, while the breathing is somewhat laboured.

CHESTER GEORGE: Why would a good girl like that get involved in all this nonsense, eh? An athlete. You - the academics - will tell us that she abandoned her sense of personal identity and lost all sense of individual responsibility. It's the crowd you'll say. The crowd is alive. It leads people to commit acts of violence that normally they wouldn't dream of committing. That poor girl is suffering from a rapid descent into mob mentality. Reasonable people no longer exist. They lose their reason in a crowd. That's contagion theory.

Chester George stands up. He points the camera around the supermarket and we get brief glimpses of the others, trashing what's left of the supermarket, knocking over shelves or smashing them in with baseball bats.

CHESTER GEORGE: Yes indeed Mr Prime Minister. We are an *epidemic* behaving with all the characteristics of a *disease*. This groupness is a *virus* and it affects the mind. The mind is *infected*. And the epidemic moves from person to person, town to town, city to city, country to country, until it's everywhere.

He stops once more for breath.

CHESTER GEORGE: The mob? The crowd? It's you. It's your culture. We see it all the time at football matches where you gather together in your different coloured shirts. The crowd. It's why we boo for some and cheer for others.

He turns the camera back on himself.

CHESTER GEORGE: Well, I hope you enjoyed our little Olympic event. Now there's no need for another Olympics is there Mr Prime Minster? Why not spend the money on the people who live here, and who don't give a shit about your Olympic Village.

There are wild cheers off camera, followed by the sound of more glass breaking.

CHESTER GEORGE: Now. Before I go it's time for a little announcement. Or should I say a big one. Very soon, I'll be calling a meeting of The Good and Honest Citizens in London. And I want all of you to be there. This meeting will take place in London's very own advertising Mecca - Piccadilly Circus.

Chester George raises a finger and things quieten down in the background. The music playing over the speakers is cut off.

CHESTER GEORGE: Now listen to this. It's time for Phase Two of our little revolution. Phase Two. I want ALL violence in the city to end – as of right now. Spread the word. Tell all the Good and Honest Citizens. There will be no more trouble on the streets from us. No more looting. No more rioting. But keep to the streets and occupy the space my friends. This is civil disobedience. But don't break any more shop windows or burn anything else down. Don't give them an excuse to stop us coming together in Piccadilly Circus. After all, the world is watching and they can't touch us if we do no wrong.

Chester George pulls the camera closer to his face. The skull design leers back at the lens.

CHESTER GEORGE: Mr Prime Minister – now it's your turn to listen. If any of your feds or soldiers try to get in the way of our peaceful meeting, then I say this to The Good and Honest Citizens – BURN this city to the ground. Burn it. And last but not least, before you turn London into a pile of ashes, make your way to Westminster, to the Houses of Parliament, and have your fun there.

Clip ends.

CHAPTER 24

#Piccadilly

Sample of Tweets - *posted 15th August 2011*

A.T Ross *@ScribblerManUK · 6m*

There will never be a better time to make our voices heard - #piccadilly

Gregory White *@MisterMaster81 · 6m*

Is the PM really going to let #piccadilly happen?

Jane Lange *@SkaYo · 7m*

Estimates from @CBCNews say hundreds of thousands of people expected at #piccadilly. Not counting soldiers and police.

Maggie June *@MJ_1962 · 8m*

Yobs organising at #piccadilly. Soldiers and police useless. What happened to your spine Great Britain?

Sadie Hobbs *@AlphaBitchSadie · 10m*

Bring back lynching. I'll even put the rope around CG's neck myself.

Jezza *@tinylilspiderman · 10m*

Chester George! Where can I get a hoodie like that? #piccadilly

CHAPTER 25

15th August 2011

They sat in a line with their backs propped up against the brick wall of Lancasterian Primary School.

Mack sat on one end of the line, watching the heavy rain, which had been coming down all morning.

Sitting next to him, Tegz was watching the Supermarket Olympics on his phone – for about the twentieth time that day. Every now and then he'd fold himself over, his body convulsing while the sound of another giggling fit rang out across the playground.

Sumo Dave sat in silence. His cap was pulled over his eyes and his head slumped forwards, as if he'd fallen asleep.

Hatchet sat on the other end of the line from Mack. He was eating a BLT, which he'd picked up from a supply drop that morning on Tottenham High Road. As he sat there chewing away, Hatchet smacked his lips constantly in enjoyment - a sound that was to Mack, worse than that of someone scraping their fingernails down a blackboard.

But Mack wasn't the first to crack.

After several more minutes of lip smacking, Sumo Dave lifted the cap away from his eyes.

"Fucking hell Hatch!" he yelled. "I'm trying to get some kip here mate and you sound like a starving dog who's just found a giant bowl of kibble."

Sumo Dave yanked his cap back over his eyes.

Hatchet shrugged. "I'm hungry."

Sumo Dave threw him the middle finger. "Sake!"

Hatchet dropped the empty sandwich box on the ground. Then he reached a hand into his rucksack and pulled out a packet of chocolate chip cookies. Tearing furiously at the top of the packet with his teeth, he opened them up and started throwing whole biscuits into his mouth.

CRUNCH.

"Jeeeees-usss Christ!" Sumo Dave said, lifting the cap up again. "You got worms or something lad? When did you last eat?"

Hatchet thought for a second. "Yesterday," he said with his mouth full. "All the cupboards are empty at home now. And I never thought to go looting for food, eh?"

Sumo Dave nodded. "What about your mum? Is she alright?"

"That old cow don't bother with food anymore," Hatchet said, picking up a few crumbs from his jeans and scooping them into his mouth. "It's vodka she wants. And there's none of that going for free down the High Road, eh?"

Sumo Dave shook his head. "Bollocks, innit?"

"What about you?" Hatchet said. "You using the supply drops yet?"

Sumo Dave grinned. "Nah. I nicked a shitload of food from Sainsburys and Tesco when this kicked off. I'm what you call a clever bastard, eh?"

Hatchet glared at Sumo Dave. "Well ain't you fucking great?"

"You were too busy nicking giant flat screen TVs mate," Sumo Dave said.

There was a moment's silence. Then Sumo Dave reached over and poked Hatchet on the shoulder.

"Hey," he said. "Anything you need mate - food and that - just pop over to my place. Yeah? I'll sort you out."

Hatchet nodded. "Yeah," he said, reaching for another cookie.

It had been Mack's suggestion to go to the school that morning. He didn't want to sit at home all day listening to his parents talking to estate agents, discussing the value of the house in Stanmore Road. All of that meant thinking about Edinburgh, and about going home, and about Rossi.

Not that he could blame his parents.

That morning as he'd made his way to the school, Mack had seen the first armoured vehicles on Tottenham High Road. Two of them with armoured spines and V-shaped hulls. They looked like something you'd expect to see only on the news, rolling across the deserts of Afghanistan, dodging blasts, mines, and bullets.

But here they were, on the streets of North London.

The riot police were all over the High Road that day. The army presence was small but significant. Still, the Good and Honest Citizens dwarfed their combined numbers at least two times over. Following Chester George's instructions, they had taken to occupying the streets in a non-violent manner. The transformation from savage violence to a peaceful occupation was quick and surprisingly coherent. It felt like everyone was working together now, and suddenly there was a goal.

And it was Piccadilly.

"Twitter's gone loopy," Tegz said, looking at his phone. "London's trending all over the world. That means the whole planet is watching, eh?"

Mack smiled. "Eager for the next instalment of London's Falling."

"Yeah," Tegz said, grinning. He went back YouTube and Chester George's voice could be heard in the background:

'It's ordinary people getting carried away in crowds and losing themselves in the mob. Doing things they wouldn't normally do in their everyday lives.'

"He's a smart lad that Chester George," Sumo Dave said. "He knows we can't just keep rioting forever. It has to go somewhere, eh?"

"Yeah," Tegz said. "He knows what he's doing."

Sumo Dave turned to Mack. "You coming with us mate?" he said. "Piccadilly? It's going to be history in the making, whatever happens."

Mack nodded. "Aye. I'll be there. That's if I'm still in London that is."

Sumo Dave leaned back against the wall. "You think they'll sell the house?" he said. "With all this going on?"

Mack looked out across the playground. "Everybody loves a bargain," he said. "My folks are willing to drop the price and sell it cheap. And when all this shit blows over, whoever bought it cheap will be laughing."

"Be a shame to miss Piccadilly mate," Tegz said.

Mack nodded. "I know."

"It's not just that," Sumo Dave said. "You only just got here, eh? I was just getting used to your ugly little mug."

Mack smiled, and fell back against the wall.

Sumo Dave scratched at a bit of dark fluff on his chin. "Yeah," he said. "Piccadilly. I can't wait for this."

"It's a load of bollocks," Hatchet said, tossing the empty cookie packet onto the playground.

"What you on about?" Sumo Dave said.

Hatchet turned towards them.

"I thought Chester George was going to tell us to up the ante," he said. "To start targeting more police stations or courthouses. Some fucking leader he's turned out to be."

Tegz sat forward. "What?"

"Are you serious Hatch?" Sumo Dave said. "Up the ante? The city's already lying in tatters. It's time for Phase Two mate."

Hatchet stared out at the rain. "No," he said quietly. "Smashing things up – that's the only way."

Mack looked over at Hatchet. Those dark eyes, usually so lifeless, were now ablaze with conviction.

"All of *this*," Hatchet said, "It only works when we're doing what we've been doing so far. Playing it our way. Smashing in shop windows, burning down shops and homes – that's the only power the likes of us have. It's about not giving a fuck 'cos we've got nothing to lose, eh?"

"It can't stay like that forever Hatch," Sumo Dave said. "We've done that. And now we've got their attention. Now that they're listening we need to have something to say."

"What the fuck do *we* have to say Sumo?" Hatchet said. "You think politicians and people that matter want to have a conversation with the likes of us?"

"That's what Chester George is doing, innit?" Sumo Dave said. "You've heard him. He knows things and he speaks for us – the likes of you and me Hatch."

Hatchet shook his head firmly. "Chaos," he said. "That's *our* language. Without it, everything will go back to normal. And I'll tell you this Sumo, I can't think of anything - *anything* – worse right now than my life going back to normal."

Hatchet turned away. He dabbed at something in his eye with his sleeve.

Sumo Dave sighed. "There'll be nothing left of London," he said. "Not if we play it your way."

Hatchet looked out at the empty playground.

"Sounds good to me," he said.

Mack didn't speak, but he was listening to every word. It was the first time he'd seen Hatchet since the confrontation in Charlie's. Nothing had been said, but for all Mack knew, Hatchet could have been carrying his dad's gun in the rucksack, along with the cookies and the BLT.

Best to keep quiet.

Tegz slipped his iPhone into his hoodie pocket. "Does that mean you ain't coming to Piccadilly Hatch?"

"Course I am," Hatchet said. "What the fuck else am I going to do?" With that, he swung his rucksack over his shoulder and got to his feet.

"I'm going back up the High Road," he said. "There's got to be some action somewhere."

"Easy Hatch," Sumo Dave said. "Listen mate, nobody's rioting anymore. We're onto Phase Two now."

"Yeah well," Hatchet said. "We ain't politicians yet, are we? You coming?"

Sumo Dave shrugged. "Nah, I'm going to stay here a while."

Hatchet gave a snort of disgust. "Sitting in a school playground?"

"I ain't budging Hatch," Sumo said.

Hatchet shrugged. "Suit yourself. Tegz?"

"Yeah, might as well," Tegz said, getting to his feet. Without another word, the two teenagers set off towards the black fence and Kings Road.

The rain was easing off at last, the downpour turning to a soft drizzle. A hint of blue sky crept slowly in between the cracks of blanket grey up above.

Sumo Dave turned to Mack. "Hatchet's got a real taste for it now," he said.

"Aye, I can see that."

"Not that I blame him," Sumo Dave said. "I mean, what else has he got, eh?"

"You think he'll stop?" Mack asked.

Sumo Dave shrugged. "Chester George needs to call a date for

Piccadilly soon," he said. "So we can show people like Hatchet that we don't need to burn the city down just to be heard anymore."

Mack started to laugh

'Eh?" Sumo Dave said. "What's so funny?"

Mack shook his head. "I just thought of something," he said.

"Oh yeah?"

Mack nodded. "I was just thinking about that line from *The Dark Knight*? You know, the Batman film."

"Yeah? What line?"

"Something that the Joker said. Reminds me of Hatchet."

"Go on then," Sumo Dave said.

Mack did his best Heath Ledger as the Joker impersonation:

"*Some men aren't looking for anything logical...some men just want to watch the world burn.*"

Sumo Dave smiled and then he turned away.

"Yeah," he said.

CHAPTER 26

Sadie Hobbs: Filthy Rich and Worth It

(Blog post by Sadie Hobbs - 17th August 2011)

CHOPPITY-CHOP. It's that time of year again. Out with the old and in with the new.

Yes, ladies and gentleman - culling season has returned to the Hobbs residence for the year 2011. This is an annual thing that takes place, usually around July or August, when I spend two or three days rifling through all my worldly possessions (and there are a lot of those), sorting the good from the bad, and putting whatever I don't need into black bin bags and giving them to charity.

I know, I'm wonderful – it's all lies what they say about me!!!!

But OMG - it takes such a long time to do this! Like I said, I have *soooo* many things to throw away and all for the sake of making room for new things!

This morning's job involved going up to the attic and looking through two massive crates of books that had been sitting up there for years. I must admit however, that it was faintly amusing to look back on the literature of my youth. Dusty old books now for the most part. But OMG, did I read some CRAP with a capital 'C'. Stories about horses and vampires – that about sums it up for my childhood. And yes I was reading about vampires long before *Twilight* made it cool to do so. And if by chance, Mummy or Daddy could find me a book about horses *and* vampires, then I was the happiest little girl in the world.

Easy pleased, that's me.

But guess what else I found in the attic today? A box that was absolutely packed with my old school stuff - books and jotters, pens and pencils and even things that I'd once made in arts and craft. I also stumbled upon the ruins of what I think was once a handmade pencil case - bright pink with green dots. I know, I know – it's probably a good thing I never got past the first round in one of my least successful reality TV ventures: *So You Want To Be A Fashion Designer?*

LOL!

I also found an old Latin phrasebook in the box. This was from my years at boarding school – I went to Downe House in case you're wondering – it was very exclusive. But God I HATED Latin!!! And as I picked up this decomposing monstrosity I suddenly thought how wonderful it would be to watch it burn in the garden. I could just imagine the look of horror on the face of old Mrs Reddan, my Latin teacher. If only she could see me do it - but I imagine she's dead now the silly old cow.

Hope so!

To my surprise, I found myself browsing through the old textbook, rediscovering old terms and phrases. Given all that's happened recently, one phrase in particular caught my eye.

Mobile vulgus – excitable or fickle commoners.

There were a few squiggles next to this term (God my handwriting was ATROCIOUS!!) But I could just about make out from my younger self that *mobile vulgus* is where the word 'mob' came from. And as I wrote back in the day, it's also described as a 'moving, shifting, dangerously directionless force'.

Does this sound familiar people?

The lower and illiterate classes are still out there, running riot on the streets of London. The number one reason for this is that the British government has been too soft with the perpetrators of these disturbances. The police are outnumbered and the army – who were brought in to assist the police - are limited in regards to what they can do. So in other words, they can't just drive a tank through the streets and shoot all the hooligans. Which would solve the problem in a jiffy.

The feral rats are refusing to crawl back into their little ghettoes. These people (and I use that word hesitantly) are individually weak. They feel important because they have strength in numbers. The Good and Honest Citizens? Don't make me laugh - they're a bunch of underwashed, undereducated plebs and oh - you should see the abuse I'm getting on Twitter for saying these things. It's delicious and I'm enjoying every single second of it so keep it coming – PLEBS!

We are dealing with the lowest class of people. But let's be fair – after all a rat can't help being a rat. Can it?

What I'm saying is this – it's up to us, the civilised people, to take charge of this situation. Too many people have forgotten that there is a great chain of being in the universe - a Divine Order that is ordained in nature. Everything in the universe has its specific place and the *mobile vulgus* have theirs. They are useful at performing certain tasks in society – they work in supermarkets, they sweep the streets, empty bins, and clean our toilets. Good on them. We couldn't get by without them. But the peasants have always sat at the bottom of the chain of being while the Kings, Queens, Nobles and Merchants are placed above them. This is the natural order of things.

So why are we letting the peasants do what they want?

It's time to do something about this. I've said it before and I'll say it again. Capital punishment must be reinstated in the United Kingdom. It's a no-brainer! Lynching these hoodlums is the only effective deterrent. And it'd be quick too – the streets would be empty of yobs in a day or two. Isn't that what everyone wants? For things to go back to normal? String a few peasants up in Hackney, leave them hanging there for a few hours and watch the others run back into their holes.

That's the solution.

NOW - contrary to what you might hear, normal people are NOT appalled at what I say. They ARE appalled that no one else is saying it. Particularly from those who claim to represent us in Parliament.

This is very important. We cannot let the *mobile vulgus* come together at Piccadilly Circus.

COME ON Mr Prime Minister!

I've met you on several occasions and you seem like a nice chap, but it's about time you grew a backbone. Our political and economic centre is collapsing. And it's too late for water cannons and rubber bullets – these so called 'deterrents' will prove ineffective.

I'm writing this as a proud citizen of the UK. I demand the return of the death penalty – even if it's only a temporary return until this infestation problem is fixed. There are many of you out there who agree with me. And I urge you all to get over to Twitter now and get behind the hashtag: #bringbacklynching

Together we can take back Britain. Let's do this, if not for ourselves, then for the sake of our children.

CHAPTER 27

18th August 2011

Archie Walker was grinning from ear to ear, as he led the two young visitors across the hallway towards the front door. The grin faded however, as he pulled the door open about an inch and a half, peering warily outside through the narrow gap onto the street.

Mack was standing behind him in the hallway. What did the old man expect to see out there anyway? A horde of masked rioters standing on the front doorstep, tapping baseball bats impatiently off the palm of their hands?

Waiting?

"Thank you for coming," Archie said to the guests. "It was lovely to meet you both."

Isabella Walker, standing at her husband's side, stepped forward. She smiled at the handsome young couple who were currently making their way outside. The visitors stopped on the doorstep and turned around to say goodbye to the Walkers. They were a pair of young professionals - Iain and Sally Burton, and approximately in their late twenties.

"It's a gorgeous house," Sally said, running a hand through her long blonde hair. "Such a shame, isn't it? That you have to go back to Scotland."

Isabella smiled and nodded. "It's a real shame."

Mack loitered restlessly in the background.

"Have there been many viewers so far?" Iain asked. "Apart from us?"

Archie shrugged - a non-committal gesture. "A few," he said. "Not a great time to be selling, is it? People are well, nervous with all that's been going on."

"Yeah," Sally said, smiling and nodding sympathetically. "But you're letting this place go for a real bargain. And things have quietened down, you know – the riots."

"For now," Iain said, giving his wife a sharp look.

"We miss Edinburgh anyway," Isabella said quickly. "My mum's up there, she's alone and well, you know how it is."

Mack almost laughed out loud. *Bullshit.*

The young couple exchanged a brief glance at one another.

"Well," Iain said. "We're definitely interested in the house." And with that he leaned closer and lowered his voice in an exaggerated whisper. "*Very interested.*"

Everyone laughed, except Mack.

What a prick.

Sally, who couldn't stop fidgeting with her hair, flicked a loose strand out of her eyes. "What we'll do is talk to the estate agent this afternoon," she said. "And I think after that - you'll be hearing from us again soon."

She poked her husband in the ribs.

"Won't they Iain?"

Iain nodded, a smug grin wrapped around his face. Mack got the feeling that Iain thought *he* was doing the Walkers a favour by taking the house off their hands. Rather than him and his wife landing the property bargain of the year in Tottenham.

Archie Walker seemed happy to play the desperate seller. He thrust an enthusiastic hand at the prospective buyers and grinned manically.

"Excellent," Archie said. "That's brilliant news."

"Wonderful," Iain said.

Sally looked past the door and smiled at Mack.

Mack smiled back.

"Well," Isabella said, hurrying things along. "We'll look forward to hearing from either yourselves or the estate agent."

They said their goodbyes, but it was only when the Burtons were halfway down Stanmore Road and almost out of sight that Archie finally closed the door – but not without another look around, both to the left and right for rioters.

Archie and Isabella stood behind the closed door, looking at one another. Their eyes beamed with excitement.

"YES!" Archie said, pumping a fist into the air.

Mack's parents fell into each other's arms, dancing around the hallway as if they'd just won the lottery.

"Well," Archie said, unwrapping his hands from around his wife. "Time to break out the champagne. The Walkers are going back to Scotland!"

Isabella smiled, but she was more restrained than her husband. "I've got a good feeling about those two," she said. "But let's wait until it's final before we celebrate properly, okay?"

Archie turned towards Mack, the manic grin still lingering on his face.

"You ready for this son?" he said. "Are you ready to go back to Edinburgh?"

Mack looked unimpressed. "You're giving this house away for peanuts," he said.

Archie laughed. "And since when did you become the expert?

We're making a loss, aye, but at least we're getting away from this madness."

Mack shook his head. "You just heard that woman say the riots were over. If you're so confident of that, why leave?"

Isabella looked at her son. "You know why Mack."

Mack stubbornly folded his arms against his chest. "No I don't."

Isabella took a step closer.

"Maclean Walker," she said in *that* voice. "YOU are the reason we're leaving London. Just as you were the reason we came to London in the first place. You think we're going to stay here with all this going on and with your recent track record? Even the slightest hint of trouble will get you locked up."

"We're just looking out for you son," Archie said.

Mack sat down on the bottom stair.

"Where will we stay in Edinburgh?" he said.

Archie smiled. "We'll stay with your gran until we find our own place," he said. "It's no problem. She'd be happy for the company."

"Gran?" Mack said, feeling nauseous. "So we're moving back to the *exact* same area of Edinburgh? To a place where everybody knows what I – what happened?"

Isabella raised a hand. "Mack, listen..."

"Why are you doing this to me?" Mack said. "Rossi's mates – they'll be waiting for me up there. They'll cut me to shreds."

Isabella threw her hands up in the air.

"What are *we* trying to do to *you*?" she said. "Nobody put that knife in your hand Mack, did they?"

Mack said nothing.

Archie Walker stepped forward, putting a hand around his wife's waist.

"These riots were just bad luck," he said. "For all of us. Nobody saw this coming. How could we have seen *this*?"

"You're going back to Edinburgh Mack," Isabella said. "Just start dealing with it."

"It might only be temporary," Archie said. "When we get back,

I'll ask the company about another transfer somewhere else. Somewhere permanent this time. We could even think about going to continental Europe. Who knows?"

Mack shook his head. He saw the future ahead of him, always the new boy in town, overcoming the same challenges.

No solid ground beneath him.

"I want to stay here," Mack said. Fuck it - what did he have to lose by speaking the truth. "I want to go to Piccadilly."

"Well we won't be around to see Piccadilly," Archie said. "As soon as this house is sold, we're out of here."

"Forget it Mack," Isabella said firmly.

Mack got to his feet slowly, determined that this conversation was now over. He turned around and started walking upstairs.

His parents weren't finished with him yet.

"You've been out there, haven't you?" Isabella said. Her voice was flat, eerily calm. "You told us you hadn't been involved in the riots, but you have, haven't you?"

He turned around slowly.

"Yes," he said, shrugging his shoulders.

Isabella walked over to the foot of the stairs.

"Why?"

"Look closer," he said. "Look at what's happening out there now. Not everyone wants to burn the city down you know. Or steal a flat screen TV. Some people are just pissed off and want their voices heard."

Isabella forced out a laugh.

"You're sixteen years old," she said. "What do *you* know about anything?"

Mack smiled. "Been out there lately, have you?" he said. "Spoke to any of these people? All you do is watch the news. I know more about the riots than you ever will."

A gleam of anger flickered in Isabella's eyes.

"Listen to me Mack," she said. "Until this house is sold and we're on our way home, you don't set one foot outside unless it's with one of us. Do you understand me? You're grounded."

But Mack shook his head. "No I'm not. I'm going to Piccadilly."

Isabella's voice was calm.

"No. You're not."

Archie Walker stepped in quickly.

"Look," he said. "If those people buy this house it's only going to take a few days for the deal to go through. You and your mum don't even have to stay down here until it's sorted. I can take care of everything. Whatever happens though, we won't be here for much longer Mack."

"You can watch Piccadilly in Edinburgh," Isabella said. "I've no problem with that. We'll even buy it for you on Pay-Per-View if it means that much to you."

Mack frowned. "Pay-Per-View?"

Archie Walker allowed himself a smile. "Aye," he said. "Apparently your Piccadilly thing - whenever it happens - is going to be broadcast live on SKAM Box Office. Twenty pounds a head."

Mack was the one grinning from ear to ear now. He couldn't help it. "Twenty pounds?" he said. "They're actually charging people to watch it live on TV?"

"What's so funny about that?" Isabella said.

Mack looked at his mother.

"No wonder the world's such a mess," he said.

CHAPTER 28

18th August 2011

The CBC News at Six

CBC News reporter Dick Ronson is standing on a dark street in North London. He's positioned directly behind an isolated block of brick wall, which is adjoined to a narrow black fence. Tall streetlights throw down much needed illumination upon the early evening, aided by the headlights of the occasional passing car. Behind Ronson, a vast array of floral tributes is attached to the black fence.

DICK RONSON: Sophie, this evening I'm in Ferry Lane in Tottenham. This is of course, the place where it all began with the shooting of Mark Duggan exactly two weeks ago. And who could have imagined back then, what would come next? We've seen the worst riots in this country in living memory; we've seen looting and criminality beyond comprehension; we've also seen countless buildings burn across the city in scenes reminiscent of the Battle of Britain, seventy years ago.

SOPHIE WALLACE: (*Speaking from the CBC studio*) It looks very quiet there tonight Dick.

DICK RONSON: Indeed Sophie. In fact, there's something almost church-like about the atmosphere tonight. Not far from here however, thousands of people have taken to Tottenham High Road - but not to riot. Instead they're initiating this so-called Phase Two of Chester George's master plan. This consists of a peaceful occupation of the streets by thousands of people who are waiting for their leader, Chester George, to call them to Piccadilly.

SOPHIE WALLACE: Are the rioters not even going home at night?

DICK RONSON: The short answer is no. The rioters, the Good and Honest Citizens - whatever you want to call them - they're going nowhere. They've take over many streets across London and it seems they're content to stay there and wait for the call from Chester George.

SOPHIE WALLACE: And given the recent food shortages, how are all these people finding enough to eat and drink?

DICK RONSON: Surprisingly enough Sophie, food and drink

supplies are being delivered regularly to theses sites of occupation across London. People are walking through the crowds, handing out sandwiches, water, and other items. Police believe these supplies are either coming in from central or west London – CR – and I suspect this myself, that these food items were looted earlier in the riots. Either way, it seems there's no shortage of food for the rioters.

SOPHIE WALLACE: And Dick, how are the police and army handling this so-called 'Phase Two'?

DICK RONSON: The police and the army are staying close by Sophie, but they really have their hands full. We're talking thousands upon thousands of people standing out on the street and refusing to disperse. It's like nothing we've ever seen before.

SOPHIE WALLACE: But there's also a new turn of events, isn't there? There's hope for the other side at last.

DICK RONSON: (*Perking up*) Yes Sophie! The counter-revolution has begun. At last, all over the country - and not just in London - ordinary people are saying NO MORE to the riots. And astonishingly, it's the nation's most infamous and loathed reality television star - Sadie Hobbs - who has become the figurehead of the fight against terror.

SOPHIE WALLACE: It started with a recent blog post didn't it?

DICK RONSON: Indeed Sophie. Just yesterday, Sadie Hobbs,

who's been an outspoken critic of the riots, wrote a blog post that reiterated earlier calls for the return of capital punishment. Sadie Hobbs believes that she speaks for the majority of ordinary decent people in Britain and that the police and army have been too soft on the rioters.

SOPHIE WALLACE: Is capital punishment likely to return?

DICK RONSON: Well, the politicians are saying very little tonight Sophie. But there's been a great deal of public dissatisfaction with the way they've handled this crisis. And if that dissatisfaction continues – well – Sadie Hobbs has already used the term 'lynch mob' on more than one occasion. And as you know, lynch mobs don't usually sit around and ask for permission to do what they do.

SOPHIE WALLACE: Two clear leaders have now emerged, is that right Dick?

DICK RONSON: Yes Sophie. And ahead of Piccadilly, the real battleground is no longer on the streets of London – it's on the Internet. It's the battle of the blogger versus the vlogger. Are you #teamChester or #teamSadie? Are you #teamPiccadilly or #teamPunishment?

Cuts to interviews with members of the public.

INTERVIEEW 1: (*Middle-aged white woman*) I'm definitely #teamSadie. I'm disgusted with the government treating these criminals like badly behaved children. Slap on the wrist and that's all they get innit? Blow 'em away, that's what I say. Bloody scum destroying this beautiful city and we're all just sitting back watching it happen. It's pathetic.

Cuts to...

INTERVIEEW 2: (*Elderly white man*) Hang 'em. Hang 'em all! Show them what happens when you misbehave.

Cuts to...

INTERVIEEW 3: (*Elderly white woman*) She just says what the rest of us are all thinking, doesn't she? I like Sadie.

Cuts to...

INTERVIEEWS 4 AND 5: (*Two thirty-something white women, dressed in business suits, jumping up and down, unleashing a football style chant into the microphone*) SADIE! SADIE! SADIE!

Cuts back to Dick Ronson in Ferry Lane.

SOPHIE WALLACE: Not a lot of support for Chester George, was there?

DICK RONSON: No Sophie. And that was a completely random survey on our part. The truth is that the silent majority are, thanks to Sadie Hobbs, beginning to make their voices heard. They want to put an end to this. They want capital punishment back. The question is, are the politicians listening?

CHAPTER 29

19th August 2011

The Paxton Show

The Prime Minister of the United Kingdom is sitting in a television studio near Westminster. Sitting across from him is the CBC's interviewer extraordinaire, James Paxton. This is Paxton's first chance to grill the leader of the country since the disturbances began in early August.

PAXTON: Prime Minister, thank you for joining us. It certainly hasn't been easy to get a hold of you lately. God knows we've tried.

PRIME MINISTER: Sorry about that James. Of course, we've been kept very busy lately.

PAXTON: First of all, let me ask you a very important question. Are you #teamSadie or #teamChester?

PRIME MINISTER: (*Laughing nervously*) Well James, I suppose if anything I'd like to think of myself as #teamUK.

PAXTON: I don't think that's trending on Twitter at the moment.

PRIME MINISTER: No, you're quite right. Unfortunately not.

PAXTON: Prime Minister, there are those who believe that two weeks of wanton destruction hasn't been dealt with by your government. What do you say to those people?

PRIME MINISTER: Well I don't think that's entirely fair James. We've brought in extra police and there are army patrols and tanks -

PAXTON: But it's clearly not enough is it? Most of the police aren't even armed and the military aren't authorised to fire their weapons. Now there's a so-called Phase Two occupation – thousands of people taking to the streets - prior to embarking on a journey west to Piccadilly. Need I remind you Prime Minister that Piccadilly isn't too far from the Houses of Parliament?

PRIME MINISTER: (*Shifting uncomfortably in his seat*) James, we can't simply ignore the fruits of a sensible, balanced approach to this problem. Hundreds of arrests have already been made. The judicial system is working overtime, round the clock, twenty-four hours to process and sentence these criminals in record quick time. We're getting the rioters off the streets and we're doing so with the minimum of bloodshed.

PAXTON: But are you aware that rioters are now travelling down to London from other parts of the country now? From Birmingham, Liverpool, Manchester and other cities? You've been celebrating the fact that trouble in those other cities has decreased, but that's only because they're all coming down here to gather in the one place. They're coming here for Piccadilly.

PRIME MINISTER: James, you're talking about Piccadilly like it's a sure thing. We don't even know if there's going to be a Piccadilly. Now I'm confident that a sensible and balanced approach to the problem will get rioters off the street with the minimum of bloodshed.

PAXTON: Okay Prime Minister. Let's talk about the death penalty because that's what people are interested in at the moment. It was abolished in the sixties. It hasn't been debated in Parliament since 1994. Why aren't you talking about it today?

PRIME MINISTER: I don't believe that the death penalty has any place in a civilised society.

PAXTON: (*Raising his voice*) But we're not living in a civilised society anymore! Half the city's been razed to the ground. And now the people responsible have taken over the streets in their hundreds and thousands. The roads are blocked off and there's very little food getting to those who need it the most. Don't you agree Mr Prime Minister - that drastic situations require drastic solutions? Several of your MPs have publicly tweeted that they're on #teamSadie.

PRIME MINISTER: It is not unacceptable to hold that view in the Conservative Party. That's up to the individual. But the death penalty brings with it all sorts of issues and historically there have been instances in which the wrong person has been sentenced to death. Or new evidence has appeared after the execution. It's complicated James.

PAXTON: Okay. I want to draw your attention to something Prime Minister. The government's own e-petition site clearly states that if any single petition gathers more than one hundred thousand signatures then it is 'eligible for debate in the House of Commons'. As of this afternoon, nine separate petitions calling for the return of the death penalty have gathered well over that figure.

PRIME MINISTER: Death penalties don't lower the crime rate James. Since the death penalty was reinstated in the United States in 1976, the crime rate has actually risen -

PAXTON: *Are* you going to debate the matter? The British public have told you that they want you to debate the return of the death penalty in Parliament.

The Prime Minister dabs at the sweat gathering on his forehead.

PRIME MINISTER: Emotions are running high James. That's understandable. But things are being said now that in the light of day, when the police and armed forces have suppressed these riots, will seem rather foolish.

PAXTON: But why not bring the death penalty back? From a general perspective. Aren't there crimes that should be punished more severely than by imprisonment. The murder of a child for example. You're a father aren't you Mr Prime Minister? And what about the murder of a police officer killed in the line of duty? And while we're at it - what about the murder of an entire city?

PRIME MINISTER: Look James, I think we need to remember that capital punishment is still illegal under EU law. As long as we remain part of the European Union –

Paxton cuts him off, turning towards the camera.

PAXTON: Well, earlier this evening we ran a Twitter vote that asked you if you'd like to see the return of capital punishment. The results are in and they're pretty conclusive. Ninety-two per cent of those who voted are in favour of the return of capital punishment. With only eight per cent against.

Paxton turns back to the Prime Minister.

PAXTON: Twitter has spoken sir. Hundreds of thousands of people are signing petitions and yet still, you don't seem interested in debating the matter. Are you sure you're not with #teamChester?

PRIME MINISTER: Look James, I don't think we should be making light –

Paxton holds up his hands.

PAXTON: Time's almost up Prime Minister. But we have time for one more question. Let there be no doubt that the army of Chester George will soon be eating its way westwards across London. Given the severity of this impending threat, will you be debating the return of the death penalty? Yes or no?

PRIME MINISTER: It won't happen on my watch.

PAXTON: Thank you.

CHAPTER 30

21th August 2011

BBM (Blackberry Messenger)

Message distributed widely across London.

'This just in from Chester George.

Piccadilly. 1st September.

It's on.'

CHAPTER 31

22nd August 2011

Mack tiptoed quietly downstairs. In one hand, he held a pair of Adidas Kicks tight to his chest, while the other squeezed down on the strap of the rucksack draped over his shoulder in order to prevent the buckles from rattling.

God, if they hear me.

Every time a sock hit the stairs it sounded like a clap of thunder. Downstairs, he could hear the TV playing in the living room. His parents were in there watching the evening news and somebody - it sounded like Dick Ronson - was talking about Phase Two and the occupation.

He landed on the hallway and crept quietly to the front door. Very gently, he pushed down the brass handle and was surprised at how cold it felt against his skin. And why was it so heavy this time? Was it just his imagination?

He pulled the door open as quietly as he could. Fortunately for

Mack, the Walkers hadn't inherited a creaky door at the house in Stanmore Road.

Stepping outside, he closed it gently behind him.

Click.

He let out a deep breath. It wasn't quite Andy Dufresne standing under the rain in *The Shawshank Redemption*, but he'd been grounded for a few days now and with everything that was going on in London, being cooped up indoors was enough to make him go at least a little crazy.

Looking up, a blanket of angry clouds was encroaching upon the early evening sunlight. It would be dark soon, but Mack welcomed the opportunity to slip inside the night, out of the reach of prying eyes, of daylight, and normality.

Twenty minutes later, he was approaching Charlie's, where Sumo Dave was waiting for him. As he walked west, he'd expected to hear the crowds on the nearby High Road. To hear something, anything - jeers, anti-authoritarian chants - any kind of noise. All those people had to be making some sort of racket, didn't they?

But there was nothing. There wasn't even the sound of traffic anymore.

And no longer were there any burning buildings on the horizon. No more orange and white lights spewing forth smoke up to the heavens.

The air felt good.

Sumo Dave was standing outside Charlie's. The lanky teenager was looking at his phone but when he saw Mack walking towards him, he tucked the device into the side pocket of his jeans.

"Alright?" Sumo Dave said. "Sneak outta jail, did ya?"

"Aye," Mack said. "Fuck it. What else can they do to me?"

Sumo Dave shrugged. "Yeah."

They started walking towards the junction where Philip Lane came onto the High Road.

Up ahead, Mack saw crowds of people gathered together under the dim streetlights. When they reached the High Road, the scene was unlike anything he'd seen during the riots. This was Phase Two. Thousands of people standing or sitting on the streets, almost in perfect silence. It was like looking upon a vigil for a fallen idol.

There were no masks anymore. No faces hidden underneath hoods.

In fact, it would have been quite civilised if not for the burned out and windowless buildings that hovered in the background. A reminder of Phase One.

Sumo Dave led Mack through the crowds. There were people everywhere, standing in groups talking quietly to one another. Black faces, white faces, brown faces – Mack saw children, he saw dogs running up and down the street.

There were tents everywhere.

Others were sitting down in small groups, gathered together to share a meal.

Mack looked up and saw people sitting on the roofs of whatever buildings were still strong enough to hold them. They were sitting over the edge, their legs dangling in the air, looking down and waving to the crowds below.

It was like walking through a street festival, but without the music. And although there was muted chatter amongst the crowds, it was still eerily silent compared to what had been going on for the last few weeks.

Sumo Dave brought Mack to the front of the Christ Apostolic Church, which had remained untouched by the violence. Up ahead, the familiar shape of Tottenham Police Station could be seen, as well as a massive huddle of people.

"Something going on over there?" Mack asked.

"You need to see it from up there," Sumo Dave said, pointing to the upper floor windows of the church.

They walked towards the door of the three-storey, brown brick building. Inside, Mack wasn't surprised to find it also full of people sitting around, talking, drinking, and smoking. It was like a giant party spread across different rooms – be it an office or storage room.

Sumo Dave led Mack upstairs to a large, spacious room on the second tier. It had a wooden floor and on the far end of the room, a large, protruding window looked down onto the High Road.

There were about twelve people inside the room. Most in their twenties or late teens at best. Sleeping bags were strewn across the floor, as were plastic bags, tins, water bottles, sandwiches and packets of junk food.

Tegz and Hatchet were standing at the large window with some of the others – typical student types with long hair, greasy skin, dressed in jeans and T-shirts.

Sumo Dave gave Mack a nudge. "Go on," he said. "Take a look."

"This is the shit," Tegz said, standing aside to let Mack in.

Mack pressed his face up against the glass. To his left, a little further up the road, he saw Tottenham Police Station. Riot police surrounded the building, some on horses, but most on foot. Dozens of police vans were parked along the edge of the street in close proximity to the station. The army were there too, with the same two armoured vehicles that Mack had seen before. Small pockets of soldiers patrolled the area on foot, carrying small machine guns in their hands.

The Good and Honest Citizens had the police and army surrounded on both sides. There were literally thousands of people down there, positioned on both sides of the police and military presence.

"Holy shit," Mack said.

"You're not kidding," Tegz said. "We're dwarfing them ain't we?"

Hatchet took a step back from the window. "We've got 'em surrounded," he said. "We've got the numbers. We could take Tottenham tonight – we could take it down. What the fuck is everybody standing around waiting for?"

"Piccadilly," Mack said.

"This is big time," Sumo Dave said. "It's gone way beyond smashing in shop windows mate."

"It's a waste," Hatchet said, glaring out of the window.

Then something happened that made Mack's blood run cold. Hatchet took a step back from the window, lifted up his hoodie and pulled out something tucked in between his waist and his jeans.

It was a black pistol.

"It's a waste," he said again. "I ain't afraid of those soldiers and their fucking guns, am I?"

He tapped the muzzle of the pistol off the glass.

Everyone else at the window backed off quietly. All except Sumo Dave, who stepped forward and grabbed Hatchet by the forearm. He tried to bundle his friend away from the window but Hatchet, who was stronger, wasn't going anywhere.

Everyone in the room was watching them.

"Are you fucking nuts Hatch?" Sumo Dave said.

Hatchet smiled. Sumo Dave let go of his arm.

"I'm gonna tell you something mate," Sumo Dave said. "And this is just a bit of friendly advice, yeah?"

He stood in Hatchet's personal space, seemingly unconcerned about the gun.

"Hotheads like you need to stay well away from the coppers and soldiers," Sumo Dave said. "You've had your fun, eh? Half the city ain't there anymore mate. But now it's time for something else - we wait for Piccadilly. We wait for Chester George. You give us that much before you start shooting the place up, yeah?"

Hatchet tucked the pistol back into the waist of his jeans. He shrugged his shoulders, and then walked over to his sleeping bag.

Mack needed a moment to regain his composure. To see a loose cannon like Hatchet wielding a gun, and knowing how much he hated Mack's guts - that was something else. His heart gradually began to slow down.

Sumo Dave came over to him, a look of relief etched on his face.

"Close one," he said quietly.

Mack nodded. He looked at the sleeping bags on the floor. "You guys staying here too?"

"Yeah," Sumo Dave said. "There's no going home anymore. Not until this is done."

"Piccadilly?"

Sumo Dave nodded.

"What'd your mum say about it?" Mack said.

Sumo Dave smiled. "She didn't try and stop me if that's what you mean."

Tegz, who was listening in at the window, walked over to them. He gave Mack a playful tap on the arm. "You'll be there?" he said. "Eh?"

Mack nodded. "Aye mate. I hope so."

He dropped his rucksack on the floor at Tegz's feet "I brought you guys some food," he said, looking at all the tins and packets scattered across the floor. "I didn't realise you were already stocked up though."

Tegz grinned. "No food shortages anymore," he said. "Everyone's working together now. Sharing."

"We'll still take it though," Sumo Dave said, grinning. He put a foot on the rucksack and kicked it towards one of the sleeping bags.

Mack took one last look out the window, at the crowds outside the police station.

"I'd better go," he said.

Sumo Dave walked him to the stairs. They said their goodbyes and Mack walked downstairs, squeezing past a group of people sitting on the steps talking about Piccadilly and the first of September.

When he was outside, Mack took a look back at the church, wishing that he could stay there with the others. Then he remembered Hatchet and the gun, and he wasn't so sure it was a good idea.

But he didn't want to go home either.

Mack walked towards the thousands of people who had filled up the streets in anticipation of Piccadilly. This carnival of smiling faces was pulling him in. Somebody was playing the guitar nearby, fingerpicking a pretty melody. Elsewhere, a child laughed. And up above, the stars were out, a gang of celestial bodies looking down in envy at all the excitement on the tiny blue rock.

Mack walked away with a heavy heart, back to Stanmore Road.

The front door was locked.

Shit.

And the living-room light was on.

Mack took a deep breath before pulling the keys from his pocket. He unlocked the door, stepped inside and closed it gently again.

The house was silent.

Trying his luck, he made for the stairs. He almost had one foot up the 'wooden hill' - as his parents used to call the stairs when he was a child - when a voice, coming from the living room, interrupted him.

"Get in here."

Isabella Walker didn't sound angry. In fact, there was no trace of emotion in her voice whatsoever, which made it worse.

Mack sighed, turning back towards the living room. Slowly he pushed the door open and saw his parents sitting on the leather couch. Mack saw that familiar look of disappointment in their eyes.

And on the floor, a suitcase.

"No more arguments Mack," Isabella said. "It's done. You're booked on a train to Waverley Station first thing tomorrow morning."

Archie pointed at the suitcase. "You're going home son."

CHAPTER 32

23rd August 2011

At precisely 9.33am on Tuesday morning, the train on Platform Four pulled out of King's Cross Station - three minutes late - en route to Waverley Station in Edinburgh. The station was especially busy that day, and almost all of the trains pouring out of London were full. In particular, as Mack had sat in the carriage waiting for his own train to leave, he'd noticed a lot of families - mothers, fathers and little kids – hurrying on the platform towards the train as if being chased by something terrible.

Mack was probably the only person in the station who wanted to stay in London.

But his parents were having none of that.

He'd fought them very little on the topic of his going home. It was a battle he couldn't win and so he hadn't wasted the energy trying. Upon seeing the suitcase on the living room floor, he'd accepted the situation quietly and gone to bed. The following morning, after a cooked breakfast courtesy of his mum, there had been a rushed and awkward goodbye with her at the door.

Mack's dad then drove him from Tottenham to King's Cross.

"Your gran will be waiting for you at Waverley," Archie said. "She'll meet you, so don't go running off without her, okay?"

Mack shrugged. "Okay."

Archie laughed. "And don't get off the train at the first station and try sneaking back to London," he said, turning to Mack. "Because you know what'll happen, don't you?"

Mack shrugged. "What?"

"I'll put you on the first train back to Edinburgh," Archie said. "And next time – your mum's going back up there with you."

The first stop was in Stevenage, about thirty miles north of London. Mack sat up in his seat and stared through the window at the unspectacular little station.

I could do it. I could get off here. I could switch platforms and get the first train back to London. Walk straight up to the door in Stanmore Road and that would show them - show them that I won't be bossed around by anyone. God, I'd love to see the look on their faces. And then I'd be there, standing in the middle of Piccadilly Circus with thousands of other people. Chester George will step onto the podium. And I'll be there to see it.

But when the train pulled out of Stevenage, Mack was still in his seat.

He laid his head upon the glass, watching the scenery roll by. Green fields stretched out on both sides of the train, lying underneath low-hanging clouds. The various names of all the stations went past in a rapid blur: Peterborough, Newark North Gate, Doncaster, and all the rest.

The thought of going back to Edinburgh preyed upon his nerves. What would all the old faces think when they saw him in school? Mack Walker, the nice middle-class boy who'd stabbed Jon Rossi and got away with it. What would they say? Not just the kids but the parents who were sometimes twice as bad.

Mack the Knife. *What would the Rossi family do now that old Macky's back in town?*

The sound of Jon Rossi screaming. It came to him late at night, just as he was drifting off to sleep. Jon Rossi, the tough guy who always acted the hardman in front of the girls. To hear him screaming that day like a little girl, his face contorting with pain as Mack crawled off his bloody chest – that was hard to forget.

Mack could still feel the warm blood running down his fingers. He could still see it falling off at the tips in thick drops, landing on the concrete with a faint, chilling splat.

Dark red raindrops.

Mack curled both hands into tight balls.

And then there was Piccadilly. He wanted to be there so badly when the Good and Honest Citizens came together in September. He didn't even know why it was so important to him anymore, but something was calling him there. It felt like everything was at stake.

He turned in his seat, looking back towards the city that everybody was running away from. The one place he wanted to get back to. The one place in the world that was starting to make sense.

An announcement came through the speakers.

"Ladies and Gentleman, the next stop will be York..."

Yorkshire already? It felt as if he'd only been on the train for ten minutes. But now they'd come all the way from London to northern England. And it wouldn't be long until they crossed the border into Scotland.

And after that...

The city of York loomed in the distance. Instinctively, as if his life depended on it, Mack got to his feet. He walked quickly over to the luggage rack and pulling the other baggage out of the way, dug out his small suitcase from the back.

Quick!

He replaced the other bags and dragged his suitcase towards the train door.

"C'mon," he said, waiting for the train to slow down. At the same time, his mother's voice jumped into his head:

You're not stopping here Mack. You're going all the way back to Edinburgh. At Waverley Station, you'll take your granny's shrivelled up hand, and she's going to deliver you into the hands of an entire city that reeks of fear and hates your guts. And Jon Rossi will be waiting. Maybe he'll smile when he sees you coming. Maybe he'll show you his scars before he gets his revenge.

Finally the train arrived at York. Mack pushed button and the doors slid open.

He was the first person off the train. On the platform, he pulled his suitcase behind him and walked further into the station, walking like someone who was seriously late for an urgent appointment.

When he finally walked outside into the afternoon sunlight, it felt like he was waking up and out of a bad dream.

Mack looked around at his immediate surroundings. A section of York's famous city wall, dating back to medieval times, was directly outside the station. This sight alone reinforced the fact that he was no longer in London.

With his suitcase in tow, he made his way down a short winding road that led past a row of small brick houses. All the while, he kept his eyes open for somewhere to sit down, somewhere he could think for a while.

Somewhere that didn't bring him any closer to Edinburgh.

He followed the road further down. Taking a left, he walked through the distinctive Micklegate Bar, a medieval entrance for historic visitors arriving into York from the South. And further down that route, he found a small traditional cafe that didn't look too busy and so he went inside.

At the counter, he ordered a Coke and a toasted sandwich from a friendly middle-aged lady. With her distinctive Yorkshire accent, she told Mack to sit down and she'd bring the food to him. He did so a corner table, tucking his suitcase under his seat.

Suddenly it hit him.

Shit. What have I done?

As Mack got to grips with what he'd just done, his eyes roamed the room, stopping at the TV fixed to the wall near the counter. The SKAM News Channel was broadcasting footage about the remarkable and 'chilling' standoffs going on in London. All across the capital, people - no longer hiding behind masks and hoods - had taken over large chunks of the city, standing in tens of thousands and shutting down large sections of London. Roads were closed, schools were shut, and hundreds of businesses were no longer open.

Phase Two.

The woman behind the counter was watching the footage as she prepared Mack's food. She shook her head in disbelief, as if she was unable to believe her eyes.

Mack sipped at his Coke, the sugar reviving his spirits a little. He followed the news, watching as the newsreader, Hugh Stanton, spoke about the 'rioters' and how they were 'holding the city hostage.' He was also saying that 'London was a time bomb ticking down until September.' They were showing images of burning buildings taken from earlier in the riots, broadcasting them as if they were something new, something happening today.

Mack extended his middle finger towards the TV.

He brought it down quickly as the woman brought his food over. She put it on the table with a warm smile and a 'there you go love' in her broad Yorkshire accent. With his hunger pangs stimulated by the smell of melted cheese, Mack bit into the soft filling and just as he did so, a familiar face appeared on the TV screen.

It was Michael King.

The SKAM crew were interviewing the intense-looking young man in Peckham. Standing behind Michael King as he addressed the camera, was a large crowd of Good and Honest Citizens – of all ages and races. The crowd filled up the street in the background and Mack recognised a similar carnival-like scene to what he'd witnessed on Tottenham High Road.

The SKAM News caption labelled the speaker as: *Michael King – Rioter.*

Mack listened intently to the interview, looking at the conviction in the young man's eyes and those gathered around him. By the time the interview was over, Mack knew what had to be done.

To hell with the consequences.

Leaving half the sandwich on his plate, he took his phone out of his pocket, found the number he was looking for, and hit the green button. As the number rang in his ear, Mack noticed that Hugh Stanton was now interviewing Sadie Hobbs in the SKAM studios.

Bitch.

He put a finger over his spare ear, drowning out the sound of the TV.

A familiar voice appeared on the other end of the line.

"Alright Mack? What's happening mate?"

"Alright Sumo?" Mack said. "You sound a bit wrecked mate. Been up all night, eh?"

"Bit of a party here last night mate," Sumo said. "Know what I mean? A shitload of vodka and Tegz's weed, that's all I remember. Bad combo."

Mack smiled. "Nice one," he said.

"So you coming round?"

"Actually I am, aye."

"Where you at then? Home?"

"York."

There was a brief silence on the other end.

"York? What like, in..."

"Yorkshire, aye. They caught me coming in last night. There was a suitcase and a train ticket to Edinburgh waiting."

"Bloody hell mate. You're going home? When?"

"Today. I was, but not anymore. I'm coming back."

"What about your folks? They'll just send you back, won't they?"

"I'm not going to their place mate. I was thinking about coming to the church and staying there until Piccadilly. If that's cool?"

Sumo Dave perked up at that. "That's my boy!"

"So it's cool?"

"Yeah of course. Get down here bro. We'll find you a sleeping bag or a blanket or something. You won't be stuck for a place to sleep, I'll make sure of it."

"I'm on my way. Cheers Sumo."

"Alright mate. See ya."

Mack hung up and put the phone down on the table. Glancing over at the TV, he noticed that Sadie Hobbs was talking about lynch mobs again. She was in the middle of yet another rant, calling on the so-called 'ordinary people' in Britain to stand up and take over from the police and the army, in other words to do their job for them.

To flush out 'the rats' who'd taken over London.

CHAPTER 33

23rd August 2011

SKAM News Channel

In the SKAM News studios in Central London, veteran anchorman, 'Slick' Hugh Stanton, is all business as the camera zooms in.

HUGH STANTON: The number of people occupying the streets of London has continued to increase today in anticipation of an appearance by Chester George in Piccadilly Circus on the first of September. Our reporter, Poppy Baskerville, is in Peckham this afternoon. Poppy, what's going on down there?

The camera cuts to a young woman of about thirty with long blonde hair. She's standing in an inner city street where large crowds have gathered behind her.

POPPY BASKERVILLE: Thank you Hugh. Well here in Peckham, all roads lead to Piccadilly, which is just over four miles across the river from where I'm standing. Next Thursday, thousands of people are expected to march west from here in order to hear the mysterious Chester George give his first public speech.

The camera zooms out to reveal a tall black man standing beside Poppy. Dressed in a jet-black hoodie and khaki combat trousers, the young man's eyes are glued to the camera as he's introduced.

POPPY BASKERVILLE: Well you might remember Michael King from his recent appearance on *The Paxton Show* a couple of weeks ago. Michael, who played a large part in coordinating the London riots, is joining us live here in Peckham. Michael, thank you for your time.

MICHAEL KING: My pleasure.

POPPY BASKERVILLE: There are literally thousands of people standing out here on the street today, and elsewhere across London. What exactly is going?

MICHAEL KING: This is Phase Two. This is the occupation. It's a true demonstration of people power.

POPPY BASKERVILLE: Has the rioting stopped altogether then?

MICHAEL KING: There were never any riots. What you saw was an insurrection. Phase One.

POPPY BASKERVILLE: Okay. So there's no more looting then?

MICHAEL KING: The looting was just a symptom of hopelessness. Now we have hope. There's no need to loot or burn anything else down. Chester George has asked us to be peaceful and we will comply with his wishes.

POPPY BASKERVILLE: But will there be violence at Piccadilly?

MICHAEL KING: The Good and Honest Citizens used violence to make people listen. You don't listen to petitions, but when you hear the sound of a shop window being smashed in, by God, you'll take notice.

With a nervous smile, Poppy Baskerville turns back to the camera.

POPPY BASKERVILLE: Michael King, thank you. Hugh, it's back to you in the studio.

HUGH STANTON: (*Smiling*) Thank you Poppy. Well, it's been a remarkable few weeks here in London. And what's even more remarkable is that a reality TV star and an unknown man dressed up like a skeleton are now more influential than the British government. Well, joining me now is the woman of the hour - Sadie Hobbs.

The camera pans right to reveal Sadie Hobbs sitting next to Hugh. She's wearing a short gold dress, which matches her orange skin and crimped blonde hair. As she's introduced, her lips ease into a relaxed smile.

HUGH STANTON: Sadie, thank you for joining us. Piccadilly – September 1st. What's your take on this?

SADIE HOBBS: Hugh. It's going to be the GREATEST day in the history of this city. It's going to be remembered as the day we took our city back.

HUGH STANTON: (*To camera*) Did you hear that London?

SADIE HOBBS: You see it's like this Hugh. I want people to stop hiding from these yobs. I want them to stop sitting in front of their TVs, cowering behind the curtains and gawking as all our buildings burn and shops get their windows smashed in.

Sadie turns to the camera.

SADIE HOBBS: Seriously! Why so PASSIVE Britain? We have

strength in numbers. Forget the police, the army, the politicians – they had their chance and the truth is, they blew it. It's up to us to put a stop to this. US.

HUGH STANTON: So what exactly are you proposing?

SADIE HOBBS: I'm proposing that we have our own march to Piccadilly in September. That we get everyone out onto the streets and show Chester George and his pet rats who has the real power.

HUGH STANTON: Are you encouraging people to become vigilantes?

SADIE HOBBS: (*Nodding*) YES! And I'll tell you something Hugh - if we'd done this earlier and stood up to the rioters - poor old London could have been spared a lot of hassle. But we trusted in our police force and our politicians to protect us. And they FAILED!

HUGH STANTON: And I hear you have a documentary crew following you around as you prepare for this counter-march to Piccadilly?

SADIE HOBBS: (*Smiling*) Yes, well with my reality TV background it seemed like a no-brainer Hugh. So yes we're filming my attempt to save the city and the show is called *Sadie Hobbs: Riot Hunter*. Basically I'll be going around knocking on doors around Britain, recruiting people for our march to Piccadilly.

HUGH STANTON: And where can viewers watch your show?

SADIE HOBBS: Right here on SKAM of course! (*Gives him a playful wink*) How could you even ask me such a question?

HUGH STANTON: I'm sorry darling.

SADIE HOBBS: SKAM One at 8.30pm, starting tomorrow night.

HUGH STANTON: So you're recruiting an army?

SADIE HOBBS: ABSOLUTELY! And we're going to exterminate these feral rats once and for all.

HUGH STANTON: (*Smiling*) Sadie Hobbs, thank you very much.

Sadie turns to the camera.

SADIE HOBBS: Remember! – *Sadie Hobbs: Riot Hunter* - 8.30pm tomorrow night. See you there!

CHAPTER 34

24th August 2011

Mack stood outside the Christ Apostolic Church on Tottenham High Road. He pressed the phone up against his ear, while surveying the crowds around him.

"Hello?" said a voice on the other end of the line.

"Mum, it's me," Mack said. "I'm back in London."

"Mack!" Isabella's voice was full of relief. "Are you alright?"

"I'm alright," he said.

"Your gran phoned us yesterday. She said you never arrived at the station. We've heard nothing since – what the hell is going on with you?"

Mack was looking over to the other side of the High Road, where a woman was sitting on the burned out shell of a police car. A young boy was sitting next to her on the roof. They were pointing at the sky, looking up at the stars.

Mack wondered if that was one of two police cars he'd seen burned on the first night of rioting.

"I'm fine," he said.

"Where *are* you?"

"I told you. Back in London."

"*Where* in London?"

A part of him wanted to tell her he was close. Real close. She was his mother and he owed her that much.

"I can't say," he said.

"Mack," Isabella said. "London isn't safe."

"Edinburgh isn't safe either Mum," he said. "Not for me."

He could hear his dad's voice in the background. Asking her to ask Mack questions.

"We're going back," Isabella said. "You have to come with us. I promise you, nothing bad will happen."

"I can't Mum."

"Are you at Sumo Dave's?" Isabella asked.

Mack smiled. "I know that's the first place you'd look."

"What are you going to do Mack?"

He took a deep breath. "I'm going to Piccadilly Mum."

"With your friends from the Broadwater Farm Estate?" she said. "God Mack, you really know how to pick them don't you?"

"What?"

"Your friends."

"Friends?" Mack said. He turned around and looked back up at the second floor window of the church. "I can count my friends on one finger Mum."

Isabella was quiet for a moment. Then she said in flat voice:

"Don't make me call the police Mack."

But Mack wasn't fooled. He stole a glance to his left, towards the police station, where the authorities were still surrounded by the Good and Honest Citizens. "The police are a bit busy Mum."

He heard her sigh down the phone. One of those deep, pitiful sighs of Isabella's that never seemed to end. He knew he was causing his mother even more sleepless nights, which ate away at his guts. But at that moment in time, there was nothing more important for Mack

Walker than getting to Piccadilly. And if he went back to the house on Stanmore Road, he'd never get there.

"He's just a loony in a skull hoodie Mack," Isabella said. "Just another screwball on the Internet. And you lot think he's Jesus. He's got you brainwashed."

"I'm going Mum."

"And then what?"

"Then we can talk, okay? I've got to go now."

"Mack! Don't you dare put that phone down on me...MACK? Are you still there? "MACK!"

Click.

CHAPTER 35

25th August 2011

Sadie Hobbs: I'm a Celebrity Riot Hunter!

Viewer discretion: this show is live and may contain some offensive language.

(Opening sequence)

The intro begins with a montage of images from the riots: burning buildings, mass lootings and vicious beatings.

The camera then zooms in on an imaginary inner city street, with buildings that are clearly made out of huge blocks of cardboard. Some of them have bright orange triangles attached to the top, supposedly signifying that the building is ablaze.

A group of actors dressed up in hoodies and wearing paper rat masks over their faces are attacking a row of cardboard shops with plastic baseball bats – swatting the fake buildings with a barrage of feeble blows.

Suddenly a lone figure appears at the far end of the street.

Sadie Hobbs.

The rioters stop what they're doing and turn towards her.

The camera zooms in on Sadie, who swaggers slowly up the street. She's wearing a bright orange pest exterminator suit with 'RIOT HUNTER' printed in capital letters on the left breast.

The fake rioters charge at Sadie, one by one. Clumsily, they swing at her with their fake bats and Sadie swats them away like flies with her bare hands. The vanquished rioters fall in a heap at her feet.

Sadie approaches the camera, stops and breaks out into a broad smile.

The title appears onscreen:

SADIE HOBBS: I'M A CELEBRITY RIOT HUNTER!

Sadie Hobbs - dressed in her orange pest exterminator outfit - is walking down Old Church Street in Chelsea. She stops outside an attractive house, which is clad in red brick and has a sparkling pink and white Mini-Cooper parked out front.

Sadie turns to the camera:

SADIE HOBBS: Hello and welcome to *Sadie Hobbs: I'm a Celebrity Riot Hunter!* This is the only show out there GUARANTEED to exterminate the pests who've been taking the 'Great' out of Great Britain.

Sadie turns around and pushes open the small gate. She starts walking up the path towards the door, turning back to the camera as she does so.

SADIE HOBBS: This show is all about YOU – the great people of Britain. I'm here to recruit you to join my march to Piccadilly in September. Okay let's start recruiting shall we?

She knocks on the door.

A few seconds later, a young woman in her mid thirties answers the door. What is immediately apparent to the viewer is how similar in appearance she is to Sadie, albeit a slightly younger version. Her blonde hair is also crimped and her skin glows the same shade of deep orange. Upon seeing Sadie at the door, she clasps a hand over her mouth.

WOMAN: OOOH MA GAWWD!! Sadie Hobbs! I've just been watching you on the telly! I didn't realise that was my street you were on. I didn't even realise that was my house you were standing outside – or my pink and white car! OOOH MA GAWWD! What am I like?

SADIE HOBBS: (*Beaming*) Hello my dear, what's your name?

WOMAN: SADIE HOBBS! No that's not my name, that's your name. I just can't believe it! You're my hero, standing on my doorstep. I LOVE YOU!

The woman throws her arms around Sadie.

SADIE HOBBS: Woah there! Easy tiger.

WOMAN: Ooh! I've read everything you've ever written. I love your blog. You're like the best writer ever that's ever written anything. PHIL, PHIL – Sadie Hobbs is at the door! I think you're one of them geniuses! You're a genius aren't you?

Sadie wriggles free of the woman's grip.

SADIE HOBBS: Okay darling, calm down. I just need a quick answer. Are you #teamSadie or #teamwhatshisname? Can I count on YOU to join me on my march to Piccadilly in September?

The woman walks forward slowly, like a zombie chasing brains.

WOMAN: I'll do whatever you want me to do. ANYTHING!

SADIE HOBBS: (*Turns to cameraman*) Okay, we'll take that as a yes. Time to go. Let's get the hell out of here Mike.

Sadie turns around, runs down the driveway past the pink and white Mini, pulls open the gate and takes off down the street. Mike, the cameraman, chases after her and judging by the sound of heavy breathing, is on the verge of collapsing with exhaustion. Eventually Sadie stops running at the end of the street. Mike catches up with her and the shaky camera footage shows her looking back in the direction they just came, making sure they're not being followed.

SADIE HOBBS: Phew! That was close. The perils of live TV.

She checks back up the street one more time.

SADIE HOBBS: Okay. Well it's not just me recruiting. I have people all over the country knocking on doors right at this very minute. Let's go to one of my minions now. Kumiko is in Birmingham – hello Kumiko!

Sadie fidgets with the earpiece in her right ear.

SADIE: Kumiko! CAN-YOU-HEAR-ME?

KUMIKO: I-can-hear-you-Sadie.

The camera cuts to a small-statured Asian woman, no more than five feet tall. Like Sadie, she's wearing a pest exterminator outfit with a 'RIOT HUNTER' badge on the front.

Kumiko speaks in clipped English, smiling pleasantly at the camera as she stands outside a row of terraced houses in a pleasant looking suburb in Birmingham.

SADIE: Kumiko? You're about to knock on somebody's door aren't you?

KUMIKO: Yes-try-one-more.

Kumiko - followed by the cameraman - walks up the driveway of the nearest house. She rings the doorbell and waits.

A black man, approximately in his mid-fifties, opens the door. He's wearing only a pair of boxer shorts and a white vest. The man stares at Kumiko for a moment, taking in her exterminator outfit with a raised eyebrow. Then he notices the camera.

MAN: Yes? Can I help you?

KUMIKO: Sir. You-on-Sadie Hobbs-show. She-want-to-know-if-you-come-down-to-Piccadilly-to-chase-evil-Chester-George-away?

The man, speaking with a strong West Indian accent, looks at Kumiko thoughtfully.

MAN: I'll be there.

KUMIKO: (*Smiling*) That-is-wonderful.

MAN: Hold on little lady. I'm going down to Piccadilly alright. But I'm going there to stand with Chester George and the Good and Honest Citizens.

Kumiko tilts her head, like a bewildered puppy.

KUMIKO: Sir?

MAN: The Good and Honest Citizens. My brothers and sisters.

KUMIKO: (*On the brink of tears*) But-why? Why-you-destroy-this-beautiful-country?

MAN: Do you really want to know why?

Kumiko fidgets with her earpiece, as if receiving instructions.

KUMIKO: Somebody-say-no-in-my-ear.

MAN: (*Ignoring her*) There are many reasons.

Kumiko throws a panicky look to the camera.

MAN: Something happened just yesterday in fact. I'd like to share that with the camera.

KUMIKO: Oh-dear.

MAN: I was looking after my grandson for my daughter. We had a full day planned together – a day of watching DVDs and just enjoying each other's company. You understand? My grandson loves sweets - and so do I - so we decided to go to the supermarket and get some treats to eat while watching films together.

KUMIKO: (*Still fidgeting with her earpiece*) So-sorry-sir-I'm-getting-word-that-we-have-to-go-back-to-Sadie.

The man is undeterred.

MAN: If you cut me off now, you will only make things worse. Do you understand?

KUMIKO: Uh...

MAN: (*Directly to camera*) Do *you* understand?

Kumiko nods while receiving instructions in her ear.

KUMIKO: Ok-we-have-time. Tell-your-story-sir.

MAN: (*Nods*) So my grandson and I are walking down the street making our way to the local supermarket. And then a car drove past us, very slowly. I looked inside the car and there's a middle-class looking white guy at the wheel. Nice suit, all that. And I couldn't help but notice the way he looked at me. The *way* that he looked at me. He leaned forward in his seat and he actually sneered at me. He *sneered* at me as I was walking down the street with my grandson.

Kumiko nods.

MAN: Now I'm not being paranoid. It was a look I'd seen before. Many times. I used to live in London and I've seen it on the faces of the police officers who used to do stop and searches on my friends and me. It was a look that said - *you don't matter*. Pure contempt. And I was so angry yesterday. I wanted to walk right up to this guy's car and pound on the windscreen with my fists. Had my grandson not been there, maybe I would have.

At this point, the camera cuts back to Sadie Hobbs in Chelsea. She's looking at the camera and shaking her head disdainfully.

SADIE HOBBS: MOAN, MOAN, MOAN! They're all the same, aren't they? Looks like you drew the short straw Kumiko. Sorry about that love. Right let's get back to talking to some normal people, shall we?

CHAPTER 36

August 26th 2011

"Hello. Tottenham can you hear me?"

The amplified voice came out of nowhere.

For a moment, everyone on the second floor of the Christ Apostolic Church looked at one another, as if to make sure they'd heard it too.

Mack got to his feet, throwing his blanket aside. He hurried over to the large second-floor window. Footsteps crept up from behind, gathering around him.

"Who the fuck's that?" Tegz asked. "Are they speaking to us?"

Mack pushed the tip of his nose onto the cold glass. It was almost dark outside, but to the left there was a dazzling white light outside Tottenham Police Station, as if a spotlight was being shone from an upper floor window down onto the street.

A woman was standing on top of a police van, clutching a megaphone. The spotlight was directed at her, but it also illuminated a small battalion of riot police and soldiers encircling the van.

The Good and Honest Citizens were moving forward for a closer look at the person who had summoned them, like moths drawn to a light.

Mack tried to get a better look at the woman on the van. She was perhaps anywhere between thirty to forty years old. He was shocked at her pale skin, translucent and ghost-like, but guessed that the spotlight had something to do with that. Still, her whiteness contrasted everything else - the dark coat, her shoulder length black hair – everything was black but that gleaming face, which now looked down upon thousands of people.

"Tottenham, can you hear me?" she said.

Her voice wavered, as if unsure of itself.

"I recognise that voice," someone said behind Mack. The speaker was a nineteen-year-old student called Simon, who'd dropped everything in his hometown of Manchester to travel down to Piccadilly. "She's been on TV before," he said.

"Who is she then?" Sumo Dave said, standing at Mack's side.

Simon shook his head. "Don't know mate. But I know that voice. I do."

"Hello Tottenham," said the woman on the police van. "My name is Marie Coggins."

Simon rapped his fist against the glass. "Fuckin' hell!" he said. "Coggins. I knew it. The old war hero bloke who got - "

"My father was Richard Coggins," Marie said to the assembled crowd. "And as some of you may know, he was murdered recently in the riots."

Tegz slipped away from the huddle of people at the window. Mack turned around and saw him climb back into his sleeping bag, where he pulled the hood of his sweatshirt over his head, stretching it as far as it would go.

Mack scanned the room for Hatchet. He found him standing on the other side of Sumo Dave, watching events unfold outside. His eyes were blank, and he might as well have been watching an insect crawling over the floor.

"I know a lot of people here have grievances," Marie said to the crowd.

She pressed the megaphone tight to her lips.

"Maybe you haven't got a job. Maybe you don't have money and feel like you've got nothing to lose by taking part in the riots or the occupation. I know what it's like – we've all struggled in some way or another with the realities of life. I know. But what I've gone through in the past with money or whatever - it was nothing compared to what I'm going through now. None of that means anything. Losing Dad – that means something."

Marie paused for a moment.

Sumo Dave gave a snort of disgust. "Bloody old bill put her up to this," he said. "They've dragged that poor girl here on a mission to beg us all to go home."

"Aye," Mack said.

Outside, Marie brought the megaphone back to her lips.

"But what's happening here tonight," she said. "And what's happening across other areas of London – it isn't going to fix our problems. Not mine. Not yours."

Sumo Dave walked away from the window and sat down on his sleeping bag. He picked up the cheese and tomato sandwich he'd been eating and pointed towards the street.

"Load of bollocks," he called out, biting into the sandwich. "Push their guilt buttons love, that's what the old bill said to her. Poor cow. Exploitation, that's what they call that."

"Well I didn't kill her dad, did I?" Simon said. "And neither did anyone here so we've got nothing to feel guilty about, have we?"

Mack looked over at Hatchet. Their eyes met briefly.

On the High Road, Marie Coggins continued to address the crowd. Her voice sounded more assertive now and she raised a clenched fist into the air as she spoke.

"My dad loved this city," she said. "And I can tell you this - it broke his heart to see London destroying itself. He was a World War Two veteran and he told me that he couldn't believe we survived the Blitz only for this to happen. That's why he was out there on the street that night. He went to Croydon, the most dangerous place in London at that time. An eighty-seven year-old man wanted to talk to the rioters. To make them see sense."

Marie stopped suddenly.

"I'm sorry," she said, rubbing a hand over her eye.

Hatchet turned away from the window. He was looking at his phone now, chuckling at something on the Internet.

"My dad was a good man," Marie continued. "He didn't deserve to be bludgeoned to death for trying to help people. He was a war hero, a husband, and a wonderful father."

Mack shuddered. He thought back to that terrible night in Croydon. He heard the muffled cries of the policeman being dragged down the alley. He saw the blood on Hatchet's hand, and felt the warmth of Rossi's on his own.

Too much had happened.

Stepping back from the window, he turned around.

Hatchet was staring at him from the other side of the room. A black heat in his doll's eyes, pointed at Mack.

The Richard Coggins thing only made it worse. Mack knew. And Hatchet *knew* that Mack knew.

Mack looked away, turning back to the window. The thought of staying under the same roof as Hatchet until Piccadilly was unnerving.

But it was either that or go home.

Outside, Marie Coggins continued to address the crowd.

"Nothing will bring my Dad back," she said, resting a hand over her heart. "But there is something we can all do to honour his memory. All of us, right here tonight. To protect our own families."

"Here it comes," Sumo Dave said. "Money shot."

"We can stop this now," Marie said. "No one else has to lose their father. But if Piccadilly goes ahead, who knows how many more fathers and mothers, husbands and wives, brothers and sisters, sons and daughters, will die?"

"Yeah," Sumo Dave said. "And how many of 'em will die if we don't go ahead, eh?"

"I urge you," Marie said, a clenched fist held aloft. "PLEASE. Just go home. Go home to your family and let's start rebuilding this city - together. Together we can work out why this has happened. Grievances will not be forgotten, I understand. But go home. Please. On behalf of my dad and my entire family - thank you very much for listening."

A small round of applause broke out, applauding at least her bravery, if not her request.

Two policemen stretched their arms up towards her, helping Marie climb down from the van. As she descended onto solid ground, the bright spotlight from the station dimmed, softening the edges of the night once more.

"WAKE UP YOU LAZY BASTARDS!"

Tegz was running from bed to bed, shaking people out of their slumber. Shining the light of his phone in their eyes for good measure.

"You've gotta see this," he said.

Mack sat up on his makeshift bed of two woollen blankets. It was still dark outside, but for the faint glow of the streetlights.

"Piss off Tegz!" somebody said.

"We're trying to sleep mate," somebody else said.

"Fuck off Tegz!" That was Sumo Dave. "Pack that shit in!"

But Tegz wouldn't quit. He ran along the edges of the scattered beds again, this time kicking people on the legs until they moved.

"GET UP!" he said.

Then he ran over to the door and switched on the main light.

Electric light flooded the room like an avalanche. The sound of groans and curses could be heard all over the floor.

"Oh you little prick," Sumo Dave said, sitting up in his sleeping bag.

Tegz stood in the middle of the room, surveying how many people were now awake.

"You gotta see this," he said. "C'mon everyone, GET UP!"

Sumo Dave rubbed his eyes wearily. "Why?"

Tegz waved his phone in the air. "So I was on Twitter just now," he said. "I was just messing about when guess what happened? The trailer for Piccadilly went up."

"Trailer?" somebody called out.

Tegz grinned. "You know what a trailer is, don't you?" He was jumping up and down, like a kid on Christmas morning. "A promotional clip. Like they do for films. Well they're doing it for this, eh? SKAM Box Office are showing Piccadilly live on Pay-Per-View TV. Charging twenty quid too, the dirty bastards."

"Twenty quid?" Sumo Dave said. "To watch it on telly?"

Tegz nodded. "Yeah. They've even given it a name: Judgement Day."

"Twenty fucking quid?" Sumo Dave said.

Simon, who was sleeping directly underneath the window, sat up in bed.

"That's the corporate media for you mate," he said. "They might hate our guts but they've no qualms about making a few million quid out of our revolution."

"Oy!" Tegz said. "Never mind that now. D'ya wanna watch this trailer or not?"

He sat down in the middle of the room, and some of the others, who hadn't gone back to sleep, slowly gathered around him.

Mack sunk slowly back into the depths of his own warm blanket. He was just about to surrender to sleep when Tegz yelled over.

"Mack!" he called out. "D'ya wanna watch this or not?"

CHAPTER 37

PICCADILLY: JUDGEMENT DAY

Official SKAM promotional Clip:

Broadcast multiple times per day on all SKAM TV channels: 26th/27th/28th/29th/30th/31st August 2011

The camera looks down upon a picturesque postcard image of London.

The sky is bright blue. 'Land of Hope and Glory' is playing softly in the background.

The camera sails through the air. It glides past several ravens floating effortlessly and carefree over the long and winding River Thames, which is a beautiful and manufactured shade of aqua.

The Houses of Parliament appear in the background. The camera zooms in on the familiar Gothic architecture, the iconic clock tower; this is a place of history.

The camera glides further on towards the London Eye - a four hundred plus foot tall Ferris wheel located on the South Bank, which also reminds us that London is a modern city too.

There are other snapshots of London: St Paul's Cathedral, Buckingham Palace, Nelson's Column, and finally, Piccadilly Circus. It is instantly recognisable with its gigantic neon advertising signs and the statue of Anteros, which is so often mistaken for his brother, Eros.

And it's at this point that the sweet 'Land of Hope and Glory' begins to slow down. The music fades and a terrible dissonance emerges, as if the melody is being slowly strangled.

The screen fades to black. The colours are gone. Everything stops.

The screen lights up again. Now it's filled with images of the recent London riots.

The pictures move in slow motion to the haunting rhythm of silence. These are the most shocking scenes witnessed over the past few weeks: the burning of the furniture store in Tottenham; the bird's eye views of smoke and fire rising above the city; the most frenzied and savage instances of looting and violence; people crying and people hurt.

The screen fades to black.

It lights up again.

The camera is on ground level, looking straight onto a post-apocalyptic vision of London. The Houses of Parliament are an ancient ruin. The Thames has run dry, leaving only a deep and foreboding valley of mud in which the wreckage of the London Eye has long since fallen.

The sky is dark grey with jagged streaks of angry clouds.

A solitary dark shape walks across the ruins of this wasteland. The camera zooms in to reveal a man dressed in a skull hoodie, carrying a spiked baseball bat in one hand. It is Chester George, or rather an actor dressed up as Chester George. At his back, thousands of masked figures appear, also wielding weapons - spiked bats, knives, chains and even guns.

They move forward, an army on the march.

Thumping drums, followed by an eerie, whispering choir, are playing in the background.

Chester George and his followers march on through the dark ruins of London. They walk with primitive, almost ape-like movements. These Neanderthal multitudes strike out at nearby buildings and businesses, smashing windows and starting fires.

They pass a sign that says 'PICCADILLY'.

Innocent bystanders flee the invading army.

Chester George and his followers arrive at their destination - Piccadilly Circus. This place is untouched by the apocalypse that has ravaged the rest of the city. Here, even the famous neon signs are still fully operational. They are the only lights left in London and despite Armageddon, the advertising screens remind us that it's important to drink Coke Zero because it has no sugar in it.

Chester George calls his army to a halt on the outskirts of Piccadilly Circus. Slowly, he raises a hand and points to something on the other side of the famous landmark.

Someone is there.

It's Sadie Hobbs.

At her back, there are hundreds and thousands of ordinary people, dressed in everyday work clothes – office workers dressed in suits and ties, mechanics dressed in blue coveralls, doctors and nurses in their uniforms, and many more - all stretching back up the length of Shaftesbury Avenue, next to Piccadilly Circus.

Sadie Hobbs takes a step forward.

Chester George does likewise.

The two leaders walk towards one another. Now they're standing face to face by the Shaftesbury Memorial Fountain, with the statue of Anteros watching over them like a tennis umpire.

A deep, rumbling voice speaks over the music:

MOVIE VOICEOVER GUY: It's TIME. Two LEGENDS. One DESTINY. All roads lead to PICCADILLY.

The screen fades to black.

MOVIE VOICEOVER GUY: (*Talking at breakneck speed*) 'PICCADILLY: JUDGEMENT DAY.' You can order this event live on SKAM Box Office for only £19.95. Enjoy all the build up to the big day with special guests and studio analysis, broadcast live to the comfort of your living room from Piccadilly Circus.

There is NO safer place to enjoy the action.

CHAPTER 38

#JudgementDay

Sample of Tweets - *posted 31st August 2011*

Hannah Day *@handaychick · 1h*

Goosebumps! #JudgementDay

Tarn Di Roma *@tarndiroma · 1h*

Does anyone have any idea what's going to happen tomorrow? #judgementday

The Prime Minister *@therealPM · 1h*

We advise everyone to stay indoors tomorrow. Police and military will be on site to supervise #judgementday and maintain order.

Michael King *@therealkingoflondon · 2h*

Remember, keep it peaceful tomorrow #JudgementDay

Lara Kordei *@KordeiLara · 2h*

It's too quiet out there. I almost miss the sound of the riots. #JudgementDay

Sadie Hobbs *@AlphaBitchSadie · 2h*

Final reminder. We meet in Hyde Park at 7am. Team talk and then march to Piccadilly to take our city back. #JudgementDay #SKAMboxoffice

Jay Squire *@squire_jay · 2h*

I'm scared. Really truly deeply shit scared.

PICCADILLY

CHAPTER 39

1st September 2011

All across London, the Good and Honest Citizens were marching to Piccadilly.

It was three o'clock in the morning.

Mack and the others spilled out of the Christ Apostolic Church, and onto the crowded High Road. Still groggy from a lack of sleep, they'd packed some food and water into their rucksacks, but had abandoned their woollen blankets and sleeping bags in the second floor room of the church.

They could always pick them up later.

The crisp autumn air landed on Mack's face, reviving him slowly. Like everyone else, he'd followed the general advice to get as much sleep as possible before the march. But it wasn't enough, and a part of him was still tucked underneath the warm blankets back in the church.

Guided by the streetlights, the Good and Honest Citizens moved in no particular order and yet with an instinctive cohesion akin to a flock of birds. Those at the front led the way in silence, with the route to Piccadilly having been worked out long in advance.

They walked along the High Road, surrounded on both sides by a neverending row of burned out buildings and mangled shop fronts.

Occasionally, a child sobbed from somewhere within the depths of the crowd. There was also the odd, muted conversation to be heard. For the most part however, an eerie silence prevailed over the Good and Honest Citizens and they moved purposefully, and without distraction.

As he walked, Mack turned around several times and saw through a chink in the crowd that the army and police were shadowing them. The authorities travelled both on foot and in a slow convoy of vehicles that maintained a respectful distance. The police vans moved at a cautious pace, flashing their coloured lights in silence. Behind them, two armoured vehicles rclled forwards at a steady pace. Surrounding them, a contingent of police officers and soldiers followed on foot.

They travelled south on the A10.

There were still lights still on in some of the buildings they passed, spread out like occasional beacons scattered across the city. Mack looked up and saw dark shapes standing huddled around the windows, peering down onto the streets below.

Some of the people were waving excitedly. Others even popped their head out of the window to shout down words of encouragement.

"GO ON!" they yelled. "STICK IT TO THE FUCKING MAN!"

As the Tottenham crowd passed through the northern district of Stamford Hill, thousands of other Good and Honest Citizens were loitering on the main street, perhaps waiting for their northern counterparts to come down.

The numbers swelled dramatically, and it continued like that for some time. The Good and Honest Citizens continued to travel south, encountering crowds from other parts of London – crowds made up of people of all ages and ethnic backgrounds.

Mack smiled. His individual resolve expanded with each new arrival, as if everyone was connected on some deep, unfathomable level.

The police and soldiers continued to follow at a distance, but they didn't interfere as the Good and Honest Citizens gradually merged across the city.

As time passed, small groups of people wandered down the edge of the crowd, calling out, asking if anybody needed anything - food and water mostly, but also medicine.

"You need anything love?" a young woman said, catching Mack's eye. She and several others were carrying bin-bags full of sandwiches, snacks and bottled water. Mack groaned at the sight of them. He'd been living off sandwiches and snacks for over a week now.

"Not for me thanks," he said.

The woman smiled and moved further down the line.

A little further back in the crowd, Mack heard Sumo Dave refuse the offer of refreshment. Tegz however, whose high-pitched voice floated effortlessly over the crowd, eagerly accepted the offer of food.

"You can't be serious Tegz," Sumo Dave said. "It's four o'clock in the morning. You already ate two bags of crisps before we left the High Road."

"They're giving it away," Tegz said. "What am I supposed to do, say no to free food?"

"You're going to regret eating all that crap Tegz," Sumo Dave said. "You're gonna be locked in the bog with the shits when Chester George is giving his speech. Eh?"

Mack heard Sumo Dave laughing.

"Hey there's a thought," Tegz said. "Are there actually gonna be any toilets at this thing? I mean, who's organising all this, eh? What if I do get a case of the shits Sumo? What am I supposed to do?"

"Use your finger as a plug mate, I dunno."

"Oh fucking hell," Tegz said. "We're going to be on Pay-Per-View TV. And there I'll be, holding in a bad case of the runs. I should have went back in the church before we left. I'll have to run up a side street or something, eh?"

Sumo Dave was still chuckling away.

"People aren't forking out twenty quid to watch you take a shit in the back alleys of Piccadilly, are they?" he said. "You've got no choice mate, you'll have to bake it. And put on your happy face."

"This is serious Sumo!"

Further down the line, Mack was laughing, as were others around him.

Daylight crept slowly through the clouds. Above the tall buildings of London, hues of red sunlight appeared, wavering and distant.

The Good and Honest Citizens were closing in on their target. The large procession was now marching onto Theobald Road, in the Bloomsbury district in the West End of London.

For Mack and no doubt others in the crowd, it was like stepping into another world. In particular, it was a surprise to see so many pubs, restaurants and shops that hadn't been reduced to ruins. To see so many windows intact. To see supermarkets where you could go in and simply buy food if you wanted to. To see signs on the street pointing to grand-sounding attractions, such as The British Museum and Shaftesbury Theatre.

It was a strange new place and yet still part of their city. It was London.

Those at the head of the procession cut off Theobald Road, leading the crowd down onto New Oxford Street, then onto Shaftesbury Avenue.

They were on the brink of Piccadilly Circus now. And just at that moment, a swarm of helicopters appeared overhead. The thick pulsing sound of the rotor blades cut through the early morning calm and it was the first sign that the silent walk of the past few hours was truly over.

Hovering overhead, the helicopters pointed their white flashlights onto the lengthy procession making its way further down Shaftesbury Avenue.

Large groups of people continued to wave frantically from windows and roofs. Women screamed. Men screamed. The occasional item of lingerie was even tossed down onto the Good and Honest Citizens as they passed by.

Early morning chants of 'Chester George' contested against the chopping, slapping sound of the rotor blades overhead.

Mack saw the riot police up ahead, lining both sides of Shaftesbury Avenue in anticipation of their arrival. He couldn't see the police or army behind them anymore. But he felt sure they were still around somewhere.

The Good and Honest Citizens marched forwards, just as glorious pink and white bursts of light emanated from the rising sun.

Despite a lack of sleep, and despite walking throughout the night, Mack had never felt so excited at the start of a new day.

CHAPTER 40

1st September 2011

Piccadilly: Judgement Day

The SKAM Pay-Per-View broadcast begins with an aerial shot of Piccadilly Circus. Despite its name, Piccadilly Circus is not a circus. It's a famous road junction that links five busy roads in the West End of London. Its fame is derived from its sheer busyness and its status as a tourist attraction, not to mention the massive illuminated billboards, which have existed there since the early 1900s. It's also famous for Alfred Gilbert's statue of Anteros, which even today is still mistaken for his brother, Eros.

It's seven o'clock on Thursday morning. Twenty-five minutes have passed since a dark red sun rose over the city.

There is a massive police and military presence on site. Police officers line the edges of both sides of the surrounding roads, not unlike human tape barriers that stretch out in a multitude of directions. And in scenes reminiscent of Belfast in the 1970s, British soldiers patrol the areas around Piccadilly, Regent Street, Shaftesbury Avenue, and Coventry Street.

The SKAM Heli-Cam flies past the famous digital advertising screens. Over the last week or two, a furious battle has taken place to secure advertising space on the big day. And now, as history is being made, the famous screens remind viewers that they should drink Coca-Cola, eat their burgers at McDonalds, and that all their electronic needs can be satisfied with Samsung.

The camera cuts to a studio interior. Two middle-aged men are sitting behind a narrow table in front of a massive window, overlooking Piccadilly Circus. The camera zooms in on SKAM's lead anchor, 'Slick' Hugh Stanton, who is impeccably dressed in a light grey suit, matching the colour of his slicked back hair.

HUGH STANTON: Good morning. It's seven o'clock. It's Thursday the first of September 2011 and you're watching Piccadilly: Judgement Day. We're coming to you live from our makeshift studio here at 25 Regent Street, just above the famous Lillywhites sports shop. Stick with us and we'll bring you the build-up to the hottest ticket in town – JUDGEMENT DAY. It's Sadie Hobbs versus Chester George.

Hugh looks at his watch.

HUGH STANTON: As we speak, our helicopters are tracking the rioters who are making their way in droves towards Piccadilly Circus. We've also got an eye-in-the-sky at Hyde Park too where Sadie Hobbs is giving a speech, prior to her arrival. Thousands upon thousands of people will descend upon Piccadilly Circus today. And none of us can possibly predict what's going to happen.

CHAPTER 41

"How are we going to get through all these people?" Mack asked. He was looking down the length of Shaftesbury Avenue. "If it's like this here, it's only going to get worse the further down we go."

Sumo Dave shrugged. "I dunno," he said. "But I'm not staying back here with the kids and the grannies, am I? Fuck that. And anyway, there's no tickets, no numbers, no allocated seating down there is there? We've got every right to be down there – we were there when this all started, remember?"

"Aye."

"When Chester George speaks this afternoon," Sumo Dave said. "I want to be up front so that he can look me in the eye. In fact, I want to be on that fountain kissing his bony white skeleton feet."

Mack looked around, his eyes adjusting to the morning light. Mostly it was families who had stayed furthest back on Shaftesbury Avenue. There were sleeping toddlers everywhere, some of them being carried and comforted in the arms of their parents. Kids of about five, six and seven too, playing with their toys as their parents set down blankets in the middle of the road, setting up space for themselves.

"So we're going down then lads?" Sumo Dave said. "Yeah? We're all up for that?"

"You lot do what you want," Hatchet said. "I won't settle for anything less than a front-row seat."

"That's my boy Hatch," Sumo Dave said. "Tegz?"

"I'm getting on that fountain," Tegz said.

Sumo Dave laughed. "In your dreams mate. But I'll send you a postcard, yeah? Tell you what it's like up there with the stars."

"C'mon," Hatchet said. "Let's stop fucking about back here in the nursery, eh?"

And with that, Hatchet threw his rucksack over his shoulder and started towards the wall of bodies that stood in between them and Piccadilly Circus. He didn't turn around to check if anyone was following.

CHAPTER 42

SKAM BOX OFFICE

HUGH STANTON: And joining me for today's coverage is a very special guest - the one and only James Paxton – who we've pinched from the CBC for one day only. (*Laughs*) Welcome James.

The camera cuts to Paxton, dressed in a sleek black suit and thin matching tie. With typical curtness, he nods at the camera.

PAXTON: Hugh.

The camera cuts back to Stanton.

HUGH STANTON: I'm just getting word in my ear that Sadie

Hobbs has apparently amassed well over fifty thousand people to her cause. And those numbers are still growing James.

PAXTON: (*Nodding*) Those are staggering numbers Hugh.

HUGH STANTON: And although we don't know exactly how many people Chester George will bring – it's estimated at well over a hundred thousand - there is one thing that concerns me James. How is everyone going to fit into Piccadilly Circus? It's not that big a location after all, is it?

PAXTON: (*Shaking his head*) I don't know Hugh. I mean, it's not the smartest move is it and you know - we keep hearing how smart Chester George is, don't we? Well I would ask him this – why not go with Hyde Park instead? Why Piccadilly Circus? It's a road junction for heaven's sake. It's not big enough.

HUGH STANTON: Not exactly a stroke of genius, is it?

CHAPTER 43

The SKAM Heli-Cam looks down upon a mass exodus of men, women and children.

The procession, stretching back for miles, is slowly moving away from a vast green space located in the West End of London.

They're now travelling east towards Piccadilly Circus.

Many of the people in the procession are waving Union Jacks, or hoisting a variety of coloured banners in the air with 'London Liberation Army' printed on the front in bold letters.

When the camera zooms in on the front of the procession, a familiar figure wearing a Union Jack mini dress is visible. She runs one hand through her crimped blonde hair as she waves up at the Heli-Cam with the other, an ecstatic grin spread all over her face.

CHAPTER 44

Mack barged his way through another group of people.

He felt his shoulder slam into someone's arm.

"Excuse me," he mumbled. He could feel their eyes all over him – *where do you think you're going?*

This wasn't going to be easy. The Good and Honest Citizens were one long traffic jam stretching the length of Shaftesbury Avenue. Mack had already walked face first into someone's elbow, but thankfully he hadn't started bleeding all over the place.

He'd never apologised so much in his life.

"Sorry."

"Sorry."

"Sorry."

Somebody tried to hand him a beer. He signalled a polite refusal to the stranger.

Later on, still fighting his way through the crowd, he thought back to that beer.

Wishing he'd said yes.

CHAPTER 45

The SKAM Heli-Cam flies over Shaftesbury Avenue.

Thousands of people fill the street below.

Some of the Good and Honest Citizens can be seen working on makeshift supply stations. These crude stands, built out of crates and boxes, will provide bottled water and refreshment to those in need. Elsewhere, others are checking out the freestanding, plastic portable toilets that have been brought in overnight and scattered throughout the area. In addition, St John Ambulance crews are on site, should they be required. As the Heli-Cam flies overhead, some of the GHC can be seen in discussion with the medical personnel.

CHAPTER 46

CBC News 24

In the middle of Piccadilly Circus, Dick Ronson is doing a live report for the CBC 24-Hour News Channel. Dressed in a light blue shirt and chinos, Ronson is sporting a slightly more casual look than his usual suit and tie job.

Except that is, for the bulletproof vest he's wearing over his shirt.

As Ronson reports to the camera, the Good and Honest Citizens are pouring into Piccadilly Circus behind him. Huge crowds swarm the area and Dick Ronson looks nervously over his shoulder before turning back to the camera and commencing the report.

DICK RONSON: Sophie, this is a high alert situation today in the city of London. Let us not forget that these same people here today, have for weeks unleashed a violent reign of terror upon the citizens of our capital city.

A man walks behind Ronson. A little girl of about seven or eight – with 'GHC' printed on her forehead - sits on his shoulders, waving at the CBC camera.

SOPHIE WALLACE: (*From the CBC studio.*) Dick, what's the atmosphere there like at the moment?

DICK RONSON: It's a giant carnival of terror Sophie! The entire area around here has been closed to traffic, which feels a bit surreal given that Piccadilly Circus is normally crawling with vehicles.

Ronson glances over his shoulder.

DICK RONSON: As you can see behind me Sophie, the rioters are currently making their way into Piccadilly Circus in their hundreds and thousands. They say they want change. But is it all just an excuse? Is there more violence to come?

Ronson is interrupted by the sound of a bullhorn blaring. An explosion of cheers follows from within the assembled crowd.

DICK RONSON: Sophie, I'll have to leave it there – I'm sorry. It's getting too intense here. I feel like a man shipwrecked on an island infested with cannibals. I'm standing over a large pot filled with hot boiling water, and right now the natives are dancing all around me.

CHAPTER 47

The four teenagers had arrived. At last, they were in Piccadilly Circus.

The first thing Mack did was look up at the famous advertising screens to his right. Unlike the roads, which had been sealed off, the screens were fully operational and at that moment, were spewing out a faster-than-a-blink-of-the-eye conveyer belt of brightly lit images: food, electronics, clothing, skincare, cigarettes, credit cards, hair products, cars, sexual enhancement drugs, beer, and banks.

It was the perfect time to sell.

Hatchet, who had been leading the way so far, didn't stop for long on the outskirts. With relentless determination, he continued to push his way forward through the seething mass of bodies.

Mack, Sumo Dave and Tegz followed, but gradually, as they fought their way forwards, the four teenagers began to get split up in the crowd.

Out of the four, Sumo Dave - due to his height - had the most problems getting through the crowd. The people who'd been standing there for hours already weren't too pleased about newcomers trying to push past them. On several occasions, while trying to slip past spectators, Sumo Dave was physically pushed back.

Mack was having more success. He showed patience in his approach, standing for long stretches, biding his time, and waiting for the right moment to make a move. It was only when something happened elsewhere – a sudden noise amongst the crowd, the arrival of a helicopter, or some other distraction – that he took a couple of steps forward. But territory was much guarded here. This was the hottest ticket in town and Mack had to be careful not to make his advance obvious.

It was slow, but gradually he began to close in on the fountain.

As he progressed further, he turned around and saw Sumo Dave falling back into the crowd. The two boys caught each other's eye from afar. Sumo Dave shrugged as if to signal that this was as far as he was going.

He raised an arm aloft, giving Mack the thumbs up.

Good luck mate.

CHAPTER 48

FIXX News

Kit McAdam, reporter and national security analyst for FIXX Media, is standing by at the Shaftesbury Memorial Fountain. She is dressed in the green khaki shirt and trousers of a seasoned war correspondent.

KIT MCADAM: Well, standing beside me now is Michael King who has been a prominent voice for the rioters since disturbances began back in August.

The camera zooms out. Michael King is standing at Kit's side, dressed in a jet-black hoodie and khaki combat trousers.

KIT MCADAM: Michael, thank you for talking to us. Tell me, what are we going to hear from Chester George later today?

MICHAEL KING: He's going to talk about Phase Three.

KIT MCADAM: Phase Three?

MICHAEL KING: Phase One was the insurrection. Phase Two, the occupation. Phase Three comes next – and that's where the real, lasting change begins.

Michael looks out over the large crowd.

MICHAEL KING: Look out there today. Look at all the

different types of people who want the same change. There are students in the crowd. There are working men and women representing the trade unions. There are middle-class people who have brought their children. There are no types – only human beings.

KIT MCADAM: Any message for the people watching this at home?

MICHAEL KING: Yes. Brace yourselves.

KIT MCADAM: (*Laughing nervously*) Wow. Okay. You've become quite a hit with the people lately Michael. Is this the beginning of a burgeoning political career?

MICHAEL KING: (*Shaking his head*) I don't care a thing for politics.

KIT MCADAM: But isn't this politics?

MICHAEL KING: No, no, this is a celebration. Look around you. People are standing around singing songs of hope. There are artists down there drawing portraits of children. There are poets speaking while people are getting their faces painted. This isn't politics - it's a celebration. Change is coming.

KIT MCADAM: And Michael, there's even a rumour circulating that *you* might be Chester George. Have you heard that one? After all, we know absolutely nothing about this man who everybody's waiting for here today. What do you have to say about that?

Michael King smiles for the first time on camera.

MICHAEL KING: Oh man. I'm not even close to the level of intellect possessed by that man. Not even close.

KIT MCADAM: But you do know who Chester George is, don't you?

MICHAEL KING: Yes I do.

CHAPTER 49

Mack was exhausted, yet satisfied. He stood in the front row, having painstakingly worked his way through a wall of people for over two hours. Now his throat was dry, clogged up with nerves and a gnawing thirst. On more than one occasion, he'd felt his legs wobble underneath him as he pushed his way forwards, his body pleading with its master for rest and nourishment.

He thought about digging into his rucksack for some water or God forbid, another sandwich. But given how tightly everyone was squeezed together at the front, pulling his rucksack off his back and opening it up was easier said than done.

No need. He wasn't going to die of thirst yet.

There was no sign of Hatchet or Tegz anywhere. He assumed they'd fallen back into the crowd along with Sumo Dave.

Mack looked over towards the fountain. The advance was over - the front row was as far as he was going. As soon as he'd arrived up front, he realised there was no chance of him getting over there onto the steps of the fountain. A group of heavies, built like tanks, were yet another human wall. They were yet another obstacle in his way, standing tall and wide, posing as security. The heavies were standing facing the crowd, acting as human barriers, and keeping the fountain steps deliberately clear of too much human traffic.

There were a few people gathered under the statue of Anteros. Michael King was talking to a female reporter, and several other, mostly black faces, sat scattered around the middle steps, and then a little further down, near the bottom there was yet another familiar face.

Upon seeing this face, Mack threw his hands in the air.

He couldn't believe it.

There was Hatchet, sitting on the stairs of the fountain.

CHAPTER 50

SKAM BOX OFFICE

Poppy Baskerville is standing in the middle of Piccadilly Circus.

POPPY BASKERVILLE: (*Touching her earpiece*) This just in Hugh. Sadie Hobbs and the London Liberation Army have arrived on the outskirts of Piccadilly Circus! As you know they've been travelling along the Piccadilly route earlier this morning from Hyde Park. They're going to want to get in here, but police are expected to try and hold them back.

Cuts to Hugh Stanton in the studio.

HUGH STANTON: Thank you Poppy. We've got our eye in the sky on Sadie Hobbs and her London Liberation Army right now.

The SKAM Heli-Cam hovers over a slow-moving, but tremendous procession making its way east along the Piccadilly road - a road that links Hyde Park Corner and Piccadilly Circus, and which runs for almost a mile in length. The street is absolutely packed with bodies marching slowly past the riot police that line both edges like a guard of honour.

The camera zooms in on Sadie Hobbs, marching at the front of the procession. She's holding hands with a boy of about five or six years of age. The boy is wearing an executioner's mask and swinging a hangman's noose in mid-air.

PAXTON: (*Voiceover*) Good Lord! Never fails to shock, does she?

HUGH STANTON: (*Voiceover.*) Look at all those people James. It's incredible. I've never seen anything like this in all my life.

PAXTON: (*Voiceover*) The battle for London has begun.

HUGH STANTON: (*Voiceover*) Look James. The authorities are indeed stepping in.

As Sadie Hobbs and the London Liberation Army approach the junction at Piccadilly Circus, several police and army units move in to intercept the march. A lengthy debate follows between Sadie Hobbs, several of her followers, and those in charge of the authorities.

PAXTON: (*Voiceover*) I'll say this Hugh. The police had better keep that lot out of Piccadilly Circus. Can you imagine throwing them in with the thousands of people already in there?

HUGH STANTON: (*Voiceover*) Doesn't bear thinking about James.

CHAPTER 51

Helicopters flew overhead.

Near the fountain, a DJ had set up, and was now playing a steady stream of classic punk and reggae tunes, setting the mood for the big moment ahead.

Frequent disturbances could be heard coming from the other side of Piccadilly Circus. Angry voices, chanting anti-Chester George songs. A tirade of abuse hurled at those who'd gathered in the centre of Piccadilly Circus.

Mack heard somebody behind him say that Sadie Hobbs and her followers had arrived on the outskirts of the famous road junction and that they were trying desperately to convince the police to let them in.

There was barely room to move in the crowd. Barely room to breathe. Mack's muscles were stiff and painful and to make it worse, the putrid smell of body odour lingered in the air.

He hoped to hell that it wasn't him.

CHAPTER 52

Back in the SKAM studio, Hugh Stanton and James Paxton have been watching events unfold with interest.

HUGH STANTON: Okay. Well while we're waiting for the big one, let's check out the results of our Twitter survey, shall we? We asked you – who is Chester George?

Paxton laughs off-camera.

HUGH STANTON: Well you've been voting all day and I can tell you the results are now in. According to the Great British public, Chester George is none other than - wait for it - Prince Harry.

PAXTON: That's very interesting. A royal connection – just like Jack the Ripper all over again, isn't it?

HUGH STANTON: Well we wouldn't put it past the little scallywag, would we? Anyway, Prince Harry topped the poll with eighteen percent of the overall vote. Coming in a close second with fifteen percent is - James Paxton.

PAXTON: (*Taking a bow*) Thank you very much.

HUGH STANTON: I only got two percent of the vote.

PAXTON: That doesn't mean you're innocent, does it? I've heard you like dressing up at the weekend Hugh.

(*Both men laugh*)

HUGH STANTON: And coming in at third place with eleven percent of the vote is...

Outside there's a sudden roar from the crowd. A resounding chorus of applause and boos - coming from all sides of Piccadilly Circus - builds quickly towards a furious crescendo.

Hugh Stanton touches his earpiece.

HUGH STANTON: Okay. I'm sorry we're going to have to leave the Twitter results there. Ladies and gentleman, I'm very pleased to tell you that the time has come. Chester George is ready.

PAXTON: My God. Listen to that racket Hugh. You'd think Churchill had just come back from the dead, wouldn't you?

CHAPTER 53

Hatchet was the winner.

Mack shook his head in disgust. Why did it have to be Hatchet? And what happened to Tegz? Where the hell was the wee man? If any of the four teenagers from Tottenham had stood a chance of slipping through the crowd and security unnoticed it was Tegz. Mack would have put his money on it being Tegz.

Shite.

It hadn't taken long for Hatchet to notice Mack standing in the front row. But to Mack's surprise, Hatchet didn't gloat – in fact, he paid Mack no attention whatsoever. It was as if he didn't exist, as if they'd never met at all.

Mack looked at the row of heavies standing in between the crowd and the fountain. How had Hatchet managed to get past them?

Little Mike Tyson was sitting at Chester George's feet.

How the fuck did he manage that?

A scattered round of applause broke out within the crowd. It spread quickly, rising in volume and intensity. Soon it had grown into an onslaught of boisterous cheers, which were accompanied by high-pitched whistles.

There were boos too, coming from across the other side of Piccadilly Circus.

All in all, it was an ungodly racket, a furious cocktail of sound that swelled dramatically, until the ground beneath Mack felt like it was literally shaking.

He looked over at the fountain.

Michael King was walking up the steps. He stopped and turned to face the crowd, saluting them before making his way towards the middle platform, a little further up from where Hatchet was sitting. Somebody else followed Michael, a short older black man, carrying a soapbox in his hand.

A thunderous roar of yelling and clapping accompanied them.

The moment had come.

Chester George stepped onto the stairs of the Shaftesbury Memorial Fountain, as if he'd materialised out of thin air.

He was dressed in his trademark skull hoodie, and carrying a megaphone in one hand. When he reached the soapbox that had been placed on the top step, he climbed upon it and stood there for a while, basking in the onslaught of adulation.

Mack couldn't tell whether the great man was smiling or not. But even from the front row, he could clearly see that Chester George's eyes were beaming with joy as he surveyed the crowd around him.

At the same time, a flood of boos, jeers, and hissing continued to pour in from the west side of Piccadilly Circus. But next to the rapturous welcome of the Good and Honest Citizens, this was no more than a faint disturbance.

It was a long time before silence came. But eventually it did, and when it came, it was a complete and perfect silence.

Mack looked over at Hatchet, sitting so close to the man himself. No wonder Little Mike Tyson was grinning.

The bastard.

Up on the fountain, Chester George took a deep breath.

He was ready.

CHAPTER 54

1st September 2011

Chester George – The Speech

"Good afternoon. And welcome.

The politicians have been trying to convince us that the voice of the streets must be respected. So here we are.

And yet at the same time look all around you - they're sending in the soldiers and the riot police to subdue us.

Why?

Because they're terrified. They're terrified of each and every one of YOU.

CHAPTER 55

Hatchet looked like the happiest man in the world. Sitting on the bottom step of the fountain, he was grinning from ear to ear, as if at last he'd found contentment at long last. Even as Chester George spoke, Mack couldn't stop looking over at Hatchet.

It was his posture; the way he flopped and reclined and relaxed. Mack had never seen the grumpy little shit so enthused or so playful.

He looked like the cat that got the cream.

CHAPTER 56

"Up until today, all you have ever been to the politicians and the businessmen is a situation that had to be controlled. And yes indeed ladies and gentleman, they had the situation under control.

Until that day in August. Until at last - Phase One.

The people who own us – the businessmen – the ones who make all the important decisions have been pressurising the politicians to get this situation under control. These are the people who own you. They own YOU. They own the land. They own corporations, judges, politicians, and all the big media that feed you bullshit for breakfast every day.

They don't care about us. And yet they own us.

Now these people are terrified. They don't want this. They didn't want you to come here today, to gather here, to educate yourself.

Why?

Because it works against their interests.

If each and every one of you were capable of critical thought, you'd start realising how much they fuck you every day of your life. Yes they do. And have been doing it every day of your life up until now.

They're terrified that you might find out. Because what would happen then?

Well there'd be a fucking riot, wouldn't there?

CHAPTER 57

Mack watched Hatchet reach into his rucksack and pull out his baseball cap. He was still grinning like a loon as he placed it over his head.

Maybe, Mack thought, he was being too hard on the guy. Maybe, just maybe, the little prick could change.

All he needed was a little hope. That's all anyone standing in Piccadilly Circus was hoping for today. A little hope.

And here it was, free of charge.

CHAPTER 58

"They want your obedience. They want you to be capable of doing just enough. Run their machines, do the paperwork, and don't ask any questions.

Brothers and sisters,

Have you heard about what's going on in Brazil right now? The authorities are pumping all their money into a football tournament. At the same time, sixteen million Brazilian people are living in extreme poverty. And all for the World Cup – something that most Brazilians don't want. They'd rather see an end to government corruption and the installation of better public services. Now the people have taken to the streets in over a hundred towns and cities to protest. And how do the authorities respond to that? With tear gas and rubber bullets.

But the people - they won't back down and you'll be very pleased to hear that they're carrying banners – banners that read 'L-2011'.

You see? The Brazilian people are with us. The Brazilian people are waking up, just like you have done.

You didn't hear that on the news, did you? Where were SKAM and the CBC when all that was going on in Brazil?

No, no, no.

The big brass knobs who own the media don't want you to hear about Phase One starting up in other countries. They want people – and especially those people over there who've marched here from Hyde Park to stop us – to think that what's happening in London is an isolated incident.

But we are not alone.

In Turkey, the people are trying to protest the demolition of a public park to make way for a shopping centre. This was a project backed by the politicians but NOT by the people. The people want a nice park for their families with grass and trees and clean air to breathe.

But trees don't generate profit.

In Turkey, like so many other places, anything green is just another corporate investment-in-waiting. So the people there started to protest peacefully, holding sit-ins and waving banners in the park. And what did the government do?

They sent in the troops to silence them. Of course.

The government forcefully evicted the environmental protestors and sparked off a revolt against their own authoritarian regime. The Turks, also hoisting their 'L-2011' banners aloft, didn't back down.

Now they're losing their eyes over there to plastic bullets, but they won't give up the fight. Half the riot police over there have switched sides so far. And joined the environmentalists.

Did you hear that officers?

Your Turkish counterparts are waking up. And I say this - you are most welcome to join us brothers and sisters. You are most welcome to join the Good and Honest Citizens.

But now the most important part lies ahead.

CHAPTER 59

The Good and Honest Citizens – those in Piccadilly Circus and thousands more stretching back along Shaftesbury Avenue – stood in complete silence. Their mouths hung open; they leaned forward and devoured every word coming out of his mouth.

Even Hatchet had clambered to his feet and turned towards Chester George.

Everyone was looking up at their leader, including Mack. They were all waiting for the same thing.

Phase Three.

CHAPTER 60

You've come here today because you have a question to ask. Where do we go from here? How do we make sure that real change is going to come?

Do you want to keep letting these rich motherfuckers elect imbeciles who don't give a shit about you?

If we back down now, they'll crush us. They'll make us pay for the rest of our lives. Look at the power we've taken back already. Look how easy it is, when you're prepared to die for it.

Shall we talk about what happens next?

Are you ready for Phase Three?

CHAPTER 61

The crowd exploded into a flurry of deafening cheers. Chester George stood tall on the soapbox and saluted the crowd from up high.

Mack was cheering loudly with the rest of them, completely caught up in the moment and ready to commit to whatever brave new world awaited them.

Instinctively, his eyes wandered over to the base of the fountain.

Hatchet was no longer smiling.

He was reaching for something tucked in at the waist of his jeans.

CHAPTER 62

1st September 2011

Mack saw it. He wanted to yell – to scream – to do something, anything, but his legs were rooted to the spot, not to mention the fact that he was jammed in alongside thousands of other people.

Nobody was paying any attention to Hatchet as he pulled the cap lower down over his face. Then, with his gun outstretched, and with the speed of a panther, he sprinted up the steps of the fountain.

The black pistol pointed at the head of Chester George.

There was no time to scream. No time for warnings. There was only a high-pitched crack, a whistle, something hard and fast. Out of nowhere.

Chester George probably never saw the boy who shot half his face off. He probably never heard the sound of the bullet speeding towards him. Or the first scream either.

The leader of the Good and Honest Citizens fell backwards, collapsing onto the steps of the bronze fountain. Michael King and those surrounding him, rushed towards the fallen man, their arms outstretched even though it was far too late to catch him.

Mack watched from the front row as a small army of security guys stormed the fountain, like a gang of enraged bulls, searching for the gunman who'd got the better of them and killed their leader. He saw nothing of Hatchet, Chester George, or Michael King in the chaos. There were too many people on the fountain now, rushing back and forth, crying and screaming, and not knowing what to do.

The screams came thick and fast. The high-pitched screams of frightened children, of mothers and fathers now separated from those children.

In the crowd, people were desperately attempting to flee the scene, unsure of whether they were at risk of receiving a bullet to the face themselves. What followed was a terrifying human stampede, and the sound of bodies colliding and heads cracking into one another at a sickening rate.

Men, women, and children – everyone was screaming now. Drowning in fear.

Mack felt the earth tremble underneath his feet. Trying desperately to control his own panic, he kept still, rather than running straight into the carnage unfolding behind him.

Behind him, a child was screaming. He turned around to see a young girl, standing about ten feet away from him, her face painted orange, white and black in a striking tiger design. She was staring at him, tears pouring down her painted face. Mack reached out to her, but at this, she turned around and ran into the madness of the crowd.

Mack was looking straight into the carnage now. And what he saw chilled his blood.

Thousands of people were charging *towards* the mass of confused Good and Honest Citizens who were still scrambling for their lives in the middle of Piccadilly Circus.

This fresh onslaught of bodies was coming from the west. The London Liberation Army had broken their chains and burst through the police and army barriers. Now they were launching themselves into the madness in their hundreds of thousands.

Thunderous roars, full of bloodlust and murderous intent spread out across Piccadilly Circus.

Mack looked for a way out – a way out that wouldn't take him through the centre of Piccadilly Circus.

He turned around, and that's when he saw Hatchet.

Like a ghost, Hatchet had slipped through the throng of angry bodies on the fountain steps. The baseball cap was gone.

Instinctively, Mack rushed towards him. In that moment, he forgot all about leaving Piccadilly Circus. There was a savage desire in his heart, telling him to cause unspeakable hurt to Hatchet.

Kill him.

He ran towards the fountain, dodging those around him, most of who were now running to join the counter-charge against the London Liberation Army.

Mack heard an ungodly roar behind him, but he didn't stop to look back.

Hatchet stood perfectly still at the base of the steps. He took a look around, surveying his handiwork, and a satisfied smile broke out on his face.

Hatchet saw Mack coming towards him. As Mack approached, Hatchet pointed at the carnage in Piccadilly Circus, like an artist presenting his masterpiece to the world.

"What did I tell you?" Hatchet yelled, his voice perfectly at ease amongst the racket. "*CHAOS*," he said. "I did that."

Mack took a step towards him, and now they were almost face to face. The monstrous din continued all around them – gunshots, helicopters, and screaming – always the screaming.

"Why?" Mack said.

Hatchet shook his head. "That's the future right there," he said. "*My* kind of future. There's no coming back from this, eh?"

"You evil twisted fuck!" Mack yelled. "Children are dying out there. Screaming! Sumo Dave and Tegz are out there too, dead for all we know. You don't give a fuck, do you?"

Hatchet reached into the fold at his waist. Slowly, he pulled out the black pistol and pointed it at Mack.

"Just one more thing," he said.

Mack's eyes darted back and forth, looking for a way out. But his legs were paralysed with fear and couldn't or wouldn't move.

Hatchet took a step towards him. He was still grinning.

Why is he grinning?

"I'm going to enjoy this," Hatchet said.

In that moment, Mack's thoughts drifted away from Piccadilly Circus – dreamlike, like particles of smoke rising above a burning building. This was it. He was about to die and yet somehow, he was calm. How could that be? He was only sixteen and yet he felt ready to let go, to surrender to his fate. Maybe it was time to turn down the noise, to go somewhere quiet. Into nothingness. To go to a place where he'd never have to think about Jon Rossi or Edinburgh again. Where he wouldn't have to feel the hot and sticky sensation of warm blood on his hands every night. Where innocent people weren't beaten and dragged down alleys by rioters in a murderous rage.

The last conversation he'd had with his mother popped into his head.

"God Mack, you really know how to pick them don't you?"

Yes Mum. Yes I do.

Hatchet took a final step forward. Now they *were* face to face, and Hatchet was standing at point blank range, with the gun still on Mack.

It was then that, out of the corner of his eye, Mack saw the blur of someone familiar running towards them. It was Michael King. His clothes were covered in dark blood, and he was hurling himself down the fountain steps, charging like a champion sprinter. He was yelling something. But Mack couldn't hear what he was saying over the noise.

But it was too late to be rescued.

And so there it was. There was only one thing left for Mack Walker to do in that moment - the one power left to him that was guaranteed to wipe the smug grin off Hatchet's face.

He stood tall, staring down the barrel of the gun with a defiant expression. Then slowly, he raised his middle finger.

"Fuck you *Harold*," he said.

Hatchet's loathsome grin faded. And then he pulled the trigger.

THE END

MR APOCALYPSE
(BOOK 2)

For Sandra and Walter
(aka Mum and Dad)

THE FUTURE OF LONDON

'The Future of London'

February 1st 2020

A man and woman are standing next to one another in a blacked out room. They look directly at the camera while two spotlights shine ominously from above, drenching their sober expressions in a shower of vivid white. The light spills onto their upper bodies, cutting out at the waist and giving the viewer the eerie impression of two other-worldly beings half-bathed in light, half in darkness.

Aileen Ure, the third female Prime Minister of the United Kingdom, is standing on the left. The tall, elderly man standing next to her is Rudyard Campbell, an American and the world's most powerful media tycoon. Amongst many other global companies, Campbell holds significant stakes in the SKAM and FIXX Television networks, as well as the majority of the world's digital newspapers. Both are conservatively dressed – Ure, who bears an uncanny resemblance to one of her predecessors, Margaret Thatcher – is wearing a blue fitted dress, while Campbell is sporting a bespoke navy suit.

RUDYARD CAMPBELL: Good morning and welcome to you all on this very special day.

AILEEN URE: Good morning everyone.

RUDYARD CAMPBELL: We're talking to you live from our studios here in Birmingham, capital city of the United Kingdom. It is a momentous occasion for us here in the SKAM family and we've been waiting a long time for this historic launch to happen. What you're about to witness – what the world is about to witness is not only unprecedented in the history of *our* television network, but in the history of television itself.

AILEEN URE: We're here today to launch The Future of London. As you undoubtedly know, TFL – as it's better known, is SKAM's new and exclusive twenty-four hour television channel that will take you inside the old city from the comfort of your living room. It's an incredible achievement on SKAM's part, but before we launch TFL, Rudyard and I want to address the concerns we've heard about this new television channel.

RUDYARD CAMPBELL: (*Showing his hands, palms out in an appeasement gesture*) We're well aware of the controversy that has surrounded this new channel ever since the planning stages were announced almost eight years ago. We've listened to your concerns and now here we are.

AILEEN URE: (*Nodding sincerely*) What happened in London in 2011 was shocking.

RUDYARD CAMPBELL: Terrible.

AILEEN URE: In the immediate aftermath of the tragedy that unfolded at Piccadilly Circus, important decisions had to be made. As the violence got worse, there was real concern that it would spread beyond the capital, creating a situation too terrible to comprehend. That's why the decision was made to temporarily seal London off from the rest of the country. It wasn't an easy decision to make and as we all recall, it was a tough one to put into practice. Hundreds of thousands of volunteers assisted the military in erecting the initial barriers around the city. Those barriers eventually became the two orbital walls that now encircle Greater London. We called them the

M25 because like the old motorway, they surround the city – and they've kept us safe ever since.

RUDYARD CAMPBELL: Of course, nobody was happy about cutting London off from the rest of the UK. Innocent people were trapped behind those initial barriers. But the truth is that sacrifices had to be made in order to preserve the safety of the rest of the UK.

AILEEN URE: And of course, we understand the suffering. Many people, perhaps *your* loved ones were still in London at the time it was sealed off. In the initial aftermath of Chester George's death, we lost our Prime Minister, the vast majority of our MPs and the Houses of Parliament were destroyed. A new government had to be built almost from scratch here in Birmingham. But it had to be done. We simply couldn't risk the violence spilling out beyond London and into other parts of the country. And I know that most of the British people out there understood the difficult decision that was made at the time.

Rudyard nods.

RUDYARD CAMPBELL: I'm guessing there's one question you get asked a lot about London Aileen – am I right?

AILEEN URE: Yes Rudyard, there sure is. People always ask me why don't we go back into London. It's been nine years, they'll say. Why don't we just pull our resources together, send in the army and reclaim what's left of the city. Save whoever's left.

RUDYARD CAMPBELL: Sounds like a plan.

AILEEN URE: Yes but unfortunately it's not that easy. London has become an extremely dangerous territory over the last nine years. It's not the London we know anymore, that's for sure. It's become a very violent, lawless place with organised gangs running amok and there's no sense of order whatsoever. There are rumours of cannibalism within the city, although these are unconfirmed.

Campbell shakes his head in disgust.

AILEEN URE: There are good people trapped in London. We know that. That's why over the last nine years, we've maintained our food and supply drops over the city. That's why we continue to send crack teams in for periodical maintenance duties, so we can supply the area with electricity, hot water and other everyday essentials. We are trying to keep the people in there as comfortable as possible until full order is resumed.

RUDYARD CAMPBELL: But don't despair. If your loved ones were – *are* – trapped behind the M25, they might still be alive. And that's where TFL can help.

AILEEN URE: TFL can help you find your loved ones. And whenever possible, when a legitimate individual who is not a threat is located, we will do everything we can to bring them home. Recovery is not impossible, but of course, you'll have to be watching to spot friends and family, won't you?

She smiles at Campbell.

RUDYARD CAMPBELL: Now there have been a few complaints about the one hundred-pounds monthly subscription fee. This is understandable.

AILEEN URE: Unfortunately, all things considering, it's necessary for SKAM to charge a high price for TFL subscription.

RUDYARD CAMPBELL: Thank you Aileen. Here at SKAM, we want to offer you an insight into London – as it is today in 2020. Covering the entire city has been a monumental task. As you can imagine, this is an extremely high-tech production and the SKAM teams, along with government-sponsored supervision, have installed the very best in miniature surveillance cameras and microphones in literally millions of locations across the old city, from north to south, east to west.

Aileen nods in agreement.

RUDYARD CAMPBELL: This, along with our fleet of SKAM Heli-Cams in the sky will give you the viewer, complete access to what's going on behind the M25, all day every day. And trust me – I've seen the early footage – it's like nothing you've ever seen before. But as you can imagine, the cost of keeping all these surveillance operations is substantial. That's why we've had to introduce the monthly subscription fee.

As Campbell speaks, subscription details appear at the bottom of the page under the heading – 'WAYS TO PAY'. These include a telephone number, website details and information about which coloured buttons to press on the remote control that will allow the viewer to add 'TFL' to their monthly SKAM TV bill.

RUDYARD CAMPBELL: Now, with all that said – what do you think Aileen? Are we ready to launch TFL?

AILEEN URE: (*Grinning*) I can't wait Rudyard.

Ure giggles. Campbell turns back to the camera.

RUDYARD CAMPBELL: Are you ready to go back to London? It's been nine years since our last glimpse of this once great city. Maybe your friends and family are still in there. But how can you be sure? Subscribe to TFL today. Do it for them.

The screen fades to black.

When it lights up again, we're looking through the lens of a SKAM Heli-Cam. The helicopter is gliding at a leisurely pace, moving over a large area of dark green fields – a pleasant stretch of land ornamented by hedges and trees, something that appears unmoving and eternal, like a landscape painting.

Something else comes into view.

The camera zooms in on a section of two gigantic walls of reinforced concrete. This is the infamous M25 – often called the 'Superwalls'. Standing close to the abandoned motorway from which it derived its name, the inner wall is just over twenty feet tall. The outer wall, built a few hundred feet behind its inner counterpart, is fifty feet high.

The Heli-Cam descends closer to the two walls.

Armoured vehicles and soldiers are stationed at regular intervals beside both the inner and outer wall. There are also elevated structures located along the top of the two walls. These observation platforms look out towards Central London, located about twenty miles away, and are scattered throughout the wall's circumference, and are manned twenty-four hours a day.

The Heli-Cam ascends once more and glides beyond the M25. A few moments later, something else is visible – a dark blur at first, no more than a shadow sitting on the vast horizon. The helicopter flies closer and something slowly emerges out of this great nothingness – a skyline. Familiar shapes and patterns appear – once towering buildings, now just empty shells. On the silent streets below, a vast network of roads is empty except for the occasional glimpse of a burned out car or some other vehicle.

The camera ascends swiftly, twisting and turning in a north-westerly direction. The River Thames comes into view up ahead, its familiar muddy brown complexion unchanged over the years. The same can't be said about the Houses of Parliament. The Heli-Cam swoops down upon the steeply pitched iron roofs of the old building, which is now a ghastly, decaying black colour. Its shape and structure – the skyline and Gothic scheme – are familiar, but the exterior has been badly damaged by fire and left to ruin.

The helicopter retreats and as it does, it takes in the shape of Tower Bridge in the distance. The two large towers at either end of the bridge, linked by two walkways, are a brief reminder of the glory days of the city's past when it was one of the most revered and visited places in the world.

A narrator speaks – a deep male voice, calm and reassuring:

NARRATOR: Come with us. Travel back to the great city of London. Subscribe to SKAM TV's newest channel – 'The Future of London' – for twenty-four hours a day, seven days a week access to the streets of the forgotten city. Our high-tech cameras will work day and night to catch a glimpse of your loved ones. Come with us. We're going to bring them back to you.

CHAPTER 1

Six months later.

He woke with a start. She was still screaming, the child, somewhere in the back of his head. How quickly those terrible screams had morphed from the cries of a little girl into that of a man – his cries. Then everything would fade and memories would drop like lead balloons into the bottomless pit of his mind. And there they would remain, at least until the next time he dared to close his eyes.

This particular nightmare was a regular bedtime companion. He'd be running through the streets of the city, searching for a way to get home and trying not to partake in the madness that was floating in the air. All around him, people attacked one another and even the children were getting in on the violence, as if they were possessed by some foul demon. He could smell fear and hate in every molecule. He could taste it in the breath of the city. It was the great sickness – the urge to hurt and kill your brother and sister for no discernible reason.

And oh God, the screaming.

In the dream he always ran harder. But his feet barely touched the ground and despite the effort he invested in his getaway, there was no feeling of fatigue in his lungs and no sensation of weakness spreading throughout his limbs. The only thing he felt was a sense of impending terror – it was in his flesh, blood, bones and spirit. Everything was fear.

The buildings of London were on fire all around him. Some of them exploded at the moment he ran past them. Out of the corner of his eye he would see them go up in a giant ball of flames and then freeze in mid-explosion, as if everything that was happening was no more than a climactic scene in a high-budget action movie and somebody watching in another realm had pressed the pause button.

Then he saw her.

The little girl with the tiger paint on her face. She was screaming and crying and calling out for her mummy and daddy to come and help her. Somehow he could hear her voice crystal clear over the earth-shattering sound of the exploding buildings beside him. And then the flames took her – not flames from the explosions, but a fire that sprang up in the middle of her body, as if she was one of the buildings and there were thousands of gremlins with matches and gasoline plotting to ruin her from within. Quickly the flames spread upon the girl, moving up and down, covering her arms, legs and her face until she was smothered in the scalding grip.

As she burned, he could see the tiger paint on her face. Its pattern remained intact throughout the ordeal, a reminder that the day had started so differently, so full of hope.

She kept screaming, even when she no longer had a mouth to scream out of. Although he tried to get away, he felt himself being pulled closer to the flames until the heat snapped at his face like a set of sharp teeth. The fire grew, wrapping around him like an Anaconda. Every time he tried to exhale, the flames would squeeze tighter, crushing his lungs and internal organs and preventing him from getting his breath back.

It was over.

Finally he screamed. Despite the fact that he was being strangled, he was still able to scream. And that's when he'd wake up. He'd find himself sitting up straight in bed, looking around the familiar sights of his bedroom. There was no exploding city, no madness or bloodlust, and no girl on fire.

He was alone.

A gentle thudding noise made him look down. Droplets of sweat trickled from his upper torso in a neat, unbroken rhythm and landed on the old bed sheets that he lay on top of.

It always took him a few moments to adjust to the aftermath of waking up. It was so real every time. Waking up didn't necessarily douse the great fire that had existed just moments earlier.

With a sigh he fell back onto the bed. He felt his body floating on top of the warm, sweat-soaked sheets. It was always the same in summer – the nights were so hot that he slept on top of the covers, his legs poking out of the fabric and grasping for something cool to soothe his skin. But there was little he could do about it. He certainly wasn't going to leave a window open overnight.

It was morning. He knew that much. Looking to his right, he saw a few specks of daylight creeping through the tightly pulled curtains.

Then he remembered. It was Drop Day. Time to get up.

Reluctantly he pushed himself off the damp bed. He walked across the worn carpet towards the hallway with the hot air pinching at his naked skin. It was a different story in winter when the house would be so cold that he'd practically be living underneath the bedcovers, fighting off the freezing air and getting up only for necessities.

He walked down the hallway towards the bathroom, grimacing at the pungent body odour that was following him. At least he could have a bath. At least there was water and it was clean. It was just a shame the house ran on gas heating or it could have been a hot bath now and then. That would be nice. But all gas supplies to the city – at least to his part of the city – had been cut off for a long time. London was electric only and in a house with gas heating that meant cold baths. Still that wasn't a problem in summer. And more importantly, it meant whoever was pulling the strings out there hadn't forgotten about them. Otherwise why would they keep sending maintenance units into the city to treat the water? Or to ensure a constant supply of electricity, not to mention the food drops? Somebody out there still gave a damn. It was these simple reminders that allowed at least a little hope to remain.

He leaned over the bathtub and turned on the cold-water tap. When the water came it was always a relief to see the clear liquid pouring out – this was the new gold, the Holy Grail as it had always been before people had taken it for granted. It was the giver of life. Sometimes it staggered a little before flowing out of the tap, but so far he'd been lucky. He didn't want to think about what he'd have to do if he ran into any problems with the water supply in the house. He'd have to leave home and venture into the city, seeking refuge in the arms of God knows what.

That's why he was frugal with the water, only filling the tub about a quarter full.

Before climbing into the cold bath, he glanced at the bathroom mirror. In his dreams, he was still a sixteen-year-old boy but it was an older face that looked back at him now. He wasn't sure exactly what age he was – somewhere in his early to mid-twenties probably. It was certainly a long time since he'd been sixteen. His blue eyes had paled in the years since then, but his white skin was at least bright and healthy. The rest of him looked a little dirty and haggard – the tawny hair had been shaved down to the bone due to the heat. He kept it down with his dad's old electric razor but he was a little lazier with the hair on his face, which permanently sported the rough stubble look.

He turned away from the mirror. Without stopping to think, he leapt into the bathtub and shrieked as the cold liquid wrapped itself around his body, which was partly submerged in the water. With his arms trembling, he grabbed the bar of soap and went to work.

Walking into the kitchen, he stood in front of the white stainless steel fridge-freezer. He took a deep breath and pulled the door open. When the light didn't come on, he felt his heart sink and quickly slammed the door shut. It was the same thing as with the water taps in the house – he'd breathed a sigh of relief every time he'd opened the fridge door and saw that light go on. But now it wasn't working anymore. It had been like that for a couple of days now and he'd tampered with the fuse, kicked the fridge, shook it back and forth, and left it alone. All the time hoping that it would come back on by luck or sheer miracle.

The fridge was dead, and that was that.

There was no way he could get by without a fridge. If he was going to make his supplies last a week in between Drop Days then he had to have some kind of refrigeration unit. He was no handyman and there was little chance of him stitching something together like some sort of post-apocalyptic MacGyver.

That left only one option available.

He'd have to find one. And that meant searching through the other houses in Stanmore Road. If he was lucky, then somebody might have had the presence of mind to turn their electricity off back in the day before evacuating. If so, then there was a reasonable chance of finding a working fridge on the street.

That was today's priority sorted then. As soon as he got back from picking up his supplies at the New River, he'd start working his way through the houses.

Fridge hunting.

In some ways he was fortunate that it was hot. The heat reduced his appetite and there was practically nothing left from the last Drop Day. He'd eaten the fruit quickly so as not to waste it. Even then some of it was still rotten but it had never been the greatest to begin with. All the ready meals were gone too, as was the bread, cheese and meat slices.

He'd eat properly later. There were some biscuits left – two shortbread fingers. He grabbed those out of the packet and walked from the kitchen, into the hallway and towards the front door. As he pulled the door open, sunlight spilled into the house and he felt the warmth touching his skin like it was a personal greeting. He walked down the short garden path, past the overgrown grass sprouting up on both sides, and towards the street. There he stood on the pavement, looking up and down the length of Stanmore Road. Looking at all the houses, it was hard to believe that he was the only person left on the street. But he'd been here since 2011 and he hadn't seen anyone else in the neighbourhood for a long time. Everyone had fled north out of London as soon as they'd heard the rumours about a barrier going up. He should have gone with them but he couldn't. Not when he didn't know where his parents were.

Such a quiet street. Sometimes he heard footsteps at night. Sometimes he heard voices – he was sure of it. It was rare but when he did, he'd be hiding in the bedroom with his fingers wrapped around the handle of a kitchen knife, waiting for sound of someone trying the front door handle. But they never did try.

As he stood on the pavement, something soft brushed up against the back of his legs. He looked down to see a little white cat rubbing its body vigorously against his calves.

"Morning Alba," he said.

He knelt down and ran a hand along her back, which vibrated like a vintage motor as she purred. As he stroked the cat, he looked at her soft coat and marvelled at its lusciousness. It was a perfect thing, like freshly fallen snow.

He'd called her Alba – it was the Gaelic world for his homeland, which had never felt so far from London as it did now. She was his family.

He'd noticed her hanging around the neighbourhood a long time ago – maybe as long as three years. One day, he'd been sitting in the front garden when she'd first appeared at the gate. It was as if she'd just materialised on the spot. She'd stood there for some time on the edge of the garden path, her bright blue eyes looking warily at him. She was barely more than a kitten at that point, her eyes a vivid and electric blue. He guessed that she was a survivor of a local litter who had since turned into an adept hunter of small creatures. And she was indeed a skilled killer. As time passed, he'd lost count of the number of dead birds and mice that she'd dumped on the front doorstep. Unlike him at least, she clearly wasn't wanting for food.

Time passed and she'd gotten braver around him. Gradually she crept further into the garden and it wasn't long before she jumped onto his lap and curled into a ball for the first time. For his part, he was delighted with the company. He got so used to having her around that eventually he would leave the back window open during the day so she could come and go as she pleased. At night, she'd often stay with him and sleep on the end of the bed. If she was late or didn't show up some nights, he'd always worry.

That morning, the little cat smooched up to him like she always did at the start of the day.

"No presents for me?" he said, scratching the back of her ears. "Nothing dead you want to boast about?" He did a brief inspection of her coat as she rubbed violently up against him. With deft precision, he pulled out a few specks of dirt that were tucked deep down in her fur and close to the skin. Other than that, the little cat was in immaculate condition, clearly thriving in this post-apocalyptic suburbia.

Whirr-Click.

He stood up straight. His eyes darted left and right. Up and down. There it was again – that noise. He'd been hearing it for months now.

He looked up at the slender black streetlights that towered above him. It was only recently that the lights had been working again after a short period of blackout. Did that have something to do with the noise he was hearing? What the hell was that noise?

It was the faintest of sounds. Perhaps it was just his imagination making up for the sheer boredom and emptiness of his life. Inventing drama for the sake of entertainment. It was possible.

Whirr-Click.

Quickly he turned back to the gate. Alba rushed ahead of him, trotting up the garden path and squeezing her way past the gap in the front door that led inside the house.

With a final look up at the streetlights, he followed her inside.

CHAPTER 2

The walk to the New River always filled him with dread.

He made his way along Stanmore Road, his hands gripped tightly around the steel handles of the wheelbarrow. It was a miracle the old thing was still in one piece. The blue paint on the tray had mostly flaked off and the tire wasn't far from being completely flat. It was long overdue for the scrapheap or at least a major reworking that might give it a second chance at life. It was worth a shot. He'd been spending too much of his spare time staring into space and thinking about the past and his parents. Maybe it was time to do something practical. To be constructive.

He travelled west. The morning air had cooled slightly and he'd decided to wear his dad's old leather jacket over his usual black t-shirt and jeans. As he walked, he could hear the helicopters in the distance. They were moving towards Central London, which meant that most of the drops in the north had already been made. The supply parcel would be there waiting for him at the river – sitting on the edge of the walkway like it always was. Maybe he'd get lucky and find two of them today.

He cut through the overgrown jungle that was once Ducketts

Common. It had once been a well-manicured public space where people had picnicked and organised community fun days – now it was wild and vaguely threatening in its unkempt appearance. The pathway that cut through the common was barely visible anymore. It would probably have been buried underneath the grass altogether if not for his once-weekly visits to flatten it out.

Just as he was leaving the Common, his eye caught sight of something lying a few feet from the concrete, half-buried by a mound of drooping grass.

It was an envelope.

He put the wheelbarrow down and stared at the white paper. It was peering out at him in between the long blades of green grass. He took a look around. Standing still made him more than a little nervous. But curiosity got the better of him like it always did. He walked over to the envelope and picked it up. It felt slightly damp and was tattered at the edges. Although it had looked white from a distance, time had dulled the exterior to a warm shade of yellowy brown.

Tucking the envelope into his back pocket, he looked around again. All clear. He picked up the handles of the wheelbarrow and continued towards the New River.

He walked down Hampden Road. It had been a long time since he'd bothered with the local sights and when he passed the old Methodist church on his right hand side, he barely glanced in its direction. Still, on more than occasion he'd felt compelled to go into that place, sit down and see what happened. Not necessarily to ask for a miracle, but *ask* for something. But he never did go in. It was a large building and there was always the possibility that someone or something was lurking in there.

He didn't linger around the houses on Hampden Road either. They were still and silent. There was something menacing about them. The gardens were overgrown wastelands with bloated hedges and wheelie bins that were drowning in grass and yet still neatly stacked in driveways. There were no cars on the street. Not surprising, most people had driven out of London back in 2011. It was the surest way of getting out in time and if you didn't have a car, he imagined that people had begged for lifts off neighbours and strangers, filling the vehicles up until they were literally stuffed with bodies.

Whirr-Click.

He walked faster, making his way to the end of Hampden Road and then towards the grassy descent that led to the New River. Parking his wheelbarrow at the edge of the road, he climbed over a short metal fence and walked down towards the water.

The New River wasn't exactly a river. It wasn't new either. He remembered back in 2011 when he'd first moved to London, the disappointment he'd felt upon seeing it for the first time. If it was a river, then it was the skinniest fucking river in the world. It had an interesting enough history – it had been completed in 1613, and it functioned as a water supply aqueduct that brought clean drinking water from Hertfordshire into North London. It was a narrow waterway, barely the width of a small canal, and with a stone footpath running alongside which made for a pleasant walk.

It was upon this stone footpath that he now walked along, his eyes searching for a glimpse of the parcel. In the early years the supply crews had dropped several parcels on this footpath alone and in the neighbourhood as a whole. These were intended for the local residents but the number of people in the area had dropped significantly and many parcels were left untouched. Now there were only one or two parcels at most. That was why it was so important that he showed up at the river every week and why he meticulously counted seven days from each drop to the next – if he were to miss one Drop Day and if the parcel was left untouched then the helicopters would probably stop coming altogether.

He walked along the path. Every thirty seconds or so he'd look back towards the fence, keeping an eye on his parked wheelbarrow. That there was no one around to steal it didn't matter. The need to protect his property was an urge that he couldn't shake off, a deep-rooted instinct that belonged to another time.

After a short walk, he found the parcel. It was sitting on the side of the path furthest from the river, close to a fence that blocked off the back of a residential area. Supplies were always dropped in the same large white sacks, which were about the size of a king-size pillow. They looked similar to the type of packaging that he recalled seeing on old news broadcasts in which aid was delivered to Third World countries during the height of a famine.

Squatting down, he picked up the bag and hoisted it over his head. The package pressed against his shoulders and neck. He took a deep breath and secured his footing on the path. Packages were heavy – they were literally stuffed with the likes of fresh fruit, bread, meat, as well as toiletry items including toothpaste and toilet paper. All bundled into one sack and designed to last precisely a week until the next drop. Of course it never did last that long. He never understood why the parcels were always bulked out with large ice pads and absorbent pads, not to mention a shitload of scrunched up paper that was supposed to protect it from damage. But there was a *lot* of paper. They could easily have done away with some of the internal packaging and put some more food in there.

He looked around for a glimpse of a second parcel. Not that he was feeling lucky but it was worth taking a moment to look. If it were anywhere it would have been dropped further down the path. It would be nice to have it if it *was* there, to have a little more food in the house for the coming week.

Still holding the parcel over his head, he hurried back down the footpath towards the fence. Once there, he forced the sack through a large gap in between the metal bars and it dropped into the perfectly positioned wheelbarrow with a thud. Then he turned around hurried back down towards the footpath.

Five minutes. But don't go too far, okay?

Okay.

By now the sun had come back out and the leather jacket on his back was getting heavier. His eyes glanced longingly at the river. What would it be like to take a dip in there? To soak his skin – would the water feel as good as it looked right now basking under the sunlight? Was this the warm bath that he'd been waiting for?

He stopped walking.

A noise. Behind him. Close – how had he missed its approach?

He spun around and his blood ran cold.

It was a man or something like a man. Staggering towards him. It was wildly bearded with hungry eyes that looked through him. It wore the tattered remnants of what appeared to be a navy suit, its colour and style long gone, the fabric bedraggled and in ruin. Half a tie swung from the collar as if someone had taken a pair of scissors and cut right through it. The red skin on the savage face was a mess – riddled with painful looking sores. Its nose was badly burned at the tip – either the result of excessive sun damage or it had been disfigured by fire. Its lips were dry, with chunks of dead skin attached. In one hand it brandished a filthy looking butchers knife and as it approached, the savage stabbed repeatedly at thin air, *back and forth*, like some sort of pre-murder ritual.

Seconds later, it lunged forwards.

He only just managed to get out of the way of its attack. He moved his feet backwards and manoeuvred his body out of range of the blade. Somewhere in the back of his mind he heard a voice repeating over and over:

'*Distance. Range. Distance. Range.*'

The savage swung the blade with little skill, but what it lacked in finesse it made up for in ferocity. It aimed at his midsection. With every reckless thrust, came a primordial grunt that sounded something other than human. He was forced to retreat backwards and at such speed that he tripped and fell onto the grass behind him. At that moment, he was vulnerable. The world was upside down. He fought furiously to regain his coordination, all the while preparing himself for the sensation of a steel blade piercing his skin.

Fortunately the savage had already slowed under the heat. Its ferocious assault was now somewhat laboured and it failed to take advantage of this opportunity to finish the fallen man. It came after him but slower, like a raggedy man plodding through quicksand. It had lost his explosiveness and its breathing was heavy. Still, it wielded the butcher's knife with the same murderous intent. That look of ravenous hunger in its eyes had not tired.

The savage squatted slightly, as if it was about to leap on top of him. But as it came forward, he launched a vicious upkick from the ground that caught the beast smack on its nose. Upon impact, the butcher's knife flew out of its hand and the savage yelped and stumbled back towards the river's edge. It put its sunburned hands over the damaged nose, which was leaking blood at a furious rate.

Quickly he rolled over to his right in order to grab the knife. But the savage was back before he could get there. The thing that was no longer human mounted him and threw down a volley of deranged punches at his face. As it did so, blood dripped from its nose and landed on his face like warm raindrops. It leaned forward, baring its rotten, yellowy teeth and snapping at his face like a vicious dog. Its breath smelt of death.

From the ground, he wrapped one hand around the savage's throat. Then he pushed its head back with everything he had, forcing those foul teeth away from his face. It wasn't hard to budge the neck – it felt as if the muscles inside the thing had wasted away, which meant it was running on little else but rage and hunger.

With the other hand, he reached frantically for the butcher's knife lying at his side.

As he did so, the savage squealed with excitement.

After several attempts, he found the handle of the butcher's knife. Without hesitation he brought it up and thrust it in a sideways motion, aiming directly at the savage's brain. He missed the target and instead of going through its head, the blade slashed across its face, carving open a long and deep tear that ran down from the eyes to chin.

The savage screamed. It was a hideous sound. Then it fell backwards, its hand trying to stem the rapid flow of blood that was gushing out of its face.

He hurried to his feet, sensing that this was his chance to finish the job. But to his surprise, the savage wasn't done yet. It charged at him once again despite the fact that its face was barely hanging on at the side.

It came forward at a manic speed. Fast and yet clumsy, like a throwback down the evolutionary ladder. It screamed, like a squealing pig hurtling towards its own doom.

He thrust the knife forwards. The blade found its home in the upper torso, entering deep into the stomach. There was no doubt now – it was over.

He took his blood-soaked hands off the blade and stepped away, his heart pounding, his lungs grasping for breath in the hot air.

The savage looked down at the butcher's knife that was stuck in its chest. At the same time its face was still leaking litres of blood. With surprising gentleness, it tugged on the handle of the knife. Then realising it wasn't going to come out, it let go again. It staggered backwards. The wild look in its eyes became something else. Serene. The fury faded to blackness. It seemed to accept what had happened and perhaps in its final moments, it remembered what it had once been.

It took another step back. This time it tumbled over the edge and fell backwards into the river. There was a loud splash and then silence.

He walked over to the edge and looked down. The body was floating in the shallow water. He stayed there for about a minute, trying to convince himself that the thing down there was indeed dead. That it wouldn't come after him.

Then he took off, running towards the wheelbarrow.

He lay under the bed sheets for hours. His body shook violently as he saw the rotten teeth snapping at his face over and over again.

He could still smell its breath in the bedroom.

He'd already been sick six times and it showed no sign of stopping, despite the fact that there was nothing left in his body to throw up. All his strength was gone. Still he went back and forth between the bedroom and the bathroom, dry retching with all his might in an attempt to feel better, to vomit the experience and memory of what had happened.

After the seventh trip to the bathroom, he collapsed on the floor. His chest felt sore and dry. All he wanted to do was to get back to bed and stay there until he felt something other than what he was feeling. He crawled out of the bathroom on all fours into the hallway, steadily making his way to the bedroom.

Then he saw it.

It was curled up, tucked in between the hallway floor and the gap under the door – the door to the room that had been his parents' bedroom. It was a hair – a simple hair, but it wasn't his. This one was far too long to have ever belonged on his head.

His mother's hair.

Gently, he reached out and clamped two fingers around the hair. He brought it towards his face and marvelled at its beauty, like someone with gold fever looking at a pan full of treasure. Such a simple thing. A single strand of tawny hair that shone in the sunlight. It could have fallen from his mother's head that same morning.

He closed his eyes and tried to remember her face. The little things. How she had looked when she smiled and even the peculiar things, like the way her top lip twitched when she was angry with him.

But he couldn't see her anymore.

All he could see were a set of rotten teeth, still snapping hungrily at his face.

CHAPTER 3

TFL: Calling London!

July 5th 2020

Georgia Perkins smiles as the camera zooms in.

The successful stand-up comedienne and television presenter is slickly dressed in a black suit and tie. She's sporting a brand new short spiky blonde haircut – something she treated herself to after beating out a number of other contenders to land the much-coveted role as presenter on TFL: Calling London! at just twenty-three years old.

Georgia is sitting on a large half-circle shaped couch in a hip, brightly coloured television studio, opposite two other people – a man and a woman. A large backdrop of London covers the wall behind the three figures – a map with red blinking lights that appear on and off again at random in certain locations of the city.

The show begins with a clip from today's top story. The studio audience gasps as the footage rolls.

In the clip, a young man is seen wrestling with what appears to be a knife-wielding tramp by the edge of a canal-like waterway. The two men are rolling around on the ground, apparently fighting for their lives. There are multiple camera angles, which capture the skirmish at distance, at close range and from both sides of the river.

GEORGIA PERKINS: (*Voiceover*) On tonight's episode of *Calling London!* Mr Apocalypse is brutally attacked in a savage ambush in North London! The world watches in horror as our favourite loner is almost murdered by an unknown assailant on the bank of the New River.

The camera returns to the studio.

GEORGIA PERKINS: Welcome to *Calling London!* The official TFL show that covers all the daily news from behind the M25. How is everyone this evening?

The audience cheers.

GEORGIA PERKINS: Wonderful! Now let's get going with today's top story and it is of course, the attack on one of our favourites – the mysterious young man we know only as Mr Apocalypse. Joining me this evening to discuss today's stories are our resident TFL expert, Johnny Castle, and the lovely former presenter of CBC News, Sophie Wallace. Okay Johnny – what the hell happened today?

The camera cuts to Sophie Wallace and Johnny Castle sitting on the other side of the couch. Wallace, the former newsreader, is now in her mid-forties and is casually dressed in a loose black sweater and jeans. Johnny Castle is twenty-seven and dressed in skinny jeans and a white V-neck T-shirt. As he turns towards the camera, a heavily tattooed hand fidgets with a pair of thick-rimmed glasses, as well as the immaculately groomed hipster beard that covers the lower part of his face and beyond.

JOHNNY CASTLE: Georgia it's been a *craaaaazy* day in London. As we saw in the clip just there, Mr Apocalypse was almost killed by what appeared to be a deranged cannibal on the banks of the New River this morning. I think we all went through the emotional ringer a little bit today didn't we folks? I mean he's become such a fan-favourite recently, which is surprising considering he doesn't really do anything in that isolated region of North London that used to be Tottenham. But maybe that's why we were so shocked today - we're not used to seeing him in dramatic situations like that.

GEORGIA PERKINS: Sophie, your thoughts?

SOPHIE WALLACE: Oh my God, it was horrifying. You forget how real it is in there sometimes don't you? Just the savagery and suddenness of the attack today – it was awful and yet riveting. When I saw that thing creeping up on him...

GEORGIA PERKINS: You're a fan of Mr Apocalypse?

SOPHIE WALLACE: Oh yes. Well I'm a cat person as you know Georgia. It's the way he looks after that little stray cat, well that just won me over. He's such a mysterious character, isn't he? Why does he stay in that house and in that empty neighbourhood all by himself? It really is like he's the last man in the world.

GEORGIA PERKINS: (*Nodding*) Wouldn't you love to have a camera inside the house right now? I say that because we haven't seen him since he came back from the river this afternoon. What's he doing now? I sure hope he's okay in there.

JOHNNY CASTLE: Georgia sweetie, you can be sure that millions of people up and down the country and all over the world are sitting in front of their TV's, laptops and phones right now, watching that house on Stanmore Road and waiting for him to reappear.

GEORGIA PERKINS: It was a shocking incident. But having said that, it was pretty cool how he handled it wasn't it? I mean, Mr Apocalypse kicked some arse today didn't he?

SOPHIE WALLACE: It was so exciting. It's absolutely tragic that someone had to die of course, but I don't remember ever screaming at the TV like for any other programme. Ten out of ten for entertainment TFL.

GEORGIA PERKINS: (*Turns to camera*) Now! If you're not following Mr Apocalypse on TFL then what's wrong with you? Go now to the TFL home page on the interactive menu of your TV, push the red button on your remote device and choose Mr Apocalypse from the menu. Simple as that – you'll have access to every single camera that's located in the vicinity of Mr Apocalypse's neighbourhood and you won't miss a thing. Unless that is, he goes inside the house – which he does from time to time. Bummer eh? You can also subscribe on the TFL website – just have your customer ID ready and you're all set to go.

SOPHIE WALLACE: I hope he's got the cat with him tonight. That'll be some comfort at least after what he's been through.

GEORGIE PERKINS: (*Laughing*) Alba, isn't it?

SOPHE WALLACE: Yes. It would make sense if that truly is a Scottish accent we're hearing when he talks to her.

Georgia Perkins smiles at the camera.

GEORGIA PERKINS: Ahhhh! It's all questions and more questions when it comes to Mr Apocalypse. But at least he's alive. Now we want to hear your thoughts. What did you think about today's attack at the New River? Visit our official *Calling London!* page on Immersion 9 and join in the Live Chat using the hashtag #mrapocalypse. Johnny, you've been tracking the I-9 chat so far. What's been the response to today's events?

JOHNNY CASTLE: Just scrolling through the comments now Georgia. Alice from Manchester says that she's worried about Mr Apocalypse's state of mind after what happened today. Aren't we all sweetie? Like Sophie, she hopes he's got the cat with him. David from Cardiff is demanding that TFL place cameras inside Mr Apocalypse's house IMMEDIATELY – and that's immediately spelled entirely in caps – because he's paying a hundred quid a month and doesn't want to look at the front of a house all night. Well you *can* choose another option on the home screen David, there's lots more going on in London.

Sophie Wallace laughs.

GEORGIA PERKINS: Well Dave from Cardiff, I guess we'll all just have to be patient. Mr Apocalypse will come out when he's good and ready. And there will be a lot of people waiting to see him again. Anyway, there's lots more to get through tonight – what else has been happening behind the M25 Johnny? More gang violence in the south I believe?

CHAPTER 4

He couldn't sleep.

Whenever he tried to close his eyes, he could hear the slow squelching sound as the curved butcher's knife slid into the savage's body. It was like poking around in the skin of a rotten peach over and over again. Not only that, but he could also feel the hot blood and spit pouring out onto his face from the facial wound.

It had been like that all day. Sleep wouldn't come and now it was dark outside. He was hungry and thirsty too. His body felt severely dehydrated because of the heat and the constant vomiting. He thought about going downstairs to get some refreshments. The supply parcel was still lying on the kitchen floor where he'd left it after the sprint back from the New River. That meant his fresh supplies had been sitting in the heat of the kitchen all day and to top it off he didn't have a working fridge to put the stuff in. He recalled the plan he'd made earlier to go fridge hunting around the neighbourhood houses. The thought made him wince. It would have to wait until tomorrow.

But he was thirsty. His head was aching and he couldn't go without water for much longer.

With a groan, he pushed back the sweat-soaked sheets. Then he went downstairs into the kitchen where he found the sack on the floor. Grabbing a kitchen knife from the rack, he cut into Hessian fabric and opened up a vertical tear.

From inside the sack, he pulled out the crumpled sheets of paper that were supposed to protect the contents. As he did so, he made sure not to touch the large ice packs that were tucked in at the bottom. The food items were separated into different plastic bags. There was a small pack of fresh fruit – apples, bananas and a few other things. Another bag contained a small selection of small pasta and rice meals that could be eaten cold or heated up in a microwave. Fortunately he still had a microwave and it was working, although he used it sparingly. A hot meal was a rare treat, and something he preferred to leave until winter.

All he wanted now was a quick snack and a drink. Something that would make him feel a little less shitty. He reached into a plastic bag and pulled out a fresh packet of the shortbread fingers that he loved. They were the best things about the supply packs – they reminded him of his childhood when his dad had gone to the cash and carry on a Friday night and come back with boxes of stuff – shortbread and other types of biscuits amongst them.

He pulled the sack away from the window and put it in the pantry. It was the best he could do for now and at least it wouldn't catch the sunlight first thing in the morning.

As he walked over to the sink to get a glass of water, he noticed the letter lying on the table. The one he'd found earlier in Ducketts Common. He reached over, picked it up and looked at the faded envelope with tired eyes. Inside was another voice from the past, begging for help. Did he really want to hear it?

He filled a glass of water and drained it in one go. Then he poured another, picked up the biscuits and letter from the table and took them upstairs.

Back in the bedroom, he sat down by the bedroom window. Grabbing a small torch from the bedside drawer, he leaned his back against the wall and slid to a comfortable seating position. His fingers tore open the biscuits and he gobbled down several shortbread fingers one after the other. He wasn't really hungry until he'd tasted the first one. He was also well aware that he was wasting a week's supply in one sitting but after what he'd gone through he didn't care. There had to be some sort of reward for still being alive.

He turned on the small torch. He'd read the letter quickly and save what batteries he had left. Batteries appeared sporadically in the supply parcels and there was no way of knowing when they would appear again.

A single word was barely legible on the front of the envelope. He hadn't noticed it earlier, but there it was, looking back at him under the glare of torchlight.

Help.

The letter had no doubt been floating around the city for years. He'd found many letters like this one that had blown from one part of London to the other – people begging for help mostly. Some of them just wanted to share their story and by writing it down, there was a chance that somebody somewhere would hear them. Maybe. Most of the letters he'd found so far dated back to late 2011 or early 2012 at most. There was still hope back then, he supposed. It was the hope that people were somehow still willing to help one another, to trust in them, believing that they would do the right thing if called upon. In their minds what happened to London was temporary and reversible.

He tore the envelope open and pulled out several sheets of folded, lined paper. The paper was dull white and the handwriting was in the same faded blue ink as that on the front.

With a sigh, he unfolded the letter and began to read.

London 2011. Precise date unknown.

God my hands are shaking but I must write this down.

My name is Jonathan Hearn.

Hunger forced me back onto the streets today. It wasn't choice but necessity that made me go. My boy is literally starving. Between that and the effects of the stab wound on his leg, we're in dire need of supplies.

Robbie was lying beside me when I awoke this morning. He's delirious. He kept asking for his mum (I pray he's forgotten what happened to her). While he did this, I tried to clean the filth from the wound on his leg but it's not good enough. God what I'd give for some antibiotics and proper dressings.

It was obvious what I had to do. I had to go out in order to find food and medicine. Although there was little hope of finding either.

I left Robbie in the ruin of our old apartment building.

I walked towards Tottenham Court Road. God, it was like walking on a different planet. It looked like a bomb had hit us. There can be no doubt that hundreds of thousands of people have died in London since the events at Piccadilly started all this. And it's only been a few weeks I suppose. All those old post-apocalyptic movies did a pretty good job in depicting what the end of the world would look like. Rotten corpses lying on the street. The fallen buildings, the ruins and the ashes – it's all there. And smoke rising – there always seems to be smoke rising in the distance. There's always something else to burn.

The smell is terrible. The rats show no fear as I walk amongst them. Good luck to them, I say.

As I walked, I heard the roar of a large crowd not too far away. People were shouting. Or screaming perhaps? On any other occasion, I would be taking my boy towards them – towards people – in the hope that there was food and medicine. But I trust no one anymore.

We are on our own.

I found the large Tesco still there on Tottenham Court Road. I knew it would have been emptied of food during the London riots but curiosity compelled me to go inside anyway. The automatic doors had been pulled off and I walked through the gap that had been left in their place.

Oh God, the smell. Everything stinks in this place. It smelled like rotten fruit for the most part, but something else too. I had a terrible feeling and so I moved quickly, scouring the naked shelves for a hint of something – anything that was edible. I tried the tinned goods aisle. Nothing. The shelves had been overturned and everything taken.

I passed through the confectionary aisle – more to reminisce over old pleasures than out of genuine hope.

And then I saw her.

She was sitting in the middle of the aisle – a young girl of about eleven or twelve. She had filthy, lank blonde hair that went all the way down her back. She was barely dressed too, except for the ruin of a summer dress that barely clung to her emaciated body.

She was sitting down on the floor with her legs crossed. It was a while before she even noticed me standing there. Well how could she? She was too busy eating her own fingers.

I say fingers, but all that was left were ten gnarled and bloody stumps. She had gone through them all. And there I was, watching as she continued to pull the fleshy tips off those stumps like they were no more than gummy bears.

Eventually she saw me. Good God – my blood ran cold. It was like the monster in a horror film looking back at me through the TV screen. Was I supposed to say something? Old rituals of civilisation had never seemed so inappropriate.

Then she smiled at me. I wanted to scream but couldn't. It was only when she started laughing and pointing at me with the dregs of her bloody fingers that my legs recalled the ability to run. And I ran home through the dead streets of London, not stopping until I was back with my boy. Back, but empty-handed.

Robbie is lying beside me now. I don't ever want to leave my home again. When my son dies, I will have no reason to live.

He folded the sheets of paper and put them back in the faded envelope. Then he walked over to a set of drawers opposite the bed and opened up the bottom one down. Inside were dozens of envelopes of different sizes, shapes and colours. The drawer was bulging under the weight of all these letters – the voices of London past.

He pushed the other envelopes down, flattening them to make room for the last words of Jonathan Hearn. Closing the drawer, he went back to the window and pulled a shortbread finger out of the packet.

Alba walked into the room. She jumped onto the dishevelled bed and immediately started kneading on the sheets.

"Hey," he said. "Have you been in the house all day?" He walked over and ran a hand over her soft white fur, down her back and up the luscious tail. She purred in appreciation.

"You want to go outside?" he asked. "Want me to open a window downstairs for you?"

The little cat's response was to curl up on the bed and close her eyes.

"Staying in?" he said, smiling at her. "I don't blame you."

CHAPTER 5

He walked back down the garden path of yet another house that hadn't delivered. It was the third property he'd tried that morning with no luck – an Edwardian house, its pristine white exterior intact, and the glass in its bay windows remarkably unblemished by the passing of time. This was one of several houses in the same row of terraced housing that his home was adjoined to. He'd even knocked on the door at first – that had made him laugh out loud, as if he expected someone to actually appear and answer him.

But here he was – three houses down and still no fridge. And to top it off, it was another scorching day in the city of London.

It had been the exact same with the first two houses – the ones that were positioned on either side of his home. He'd tried the doors and of course they were locked. Then he'd walked to the end of the block of terraced houses, jumped a brick wall and landed in the back garden of the furthest house down. After that he'd climbed several fences and located his own garden so that he knew exactly where he was. Then he started around the back of the next-door neighbour's house. Start as close as possible, that was the plan. If he was going to be dragging a fridge out of any of these houses on Stanmore Road, he wanted it to be the one nearest to his house.

He'd walked towards that first house, traipsing through a small rectangle of grass and weeds that had grown to at least five feet tall.

He peered through the back window into a deserted living room. He saw a cream coloured sofa and two armchairs, spread across a room covered by a dull white carpet. A circular coffee table sat in close proximity to the sofa, on top of a small psychedelic coloured rug. There was a flat screen TV mounted on the wall and in the corner of the room there was a plastic pot with rotten debris hanging over its edges. Apart from the withered corpse of this rotten plant, the room looked normal. The owners could have been out for the morning, at work or running errands in the city.

He tried the back door and it was locked. There was nothing else for it – he'd have to break the glass. Fortunately he'd noticed a small pile of bricks lying on this side of the wooden fence, half-buried under the towering grass.

Tossing a brick through a window – little had changed since 2011.

He found the brick and threw it at the window. He winced at the high-pitched smashing noise as the glass caved in to the force of the missile. After this, he stood silent for a moment waiting to see if anyone or anything would respond to the noise.

As he stood waiting, he thought about yesterday's encounter at the New River. Something was still nagging at him and surprisingly enough it wasn't the act of killing another human being that troubled him. What bugged him most of all was the fact that he'd found another person wandering in the neighbourhood. *His* neighbourhood. For so long, this area had been his place and even if others had passed through they hadn't lingered and there was no contact with them. All that changed yesterday when the savage gatecrashed his routine.

Hopefully it was just a one-off.

Stepping forward, he slipped his hand through a jagged gap in the glass, reaching for the handle on the inside and hoping it wasn't locked. It wasn't. With a sigh of relief, he released the handle and pulled the broken window outwards.

He climbed inside. A terrible odour shot up his nostrils. It was something ungodly and he covered his nose and mouth with his hand, pressing down as hard has he could. He would suffocate rather than inhale that again.

"Hello?" he said in a muffled voice. "Anyone here?"

Idiot. There's no one here. There's been no one here for years. Now stop knocking on doors and talking to ghosts.

The only way to get through it was to keep moving. Don't linger, he kept telling himself. So he didn't. He hurried through the living room and into the hallway, his eyes searching for the kitchen.

The kitchen was on his right hand side. The door had been left open and he could see inside the narrow room. There were bugs everywhere – flies buzzing, cockroaches crawling across the worktop and all sorts of other creepy crawlies that had made a home here.

He walked inside. He might as well have been walking into the Chernobyl Nuclear Power Plant. This was a terrible place. Approaching the white fridge freezer at the far end of the room, he buried his mouth and nostrils into the flesh of his forearm. He opened the door. The light was off – it wasn't working. That should have been enough to send him on his way but he stood there, some part of him equally fascinated and horrified by the contents of the fridge. It had been full when the house was abandoned. It might even have looked good once, but all that was left now was a pile of gut-churning waste. The walls of the fridge were covered in dark spots of purple and green mould. Something that might once have been yoghurt had fallen to the bottom shelf and had congealed into a shapeless grey mound that looked like Kraken vomit. The flies couldn't get enough of it.

He felt a lurch in his stomach and slammed the door shut.

The fridge was still hooked up at the wall and switched on, which meant that it was either a fuse or that the appliance itself was a goner. Given the state of its interior and the prospect of cleaning it out, he was happy to let this one go anyway. Still covering his nose and mouth, he hurried back to the living room window and climbed outside. He fell onto the long grass and lay there for a while, his lungs grasping at the fresh air like a drowning man reaching for a life raft.

It had been a similar story with the next two houses. Smash the window, climb into a ghostly interior only to have an encounter with the fridge from Hell. After that he'd returned out the front door of the third house and onto the street for a break – there was no way he could take that smell again so soon.

He decided to lie down in the middle of the road for ten minutes and bask in the sunlight.

No wonder he'd stayed away from the other houses in the street all these years. He'd never needed anything in the early months after Piccadilly – there was enough food at home to last a long time and everything appliance-wise was working fine. Then by the time his own supplies had started running low he'd developed a peculiar fear of the empty houses that surrounded him. It was almost as if they were the incarnation of everything terrible that had happened. They were so still and quiet – a cruel reminder of all that was lost. They were giant, cursed idols – something to be respected but avoided.

But now he couldn't avoid them. He needed a fridge. There was no way around that. It was something he couldn't possibly go without if he wanted to stay where he was. And the thought of leaving home and venturing out into the rest of London was the one thing that frightened him more than breaking into the empty houses.

With a sigh, he got back to his feet and looked at the row of untouched houses.

House number four. He looked around at the weed-infested garden, two doors down from where he lived. As he approached the gate, he recalled seeing the family who had once lived in the house. He remembered the woman of the house, an attractive blonde lady who had tended to the garden at every opportunity. How neatly she'd kept it too, with its charming display of potted plants and garden gnomes, all of which were now buried under a tall blanket of weeds.

Whirr-Click.

Ignoring the sound, he threw open the gate. He walked down the path to the house. He tried the handle and to his surprise, this time it was unlocked.

As he walked in, he braced himself but still the odour caught him unawares. Something different this time. Filth and decay, but it was also distinctive and even sickly-sweet. It wasn't just rotten food and the scent of decay. It was a peculiar, yet disgusting smell. Stepping forward, he realised that it was at its most potent around the staircase. He looked upstairs – fearful of what was up there, but also curious.

Once again, he covered his nose and mouth with his arm. Before he knew what he was doing, he had started up the staircase.

You're not going to find a fridge up there.

Too late. He reached the top of the stairs and stepped onto the landing. The bathroom was directly in front of him and walking inside, he saw and heard the flies everywhere – hundreds of them. The toilet seat was lying open and there were bugs crawling around the interior as well as inside the bathtub. Brown mould dotted the white walls like unimaginative graffiti and damp patches clung to the ceiling.

There was a closed door to his right. Trying to ignore the fear tingling in his legs, he moved towards it, all the while trying to avoid the giant cockroaches at his feet. He forced himself to take a gulp of air, but it was so hot and disgusting inside the house that he was sure he'd pass out.

With a trembling hand, he pushed the door open. Inside the room, the curtains were pulled shut and everything was shrouded in a grey darkness. But he could see well enough to make out the decorations that someone had once put here. The wall was plastered entirely with posters featuring a variety of pop stars – the names of which he'd almost forgotten but not quite. Jessie J and Katy Perry – they were two of them at least.

He walked further inside the room. There was a single bed, which had been left neatly made. A flat screen TV sat atop a chest of drawers. A small stereo flanked by two tiny speakers was on the floor, surrounded by a pile of CD cases. The wardrobe door was lying half-open. He looked inside and found a treasure trove of female clothing inside – dresses, blouses, t-shirts and jeans – all hanging in perfect symmetry.

Thinking back, he tried to remember the girl who'd lived in this house. Hadn't he seen her walking past the window of his home on a regular basis? She had probably been about his age give or take a year. Gradually her face returned to him – she was blonde and pretty – a miniature version of her mother, but with a shy demeanour. He remembered now. She had always looked towards the ground, so intense, as if she was concentrating on something – on solving some unseen crisis that existed in her mind. She'd had the studious look about her – a bookworm perhaps, but she was cute and instinctively he'd liked her.

He closed the bedroom door and walked along the hall to the next bedroom. Opening the door slowly, he peered into a room that had been turned into a shrine to Tottenham Hotspur football club by its occupant. The wall was covered in this one too but instead of pop stars, there were posters of Spurs team members past and present on all sides. The carpet was spotless but he noticed that a variety of Dr Who memorabilia had been placed on the top of the chest of bedside drawers like a mini exhibit – the Tardis, several manifestation of the Doctor, Dalek figures, and other characters from the seminal science-fiction show. All of them covered in flies.

He couldn't remember anything about the other kid who'd lived here. Her little brother perhaps? A sister who'd been mad about football?

He stepped out of the bedroom and closed the door behind him.

There was one room left at the end of the hallway. He stood

outside the closed door, brushing a swarm of flies from his face. Somehow he already knew what was in there. Still, he pushed the handle down with one hand and covered his nose and mouth with the palm of the other. The hinges made a terrible creaking sound as the door swung open. Inside the curtains were shut and the interior was mostly cloaked in a murky grey darkness. But a few shafts of light were coming through a chink at the window, shooting thin golden beams across the room, allowing him to see what was in there.

They were huddled together underneath the bedcovers – all four of them. Heads and fragments of shoulder were the only thing visible and the rest was hidden underneath the sheets. But he could see enough of their faces to tell that they no longer had faces. The insects had made short work of their rotten flesh and the four skulls had been picked clean over the years.

The two adults were lying on the outside and the children were tucked in between them. That's how they'd chosen to die – together.

He stood at the door, his eye fixed upon a few remnants of hair that were still attached to one of the middle skulls. Blonde? He wasn't sure, but he tried to picture that girl's studious, concentrated expression upon that empty face. To imagine her walking past his house – going to the library or wherever it was she had gone in 2011. Perhaps they would have been friends if things had turned out differently. Perhaps more than friends. She might have been exceptional at something. She'd deserved the chance to find out.

There were bottles on the bedside cabinets. Empty pill containers and dark glass bottles sat side by side. His best guess – they had used a combination of poisons to ensure a certain death. The children first and then the adults.

He looked at them, unsure of what he was supposed to do.

By now, the heat was unbearable. The rancid smell wasn't helping either. With one last look at the dead family, he shut the door behind him. Then, brushing the flies away, he hurried along the hallway towards the stairs. He'd had enough. Fridge hunting was over for today. He'd try again tomorrow but for now he had to get out of this godforsaken tomb and back into the sunlight.

He stopped at the top of the stairs. There was something outside. A noise.

An engine? It *was* an engine. He could hear an engine outside – not somewhere in the distance but directly outside on Stanmore Road. Could it be? Could it be the maintenance people? Had they come to do some repair work on his street? Perhaps they were coming to fix whatever it was that kept making that whirring and clicking sound.

He hurried downstairs, two or three steps at a time, but stopped at the front door. His hand reached for the handle but something held him back. It was as if some part of him was reluctant to go through with this. *But listen.* It was an engine. There was no mistaking it. A car? A truck? His heart was on fire, his mind racing back and forth, filling with questions. If they saw him would they take pity on him? Would they take him out of London? If they realised that it was just one guy living alone and no one else then they'd probably be willing to help him. Wouldn't they? What harm could it do to take one person out of London?

But what if it wasn't somebody from the outside?

That's what's holding you back.

What if it was a gang of flesh-eating cannibals? An entire squad of suited monsters like the one he'd tussled with yesterday at the river?

Who drives a car in London anymore? Did people still drive cars on the inside of the walls? Where would they get the fuel? If someone had gone mad with hunger to the point of eating human flesh, were they still capable of everyday things like driving a car?

Was he going to open the door?

If only he knew more about what was out there.

But it was the thought of his parents – of seeing his long-lost parents again that tipped him over the edge. If it was a maintenance crew then this was his ticket beyond the M25.

The sound of the engine was receding into the distance.

Without another second's hesitation, his fingers pushed down on the metal handle. He ran out of the house and took off down the garden path at full speed. He almost gagged as the stench of death spilled out the door behind him like a pungent mist.

When he reached the middle of the road, he stopped and looked both ways. Empty. There was nothing there. Stanmore Road was the same concrete desert it had been for the last nine years. No car, no truck – there was nothing.

"Stop!" he yelled, looking both ways. "Please. Please stop. I'm here, I'm here!"

He started running down the street like a sprinter out the blocks. Whatever it was, whoever it had been – they couldn't have gone far. He ran about a hundred metres in one direction, fully aware that he was probably going the wrong way. But it was a fifty-fifty chance and doing something was better than doing nothing.

The heat pressed down on him. He was blowing hard and fighting hard to get enough oxygen into his lungs. But it was too hot. His legs were tired and realising that he was slowing down and getting nowhere fast, he dropped to his knees in the middle of the street.

Whirr-Click.

He looked up towards the sky, shielding his eyes from the sun. That noise again. And then a troubling thought occurred to him – what if there was no car? What if it had been a fantasy in his head – a reaction to the sight of the dead family, an overload of sensory information that had caused his fragile mind to create an audible illusion? And if so, he'd created it in the form of an escape route.

No, there was a car. He was sure of it.

"Fuck!" he said, breathing heavy. It felt like his insides were shrivelling up and turning black. He needed water.

He pushed himself up off the road. It was time to go home, pull the curtains and crash on the bed for a while. Let the warm day pass and think about things when it was cooler.

He started the short, laborious walk back to his house. It felt like an invisible hand was weighing him down in both body and mind. Thank God he could see his house up ahead.

Then he saw something else – something lying underneath the hedge of one of the houses to his right. It was a white, rectangular sheet of paper. It was another envelope.

"No," he hissed. It was like he was a vampire who'd just caught sight of a silver crucifix.

He understood the pain already. He'd read enough of those godforsaken letters to get it – times were hard in the city of London after Piccadilly. He didn't need to keep reading these fucking whiny letters to know that all the people who wrote them were long dead and that their bones were out there somewhere, picked clean by the local insect population and denied a proper send-off. They were dead. He didn't want to get to know them through their last words. They had died in horrific circumstances and that's all there was to know.

He tried to ignore the envelope. To keep walking. Let a gust of wind come along and blow it into somebody else's hand. But as always, curiosity or loneliness got the better of him. Without trying to talk himself out of it any further, he walked over to the wooden gate, scooped up the letter and tucked it into his back pocket.

Then he straightened up and looked around. He wouldn't admit it, not even to himself, but he was still hoping to see the faintest glimpse of a car receding into the distance.

CHAPTER 6

TFL: Calling London!

Georgia Perkins and Johnny Castle are hosting a ten-minute segment of questions taken from the studio audience. This is a regular part of the show and it takes place after the day's top stories, discussions and special features have been concluded.

GEORGIA PERKINS: Right you lot! Let me see some hands in the air. (*Turning to camera*) Don't forget if you guys at home have a question, leave a comment on our I-9 page using the hashtag #CallingLondonQ&A

Georgia points to a young woman in the front row with her hand raised.

GEORGIA PERKINS: Yes mate. Fire away.

YOUNG WOMAN: Hello. I want to ask a question about the Lovebirds. I know that Mr Apocalypse is a big deal these days but it seems like everyone's forgotten about the Lovebirds, haven't they? I mean they were at one point the most watched thing on TFL, but after what happened it's like no one's talking about them anymore. Know what I mean?

JOHNNY CASTLE: Oooh, I loved the Lovebirds sweetie.

YOUNG WOMAN: Me too. They were such a beautiful couple. I used to stay up all night watching them as they walked across London. They were good people for sure – we saw them give food to strangers, we listened in on their most intimate conversations and let's be honest – none of us turned away that time they had sex in Hyde Park, did we?

GEORGIA PERKINS: Great telly wasn't it?

YOUNG WOMAN: It was. Right until the moment he strangled her on live TV. But my point is this – nobody's talking about the Lovebirds anymore. Why? It's all about Mr Apocalypse today. But Mr Apocalypse is just flavour of the month and no one will remember him when the next thing catches on. I can't believe that we've forgotten the Lovebirds so soon, can you? She died in such terrible circumstances. I was gutted. I'm still gutted by what happened. I thought he loved her.

JOHNNY CASTLE: It was a terrible thing.

GEORGIA PERKINS: Such a cute couple weren't they? And young too. A real tragedy but what's your question again mate?

YOUNG WOMAN: We've got to draw a line. Don't you think we should draw a line somewhere? Yeah it's great TV and all that, but I don't want to see people being murdered. Especially people I've grown so attached to.

JOHNNY CASTLE: You're right – the camera didn't cut away from the act of murder. But you still watched it didn't you?

YOUNG WOMAN: (*Nodding*) Yes I did. I couldn't believe what I was seeing and by the time it had sunk in it was all over. That poor girl was dead. And now nobody's talking about it anymore. Everyone's moved onto Mr Apocalypse – this mysterious loner dude in the north. Why aren't we asking questions about the Lovebirds? Does nobody want to know why this young man did what he did?

JOHNNY CASTLE: Of course we do. And it's understandable that you're shocked by what happened. We all are. But as you know,

TFL is a television show unlike any other in history. These are real people living in extraordinary circumstances. Maybe he did it out of some sense of warped nobility – to protect her from the ugliness of the world. Maybe he just snapped. Who knows? We are witnessing fascinating sociological developments behind the M25, but if you don't like it – you *can* stop watching at anytime.

The audience gives Johnny Castle a round of applause.

GEORGIA PERKINS: Okay, very interesting points made there. Moving on, uhh yes you, the chap with the red t-shirt on.

A young black man with long dreadlocks and a dyed blond goatee gets to his feet. There is a yellowish glimmer in his eyes as he looks down upon the two hosts sitting on the couch.

YOUNG MAN: I have a question. It has nothing to do with what happened in London today because I don't and never will subscribe to TFL.

GEORGIA PERKINS: (*Laughs nervously*) Uh-oh. We've got a live one here Johnny.

YOUNG MAN: Yeah. There are many charities out there raising funds to provide a better quality of life for people trapped in London. What I would like to know is this - why is the vast majority of money being raised by these charities not getting past the M25?

JOHNNY CASTLE: (*Shaking his head*) Look we don't have time to discuss conspiracy theories mate. That's Internet speculation isn't it? I've heard this before but nobody ever seems to have any evidence, do they? Do you?

YOUNG MAN: Conspiracy theories? People are starving. Why are they starving? There's cannibalism and cases of clinical vampirism in London for God's sake. People are eating human flesh and drinking blood. And it's clearly born out of starvation and madness because these people aren't being provided for.

GEORGIA PERKINS: Calm down a bit mate, yeah? No need to use that tone...

YOUNG MAN: It costs people one hundred pounds a month to

watch the Londoners starve, right? To watch them go mad and turn into monsters. That's a lot of money, innit? Combined with what charities like London Aid are raising, that should be more than enough to provide food and supplies and make life bearable. Yeah?

Georgia Perkins and Johnny Castle exchange nervous glances.

JOHNNY CASTLE: Look mate, there are other costs to consider you know? For example, do you have any idea how expensive it is to maintain the TFL set?

The young man with the blond goatee laughs.

YOUNG MAN: Set? Is that what we're calling London now? A television set?

JOHNNY CASTLE: You have the purchase price of technology to consider. You have the upkeep of that technology, not to mention the military presence and the maintenance of other things such as a constant supply of electricity and clean water – these things are costly beyond comprehension. I don't think a hundred pounds a month is that steep when you take all these things into consideration.

The audience applauds, but the young man raises his voice and talks above them.

YOUNG MAN: What absolute rubbish! Charities aren't raising money for these things – they raise money to provide food for hungry people. They're not supposed to be paying for any more surveillance equipment. I remember six months ago when this abomination was launched – Rudyard Campbell and the Prime Minister told us that TFL was there to help people find their loved ones. I haven't heard of a single person being relocated from there to here. Have you?

JOHNNY CASTLE: Well it's hardly Rudyard Campbell's fault that nobody's spotted anyone they know, is it?

YOUNG MAN: You're a liar. And this is a travesty. But I'm telling you this – all of you. The Good and Honest Citizens will return and clean up this mess. We're gonna finish what Chester George started in 2011. Just you wait and see.

The young man barges past the others sitting in the row alongside him and storms towards the exit. At the same time, two security guards move in and shadow his movements.

GEORGIA PERKINS: (*Smiling at the camera*) Well, well, well. I don't know about you Johnny, but I do love a good conspiracy theory, eh?

CHAPTER 7

He pressed his face against the glass. He'd been unable to tear his eyes away from the bedroom window for most of the day. If that was a car he'd heard in the neighbourhood yesterday, then it might go past again. Maybe it was doing the rounds, day and night, looking for signs of life in the old neighbourhoods of Tottenham.

It was a plausible scenario.

But nothing happened. No one came, no engines growled down on the street. Perhaps it was true – there had never been a car out there in the first place. After all, he was hearing things on a regular basis now.

Still, he stayed by the bedroom window. Another five minutes – that's what he'd been telling himself for the last few hours.

Eventually he did give up. It was getting dark outside and he drew the curtains. He decided to go downstairs into the living room for a while. A change of scenery – live it up a little in the new London. Inside the living room he pulled the curtains and brought out one of the rustic pillar candles that came in the supply packs every other week. Apparently light bulbs were too fragile to survive the impact on Drop Day.

It didn't matter. He liked these candles. There was something comforting about the faint glow of candlelight. Not to mention it was safer as the light was bright enough, but not too bright that it could be seen from outside. He made a point of checking this with every new candle that came in a supply parcel. He couldn't risk showing any signs of life in the house.

He sat down on the leather armchair. A small part of him was still listening for the sound of an engine outside on the street. Just in case. He tried to switch off but what else was there to do except think? He looked around the living room. Like all the rooms in the house, he knew the layout better than the back of his hand. Alba was curled up in a ball on the end of the wrinkled leather couch. The TV was where it had always been, sitting on the other side of the room. What a pity it no longer picked up a signal these days. He'd enjoyed watching television and would have given anything to be able to kick back and watch his favourite shows again, especially the great comedies such as *Red Dwarf* and *The Office*.

Back in 2011, he'd spent a lot of time watching news reports about the early days of the London riots. He recalled the shocked reaction of his parents who'd sat on the couch where Alba now slept. They'd watched the documentaries with all the experts and talking heads, listening to a variety of sociological theories – feeble attempts made by academia to understand the root cause of the riots. He remembered one expert in particular who'd compared the contagious fervour of the rioters to a rat king – a strange phenomenon in nature in which multiple rats become intertwined at the tails, like a super organism glued together by blood, dirt and shit. He always remembered that theory because it sounded so stupid – like something out of a horror film.

He looked down at the coffee table. The letter was lying there, still waiting to be opened. The words 'PLEASE HELP' had been written across the front in large blue ink letters. Most of the letters he found had something similar written on the front – a headline crying for attention – but there was something about this envelope that made it different. He'd noticed it almost immediately after bringing it home. It was so well preserved. All the others had been tattered, faded and ravaged by the weather and years. Not this one. The white colour of the envelope was still pristine white and to look at it, you could believe that it had been purchased in a shop that same day. Not to mention the blue ink on the front was bright and clear.

That aroused his curiosity. But it was still with some reluctance that he tore the envelope open. What fresh horrors awaited him now? He pulled out a folded piece of A4 paper from within and unravelled it. There was handwriting on both sides of the sheet and his first impression was that it was remarkably neat. He looked at the left-slanting, wide penmanship and instinctively thought it belonged to a woman's hand.

Across the room, Alba stood up briefly and stretched her legs. Without fully opening her eyes, she did a full turn, rearranged her sleeping position and went immediately back to sleep.

He looked towards the window. No cars, only silence. Returning his thoughts indoors, he gave his full attention to the letter.

Please help me. I'm running out of time.

I'm in Tottenham, North London. If my numbers are right then the year is 2020.

I'm trapped. They've got me surrounded outside the house and I'm writing this letter while they're quiet. Perhaps the night breeze might carry it to someone who will help me. I have to try.

Whoever you are – help me please. I'm trapped upstairs in 15a Langham Road, Tottenham N15. My name is Cristiane Barboza and I'm probably 28 years old. I can't go outside anymore. Four men have been laying siege outside my house for two days. I think they're rogues who have broken away from a pack and are now scavenging the area for food. So far I've been able to fight them off, but there's too many of them and they keep coming back. They've broken all the lower windows at the front of the house but I've got a knife and have cut them when they try to get close. I got one of them good in the arm. They're wary and it's bought me time but that won't last.

Help me please.

I've been living here for about two months on my own. Quite happily until now. I came up from the hellhole that is South London. Unlike so many others I survived the journey and I thought I'd found a quiet place here in the north, somewhere I could live in peace and within reach of a regular supply drop. And it was peaceful for a while. But then a couple of days back – on the last Drop Day at the New River – they saw me. Five of them - wild-looking men - two of them dressed in tattered suits. I dropped the sack and ran back here. They chased after me. Four of them made it back. I don't know what happened to number five.

I don't have much food left. Running back to the kitchen to refill my water supply is getting too dangerous. I can't let them out of my sight for too long.

I can't stop thinking about my family back in Brazil. I came to London to study in 2010 and thought I was going to something better. Last I heard back in 2011, my mother was ill. They must have given me up for dead by now – I mean, what chance does anyone have on their own out here?

I'm sorry to ramble on. But I can't stop thinking that this piece of paper might be the last trace of me that ever exists. I won't have a headstone and I want to leave something of myself behind. I studied music at university. I practiced the martial art of capoeira from my beloved Brazil. I have had four boyfriends in my life. I believed that I was going to be happy in London.

I must eat something. I need to stay awake, but I know this stand off is coming to an end. What would be the kindest thing for myself? To end it before those flesh-eating brutes get near me? I won't risk the terrible sensation of their teeth biting into me.

Please God.

You will come for me, won't you?

Cristiane Barboza.
15a Langham Road.

He put the letter down on the table. Immediately his eyes returned to the top of the page and specifically to the number that she'd written there.

2020.

Was that this year? Had nine years passed since the events of 2011? And if so, how old was this letter?

He knew Langham Road. It was about five minutes walk from where he lived. If this letter was recent, then somebody else had been living in the same area for the past two months. That was a shocking possibility. Granted, he never travelled anywhere near Langham Road and if she'd been trying to lay low then he would never have heard or seen anything. But like him, she'd been going to the New River on Drop Day – had she been taking the second parcel from him all this time? His mind was filled with questions. But the most important question remained – was it 2020? And was this letter brand new?

She's dead. Forget it.

The letter had probably been floating in and around Stanmore Road for months. She *was* dead. Undoubtedly it had been written recently and it was a tragedy, but it was too late to do anything for her. She would take her place with all the other tragedies lying in the drawer in his bedroom upstairs.

You could go take a look. It's only five minutes walk.

No.

His eyes returned to the letter. He leaned forward, skimming the passage about her attackers and in particular about the two 'rogues' in the suits. Just like the savage who'd attacked him two days ago. He felt his heart beating faster. *Jesus Christ.* What if she'd been down at the river that day before him? Perhaps the parcel he'd picked up had been the same one she'd dropped. If one of those savages or rogues had lingered in the area, then what happened to him would make sense.

He looked over at Alba. She opened her pale blue eyes and stared across the living room at him.

"You've been out there," he said. "What's a 'pack'? What's a 'rogue'? What do these words mean?"

Alba held his stare, but remained motionless like a cat mannequin.

"Oh no," he said, shaking his head. "I'm not going anywhere. She's probably been dead for months if not years. It's nothing to do with me. You know what I need to do Alba? I need to stop reading these letters, that's what I need to do. It's not good for me."

He sat back in silence, still staring at the letter on the table.

"No!" he yelled.

Moments later, he jumped to his feet and shoved the piece of paper into the back pocket of his jeans.

Rest in peace.

He felt better with the letter out of sight and sat down again. His eyes were heavy with all that watching and waiting he'd done. It felt like a good time to sleep so he leaned over and blew out the candle. The room fell into a warm and pleasant darkness. He hadn't slept in the living room for a long time but he didn't feel like getting back up again.

He closed his eyes. It didn't take long to fall asleep.

It was dark. He was standing on something soft and spongy. It was an unfamiliar environment, somewhere warm and wet. Immediately dangerous. There was a faint stream of light pouring in from somewhere up ahead and for a moment he thought he was standing in the middle of a short tunnel looking towards the exit and onto daylight. Instinctively he started walking towards the light. Fumbling around in the hot damp, his hands groped in front of him. He touched something that felt like teeth – giant teeth. Hard and pointed. That was all he needed – now he knew where he was. There was no doubt. He was trapped in something's mouth. Something big. He panicked and made a dash for the exit – the faint glimmer of light that formed an odd arch-like shape up ahead. As he ran towards the light, everything became clearer. He saw four gigantic incisors going up and down in a mechanical rhythm, barely missing him as he stumbled his way towards the end of the fleshy tunnel. But it was no use. Running wasn't working. Whatever had a hold of him, it was too strong and despite his best efforts, he felt himself being pushed further to the back of the mouth, back into darkness and towards the throat.

He couldn't breathe. Blackness threatened to overwhelm him.

In the moments before plunging down towards the stomach, he saw something through the opening of the mouth. It was a television set – his television set, the same one that was located in the living room of his house. And it was working. There was something on. Somebody in a documentary was dressed in a tattered suit. They were talking directly at the camera:

'A rat king is what happens when multiple rats become intertwined at the tails. This can happen when the tails become knotted but blood, shit or dirt can also cause entanglement. Rat kings aren't like conjoined twins – they are not born physically a part of each other. Much like the rioters in our inner city communities, they grow together after birth. Most rats probably get stuck together because so many of them are gathered into one place. It just gets too crowded. Whether it was by knots, blood, shit, dirt or freezing, some of those individuals got sucked into one big super organism and now they're consuming everyone in their path.'

The television screen went blank. Everything went blank. He felt his skin burning up as if he was brushing up against the flames of eternal damnation itself. This was it. He was being swallowed alive. He was being consumed. It was the end of his life and there was barely time to scream.

He awoke in the pitch black. He was breathing heavy and on the brink of yelling out for help when he realised that he was sitting in the armchair in the living room. There was no mouth. He was not being eaten alive.

With a sigh of relief, he sat up straight in the seat. His heart was banging in his chest like a drum. The familiar sensation of his body swimming in its own sweat made him groan.

Reaching for the coffee table, he groped around and found the candle and the box of matches. His hands were trembling and he struggled to light the match. It took a while, but eventually he found the wick and a faint orange glow washed at least some of the darkness out of the room.

Alba was no longer on the couch.

"I'm going crazy," he said. "I'm going crazy girl."

He scratched furiously at the back of his hand. He stopped when he realised it wasn't itchy. A moment later, unable to sit still, he got up and walked through to the kitchen and turned on the cold tap. This time he threw caution to the wind and let the water gush out at full force. He placed his open palms under the icy liquid, gathered up a small puddle and threw it at his face. Then he opened his mouth under the tap and drank as much as he could.

When his thirst was quenched, he walked upstairs to his parents' room. Using torchlight to guide him, he went to work, digging out a few things from the back of the wardrobe and throwing them into a plastic bag. All the while, he tried not to listen to the voices in his head telling him that what he was doing was a bad idea.

It's not a bad idea. It's a fucking ridiculous idea!

Once he'd found everything, he took a step back and caught sight of his ragged reflection in the full-length wardrobe mirror. He looked pale blue, almost ghostlike in the moonlight.

"Nobody's going to be there," he said to the man looking back at him in the mirror. "You're wasting your time."

CHAPTER 8

TFL: Calling London!

July 7th 2020

GEORGIA PERKINS: Good evening and welcome back to *Calling London!* In case you missed it, Mr Apocalypse has just stormed out of his house and is at present making his way to an unknown location. Johnny, we've never seen him do anything like this before have we? Especially after dark.

JOHNNY CASTLE: Wow Georgia. We've absolutely no idea what he's doing tonight. This is completely out of character. (*Turns to camera*) Now we understand that you guys at home watching the show will also want to keep an eye on what Mr Apocalypse is doing. If that's the case then choose the split-screen option on your TFL home page. That way you can watch *Calling London!* and keep an eye on Mr Apocalypse at the same time.

Johnny Castle touches his earpiece. He turns around to face a video screen behind him on the couch, which is currently showing Mr Apocalypse making his way through a murky suburbia.

JOHNNY CASTLE: As we can see, he's on Langham Road at present. That's just a short walk from his house so he hasn't wandered too far yet. I wonder what's in that plastic bag he's carrying, eh?

GEORGIA PERKINS: Lots to talk about Johnny. But we'll come back to Mr Apocalypse in a few minutes. Before we do that, we'd like to take a moment to speak to you – the studio audience and the viewers at home. This is about something that happened on yesterday's show.

JOHNNY CASTLE: Yes. Now you might remember the hot-tempered young man who was hurling accusations about charity donations on last night's programme. We've had a lot of feedback about this and quite frankly, some people are worried that there might be some truth to what he said. Well, Georgia and I would like to address those concerns before we go any further. The first thing I want to say is that these accusations were made with no evidence whatsoever.

Georgia Perkins nods. Her eyes move back and forth between Johnny Castle and the television screen behind her, which is still following Mr Apocalypse.

JOHNNY CASTLE: We want to assure you – the general public – that every penny raised for the people of London *goes* to the people of London. That's guaranteed by all of us here in the TFL family and none more so than our CEO, Rudyard Campbell.

GEORGIA PERKINS: (*Turning back to the camera*) But we don't just want to tell you how committed we are to the people of London. We want to show you as well. So tonight, Johnny and I will be doing something extra-special for your viewing pleasure. It's something I'm dreading but as long as you lot are willing to donate money to London Aid, I'm going to do it. You got it?

The studio audience gives a round of applause.

JOHNNY CASTLE: Yes indeed. All the staff and our audience members have agreed to make a donation of ten pounds to London Aid if Georgia and I will partake in our little venture this evening. We hope you at home are willing to do the same. After all, London gives us plenty of entertainment. Let's give something back yeah?

GEORGIA PERKINS: So what are we going to do? Well I'll tell you. Do you remember the ALS Ice Bucket challenge back in 2014? Back then, random people and celebrities were doing silly things, making videos of themselves dumping buckets of ice and water over their heads to promote awareness for ALS. Remember?

JOHNNY CASTLE: Well coming up is our London-themed version of the ALS Ice Bucket Challenge – and it's one that symbolises the violence and hunger that are such an unfortunate aspect of everyday life for the people in modern London.

Georgia and Johnny stand up. She offers him her hand.

GEORGIA PERKINS: Let's do this Johnny.

The two presenters walk over to a makeshift stage area located near the audience. Upon the platform, two wooden chairs have been positioned side by side, facing the crowd. A small plastic bucket sits behind each of the two chairs while at the front, a small paper plate with a gnarled looking apple on it has been placed on the floor.

GEORGIA PERKINS: Ladies and Gentleman, we bring you the 2020 TFL Knife Bucket Challenge!

Another round of applause.

GEORGIA PERKINS: As we all know, knife-related violence is a big problem in London. And hunger is often the reason for this.

JOHNNY CASTLE: Well tonight we want your money boys and girls. Of course we don't want it for nothing. These two buckets you see are filled to the brim not with ice, but *knives*. And we're not talking disposable plastic knives either – these are steel table knives – this is the real deal and what we're about to do is going to hurt like crazy. But if tipping a bucket of steel knives isn't enough to make you donate, then don't fret sweeties. Once that's done we're going to eat that piece of disgusting looking fruit you see on the plate on the floor.

The audience responds with a unified 'Oooooooh!'

JOHNNY CASTLE: The rotten fruit isn't just for decoration either. It symbolises our commitment to raising money in order to provide a better quality of food to the people of London.

GEORGIA PERKINS: What do you say? Are you with us?

The audience roars its approval and the studio vibrates with excitement.

JOHNNY CASTLE: Okay. Text FEED LONDON to 345 and voilà! You have donated ten pounds to a very worthy cause.

GEORGIA PERKINS: Right Johnny, you're up first.

Johnny Castle smiles nervously. He sits down on one of the two wooden seats and faces the studio audience. Georgia steps behind him and picks up the bucket. She tilts it towards the camera with a mischievous grin, showing that it is indeed full of silver table knives.

GEORGIA PERKINS: Bloody hell this is heavy! You ready mate?

JOHNNY CASTLE: Ready!

The audience counts them down. 3-2-1…

JOHNNY CASTLE: (*Grimacing*) I'm doing this for you London!

Georgia tips the bucket over Johnny's head. There is a fierce clanging as the knives crash land onto Johnny's well-groomed head. He winces in pain while the audience howls with delight at the spectacle. Johnny keeps his head down until the last knife has fallen. When it's over he looks towards the camera and gives a weary looking thumbs-up. Then taking a deep breath, he picks up the paper plate and bites into flesh of the rotten apple. He eats most of it in less than a minute, screwing his face up like he's just been force fed a fresh rat turd.

GEORGIA PERKINS: You're not allowed to be sick Johnny! Or you'll have to do it all over again. Them the rules mate.

Johnny looks up at the camera again. Although he looks a little worse for wear after eating the apple, he smiles and gives another thumbs-up sign. This earns him a tremendous round of applause.

JOHNNY CASTLE: Oooh that apple, oh my God – I feel like I just bit into some fat bloke's sweaty testicles!

Georgia Perkins doubles over with laughter.

JOHNNY CASTLE: I don't know what you're laughing at. You're up next Georgia.

Georgia nods. She hurries into her seat, keeping her eyes closed all the way.

GEORGIA PERKINS: Do it! Do it quickly Johnny.

Johnny picks up the bucket and tries to hoist it aloft.

JOHNNY CASTLE: Bloody hell, this weighs a ton. You must be stronger than I am Georgia. You ready for this sweetie?

GEORGIA PERKINS: Do it!

He gently tips the bucket of knives over Georgia's head. She screams as they come crashing down on top of her. When it's done, she doesn't hesitate to start the second part of the challenge. She wolfs down the apple as quickly as she can, gagging a couple of times in the process.

The audience howls with laughter.

She hurries back to her feet, running a hand through her spiky blonde hair.

GEORGIA PERKINS: Am I cut? Oh my God! Them bloody knives mate!

JOHNNY CASTLE: You made it darling – safe and sound. I can't see any blood.

GEORGIA CASTLE: (*Turning to camera*) Woo-hoo! We did it. Right, now pay up you lot. Text FEED LONDON to 345. Ten pounds from each and every one of you will make a massive difference to the people living behind the M25.

Johnny Castle fidgets with his earpiece again.

JOHNNY CASTLE: Hold on! I'm getting word about Mr Apocalypse.

GEORGIA PERKINS: What? Is he still outside?

JOHNNY CASTLE: (*Listening to the voice in his ear*) He's still outside yeah.

GEORGIA PERKINS: Well what is it? What's he doing?

JOHNNY CASTLE: Let's go and sit down Georgia. I think we'd better take a closer look at this.

CHAPTER 9

He walked along Langham Road. It was such a strange sensation to be out at that time. He felt like a man taking his first steps on the moon – an explorer embarking upon a journey within some terrifying and fantastic virgin territory. Every couple of seconds he'd glance over his shoulder, half-expecting to see someone or something standing behind him.

He kept to the middle of the road as he walked. There was less chance of anyone taking him by surprise if he stayed out in the open. Had he chosen to walk on the sidelines, an assailant could easily leap out at him from behind a hedge or closed gate of one of the many houses that lined both sides of the street. The ambush by the New River had forced him into being extra vigilant. Like he'd been back in the early days before getting complacent. He had to be aware of all possibilities if he wanted to stay alive.

With one hand, he clutched at the handle of a plastic carrier bag. The other hand held onto a large kitchen knife, which he held out in front of him, like the jabbing arm of a boxer trying to keep the opponent at bay.

It didn't matter that he was only five minutes from his house –

he'd never felt so exposed in all his life. This was an alien suburbia. It was another world and it was strange and frightening. All he wanted to do was turn around and go home. He didn't even know what he was doing out there. But something forced him to keep going forwards. Some faint voice in the back of his head resisted the urge to go back.

The streetlights cast a pale glow over the neighbourhood. On either side of the street, the houses were dark and foreboding shapes with windows like eyes that watched him go past. Were they empty buildings? He could feel someone or something watching him. He was sure of it. Or was that just his imagination again? Another sign of his slow descent into madness.

90, 88, 86...

He counted down the houses as he walked past.

Soon he arrived at the intersection between Langham Road and Belmont Road. The path forwards began to narrow so much so that it looked more like a lane than a street up ahead. The abandoned houses, the fences, the hedges and garden gates – they were all bearing down closer now.

A thunderous roar from the sky came out of nowhere. He screamed. Quickly he dropped into a crouching position, pointing the knife blindly towards the darkness above him. About thirty seconds passed and nothing happened. Finally he dared to look up and saw the flashing lights of an aeroplane soaring across the night sky.

He breathed a sigh of relief.

Sitting down in the middle of the road, he stared up at the green and red lights in the sky. For a moment, he was lost in the colours. The rhythmic blinking of the plane was strangely soothing.

He wondered where the aeroplane had come from. Was Heathrow Airport still open anymore? He couldn't recall whether Heathrow had been located inside the M25 or not. Had Gatwick become the major airport in its place? Or was Gatwick gone too? Was there still any need for an airport in the London area?

He stood there watching the metal monster with its flashing

lights like beacons from another world. He'd been on a plane three times in his life. Family holidays to Spain, France and Majorca. Trips abroad were rare because his mum had hated flying with a vengeance. She'd always been so nervous in the moments immediately before take off. Each time she'd taken Valium to get through the experience and he recalled sitting beside her, teasing her about it and even joking out loud about all the things that could go wrong. That had pissed her off and rightly so. What a little arsehole he'd been to do that. Still he'd inherited none of her fear of flying. In fact, he'd always enjoyed the experience of sitting on an aeroplane, looking out of the window from forty thousand feet, down onto microscopic cities that looked like a panel of lights embedded on an Earth-sized circuit board.

Someone up there was probably doing the same thing. Looking down over London, the corpse of an entire city? And if London was a corpse, what did that make him and all the rest of its inhabitants? The worms, the flies and maggots feasting on its rotten flesh?

The plane disappeared into the dark sky. The noise of the engines faded and a gradual silence swept across the neighbourhood. It was a terrifying sound.

He continued to walk down Langham Road.

32, 30, 28...

Moments later, he heard it – the excited grunts and snarls. With his heart in his mouth, he edged forwards along the narrow street until he saw them.

Four people were standing in the middle of the road. Dark shapes. One by one, they rushed towards one of the houses before stopping and retreating back, as if they'd suddenly changed their minds. He tried to see the place they were going after. It was a large white building with two gable roofs that appeared to split the property neatly into two separate houses or apartments. At the front of the house, a wildly overgrown hedge spilled out from the garden path onto the pavement.

He was still standing in the middle of the road. Recognising how vulnerable he was, he took cover behind the nearest garden hedge and settled into a surveillance position.

Looking down, he saw that his hands were shaking.

From behind the hedge he took a minute or two to process the fact that it was real – the letter, the girl, the situation. Then he peered over the top of the hedge towards the white house.

They looked like tramps – filthy long hair and beards stretching far beyond their chin. Most of them were dressed in ragged coats and torn jeans, but one of them was clearly wearing the remains of what had once been a tattered suit. It looked similar to the savage in the suit that he'd encountered at the New River two days ago – so similar that he felt a cold chill just looking at the black shape.

One of the savages laughed. Another let out a guttural howl. He could hear something else too mixed in with all of this – a woman's voice. She was yelling what sounded like muffled obscenities, telling the savages in no uncertain terms to get away from her house. *To get the fuck away from her house.* There was anger in her voice, but it could easily have been interpreted as fear.

No wonder they had built the M25 around London. People had gone crazy. The smartest thing he ever did was to stay away from all this. But now it had come to him.

Fuck.

The savages continued to try and get closer to the house. He heard them panting like rabid beasts on a mission. But their clumsy charges would always fail and they would be forced to fall back onto the street. She was fighting them off with courage – a dark, slender shape hovering at the edge of the garden. She held something aloft – a weapon of some sort and she was brandishing it at her attackers with gusto.

He fell back against the hedge. Why weren't the savages attacking as a unit? Four against one, it should have been easy. Perhaps they had lost the ability to think strategically. The madness and the heat, not to mention the hunger had blinded them to reason. If that was true then it had kept her alive. So far.

The savages were waiting it out. They would get what they wanted and it was only a matter of time. He'd sensed how exhausted she was just by reading the letter. And that was how long ago now?

He looked inside the plastic carrier bag. Immediately he threw it back down again and groaned. It had seemed like a good idea at the time. Creative. But now that he'd arrived on site and having seen the things he'd brought with him, it was obvious this was the worst idea he'd ever had.

But what choice did he have?

Reaching inside, he pulled out his mother's high-heeled shoes, followed by her black evening coat that had been folded up into a bundle.

"Shit," he whispered. "What am I doing here?"

He would become a damsel in distress. If those things were so turned on by chasing after a woman, then wouldn't they try chasing after another one? It wasn't going to pleasant, but he could at least draw them away from the girl. It would give her a fighting chance to run. Then he would kick off his mum's shoes, make a run for it and get back to his own life, knowing that he'd done the right thing.

With a sigh, he pulled off the socks and trainers that had once belonged to his dad. Then he tried to force the heels onto his feet.

"Jesus Christ!"

He winced as the shoes bit into his skin. It felt as if they were cutting strips of meat off his feet as he pushed down. Why did women put themselves through this torture? But the hardest part was standing up. As he did so, he almost tripped over his feet and toppled through the hedge. Fortunately he regained his balance at the last moment.

Then he took a deep breath.

It didn't matter. The shoes didn't need to be on for long – just a few seconds to divert the savages away from the house. And when they came running after him, the girl would either take her chances and get out of there or she'd freeze and stay there until they came back. But that wasn't his problem. He would help her once and then he was getting out of there and back to Stanmore Road.

He tucked the carrier bag and trainers into the base of the hedge. If needs be, he would come back for them in the morning. Then he straightened up again and put on his mother's evening coat. Thank God he couldn't see himself.

He staggered on his feet like a drunk, swaying from side to side.

"Cross the street," he said, pulling the neck of the coat up to try and conceal his shaved head. "Let them see you. They'll come running. And get the fuck out of there."

He tucked the kitchen knife into the sleeve of the coat, blade first so that he could keep a solid grip on the handle. That way he could pull it out quickly if he had to.

Without any further hesitation, he stumbled onto the street. Doing his best to retain his balance, he pushed the heels hard into the concrete so that the savages would hear the clacking sound over the rest of the noise.

He hurried across the street.

Silence. The assault on 15a Langham Road came to a sudden halt. He kept most of his face hidden behind the coat, but he managed to peer out and felt his blood freeze.

The savages were looking at him. All of them.

They would come. Any second now. Still the damsel in distress kept moving, staggering clumsily across the street. All the while he tried to ignore the searing pain below as the shoes mutilated his feet. He only hoped that he'd be able to kick off the heels in a hurry when it came time to run for his life. He didn't want to die like this – wearing a woman's coat and a pair of high heels.

But to his surprise, nothing happened.

The savages weren't coming after him. He had their attention and that was all. They were looking down the street at the fleeing damsel but doing nothing. Perhaps they weren't convinced by his less than stellar performance. Who could blame them? As he staggered across the street in his mother's high heels, he looked less like a damsel in distress and more like a geriatric Swamp Thing on its last legs.

He couldn't believe it. They were letting him go. He stopped moving in the middle of the street and turned back to them, watching as the savages renewed the assault on 15a Langham Road with a fresh barrage of missiles. The young woman charged at them again, running out towards the street, pointing her knife at them.

Wincing in pain, he pulled off the shoes. It felt as if his feet had been through the grinder. He wanted to throw the heels away but he couldn't because they had been his mum's. Were *still* his mum's. He let the knife slip through the coat sleeve of the jacket. Then he removed the garment and laid it down beside the shoes.

It had been a ridiculous plan. Maybe he'd underestimated the intellect of the savages. Maybe there was still something going on up there in the brain after all. Something human. It didn't matter – he had to try again and there was only one option left to him – he'd have to charge and fight them off. It was either that or abandon the girl to her fate and then he'd be forced to see her in his nightmares alongside the girl with the tiger paint on her face.

He grabbed the knife and hurried back across the street in his bare feet. He pulled the plastic bag out from under the hedge and put his socks and trainers back on. Then he put his mother's shoes and coat back into the bag and pulled out the second of two kitchen knives that he'd brought along.

Now he held a knife in each hand. He knew that he was capable of doing what had to be done. He had killed by the New River yesterday and he could do it again. Killing was no longer the same thing that it used to be.

He took off, tearing along Langham Road towards the white house. He let out a scream of mixed emotions, his voice ripping a hole through the night air. In that moment, something happened in his mind. A switch went either on or off. He felt otherworldly and knew that he would succeed. It was as if some sense of indestructibility had entered his body, mind and soul and taken control. He would kill them all. He would go through them or die because they had come into his territory.

The savages saw him coming. He saw the uncertainty in their black eyes. They took several steps backwards but he picked up the speed, no longer caring whether he saw another sunrise or not. It was all or nothing.

Three of the savages turned and ran. But one of them – the man in the suit no less, charged to meet him in the middle of the street.

There was no stopping. He ran through the savage – who was a big man with broad shoulders, built like a welterweight boxer at the peak of his powers.

He brought both knives down, aiming for the thing's forehead. He missed and saw the savage roll away, quite expertly so, and get back to its feet. This one seemed more agile than the sloppy tramp he'd encountered by the New River. For a moment, he was concerned. It was going to be a tough fight.

But then something happened. Without looking back, the beast in the suit turned and ran after his three colleagues. That brief skirmish had been enough to send the thing on its way. There were cries of fear – feral whimpers, as if the savage didn't understand the need for such brutal treatment at the hands of the stranger.

But he wasn't satisfied with letting them get away. They would do the same thing to someone else or more likely they'd be at the New River waiting for him on the next Drop Day.

He ran after them, still in a daze, still hungry for the kill.

"Hey!"

Her voice went through him and he stopped in his tracks. Slowly he turned around and saw her standing in the middle of the street.

Cristiane Barboza was walking towards him. She carried two knives, one in each hand. There was a strange look in her eyes. Something in between fear and suspicion – unsure of whether the man standing in front of her was friend or foe. Was he someone to be grateful to or was he someone to kill?

"Hello," she said, stopping a few feet away from him. Her body was as rigid as a statue. Her eyes looked him up and down, from head to toe.

He hadn't seen a woman in a long time. He recalled reading something about Brazil in the letter and certainly she looked like someone who hailed from that part of the world. She was about 5'6 or 5'7, with black hair, a slim build and warm olive skin with a yellowish-gold hue. She was dressed in a grey vest top and black jeans – the vest was soaked in grime and sweat, a testament to the battle for survival that she'd undergone the past two days.

"Who are you?" she said. Her accent was faint, but exotic nonetheless.

"I – I got your letter," he said.

You're talking to a real person.

Her posture loosened a little.

"You found it? You read it?"

"It was on my street."

"Your street?" she said.

"Aye," he said. That was all the information he was willing to share. He certainly wasn't going to give her the address.

"They'll come back," she said, looking towards where the savages had run off. "They know I'm here now."

He said nothing.

"I'm Cristiane Barboza," she said.

"I know."

"What's your name?"

He shook his head. "Does it matter?"

Barboza raised her eyebrows. "You still have a name, don't you?"

He nodded.

"Walker," he said. "My name is Walker."

CHAPTER 10

Immersion 9 – Live Chat Rooms
Hot Topics - #MrApocalypse

Dennis D: Hoooleeeey shit!

Gracie: Dude just got himself a GF!! Future Mrs Apocalypse?

Dennis D: True dat. U cant script the awesomeness of real life.

Jack Burton: Never knew that girl was living there! Neither did TFL obviously until those rogues turned up at her front door. Fuckwits! Been watching her since the siege started - man she's tough but I thought she was dead for sure. Them fucking animals were going to rip her to pieces.

Immersion 9: (ADVERTISEMENT) Hey guys. Is all the excitement in London tonight making you hungry? Click *here* for a 25% discount on Pizza Farm delivery.

Gracie: Fuck off I-9!

Dennis D: Any word on TFL getting cameras INSIDE Mr A's house? I don't want to miss what happens next. It's sexy time!!!

Jack Burton: @Dennis D - No! Everyone keeps asking but @TFLOfficial always come back with the same thing – 'we're exploring the possibilities' – blah blah blah.

Dennis D: @JackBurton @TFLOfficial – Get a tech in there to install cameras. How hard is that? Wait till Mr A goes to the New River and get it done in 20mins tops. Have you seen how fast those guys work when they have to? These techs are fucking wizards.

Gracie: I want cameras in there! I pay £100 a month and the customer is always right.

Jack Burton: Tonight's developments will only increase demand. Mr and Mrs Apocalypse! Lol. @TFLOfficial – well? We're waiting?

CHAPTER 11

What was he supposed to do? Was he supposed to offer her something? A drink or a bite to eat? Wasn't that how it was done back in the day? But there wasn't much to give besides water. They did put teabags and coffee sachets in the supply parcels, but he'd never cared much for those kinds of drinks as a teenager and had never bothered with the kettle, which he'd discovered some time ago was broken.

There was some food in the house but he was hesitant to offer her anything like that. It was a big ask. Every morsel in the kitchen was precious and more so now considering the lack of refrigeration. He simply didn't have the food to spare, at least not for someone he knew so little about.

Maybe she'd take a multivitamin pill? They always put a lot of those in the supply parcels and there were too many of them lying around the house. But was that enough in terms of hospitality? Would that be considered rude?

What was he supposed to do?

"Can I get you something?" he asked. Barboza was sitting on the edge of the leather couch in the living room. Her fingers moved restlessly on the arm of the couch, as if she was trying to scratch something off that wasn't there. Walker figured a part of her was still back there on Langham Road, fighting off the savages. It was understandable. That had been her life for the past two days with little respite.

He was standing at the doorway, awkward and as uncomfortable as he'd ever been in the house.

"Water please," Barboza said. "Just a glass of water would be great. Thank you."

He nodded, thankful that she hadn't asked for food.

In the kitchen he poured two glasses of cold water. He thought about bringing some biscuits into the living room and then decided against it. If she asked for food then he'd provide it; otherwise he'd show the bare minimum hospitality. She was probably more interested in getting her breath back anyway – at least that's what he told himself.

Walker returned to the living room. He handed her one of the glasses and she drank it down greedily, like someone who'd just walked out of the desert.

"Sorry it's not colder," he said. "No ice. My fridge-freezer isn't working. But I've been trying to find one in the neighbourhood here. Not that I really want to go looking in any of them but that's the current project anyway, you know?"

The words felt clumsy. They stumbled out of his mouth like a drunk leaving the bar at closing time. In comparison his thoughts were so fluid, but he found that articulating them into speech – to anyone other than Alba – was harder than he could remember.

"It's fine," she said. "Sit down please."

He liked her accent. The vowels came out long and slow.

Seet down pleeeeze.

"You're from Brazil?" he asked, sitting down in the armchair.

She nodded. "From Curitiba. You know it?"

He shook his head.

"It's in the southern part of Brazil. I come here to study. But you know that. I said so in my letter, yes?"

"I can't remember everything," Walker said truthfully.

She looked longingly into her empty glass. Walker got up and refilled it in the kitchen and then brought it back to her.

"Obrigado," she said. "*Thanks.*"

He sat down in the armchair. "What are those things you were fighting? I mean, I know they're people but how did they get like that? It's so fucked up. Wanting to eat other people?"

"They're rogues," she said. "Most people call them rogues."

"Rogues?"

"Yeah. They drifted away from the pack. Scavengers."

"The pack?" he said. "What's that?"

She frowned. "You don't know?"

Walker shrugged.

"You know – like people working together. They do better in a pack than being alone."

"Like a rat-king," he mumbled to himself.

"What?"

"Nothing," Walker said. "So they're cannibals? You're talking about cannibals?"

Barboza nodded. "Strength in numbers," she said. "I guess they don't like the supply parcels, huh? Not when there's food in the streets."

Walker grimaced.

"I don't know," she said, staring into the glass. "Somewhere along the way they figured out that it's more satisfying to hunt their own food instead."

"Are they mad?" Walker asked.

Barboza shook her head. "No," she said. "Only the rogues are mad if that's the right word. But these other people are more dangerous than that. I'm talking about intelligent people trying to survive in difficult times. People you'd never expect to be doing that sort of thing. They might say we're the ones who're mad for living off the scraps from the outside."

"Are there a lot of packs?" he asked.

"I don't know," she said. "They live in smaller communities but then join forces sometimes, once or twice a year for a big hunt in the city. You don't want to be out on the streets when that happens. Although staying in isn't enough sometimes either."

Walker took a sip of water. He'd done the right thing by staying put – by avoiding the rest of the city. No doubt about that.

"I saw one of them yesterday," he said. "A rogue I mean – by the New River. He was wearing a suit just like the one outside your house tonight."

"What happened?" Barboza said.

"He jumped me," Walker said. "I had to kill him."

Barboza smiled. "Good job," she said. "So that's what happened to number five. The motherfucker."

"Aye."

She drank slowly from her second glass of water.

"Anyway you've read my story," she said. "What's yours? And how come you know so little about what's going on out there in London?"

Walker winced. Alba never asked him this many questions, even when he imagined that she could speak like another human being.

"2020," he said. "Is that right? Is that what year it is?"

"For sure," she said. "I count every single day in a journal. I put a tiny little ink notch on the paper for each day. You know – like you see prisoners do on the wall of their cells in the movies. It's the first thing I do in the morning. It's a one-year journal from 2011 but I've managed to make it last for nine years by doing it that way. I even know the exact date, I think."

Walker listened in fascination. "What is it?" he asked.

She smiled. "It's the 7th July," she said. "And today is a Tuesday."

"Tuesday," he said. It had been a long time since he'd put a name to any of the long days and nights. And yet still, it was somehow good to know.

"So what's your story?" Barboza said. "Or are you deliberately avoiding the question?" She ran a hand through her jet-black hair. It was gleaming with sweat in the candlelight.

"I exist," Walker said. "That's about all there is to tell."

Barboza looked at him. She rolled her eyes, unsatisfied with the response.

"Have you been here since Piccadilly?" she said.

Walker gave her a curt nod.

"You didn't try and make a run for it?"

"I came here first," Walker said. "To look for my parents."

She nodded and then put her glass on the floor. "How old were you?"

"Sixteen."

"And did you find them? Your parents?"

He hesitated. "They were gone."

"But where were you?" Barboza asked.

Walker took another sip of water. "I was at Piccadilly."

Barboza's jaw dropped. "You were there? September 2011?"

He nodded.

"You know I've never seen the M25," he said. "And I only live about ten miles below it. When it happened in 2011, I heard people talking about an emergency barrier going up around London. Rumours, I thought. Something to contain the violence temporarily – to keep it in check. I doubt everybody tried to get out of London because they thought it was only going to be a short-term thing. It'd be gone in a week once everything had calmed down – that's what they were saying I bet. That's what my parents were probably thinking. That's why I don't think they went north after it happened. I think they came looking for me because they knew where I was. They must have been worried sick."

Barboza leaned forward. "You saw it happen? Chester George?"

"I had front row seats," Walker said.

Her eyes were wide with excitement. "Who killed him? Was it the government?"

"It was one person, acting alone."

At that moment, Alba walked into the living room. The little white cat stopped in the middle of the floor, sat down and gave Barboza the hard stare.

Walker smiled. "You're sitting in her spot."

Barboza shifted along the couch. "I'm sorry kitty," she said, tapping the edge of the leather armrest. "You wanna come up?"

Alba just sat there, ignoring her. She looked at Barboza for another ten seconds before swaggering back out of the living room. Walker heard the light tapping of her footsteps on the stairs, the gentle rhythmic thud, and knew that he'd find her asleep on his bed later.

"She's your cat?" Barboza asked.

"I'm *her* human," Walker said.

"You were saying? About Chester George. It was one person that killed him?"

"Aye," Walker said. "It was."

"I'd like to know who it was," Barboza said. "Is that okay?"

Walker sighed.

"He was waiting on the memorial fountain," he said. "You remember? That was where Chester George gave his final speech. As soon as Chester George started talking about Phase Three – and that's what everyone was waiting to hear – that's when the killer ran up the stairs and shot him, once in the head."

"Who?" Barboza asked. "Who was it?"

"Doesn't matter," Walker said. "It wasn't the government. And it wasn't anybody from the other side, Sadie Hobbs, all that lot. Chester George was killed by a nobody."

"You knew him?" Barboza said. "The killer?"

Walker nodded, feeling ashamed at the connection. This was the first time he'd ever spoken about it, although it was always there – a whisper at the back of his mind, taunting him.

"They called him Hatchet," he said. "He was the friend of a guy that I'd just met. I was new to London in 2011."

Barboza gasped softly. "So this Hatchet was a friend of yours?"

Walker shook his head. "I wouldn't go that far," he said. "We hung around together for a few days. There were four of us. He didn't like me and I didn't like him, and that's putting it mildly. Guess my instincts were right in the end, eh? This mess, everything. It's down to that motherfucker. There's rarely a day goes by when I don't wish a slow and painful death upon him, wherever he is."

"Yeah," Barboza said. "Hey. Did you know that there are people in London who think that Chester George is alive? They walk the streets of the city looking for him. They're convinced that he's alive and hiding out somewhere. They think he's the only one who can save them from all this – that by initiating Phase Three he can change things. Bring down the superwalls and start the revolution all over again."

Walker shook his head. "I saw his head explode," he said.

Barboza fell back into the soft leather couch.

"You wouldn't recognise the city now," she said. "South London is the worst of it. God. Most people call it The Hole. You've got murder, rape, cannibalism and all kinds of things going on down there. I'm talking about a real post-apocalyptic wasteland man – everything burned to shit."

"What about the rest of the city?" Walker said.

"There are four zones," she said. "The Hole is the South. The East and West are smaller, not really important and there are less people, but the North is the safest place to be. I don't know - I suppose there are only two zones that matter. North and South. You did the right thing by staying here Walker. At least up here they've got someone who keeps all the gangs under control."

Walker sat forward, sliding towards the edge of his seat. "Up here?"

Barboza nodded. "Michael King. He was a friend of Chester George back in 2011."

Walker almost smiled. It had been a long time since he'd heard that name. He remembered a tall, wiry black man speaking eloquently on television and defending the rioters of 2011. Most of all, he recalled seeing Michael King at Piccadilly that day – before and after the killing of Chester George. He couldn't have been more than twenty-one back then.

"Where is he?" Walker asked.

"His organisation is based out of Liverpool Street Station," Barboza said. "Close to the river. That way they can deal with the raids that come out of The Hole. You get all sorts of shit man – rogues crossing the river, sometimes try to swarm into the north. Sometimes the gangs try their luck breaking into northern territory. There's constant tension between North and South London. Don't get me wrong, Michael King and the gangs aren't perfect by a long shot, but they're a lot better than the filth that crawls out of The Hole."

Walker stood up and went over to the window. Pulling the curtains back an inch, he peered outside onto the darkness of Stanmore Road. His meagre existence living alone on the streets of North London seemed smaller now. Much smaller.

"It's sick," he said, looking north. "Why don't they just send a cloud of poisonous gas over the city? Put us out of our misery?"

Barboza shrugged. "Beats me Walker."

Walker kept his eyes on the street. Waiting for something.

"You know Hatchet tried to kill me," Walker said. "Right after he killed Chester George. He probably knew that I'd seen him do it. It didn't matter – he hated me anyway and why not get me out of the way at the same time? Who'd notice another dead teenager with all the shit that was going on that day?"

He let go of the curtain, turned around and looked at Barboza.

"He held the gun to my face," Walker said. "It was almost touching me. He was smiling because he knew that I was about to die."

"Jesus," Barboza said.

"He pulled the trigger," Walker said. "But the gun was empty. He must have shot his way off the fountain and lost track of how many bullets he'd used up. It was Michael King who ran over and jumped Hatchet after that. I saw them crashing to the ground together. Fighting. And that was the last I saw of either one of them.

There were so many people going crazy. So much noise, you wouldn't believe it if you weren't there. I had to get out of there. It took me a couple of days before I got back to North London, but eventually I came here. And I've never left since."

Walker closed his eyes.

"You should get some sleep," he said to Barboza.

"Yeah," she said. "That's a good idea."

He walked over to the door. "I'll make up the spare bed. Everything's clean. I keep the sheets sealed up in a bag, you know?"

Barboza's eyes were already closing and she might have missed that last part. Still, she managed a brief smile before pushing herself up off the couch. She walked towards him, offering her outstretched hand.

"Obrigado Walker," she said. "Thank you for saving my life."

CHAPTER 12

Walker slept with both eyes open that night.

He could hear her in the house. She kept getting up and moving about – in *his* house. It was the sound of another person's footsteps downstairs. Jesus Christ, it was unnerving. She must have been dehydrated because he heard her running the tap in the kitchen at least ten times. She didn't hold back with the water either – he could hear it gushing out and it felt like the house was vibrating under the pressure.

Walker lay on top of the sheets, his skin soaked with perspiration. Another hot night and yet Alba was curled into a ball, sleeping soundly at the bottom of the bed like she always did.

He thought about getting up. Talk to her – was that the right thing to do? No, he thought. It was probably best to back off and give her some space. She needed time to process the last couple of days and all the crazy shit that happened to her. And to appreciate the fact that she was still alive – if being alive was still something to be appreciated.

After some time, he heard Barboza coming back upstairs. Her footsteps came creeping along the hallway and as they did so, his hands reached for the kitchen knife that he kept on the bedside table. But she continued to walk quietly past his door. The floorboards creaked. The bedroom door opened and closed again and he could hear her climbing into bed.

Walker breathed a sigh of relief. But he kept the knife close and went back to staring at the ceiling.

He dozed on and off until sunrise. Mostly off. Eventually he got up and did some push-ups on the bedroom floor, hoping that the exercise would rejuvenate him a little. Then he went into the bathroom and washed his face and body, and brushed his teeth. After getting dressed in a pair of jeans and black t-shirt, he crept downstairs towards the front door, stopping into the kitchen for some water.

While he was in there, he checked the apples from the last supply drop and noticed hints of brown mould on the skin of the fruit.

"Shit," he said.

He had to get a fridge sorted. It was getting so hot both inside and outside that the fruit was bound to go off sooner. And it wasn't just the apples that were the problem. The wafer thin meat slices were beginning to reek a little.

"Damn it."

He took one of the sickly looking apples into the front garden. Walking down the path, he sat on the kerb and lifted his face towards the morning sun. Another clear blue sky. Another hot one. How long had it been since the last rainfall?

He chewed nonchalantly on the apple, which tasted faintly of chemicals.

No wonder people are eating one another.

He heard movement behind him from the house. A moment later, Barboza opened the front door and he listened as her footsteps – the same footsteps he'd spent most of the night listening to – came walking down the garden path towards where he sat on the kerb.

"Good morning Walker," she said.

"Morning," Walker said, turning around.

He almost gasped out loud.

Barboza was wearing a fresh white vest top, like the one she'd worn yesterday. But to Walker's surprise, only her underwear was covering her modesty from the waist down. He could feel his eyes being pulled towards her body like a magnet. It had been so long since he'd been around a woman of any sorts, let alone such an attractive one who went around half-naked. And she was impressive too – her brown thighs were thick and solid, and her calves muscular. She had the legs of a professional athlete, and he recalled reading something about martial arts in her letter.

"Is everything okay?" he asked, turning quickly back towards the street.

"It's all good," she said. "I was a little restless last night."

Barboza laughed.

"Can you believe it – I even thought about going back to my house at one point," she said. "I wanted to find those rogue bastards. What do you think? Between the two of us we could wipe the floor with them, no? That's what they deserve."

Walker shook his head. "I'd just as soon never see them again."

"Well I hope I see them," she said. "I want *them* to know what it feels like to be hunted for a change. Those chickenshit bastards."

Walker put the apple down on the pavement, half-eaten.

"That's what you were doing last night?" he said. "Plotting revenge against the rogues?"

"I was just thinking," she said. "About everything you were telling me too – about Piccadilly and the murder of Chester George. About this Hatchet guy."

She sat down beside him on the kerb. They were so close that their bodies were almost touching. Walker sat up straight. Was it just his imagination or was she flirting with him? Maybe she was just lonely. Maybe he was thinking too much.

"Can I get you something to eat?" he said quickly. "There's not much but I could make you a passable sandwich. There are a couple of ready meals in there too. The microwave is old but it works."

He looked at the apple on the pavement and shoved it away with the flat of his shoe. It rolled slowly towards the middle of the road before coming to a gradual stop.

"Don't eat the fruit," he said. "It's minging."

She turned towards him and smiled. Her brown eyes were soft. Her teeth were in good shape too – pearl white, small and perfectly straight. She'd obviously taken care of herself in the past nine years.

Walker felt himself blushing and looked away.

"Take anything you want," he said. "From the kitchen I mean. Help yourself."

"Obrigado Walker," she said. "But I'm not hungry yet. I'm still thirsty though – can't seem to quench my thirst."

"Yeah I heard you last night. You sounded thirsty."

"I'm sorry Walker," Barboza said. "I didn't mean to disturb you."

He shook his head. "It's too hot to sleep anyway."

"You're from Scotland?" she said. "Aren't you?"

He felt Barboza edging closer to him on the kerb.

Walker kept his focus on the street and on the houses opposite. "What gave it away?" he said. "Was it my pale blue skin?"

She laughed and slapped him gently on the knee. He almost yelped.

"It was your accent dummy," she said. "I knew some Scottish people at university." Barboza sighed and closed her eyes, as if remembering the past. Revisiting old faces and places – Walker had done the same thing many times.

"I always liked Scottish people," Barboza said. "But I never got the chance to go there. It was always on my list you know?"

"There's some history between the two nations of Scotland and Brazil," Walker said. "Football history at least. You know, the English are always quick to claim they invented football and that they spread it worldwide and all that. But it was us – the Scots who took the game to Brazil. A man called Thomas Donohoe, a Glaswegian, organised the first football game in Rio in 1894. And then Charlie Miller, whose dad was a Scot, came along and he organised a team and set up the first football league in Brazil. So there you go, you learn something new every day."

Barboza raised her eyebrows. "Didn't know that."

"I memorised it," Walker said. "When I moved to England in 2011, I was going to wipe the floor with all the English kids who said otherwise. That was bound to win me some friends in the playground, eh?"

She laughed again.

Walker felt dizzy, as if he'd just waken up in a strange room after being drugged by rhinoceros tranquilisers. She was sitting too close. He hadn't been this close to another person in a long time. She might as well have been smothering him with a pillow.

"Well I'd better crack on," he said, getting to his feet. "Things to do, eh?"

"Things to do?" she said, looking up at him. She was shielding her eyes from the sun with her hand. "What is there to do in the world anymore? Have you got a job waiting somewhere?"

"Sort of," Walker said. He pointed to the houses on the other side of the street that he'd been looking at. "I need to find me a fridge. And then if I manage to do that, I've got to get it back to my house."

"Haven't you looked in these houses already?" Barboza said. "In nine years?"

"Some of them," Walker said. He didn't want to tell her that about his overwhelming fear of going anywhere near these houses. She wouldn't be flirting with him if she knew about that. "Didn't like what I found."

He saw a flicker of uncertainty in her eyes. "What do you mean?"

"A tomb for starters."

"Where?"

Walker nodded in the direction of the house with the dead family inside. "Mum, Dad and the two kids," he said.

Barboza turned around and looked at the house-shaped tomb.

"Oh God," she said. "That's terrible."

"Aye," Walker said, looking at her – a bronze statue basking in the sunlight.

Whirr-click.

Walker took a step onto the road. He looked up towards the sky, at the sleeping streetlights, and the trees that lined Stanmore Road in odd intervals on both sides.

"Did you hear that?" he said.

Barboza glanced back and forth between Walker and the tomb. "What?" she said. "What did you say?"

"You don't hear it?"

"Hear what?" she said.

Walker stepped back onto the kerb.

"You didn't hear that noise second ago?"

She shrugged her shoulders, as if to apologise.

"I hear it all the time," he said. "It's like machinery or something, but up there somewhere. It's nothing natural, like the wind or the birds singing. Damn it, I swear it's real."

Barboza looked up towards the sky, searching for the source of whatever he was trying to describe. But she didn't say anything and it was clear by the blank look on her face that she had no idea what he was talking about.

Walker didn't press the matter further.

"Hey maybe I can help you today?" Barboza said. "What do you say Walker? Let me help you find a fridge for your kitchen. It's the least I can do after what you did for me last night. Let me return the favour, no?"

"You're not too tired?" Walker asked.

She shook her head. Then with a smile, she pointed at the piece of discarded fruit that Walker had left lying in the middle of the road. The discoloured section of the apple that he'd bitten into was festering under the sun like a gangrenous wound.

"It's not sleep that I need," Barboza said. "I don't like the taste of rotten apples any more than you do."

CHAPTER 13

KNIFE BUCKET FRENZY GOES GLOBAL!

EntertainmentNewz.Com – Top Stories, July 8th 2020

By Stephanie Chambers

Jinkees Velma! Who on Earth could have predicted that? TFL's little brother show *Calling London!* has only gone and started a global phenomenon. Just a few hours after last night's TFL broadcast, Georgia and Johnny's one-off stunt has turned out to be more contagious than an outbreak of Spanish Flu in 1918!

Okay. Maybe your head was buried under a rock last night? Maybe you woke up this morning, went browsing on your I-9 news feed and wondered what all the fuss was about? Well this is what's happening and here's why you should get on board. The world is working together to bring aid to hundreds of thousands of Londoners trapped behind the M25. Following last night's broadcast, people all over the world have been getting involved, mostly by posting videos of themselves or their loved ones doing the KBC on I-9.

What is the KBC? The challenge itself is not a pleasant one ladies and gentleman. First of all, participants have to pour a bucket of table knives over their heads. Ouch! Then they have to wolf down a piece of rotten fruit as quickly as possible without throwing up all over the floor. Throw up and you have to repeat! Once you've done that, post your clips onto your I-9 page using the hashtag #KBC, and don't forget to tell people to donate ten pounds (or the international equivalent) to London Aid.

Celebrities from the world of sports, music and movies have been joining in with the fun. Even the President of the United States has promised to post a video over the next couple of days on her I-9 page. If it keeps going like this, the KBC looks set to rival or even top its predecessor, the Ice Bucket Challenge, which raised millions of dollars for ALS back in 2011.

But there are always trolls, aren't there? Many KBC participants' videos have been bombarded with negative comments. These killjoys – who affiliate themselves with the long dead Chester George and his band of merry men – suggest (repeatedly!) that little of the money that is being raised will ever get past the M25, blah blah blah!

We've heard it all before chaps. Nobody's listening.

In fact, a group of UK students have already launched a campaign to stage 'The Biggest KBC Ever!' The aim here – according to their brand new I-9 page is to get as many students as possible – hundreds, preferably thousands – in one place and to perform the largest Knife Bucket Challenge in the world. Elsewhere people are doing the KBC on mountain summits, beaches, in the water, underwater, and there's even one scheduled at the North Pole later today. One thing's for sure – with campaigns such as these, not to mention oodles of celebrity participation, the Knife Bucket Challenge has literally become an overnight sensation. We don't know how long it's going to last but climb on board and get posting your vids – 'cos there are people in London who need your help.

UPDATE: *Still on the subject of TFL – an exciting announcement was made this morning on the official TFL website. Due to a heavy increase in popular demand, an attempt will be made to install* *cameras* INSIDE *the house of Mr Apocalypse at the first available opportunity. The website states that 'this difficult decision is deemed justifiable by the increased interest triggered by the recent arrival of a companion in the life of Mr Apocalypse.'*

Keep your eyes peeled for this brand new feature coming soon.

CHAPTER 14

Walker and Barboza stood in the middle of Stanmore Road. They were staring at the row of terraced houses on the other side of the street from Walker's house.

It was late morning and the heat was gruelling. Walker knew that it would be intolerable by mid-afternoon. If they were going to get this thing done then they had to do it quick.

Prior to coming out, they had both eaten a little bread, butter and sliced a few strips off the hard block of cheese that would have tasted much better had it been stored in a fridge. After drinking plenty of water, Barboza had gone upstairs and put on a pair of denim shorts and shoes.

Now they were ready to go fridge-hunting.

To Walker's surprise, Barboza seemed enthusiastic about their upcoming venture - about rifling through the houses that had creeped him out for nine years. Walker was impressed with Barboza's general resilience. She'd just gone through hell and she was showing no signs of any ill effects whatsoever. Even as they'd been eating breakfast, she was still talking about going after the rogues and getting her own back. Clearly her experiences in London had inoculated her against any form of post-traumatic stress disorder. And to think, he'd been out of action for an entire day after his battle with the rogue at the New River.

"You ready?" Barboza asked.

"Aye," Walker said. "Ready."

"So how do we get in?" she asked, pointing at the nearest house.

"Try the front door first," Walker said. "If it's locked, then we go around the back and break in through the window."

Whirr-click.

Walker glanced upwards but didn't say anything.

"It's just a thought," Barboza said. "But my kicks are pretty strong you know. I might be able to break the door down."

Walker smiled. "I get it. You're Supergirl."

She laughed. "Might save us some time rather than going around the back," she said. "No?"

"Let's do it my way," Walker said.

Barboza nodded. "Whatever you think," she said.

Walker led the way. They approached the nearest house and walked down a small path that was choking under the weight of yet another garden turned jungle. He tried the door handle. It was locked.

"Okay," he said. "Round the back it is."

"Let's do it," she said.

They walked down the street until they reached an intersection in Stanmore Road, where the row of terraced buildings came to an end. Then they climbed over the five-foot wooden fence that led them into the back garden of the first house. Both Barboza and Walker scaled the fence easily. They landed in something else that had once been a garden, now a stretch of long neglected grass, fenced off on both sides with a small wooden shed tucked away at the bottom.

"We'll start here," Walker said. "Work our way down the row. Cool?"

"Yeah sure," she said, eyeing up the house and backyard. "Jesus, look at this garden Walker. It's so sad, no? This was somebody's home once."

"I know," he said, walking over towards the back door. He tried the handle and it was locked. Then he searched the garden, looking for something to break into the house with. After searching near the fence, he found some rocks buried beneath the grass. It looked as if a small rockery had once existed there. Lucky for him.

He picked up one of the smaller rocks off the pile and walked back towards the house.

"Stay back," he said to Barboza.

Then he took a deep breath, stood back and hurled the rock through the window.

There was a crashing sound as the glass caved in. A faint ringing sound, like an echo lingered in the aftermath. Walker stood his ground throughout, even managing to grin at the large hole he'd busted in the window with one shot. He was getting good at this – at least the breaking in part if not the finding the fridge.

He reached an arm through the jagged gap in the glass and opened the window from the inside.

From there, the same frustrating pattern of events unfolded that Walker had encountered in his first search for a fridge. An empty house, the gut-churning smell of rotten food - and it was all for nothing. The first three houses that Walker and Barboza searched were of no use in their suburban quest. They all had a fridge but the interior remnants of the long-since abandoned appliance were a smorgasbord of rotten foodstuffs. They looked and smelled disgusting.

The first three fridges had also blown their fuses. Either that or they'd broken down in some other way.

In short, they were all disgusting and broken.

The third house was the final straw for Barboza. She ran outside ahead of Walker, stopping only at the bottom of the garden. Then she doubled over by the fence and threw up all over the grass.

Walker looked away.

"Oh Jesus Christ," Barboza said, in between large gulps of air. "*Filho da puta!*"

While Barboza recovered, Walker went back into the third house. He bypassed the kitchen and looked upstairs in the wardrobes and drawers for anything of any interest – clothes, shoes, tools, but there was little there that would have been much use to him. This house was particularly empty, as if everything had been stripped meticulously prior to evacuation. He did find a digital *Star Wars* clock in one bedroom and was surprised at how much pleasure and sadness this object brought to him. Sitting down on the bed, he wasted a few minutes trying to get it working, hoping that the clock might play the theme music from the film. He tried plugging it into one of the sockets but nothing happened – no flashing lights or music. His disappointment was profound.

With a sigh, he put the clock back where he found it. Then he went back downstairs to check on Barboza.

She was standing at the back door waiting for him. Her skin looked yellow and dry, like it was in the early stages of shrivelling up.

"You alright?" he said.

"Sure thing," Barboza said. "Sorry – I guess my stomach can only take so much of that fucking smell."

Walker nodded. "I'll do the next house on my own. You sit this one out."

Barboza shook her head. "No way man. I'm okay now."

"You sure?"

She nodded. "Let's do this."

They climbed over the fence and moved onto house number four. This was the house directly opposite Walker's home – the first one they'd tried before moving around to the back of the row of terraced houses.

Walker tried the back door and to his surprise, this one was unlocked. He turned to Barboza, who still looked a little green around the gills, and smiled.

"Why didn't *they* lock the doors?" Barboza asked.

Walker shrugged. "Maybe whoever lived here, they knew they weren't ever coming back. Who stops to the lock the door when you're running for your life?"

"Who did live here?" Barboza said. "Do you remember?"

"No."

Barboza took a tentative step towards the door. She was looking past Walker, as if she'd just arrived outside Count Dracula's castle – the special guest who'd just been delivered to the castle courtesy of a riderless carriage that had found her in the middle of a Transylvanian forest, full of distorted and twisted forest trees.

"What if someone's in there?" she said. "Maybe that's why it's unlocked."

Walker laughed softly. "I doubt it," he said. "I've lived here for nine years remember. You think I wouldn't have noticed somebody living directly across the street?"

Barboza sighed. "Fine. Let's just do it, huh? This is creepy, no?"

"How about a moment before we go in?" Walker asked.

She smiled. The colour returned to her face.

"I think my stomach would appreciate that."

Walker took his hand off the door handle and stepped back. While he waited for Barboza to get ready, he looked over the garden. There was a steel shed located near the bottom, surrounded by an abundance of wreckage – mostly old plant pots and plastic tubs. The pots were spewing out thick monstrous weeds but despite the ruin, Walker could envision that a well-tended garden had once lived here.

He turned around to check on his companion. Barboza was sitting on the doorstep, looking at him thoughtfully.

"Stanmore Road is your sanctuary," she said. "Isn't it? I mean, given everything else that's going on in this city – this life you have here, it's okay. No?"

Walker walked over to the back door.

"Sanctuary?" he said. "It feels more like a prison to me."

Barboza shook her head.

"Believe it or not Walker," she said. "You've got it pretty good here. You're alive at least."

Walker felt the heat pouring down onto his face. Considering that it had been an unusually hot summer, he wondered if they would start putting sunscreen in the supply parcels? God knows, with his white skin he could use it. Or was it more convenient if people in London died off with skin cancer? He thought about how hot it had been this summer and wondered what was going on with global warming and all the panic he recalled from the time before 2011. Was this heatwave a sign of things to come? Was the world already dying?

"Aye, I'm a real success story," he said, turning back to Barboza. "Some kids grow up wanting to travel to outer space. Some want to be a footballer. Not me, I got this – a half-life locked inside the walls of a high security city-prison."

Barboza smiled. She got to her feet and pinched her nostrils shut with her thumb and forefinger.

"Ready," she said.

Walker opened the back door and stepped inside the house. He braced himself for the inevitable smell, but when it didn't come he relaxed and grew concerned at the same time. The air inside the house was mouldy, but it was far from the horrors of what he'd been expecting and nothing like what he'd encountered in all of the other houses so far.

He moved further into the kitchen. To his left, there were several white oak cabinets sitting over a long granite countertop. The countertop was covered in a combination of dust and a small assortment of dead insects. Even so, it was still an attractive and compact kitchen with a modern cooker and besides that, the Holy Grail and the Golden Fleece all wrapped in one – a tall fridge freezer.

Walker smiled. He had a good feeling about this house. Maybe it was just the lack of a pungent odour but he allowed himself the luxury of thinking that he'd come to the end of the long and arduous road.

The fridge looked perfect. It might as well have been sitting in a retailer's showroom. There it was – a slim, stainless steel fridge-freezer, tucked in close beside the door that connected the hallway with the kitchen. At the end of the hallway, Walker saw the front door that they'd tried to open at the beginning of their adventure that day.

He walked towards the fridge, shorn of that sense of impending doom that had accompanied him in all the other kitchens.

He heard Barboza creeping into the house behind him.

"It smells not too bad in here," she said. "What does it mean?"

Walker kept his eyes on the prize. "I'm hoping it means that whoever lived here switched it off before they buggered off," he said. "That what we have here is a perfectly good working fridge-freezer, just waiting to be transported across the street into my kitchen."

"You think?" Barboza said.

Walker shook his fingers loose. Then he reached for the dust-splattered handle.

"Only one way to find out."

As he gripped the handle, he caught sight of a multi-socket adaptor lying on the kitchen counter. There were several plugs scattered around the adaptor – one that looked as if it was attached to a toaster. The other seemed to lead towards the kettle. But the one on the right, a long black lead – that seemed to be stretching up from behind the fridge. It was also unplugged.

Walker felt a surge of hope. With his other hand, he reached over and fixed the right hand plug into the socket. Then he switched on the adaptor at the wall and heard the greatest sound he'd ever heard in his life. A thudding noise, a jolt of something, quickly followed by a monotonous hum.

That hum was the miracle he'd been waiting for. The fridge was alive.

Walker tightened his grip upon the steel handle and pulled it open. The fridge lit up, revealing its contents or in this case its lack of contents. The shelves were empty and clean, as if they'd been scrubbed that same morning.

"It works," Barboza said. There was genuine excitement in her voice. "Congratulations Walker."

Walker put an arm inside the fridge. The cool air soothed his burning skin and if he could have, he would have climbed inside the fridge and shut the door.

He took his arm out and turned off the fridge at the main socket. Then he pulled out the plug. He was grinning and for the first time in a long time, there was even a hint of contentment in his heart.

"I'll take this one thank you very much," he said. "Now we just need to drag it across the street."

He turned around but Barboza wasn't there. For a moment, he thought she'd gone back into the garden, but then he heard something – a slight movement coming from somewhere inside the house.

"Barboza?" he said. "You in here?"

Why didn't you bring a knife?

"Yeah it's me," she called out.

Walker breathed a sigh of relief. He followed her voice into the hallway, towards a large living room area on the left. Barboza was in there, standing next to an antique wooden mantelpiece, which was holding up several framed photographs running from one end to the other.

Walker was impressed. It was a picturesque room with white walls. The antique mantelpiece was a perfect accompaniment to the overall theme of collectible furniture, the most notable of which was an old fashioned sofa made of oak, with a large padded cushion and arms. The floor was wooden and there were a variety of ornaments, such as ceramic vases and porcelain dolls, scattered throughout the room, on the window ledge and elsewhere. It was like something from another world – almost like walking into another century.

"Look at this," Barboza said.

She lifted one of the framed photos on the mantelpiece. In the picture, an elderly looking woman was squatting in the grass, surrounded by three young children. They were all smiling and the kids were laughing and it looked like a summer's day not unlike the day outside. Walker knew right away that the woman in the photograph was the owner of the house. Somehow it just felt right. He also recognised the steel shed at the bottom of the garden lurking in the background of the photograph.

The same woman appeared in several other photographs. In each one she was smiling that same beautiful smile, whether she was with grandchildren or other adults who might have been her children. There was a dog in the majority of photos too – a healthy looking border collie, and it was always there, a constant companion at the old lady's side.

Walker stood beside Barboza at the mantelpiece. He picked up a black and white photo, which featured a much younger version of the woman. The smile was instantly recognisable. In this one she had a handsome young man locked onto her arm. He was dressed in an RAF uniform and with his slick black hair and pencil thin moustache, he looked like he'd just stepped out of a World War Two movie. There was no sign of the man in the colour pictures. Walker wondered whether he had survived the war or if the woman had been forced to go on without him.

"This is a nice house," Barboza said. "I like it. You should move over here."

Walker put the photo back on the mantelpiece. "Aye," he said. "Might just do that."

"Maybe we should take a look around?" Barboza said. "I mean, there might be something else worth taking. What do you think?"

Walker shook his head. "I think the fridge will do me. Antiques are nice, but useless."

But Barboza was already walking towards the living room door. "Mind if I take a quick look anyway?" she said. "I'm curious."

Walker shrugged. He heard Barboza walking upstairs and then the sound of the floorboards creaking above him.

As Walker waited, he went over to the living room window,

which looked onto Stanmore Road. He saw his house – his *sanctuary* as Barboza had called it – directly opposite on the other side of the street. What a cold looking sanctuary it was. Strange to think he'd hidden in that little building for the last nine years of his life. And yet despite all those years, he felt like a stranger casting an eye upon the house for the first time.

His thoughts were interrupted by the sound of Barboza coming back downstairs.

"Look at this Walker," she said, coming into the living room. She sounded excited, like a kid showing off her favourite present on Christmas morning.

Walker turned around. Barboza was holding a vintage record player in her arms. It had the wooden base and most noticeably, the big horn that was most commonly associated with old gramophones. Walker had no idea whether it was a genuine antique or a replica but given the quality of the old woman's living room, he had a feeling it was probably the real deal.

Barboza was grinning from ear to ear, like she'd just found her heart's desire.

"I think it's real," Barboza said, as if reading his thoughts. "My parents had something like this when I was younger. We used to play records on it all the time."

She put it down on the floor and looked it over. After inspecting the needle, she checked the record that had been left on the turntable. Barboza lifted it up and then put it back down again, with the spindle of the machine going through the hole in the record. There was a brief cranking sound and then slowly, Barboza released the brake lever at the side. Then came the wonderful cracking sound of old vinyl, followed by the arrival of the music itself.

"It's 'The Lark Ascending'," Barboza said, as the music opened with a set of sustained chords from the string and wind section. "It's very famous. Very beautiful."

Walker was intrigued. God knows how long it had been since he'd heard the sound of music. He stared at the gramophone as a violin entered the piece, ascending at repeated intervals and flurrying with a series of nimble and elongated arpeggios.

Barboza sat down on the old fashioned sofa. She tilted her head back, closing her eyes.

"I like this old lady," she said. "She has style, no?"

Walker turned back towards the window. He looked at the house across the street and tried to recall his parents' faces. They were always fading in his mind and he wondered how much of the images that he conjured up in his mind were real and how much his imagination had fabricated. The details were darker, less clear than ever.

He only realised that his eyes were full of water when a single teardrop came rolling down his cheek. He slapped it away quickly.

Damn music.

He didn't want Barboza to see him like that. He glanced over his shoulder and fortunately she was still reclining on the sofa, her eyes closed, her mind absorbed in the music.

Walker hurried quietly out of the room.

He walked through the kitchen, out the back door and into the sun-drenched garden. The hot air clung to his skin. But he was still walking, running almost, and he didn't stop until he'd bounded through the tall weeds and was standing in front of the steel shed at the bottom of the garden.

Walker stood there, dazed and confused. He wasn't sure how he'd gotten there. It was as if he'd just caught himself sleepwalking and now he had to figure out where the hell he was. It was by sheer chance that he noticed the bolt on the shed door was unlatched. Then something pulled him closer, forcing him to reach for the bolt and pull the door open.

The smell hit him first, followed quickly by the fierce buzzing of the flies. And then he saw what was left of her. There was a pile of bones scattered on the hard floor, including a distinctive human skull positioned front and centre. Looking up, he saw where a scarf had been meticulously tied around one of the beams on the roof. But at some point her remains had fallen away from the knot. The flesh had long since been picked from the bones, but still the insects worked ceaselessly on whatever microscopic morsels might have remained.

Hatchet. You did this.

Walker's heart sank like a stone. Behind him, he heard the violin of the 'The Lark Ascending', its sweet melody soaring to the sky, oblivious of the horrors that inhabited the world below.

Then he saw something else on the floor of the shed close to the woman's remains. It was a large dog bed. It was also full of bones.

"Walker?"

Barboza was at the back door of the house. He heard her footsteps, walking down the garden towards him. Towards the shed.

"Are you okay?" she asked. "I opened my eyes and you..."

She stopped talking and covered her nose.

"Jesus," she said. "What's that smell?"

Walker stepped outside and pulled the shed door closed behind him. Then he bolted it. After that, he trudged through the long grass towards her.

"What is it?" Barboza asked. "What's that smell?"

"It's her," he said. "What's left of her. The dog too."

Barboza winced. "Oh no," she said. "That poor woman."

Walker gestured towards the door of the house. He wanted to go inside, or at least to get as far away from the shed as possible.

"C'mon," he said. "We'd better turn off that music."

Moving the fridge hadn't proved as problematic as Walker had feared. Fortunately, the front door of the old woman's house had unlocked from a catch on the inside and although there were many false starts, they'd managed to tilt the appliance at various angles and eventually ease it through the front entrance. Once it was outside, they took an end each and progress to their final destination was slow but steady.

It didn't matter – Walker had a fridge.

The early afternoon heat was brutal. Walker's t-shirt was soaked through and he knew he was going to have to force himself into a cold bath later. But at that moment, it didn't seem like such a bad thing.

When they were close to Walker's house, he asked Barboza to put her end of the fridge down. They stopped in the middle of the street and Walker turned back and took another look at the house they'd just come from.

It had been a victory. He had a fridge and yet how could he enjoy the moment after what he'd found in the garden shed?

"I wonder if they turned her away?" he said. "From the M25."

Barboza looked at him from the other end of the fridge.

"What? You say something Walker?"

"Was she too late?" Walker said. "Had the first barrier already gone up by the time she got there? Or did she even go at all? Maybe she chose to stay here and take her chances in her beautiful antique home."

"She didn't deserve to die like that," Barboza said, looking at the house. "And she seemed like a nice person, no? From the photographs I mean."

Walker turned back to the house. There was no way he could leave it at that. She had given him a fridge after all – a lifeline in this hellhole and what sort of person would he be if he didn't thank her for it?

"Walker?" Barboza said. "Are you okay?"

"I'll go back later," he said quietly. He was talking to himself. "I'll bury her in the garden. Her dog too."

CHAPTER 15

Transcript of a video uploaded to Immersion 9 - posted on *July 9th 2020*

The broadcast begins with 'Death or Glory' by The Clash. The song is playing over a montage of bloody and brutal clips showing the violent aftermath of the 2011 event known only as 'Piccadilly'. It was on this day that Chester George was murdered in cold blood on the Shaftesbury Memorial Fountain. It was on this day that the streets of London descended into the worst widespread violence that any major city has ever seen in living memory.

Then silence. A black screen.

Moments later, the lights go up.

The people are sitting in a dark room, staring back at the camera. They are all disguised in the same manner – one that is instantly recognisable to those who can recall the last days of the old London before the superwalls. The black skull hoodie zipped all the way over the head, the luminous yellow and ghostly face leering back at the camera – it is the look made famous by Chester George.

The silence lingers.

The masked figure in the middle begins to talk and it is a woman's voice. The voice is well spoken, but cold and detached. Almost metallic.

'It has been nine years since our last broadcast. As we all know, that broadcast – the last ever made by Chester George – was interrupted by a single gunshot. After that, the founder of the Good and Honest Citizens lay dead on the Shaftesbury Memorial Fountain and the promise of Phase Three and a better world was in ruins.

Nine years have passed.

We have returned, better late than never.

Our first duty upon returning is to warn you – the people of the United Kingdom and beyond. You are being fooled and if you already know this then you are as guilty as the ones doing the fooling. Why? Because you have done nothing to fix the problem. People equipped with a social conscience – a rarity in this day and age – have been telling you for years that the money you donate to charity – hundreds of thousands, *millions* of pounds – will never make it past the atrocity that is called the M25. This is the truth and there is a very good reason behind it. Not only do Rudyard Campbell and his goons at SKAM Media want to keep people behind those walls forever, but they also want their prisoners to suffer and to remain as uncomfortable as possible.

Why?

Because otherwise it's boring.

Some of you are beginning to listen, to *hear*, to wake up and recognise the truth. Some of you do nothing but others have declared a willingness to fight. This willingness to fight is of grave concern to the people who *do* receive the bulk of London's charity money – namely Rudyard Campbell and his friend Aileen Ure, the Prime Minister.

So how have they responded to these rising concerns? How have they managed to distract you from making further enquiries?

They call it the Knife Bucket Challenge.

The speaker pauses.

'Here is the great smokescreen of our times. People all over the world are taking part in the Knife Bucket Challenge. Your favourite movie star is doing it. Your favourite rock star is doing it. And let's not forget all those talentless Z-list celebrities that you love so much. I even hear that a group of British students are currently organising hundreds of people into attempting the largest Knife Bucket Challenge in the world. And they want to do it in sight of the M25 – as if the walls were nothing more than a pretty backdrop to this viral circus.

Yet it continues. And no matter how much money it raises, it will do nothing to alleviate the suffering of those trapped within the remains of London.

The work that we began in 2011 is not over. Phase Three is still a reality.

The first order of business is to bring down the M25. This will not be easy but The Good and Honest Citizens pledge to free the people of London – many of who are the original Good and Honest Citizens, who have been conveniently out of action since 2011.

To Rudyard Campbell and Aileen Ure, I say this – you built your walls, you turned your backs on the people and created the world's most twisted television show.

You've had your fun. Now you will pay.

End of message.

CHAPTER 16

Drop Day couldn't come fast enough.

Despite the addition of a new fridge in Walker's kitchen, the majority of supplies from the previous drop had succumbed to the heat quickly. The bread was now peppered with nasty looking green dots. The crusts were so feeble that it was impossible to make a sandwich without every slice collapsing in his fingers.

The fruit was beyond redemption. The flesh of the red apples had at first turned brown before metamorphosing into a ghoulish shade of dark green. The ready meals – usually a flimsy looking carton of fish and salad dishes, or potatoes and vegetables, were more liquid than solid. And these had to be shared between Walker and Barboza, leaving neither one of them satisfied. Barboza had continued to insist that she wasn't hungry and tried to pass more food onto Walker, but by the look in her eyes, he could see that she was every bit as famished as he was. Despite her stubbornness, he insisted on equal rations as they sat through the long countdown to Drop Day.

Four days had passed in between the acquisition of the fridge and Drop Day. Walker and Barboza had spent that time getting to know each other a little better. They'd sat out in the front garden or on the street, chatting lazily under the hot sun and trying not to expend too much energy. She'd helped him with various little routines around the house. One of these was the periodical necessity of taking the rubbish bags down to the skip. As he'd always done, Walker had a habit of collecting the rubbish into old plastic bin bags and stashing them in the garden shed until three or four bags were piled up. Then, to avoid attracting too many insects and God knows what else, he'd put them in the wheelbarrow and taken them down to a skip, which was located not too far from the New River. Once there, he'd empty the bags into the metal skip and bring them back for reuse.

Barboza accompanied him to the skip this time. It was during this trip that he realised he was beginning to enjoy her company. He wasn't sure whether it was a safety in numbers thing or if he had taken to her unique personality, which for the most part was fearless and full of bravado. Those past four days, she'd continued to badger him about looking for the rogues that had held her hostage. All of them. Walker had learned that it was best not to say anything during these verbal outbursts – he had no intention of rogue hunting and he wanted Barboza to know it.

When she wasn't obsessing about revenge, Barboza was busy entertaining herself with the vintage record player that she'd taken from the old lady's house across the street. At Walker's insistence, she played the music – mostly classical – at low volume so it wouldn't attract unwanted attention and because music had a way of tapping at Walker's memory like a crow's beak. It was making him think too much, opening doors that he didn't want to look inside.

Barboza had also tried to teach Walker a little capoeira. They'd stood in the middle of the street, while she demonstrated kicks with exotic sounding names such as meia lua de frente and martelo de negative. But the moves required a level of flexibility that Walker simply didn't possess. Barboza however, moved with the grace of a dancer, showing off a variety of techniques that demonstrated her impressive agility. For Walker, it was like watching someone in a martial arts movie. But when he tried to get his leg up to perform even the most basic of manoeuvres, it often ended with him falling onto his backside in the middle of the street.

"Nice try Walker," she'd said, laughing into the back of her hand.

"Hey," he said, feeling the hot road on his backside. "Who needs this when you've got a butcher's knife in your hand, right?"

But physical exercise was kept to a minimum. Walker held back with his regular push-ups too, as there wasn't enough food to sustain their need for fuel. Generally they stayed as inactive as possible from one day to the next, like two snakes waiting out the long winter.

Then Drop Day came at last

It was a warm morning as they travelled towards the New River to pick up their supplies. Walker pushed the wheelbarrow and Barboza walked behind him. She was wearing a blue sleeveless t-shirt and a fresh pair of denim shorts. It surprised Walker to see how many different t-shirts and other items of clothing that Barboza had in her collection – he wondered if she'd collected these over the last nine years on her travels across London.

For his part, Walker didn't care much for clothes. He wore a black t-shirt and a pair of jeans – the same thing he always seemed to have on these days. These were the clothes that his father had worn and thank God he'd grown up to be a similar size and shape as Archie Walker.

They'd heard the helicopters buzzing around London early that morning. That meant the supply parcels had been delivered along the New River and Walker wanted to get there and back as quickly as possible. Despite everything else that had happened, he hadn't forgotten about the rogue attack on the last Drop Day. And there was always the real possibility that Barboza's rogues might still be in the area. To make him feel a little better, Walker had tossed a kitchen knife into the wheelbarrow. If something happened this time, he'd be ready.

They took Walker's familiar route to the New River – cutting through Ducketts Common and out onto Hampden Road, walking past the abandoned houses, the church and the hair salon. Further down, they crossed the intersection with Wightman Road, passing alongside the impressive mosque on their right. Then they approached the fence. Behind that was the grassy hill that led down to the river.

Walker dropped the wheelbarrow at the fence. Then he took the knife out of the tray and clutched it tightly to his chest, as if making a silent pact with the weapon that they would stand by each other no matter what. As he did this, Barboza was already climbing the fence, hauling her legs over and dropping down onto grassy slope.

Walker passed the knife to her though a gap in the steel bars. Then he climbed the fence and landed on the grass. She handed him the kitchen knife and they walked rapidly down towards the river path.

Walker kept his eyes open for signs of anything unusual.

"I hope those bastards show up," Barboza growled, keeping pace with Walker's hurried stride. "It's with great pleasure that I'm going to drown them one by one in the river. No police here, right? No such thing as murder in the new London."

Walker didn't want to talk about it. Truth was he didn't want to talk at all. What he really wanted to do was pick up the parcel, be it one or two, and get away from the river, unharmed and in one piece. Drop Day was no longer what it had been. It felt like he was walking in a different place since the attack last week. There was an underlying sense of danger, something unwelcoming about the New River now. There were other people on the scene. Barboza had been coming there for months. The rogues were there too. It was no longer his place.

"How far along do you usually go?" Walker asked.

"Not far," Barboza said. "I come here super early. Sometimes even before the helicopter."

"Aye," Walker said. "You've been taking the first parcel. No wonder I've been walking so far along this bloody path lately. I must have been picking up the second parcel all along."

"Aye," Barboza said, teasing him.

Walker managed a smile. "You know something?" he said. "I've heard some terrible impressions in my time. But that was actually – the worst ever."

It was about a five-minute walk to the first parcel. It had been dropped safely at the far edge of the winding path that ran alongside the river. Upon seeing it, Walker grabbed it, hurried back to the wheelbarrow and dropped it there. He insisted that Barboza came back with him to the fence, although she had wanted to stay on the path and wait for him to return.

Now Walker and Barboza were back where they started. They stood with their backs to the fence, looking along the river path. From somewhere nearby, Walker heard the familiar *whirr* and *click*. But he didn't say anything.

"We need that second parcel," Barboza said. It was as if she sensed his desire to go back.

Walker squeezed the knife handle. He knew that the extra food rations would be crucial but damn it, he just wanted to call it a day and go home. Get a successful Drop Day under his belt and then he wouldn't be so jittery next time. But of course Barboza was right – two parcels were better than one. There was no getting around that. They might even be comfortable for a little while if they could get that second parcel, if not quite swimming in luxury.

"Let's get it over with," Walker said.

"Vamos," Barboza said.

They left the wheelbarrow with the first parcel inside. Then they made their way back down towards the river path. With each step, Walker felt increasingly nervous. He could see nothing up ahead and there was no noise to indicate that anything was out of the ordinary. All he could hear was the gentle flow of the river and the occasional burst of bird song. If he hadn't been so anxious, Walker might have been able to enjoy the surroundings. Nature seemed so benign sometimes, but there was always the threat of something terrible lurking around the corner.

Whirr-click.

"Can you see the parcel yet?" Barboza asked.

"No," he said, looking up at the trees. "Keep an eye on the other side of the river too."

"Relax Walker," she said. "You're making me nervous."

Walker paid no attention to her. Instead, he held the knife out, his arm extended and ready for the rogues. They travelled further along the river path. The blue sky reflected off the water surface, transforming the New River into an endless sheet of icy mirror glass. The leaves on the trees were bright green and sometimes yellow, basking in mid-summer bloom. Occasionally a perching bird would leap off the rattling branches, and it sounded like cannon fire in Walker's head.

They approached a gradual turn that veered to the right. Out of nowhere, Walker heard Paul McCartney's voice in his head singing 'The Long and Winding Road'. And so it was. None of this terrain was familiar. Walker realised that this was the furthest he'd been from Stanmore Road since 2011. His eyes went back and forth, looking for a hint of something comfortable. He saw a row of wooden fences on both sides of the river, beyond which he could see the roofs of houses in the distance. But he didn't know them. He didn't know where they were.

He stopped walking all of a sudden.

Barboza slowed down and turned back to him. "Are you alright?" she said.

Walker shrugged. "I don't know."

"Do you want to keep going?" she said.

"Something's not right," Walker said. "I feel like we're wading into deep water. It's all wrong."

She touched him gently on the arm.

"Just a little longer, okay?" she said. "We need that parcel Walker – if it's here. And screw those rogue bastards – if we find them, we kill them. Right?"

Walker nodded. How could she be so nonchalant about killing? It had to be all the things she'd seen on her journey from one end of the city to the other. It had hardened her. Toughened her up in a way that Walker – who'd been hiding out for the past nine years and who'd just killed a man one week ago – couldn't imagine.

"Okay," he said, sounding less than convinced.

They followed the path as it veered towards the right. Walker lapsed into a daydream. He thought of Alba and how much he wanted to get back to her. Back to Stanmore Road. He heard Barboza's classical music playing in his head, showing him faces that he'd forgotten from the past. Walker didn't need anything outside the boundaries of his neighbourhood. It was all there – from Stanmore Road to the New River. That was his life, his universe. But how could it ever be the same again? With Barboza, the rogues, and whatever else was drifting north invading his territory.

His thoughts wandered from the path, away from the parcel and the rogues.

Then Barboza screamed. Walker snapped out of his daydream and returned to the New River in a heartbeat.

There was a tiger on the riverbank, no more than a few feet away.

When Barboza screamed, the big cat jumped and turned towards them. Its lithe, muscular body twitched slightly and then froze like a statue. It held them in his eyes, casting a spell of enchantment that rendered them unable to move.

Walker couldn't believe what he was seeing. This was a tiger. A real fucking tiger. He'd been so wary of running into other people, into the rogues, that this sort of threat hadn't even entered his mind. How could it have? Once again, the New River had got the better of him.

The tiger's yellowy-gold eyes never left Walker and Barboza. It was creeping towards them now, or at least it appeared to be.

Walker felt his body trembling. He looked quickly at the fence to their right. If they could reach it, they could jump over and it would lead them into a residential area. They could come back for the wheelbarrow and the parcel. But there was no time to run. It was too much of a risk to even move – it was at least twenty feet to the fence. And if they ran, which they'd have to do to in order to stand a chance – the creature would be on them, or at least one of them, before they'd cleared the fence.

Barboza spat out a few words, repeating them over and over again like a demented mantra.

"Jump. Jump in the river. Jump."

Her voice sounded different, like it was somebody else talking. Probably she was just as shit scared as he was.

"Jump in the river," she said. "Walker?"

"No," Walker hissed. He kept his eyes on the silent monster in front of them. "Tigers can swim," he said. "If it follows us into the river then we're fucked. It's not even that deep anyway. It'll probably slow us down more than him."

"Oh Christ Walker."

The tiger crept forward. Its ears were pinned back against its head and unless Walker was mistaken, it looked pissed off. As the two human invaders had done nothing to suggest that they were a threat, it grew bolder. Now it was stalking them, edging its way forwards as if through some unseen tall grass in the jungle. Walker had seen Alba do the same thing in the long grass of the neighbourhood gardens on multiple occasions – stalking birds and getting ready to pounce. Getting ready to kill. But this big cat, unlike Alba, had the power to crush human bones in its jaws.

The tiger leapt at Barboza.

Walker acted out of pure instinct. He didn't think, he just did. As the tiger sprang at Barboza he shoved her off the edge and sent her crashing down into the water. She didn't even have time to scream.

The tiger came down and its claws raked into the flesh on Walker's arm. Walker howled in pain and instinctively brought his other hand up, slamming the knife down upon the tiger's back with every ounce of strength he could muster. The blow didn't land clean, but he felt the blade cut through the hard muscle. This was confirmed when the tiger roared in pain.

Walker hurried backwards, creating space between himself and the tiger. *Distance, distance, distance.* As he did so, he showed the tip of the knife to the creature. The top half of the blade was now covered in blood – the purest red that Walker had ever seen. The tiger, perhaps sensing its own vulnerability backed off a little. There was no longer a meal standing in front of it, but rather a threat had emerged from the thing on two legs. The tiger's ears were down and it continued to display its sharp upper canines, two massive daggers growing out of its mouth, pointing at Walker.

The golden eyes of the beast shone in rage. Walker knew that he had to stand tall and from somewhere deep down, he felt an unexpected surge of strength. It was the same sort of feeling he'd experienced when charging at the rogues outside Barboza's house. He was winning. He had hurt the tiger worse that it had hurt him. There would be no running – he would stand his ground or die. This was *his* river after all. No more rogues and no more fucking tigers allowed.

"Jump Walker!"

Barboza's voice came floating up from the water. But there was only the tiger and the knife in Walker's hand. These were the things that mattered. He kept his blade raised, ready to anticipate every move that the creature might use to get past the knife. He took a step forward, knowing that he could die at any moment. But somehow he knew – he was getting the better of this creature. He could see it. He could feel it. He was the one with the upper hand.

Walker came forward, increasing the pace and holding his arms out to make himself look big. The tiger went backwards.

Walker jabbed viciously at the creature with the weapon – the tiger didn't like that and both blinked and snarled with each thrust of the blade. Those yellow eyes seemed to curse Walker's courage and it was both a terrible and wonderful sight to behold, such a magnificent creature shrinking before him, hovering on the brink of defeat.

Walker chose that moment to halt his advance. It was time to let the tiger back off to a safe distance, which it did. It continued its retreat back along the river path at a steady pace. Staring and growling. Moments later, it sent one last snarl Walker's way and then turned and took off, trotting down river path, following the bend to the right until it was out of sight.

Walker watched the tiger go. He stood rigid, with his knife arm pointing outward like a signpost. He didn't dare blink. Gradually, he became aware of a sharp pain eating into his left arm. His heart was thudding in his chest and a gallon of sweat was dripping down his face. It felt like the adrenaline was wearing off quickly.

"Walker!" Barboza yelled. Her voice was shrill. "Are you there?"

Slowly, he lowered the knife. The tiger was gone, at least for now. With his entire body shaking like a leaf, he staggered over to the edge of the river and looked down. Barboza was standing in the water, which went up to her shoulders. She was looking up at him and her face lit up with relief when she saw him.

"Filho da puta!" she yelled. "Are you okay?"

"It's gone," he said, barely getting the words out.

Barboza trudged through the shallow water to the edge of the river. She reached her arm up towards him on the path.

"Help me up Walker," she said. "Please."

Walker got onto his belly and reached down for her with his good arm. He pulled her up out of the water and she dropped down onto the warm concrete path beside him. Barboza was breathing frantically, but Walker was eerily still.

She put her arms around him and squeezed tightly. "Thank you," she said.

"Ouch!" Walker said, feeling a hot stinging sensation in his arm.

She let go of him.

"Give me your arm," she said, looking at his wound.

Walker reluctantly raised his sore arm and Barboza took a closer look. He forced himself to take a quick glance at the damage. The fabric of the t-shirt above the wound had been torn to shreds, but there was only one laceration in the skin. It was long but it wasn't deep. Nonetheless, it stung like a bitch.

Barboza was looking at him. Her eyes were peculiar, almost

unrecognisable. They were pleading and apologetic. He got the feeling that she was trying to say something to him, something profound that went beyond words.

"I'm sorry," she said. "I'm so sorry Walker."

Walker shook his head. "What do you mean?"

Barboza hesitated. She appeared to be on the brink of saying something, but then stopped.

"I don't know," she said. "I don't know what I'm saying. I meant – sorry for hurting your arm just there."

"Am I dreaming?" Walker said, looking back at her. "Or did we just see a tiger roaming around north London like it was the middle of the fucking jungle."

Barboza pushed a clump of damp hair away from her face. "From the zoos," she said. "They come from the zoos."

Walker sat down on the path, exposing his wound to the great fiery orb in the sky.

"You mean they escaped?" he said.

"More likely they were let out," she said. "Don't you think?"

"I suppose," he said. "But what do I know?"

Walker noticed that Barboza was staring at him again. Not just looking, but staring. It was uncomfortable to say the least. She seemed unaware of it but there it was, that same intense look in her eyes. Like two brown lasers penetrating his soul.

"You saved my life Walker," she said. "That's the second time you've done that."

CHAPTER 17

Immersion 9 – Live Chat Rooms

Hot Topics - #MrApocalypse #Barboza #TigerAttack #StudentKBC

Keanu: That was seriously fucking badass!! My man Apocalypse – he just squared up to a tiger!

Miesha P: Knew there was something special about that guy. Class act. Disappointed with Barboza's reaction tho. Thought she was this tough chick the way she's always talking about getting revenge on the rogues – u see her face when she saw that tiger? That bitch nearly shat out the kitchen sink!

The Iceman: @MieshaP - To be fair, it was a TIGER!!!

Miesha P: @TheIceman - She's a bitch coward!

Keanu: Great start to the day's entertainment tho. Fuck it I'm pulling a sickie at work and staying home to watch the #studentKBC at the M25. Anyone else?

The Iceman: I'm there brother!

Miesha P: Yeah I'm watching at work lol! Choosing split screen so I can keep watching Mr A/Barboza and the students making tits of themselves for charity. Mr A looks like he's in pain. Arm still bleeding. Wonder how bad?

Keanu: Barboza looks worse – not hurt but fucked up in the head. Guess running into a tiger will do that.

The Iceman: Here come the students! I was supposed to be there at the M25 with some of my mates from uni. Not happening tho. My folks are visiting from Manchester this week and I had to bail. Typical fucking shit luck! Could have had my name in the book of world records with this lot. Will watch 'em online tho. Should be a giggle.

Miesha P: Don't forget to donate...lol!

CHAPTER 18

Walker pushed the wheelbarrow down Hampden Road. His mind raced back to the wheelbarrow races he used to take part in on school sports days. Two teammates – one playing the role of driver and the other as the wheelbarrow – racing down the football pitch accompanied by the ecstatic cheers of all the mums and dads standing on the sidelines. He recalled those sports days and how there was this one guy – Stephen Laing – who used to always win everything every year.

Lanky, athletic Stephen Laing. The smug little prick.

It went on for years – Laing winning everything – until one day little Mack Walker, who'd always come a close second, beat Laing in everything – the one hundred metres, the egg and spoon race, the sack race. He was on fire that year. In fact, he was well on his way to being crowned the school sports champion when the heavens opened and the rain came falling down in buckets. Everyone but Mack Walker had run for shelter. Just a few events left to go and school sports day was promptly cancelled.

He never did get his hands on that trophy.

But look – look how useful all that training in the wheelbarrow race had turned out to be. Look how fast I'm going now.

Walker almost laughed out loud. The things you think about when you've been attacked by a tiger.

The pain in his arm had subsided. Three red lines ran along the length of his forearm but they weren't deep. The wound would make for an interesting scar if nothing else. He got lucky – his arm should have been hanging off in shreds.

Whirr-click.

Barboza kept up with Walker as he led them back through the empty streets of Tottenham. He alternated frequently between walking briskly and all-out running. He had to be ready for anything. The tiger might have followed them home, unwilling to give up on its lunch, or the rogues could have been lying in wait for them somewhere.

The streets might have been empty but they were still full of danger.

A terrible silence had swept across the neighbourhood. Neither one of them had said a word since leaving the New River. The only thing Walker could hear apart from the constant whirring and clicking was the sound of their heavy breathing. Even the birds had stopped singing, or so it seemed. The day's normal rhythms had stopped to let them pass.

Whirr-click.

Finally they returned to Stanmore Road. Walker saw the house – his sanctuary – and pushed the wheelbarrow towards it but as he staggered forward, he wobbled from side to side like a drunk trying to walk in a straight line. His legs had turned to jelly and he was forced to stop in the middle of the road. As he paused, he let go of the wheelbarrow with the wheel still turning. The wheelbarrow ran away from him, driverless, before tipping over and landing on the hot concrete with a solid thud.

Walker dropped to his knees. He buried his face in his hands, which were damp with sweat.

Whirr-click.

He heard Barboza's footsteps running up behind him. He felt her hand on his shoulder.

"Walker?" she said. "What is it? Is it your arm?"

Walker removed his hands from his face. He looked up at her. She was at that moment, a giant blur standing over him with the burning sun at her shoulder.

"Don't you hear it?" Walker said.

"What?" she asked.

"I can't get away from it. Here, down by the river – I'm hearing it in the house too. You can't hear that noise?"

Barboza didn't answer.

"It's me, isn't?" Walker said. "This thing. I keep thinking it's a tumour or something. That it's some weird form of tinnitus – is that even the right word? What do you call it when you're hearing things all the time? I don't know – I never got a chance to learn this stuff. I was only sixteen for Christ's sake. I don't know anything about tinnitus or if it's you know, some kind of mental illness. This is all I know – living in this street, or not living in this street. I don't know."

Barboza's voice was trembling. "Walker we need to go into the house now okay?" she said. "We need to clean your arm."

"But you don't hear it?" he said.

She tightened her grip on his shoulder.

"Get up Walker," Barboza said. "That's an order. Get up. Let's go into the house, put the supplies in the fridge and let me clean that wound. Can you do that for me?"

Despite the sun pressing down on him, Walker managed to climb back to his feet. He took a couple of steps towards the wheelbarrow. It lay toppled over on its side and the brown parcel with its crucial life-giving contents had slipped onto the road. But Walker ignored the wheelbarrow and the parcel and walked towards the house. He unlocked the door and went into the living room. It was cooler there. Inside, he sat down in the leather armchair and closed his eyes.

Whirr-click.

God forbid his parents were still alive in this hellhole. Living amongst the packs, rogues, and escaped zoo predators – it didn't bear thinking about and they were better off dead. Their faces were disappearing further from his mind's eye. He didn't even have any photos of them lying around the house to remember them by. Back in 2011, the Walker family had travelled down to London by car and to save room, a large chunk of their personal belongings had remained behind in Edinburgh, to be transported down later. All that later stuff had included the photo albums, the ones with the old pictures of his parents with their dodgy hairstyles getting married in Edinburgh back in the early 1980s. They still existed somewhere, but here in London there was nothing left of them. He had their wardrobes to remind him of what clothes they'd worn and only the faintest trace of their odour – a whiff of perfume, skin cream or aftershave – remained on their clothing.

Unless he was imagining that too.

He heard Barboza at the front door. She walked into the house and her soft footsteps went towards the kitchen. For the next few minutes, Walker listened to her as she opened up the supply parcel and put the most urgent items into the fridge-freezer, which now stood awkwardly in the middle of the kitchen.

Then she appeared at the living room door. Her hair, which had been soaking wet after her fall into the New River, was now bone dry and she had tied it back into a ponytail.

"Walker?" she said. "Maybe we should clean your wound, no?"

Walker looked at his arm. At that moment, he couldn't have cared less about what happened – let it get infected, turn green and fall off at the elbow. One less part of him for the cannibals and tigers of London to eat.

"It's just a couple of scratches," he said.

She walked over to the chair. Leaning down, she ran a finger over the wound and nodded gently, which suggested to Walker that she agreed with his evaluation that the cuts weren't going to be a problem.

"You're not crazy Walker," she said, still looking at his arm. "About the noises I mean. Whatever else you do you've got to stop thinking like that. Okay?"

Walker shook his head.

"I've been hearing that shit for months," he said. "Thinking it might have been something real. And then you came along and told me there's nothing there. Game over. Fuck it, I lose."

Barboza wiped a tear from her eye.

"Christ Barboza," Walker snapped. "What are you getting so emotional about? You've crawled through the shit out there and survived. You're the tough one – the one who wants to go after the rogues and crack their heads open. I've just been hiding out here like a coward for nine years, avoiding everything and look at us – you're the one that's crying and I'm the one who doesn't feel a fucking thing. Maybe that's one of the advantages of going nuts. Not giving a fuck."

Walker got to his feet. He was about to walk out of the room when Barboza leapt to her feet and grabbed his shirt. She pulled his head towards her face. He felt her hot, dry lips pressing down upon his mouth. Biting softly, pulling at his flesh – she was frantic and tasted like a gust of hot fire.

Walker didn't know what to do. Some part of him wanted to surrender to her advances. God knows, he was overdue some human affection. Why not just give in? What did he have to lose by letting go?

But it was Barboza who pulled away.

"Fuck," she said, walking away from him, towards the couch. "I can't do this Walker! I can't do it anymore."

Walker felt a sudden burst of rage spilling over inside him. He was embarrassed and furious and God knows what else was bubbling up in there. He stormed across the room and slammed Barboza's back up against the wall. Her body thudded against the hard surface and Walker kept her there by seizing both her arms. Walker was still aroused, but this arousal was giving way to something else. Anger. Hatred. Something worse than that. Not specifically aimed at

Barboza but at everything that had gone wrong in his life. She just happened to be there – a manifestation of London itself.

As he pinned her up against the wall, Barboza looked at him. There was a silent acceptance in her eyes, as if whatever he was about to do was justified.

"What the fuck is going on here?" he yelled. "One minute you're the toughest bitch in town, then you're crying, and then you're horny? What the fuck?"

He let go of her arms. Barboza slid down the wall, doubled over and buried her face in her hands.

"I can't do this," she said, sobbing into her hands.

Walker noticed her eyes looking up, wandering across the room – to the wall, to the ceiling. Looking for something.

"I quit," Barboza said. "I won't do it anymore."

Walker took a backwards step away from her. He heard it now, crystal clear. It was something obvious that he'd missed during the initial shock of seeing her fall apart.

The Brazilian accent was gone.

Barboza climbed slowly back to her feet. She was still staring up at the ceiling and the walls. It was as if she was convinced that someone was hiding up there, living in between the cracks. Walker noticed it and felt sick to his stomach.

"What happened to your accent?" Walker said.

Her eyes came back to him. She shook her head.

"You saved my life Walker," she said. "For real this time. And I can't keep lying to you like this. I can't."

Walker backed away further. "What the hell's going on here?"

Barboza's eyes were tired and sore.

"You're a good man Walker," she said. He couldn't believe it – she was speaking in an English accent. It wasn't quite a London accent by the sounds of it, but it was most definitely not a Brazilian accent. Not even close. "You were just a job you know?" she said. "And this – you and me – it was all manufactured to entertain millions of people who we don't even know. It's a lie, and I can't do that to you. Not now that I've been here. Now that I've seen it for myself."

"What the fuck?" Walker said. "What is this?"

"My name is Sharon," she said. Her voice was calm. Her eyes were bright and clear. Walker sensed that she'd just relieved herself of a heavy burden. "I'm an actress," she said. "And yeah, I'm English. I've never been to Brazil in my life. I'm so sorry Walker."

Walker couldn't speak. The questions were stuck in the back of his throat, like cars on a gridlocked motorway.

"Listen to me," she said, taking a step towards him. "Of course I can hear the same noises as you. You're not crazy Walker. It's real – everything that you've been hearing is real. They're cameras. They're everywhere in this city. Millions of 'em. You're on television mate. I'm sorry. You've been on television every minute of every day for the past six months."

CHAPTER 19

TFL ANNOUNCEMENT

Mr Apocalypse is currently unavailable.

We apologise for this break in service and will resume scheduled programming as soon as possible.

In the meantime, please choose another option from the Home Menu.

Thank you for watching The Future of London.

CHAPTER 20

Immersion 9 – Live Chat Room
Hot Topics - #MrApocalypse #Barboza

Sally Cinnamon: Get the fuck outta here!!

Emperor X: An actress? Did I hear that right?

Sally Cinnamon: C'mon, Mr Apocalypse is down? Tagging ***TFL***. Technical glitches are non-existent these days. You've just given us access inside the house and now you're taking it away? Let us watch! Don't fuck about! WTF did we just hear?

Look Skywalker: Talk 2 us ***TFL***

Emperor X: ***TFL*** – is she fake? Makes sense those eh? I was wondering why the cameras had never picked Barboza up before the rogues laid siege to her house. They said it's because she rarely left the house, took secret routes to the New River, travelled at weird times and the producers/viewers didn't notice – it's all bullshit! She was never there. She's fake!

The Big Tasty Grill: (SPONSORED) Hey guys. While

you're waiting for Mr Apocalypse to return, why not treat yourself to a bucket of delicious fried chicken from The Big Tasty Grill. Click *here* for an incredible one-off 80% discount AND free delivery on orders made within the next hour.

Look Skywalker: Answer the question ***TFL***!

Sally Cinammon: 80% discount?

TFL Official: Thank you for your interest in TFL. We regret that Mr Apocalypse is unavailable for the time being. To answer your question, we believe Barboza's reference to an actress was metaphorical. Please be assured we are dealing with an emergency situation at the site now. More information to follow.

Look Skywalker: Bullshit!

Emperor X: Not buying it! C'mon ***TFL***. We need more than that.

Sally Cinnamon: Chicken bucket ordered. I know it's still morning but fuck it, eh? What can you do? That's breakfast, lunch and dinner sorted! Going to sit back in the meantime and watch the students drop knives over their heads at the M25. And ***TFL*** – when that's over Mr A had better be back on.

CHAPTER 21

TFL: Calling London! – The Knife Bucket Challenge Special

July 12th 2020

The SKAM Heli-Cam flies at approximately eight thousand feet over the northern tip of the vast green belt that surrounds London. The green belt – a wide ring of countryside – was originally designed as a policy to prevent the spread of urbanisation and to maintain an area of agriculture, forestry and openness. In other words, to keep the city at bay.

It is a warm summer's morning as the Heli-Cam flies over this picturesque rural landscape. There isn't a cloud in the sky and the giant mechanical bird flies without a hint of turbulence, moving closer to the two towering walls of the M25 in the distance.

At this point, the camera cuts to the interior of the helicopter. Television presenter Johnny Castle, dressed in a V-neck Gucci sweater and jeans, is sitting in the back directly behind the pilot, clutching a microphone in one hand.

JOHNNY CASTLE: (*Shouting to camera*) Hello everyone and welcome to this very special edition of *Calling London!* Today, courtesy of Britain's finest students, we're bringing you the largest Knife Bucket Challenge in the world – you will not see a bigger KBC anywhere else guaranteed! Not only that, but this challenge will be performed *inside* the M25, the first time anything like this has taken place behind the superwalls since they were first built in 2011. Now let's go to Georgia – she's already down there at the M25. Georgia, can you hear me?

The camera cuts to Georgia Perkins on the ground. As she waves to the helicopter flying overhead, she is surrounded by hundreds of young people. They greet the camera with an assortment of smiles and silly faces. All of this takes place amidst a carnival-esque background. There are brightly coloured banners. Flags. Painted faces. Loud rock music can be heard somewhere in the background.

Behind Georgia, the massive outer wall of the M25 is clearly visible. It is a towering concrete presence and one that looks utterly impenetrable in the morning light. As if the wall itself wasn't enough of a deterrent, a large military presence is on stand-by on the outskirts of both the inner and outer walls. A huge swinging gate, which has been built into the base of the outer wall, can also be seen. There are several of these entrance points on both walls, which serve the purpose of allowing maintenance and military vehicles to pass through as they travel to and from the city. Several armoured vehicles are making their way through the gates at that moment. Cushioned in between, are several busloads of people, all of them waving enthusiastically in every available direction.

GEORGIA PERKINS: I hear you Johnny! Hello everyone and welcome to the M25. Over one thousand students from a variety of universities and colleges across the United Kingdom have put their institutional rivalries aside and will come together this morning to make history. And as Johnny said, this remarkable event will be performed a few feet in front of the inner wall of the M25. In other words, this historic event is going to happen *inside* London.

The crowd goes wild with excitement. Several people are blowing whistles and trumpets in the background.

GEORGIA PERKINS: Now just before we continue, I want to address the current situation with Mr Apocalypse. Unfortunately that service *is* still down for the time being. The people upstairs have told us that there's an emergency situation going on in the neighbourhood and that this has caused a technical glitch, which in turn has forced TFL to turn off the cameras for safety reasons. We'll let you know more about this when we can but don't worry – it's being dealt with.

The camera cuts back to Johnny Castle in the Heli-Cam.

JOHNNY CASTLE: Now forget all about Mr Apocalypse, yeah? You lot are about to see something very special – something that you've never seen before. You're about to see history in the making.

CHAPTER 22

Walker looked at Barboza. He'd been less frightened back at the river, staring into the yellowy-gold eyes of the suburban tiger, than he was now. There had been nothing hidden underneath the surface of that primal encounter – it had been man versus beast. Simple. An age-old battle of different species. And when it was over it was over.

But this was different. Now he was standing on the edge of a dark crevasse – looking down into the unknown. And Barboza's words were the hands that would push him over that edge, tumbling into the deep fracture in the ice, towards his doom.

But he had to hear them.

"You better start talking," he said to Barboza.

Barboza hung her head. She walked past him and sat down on the couch. There was an eerie calmness about the young woman now, far removed from the raw emotion that had been on display just moments earlier. Now she was little more than a mannequin speaking in quiet voice.

"What do you want to know?" she said.

"Everything," he said.

She shook her head. "Everything? Are you sure about that

Walker? Because this is your last chance to live in blissful ignorance. If I go now, that'll be the end of it. Just forget what you heard and go back to living your life. There's still time."

"Everything," Walker said.

Barboza sat up straight, almost formally, as if a job interview was getting underway.

"Okay then," she said. "My name is Sharon Freeman. I come from Leeds originally, but I moved to Birmingham in 2015 to pursue my acting career. This – what I'm doing here – is a job. I was put here for several reasons but the most important thing was to get into your house."

Walker tried to comprehend what he was hearing. But he felt lightheaded. He could see tiny white spots drifting aimlessly around in his field of vision. He wasn't sure whether it was all the physical activity that morning or Barboza's words alone that had triggered it.

Whatever it was, he decided to sit down on the armchair. As he looked across the room, he shielded his eyes from the sunlight pouring in through the window.

"What about the letter?" he said. "What about the rogues outside your house?"

Barboza was looking at the floor.

"They were actors too," she said. She spoke in a dispassionate voice, like someone reading out the TV listings in a magazine.

"Oh Christ," Walker said. He pictured himself walking across Langham Road in a pair of his mother's high heels. "What about the one I killed at the river last week?" he said. "Was that an...?"

Barboza shook her head quickly.

"Actor?" she said. "No. That was the real deal. Why do you think they dressed the one outside my house like they did? They got the idea from your guy. Maybe they hoped that seeing the actor dressed in that way would convince you to help me because of what happened to you. Empathy or something – I don't know. But no – you killed a rogue. A real one."

Walker gasped with relief. He'd still killed a man of course, but the thought that he'd stabbed a working actor to death instead of some crazy bastard who was trying to eat his flesh, that would have made things a lot worse.

"The letter was planted," Barboza said. "They dropped it here on the street so that you'd find it."

Walker thought back to that day. He recalled finding the family of corpses several houses down and then, just as he'd been on the brink of leaving that house, hearing the sound of a car engine coming from the road. Walker had convinced himself that he'd imagined that sound – that the dead bodies had messed with his mind and that it was just one more thing on his list of reasons for being crazy.

"There *was* a car that day," he said.

Barboza nodded.

Walker looked at her, sitting across from him. He wasn't sure what to think of her. He wasn't sure what to feel. Was he supposed to be angry? Was he supposed to hate her? If anything he was numb, in a dreamlike state where everything felt transient and without roots. It was only just dawning on him however, like a slow realisation, that she'd been deceiving him ever since they met. Since before they met. And yet here she was, spilling her guts, telling him all the forbidden truths that he was never supposed to find out. Whose side was she on? What chain of events had she set into motion with this sudden confession?

"You said they put you here to get into my house," Walker said. "Why? What's so important about getting in here?"

Barboza hesitated.

"Cameras," she said.

"Cameras?"

"Listen to me Walker," Barboza said. "This is what's going on. You're part of the biggest reality TV show that the world has ever seen," she said. "All of you – everyone who still lives in this shithole of a city is a member of the cast. It's called The Future of London. TFL for short."

Walker sat motionless. He felt a shrill, icy sensation seeping into his soul. Was this what they called awakening? Enlightenment?

Barboza edged forwards in her seat. "About seven or eight years ago they started planting millions of high-tech, hidden cameras throughout the city," she said. "Now they're everywhere. And they use these cameras to film you and all the people doing whatever it is you do in a city with no laws, no government, no police – no anything. The people who watch – they can't get enough of it. That's why they pay for it."

Walker sat back in the armchair, trying to process. "Go on," he whispered.

"Think of it as a social experiment," Barboza said. "At least that's how they justify it to themselves and to us. They also say it's a humanitarian thing – that they can use the cameras to find people and get them out. Surprise surprise, it hasn't happened yet. You don't hear many people talking about TFL's original bring them home premise anymore. It's entertainment and nothing else. We all know it and we're all responsible."

Barboza shook her head.

"There are cameras embedded in the streetlights, in the walls, in the trees, in the rocks, in the parks – they spent all those years filling up the city with electronic eyes. That's what the techs call the cameras – Eyes. I didn't know that until last week."

Walker looked her dead in the eyes. "So you put a camera in here?"

Barboza nodded. She pointed towards a section of the living room wall, where an empty picture hook hung on a sea of white paint.

"See that hook?" she said. "It's not the same picture hook that was here when I first moved in. I replaced it on the first night. Fortunately you're not the type of person who notices little details like that."

Walker stood up and went over to the wall. He leaned forward, staring hard at the mounted hook. At the top of the hook, front and centre, there was a screw looking back at him, like the eye of a Cyclops. It couldn't have been more than 3 millimetres in diameter.

"*That's* a camera?" Walker said.

"Sure is," she said. "The screw lens is one of the best ways to disguise it. They've got thousands and thousands of these scattered across the city. Pinhole spy cams – they use them too – but it's probably the screw lens that you're hearing out on the street. Only someone living in a quiet place like this would notice. I didn't know anything about it until I got the crash course on how to install the screw lens. It was like research for the part you know? Same thing with capoeira. Good job I was already flexible or I would never have got the part."

Walker was still looking at the picture hook. *That* tiny little thing?

"I'm sorry," Barboza said. "I had no idea what it was like in here. You're a good bloke Walker. You took that old woman's bones and buried them with her dog. That was a nice thing you did."

Walker glanced at the vintage record player on the floor.

"I can't do it anymore," Barboza said. "I can't just sit here and let you think you're crazy."

"And I thought you were just thirsty," Walker said. "The first night you stayed here I mean. But you were putting cameras up in my house, weren't you?"

Barboza nodded.

"How could I have been so stupid?" Walker said.

Barboza smiled at him, trying to send something positive his way. "No," she said. "It's not your fault. How could you have imagined they'd do something like this?"

"So nobody in London knows they're being filmed?" Walker said.

"I'm almost certain you're the first," she said.

"Incredible," Walker said.

"You're living in a contained apocalypse Walker," Barboza said. "You're entertainment. You're an experiment. The government and a big media corporation called SKAM control your life. You make for good TV and that's all there is to it. Ratings and money. *That's* why you have electricity inside the M25 – because the studio must be lit at all times. *That's* why helicopters and armoured vehicles bring maintenance crews into the city. It's not for your benefit – it's for them. You understand? They saw an opportunity in London's suffering."

"So they watch us?" Walker said. "They watch me? Doing nothing all day?"

"You'd be surprised what garbage people watch," Barboza said. "No offence. People will pay to watch nothing. Some people can't get enough of it. They've even given you a name to make you sound more exciting – Mr Apocalypse."

Walker almost laughed out loud.

"What?"

"They ran a competition on I-9 to name you," she said. "A little kid won. They paraded him around on TV and he gave you your name live on air – Mr Apocalypse. Because you live like you're the last man on Earth."

Walker looked again at the picture hook on the wall. "I-9?" he said.

"Social media," Barboza said.

"Like Facebook? Twitter?"

"Yeah," she said. "But I-9 gobbled up all the old websites. Rudyard Campbell owns them now – he owns SKAM TV too. Everything is on I-9 – news, family stuff, videos – everything like that."

Barboza pointed to her shoes, a pair of black casual ballet flats.

"Look at these things," she said. "Do they really look like the shoes of someone who's been living inside the M25 for nine years? I'm a walking billboard. I get extra money for wearing these."

"And what about the flirting?" Walker said, not even looking at the shoes.

Barboza looked away quickly.

"There's a big audience for you Mr Apocalypse," she said. "Somebody at TFL figured there'd be interest in a romance. So they invented Cristiane Barboza – the tough, exotic survivor chick.

Brazilian girl. Good thing my mum was Spanish, eh? Not much chance of me losing this role to some dumb blonde girl with big tits."

Walker didn't respond. He was looking at the picture hook again.

"And to think," Barboza said. "The casting people said I was perfect for the role. I picked up the capoeira moves fast. My accent was good. You're perfect for the role, they said. I bet they're not saying that now."

"Take the camera out," Walker said, nodding at the picture hook. "And any others that you put up – get them out too. Is there one in the bathroom? Has the entire world been watching me take a shit for the past week?"

Barboza's face wore a grim expression. She shifted uncomfortably in her seat.

"I can't do it," she said. "I can't take them out."

Walker glared across the room at her.

"You put them in," he said. "Take them out and then get the hell out of my house."

Barboza shook her head.

"It doesn't work like that Walker," she said. "Once the Eyes are activated they have to be switched off at the Control Station – that's in Birmingham. It's a way of protecting them from local interference. That is, if somebody in London does realise what they're looking at someday, then they're unable to disable it. It's insurance."

Walker turned back to the picture hook on the wall. He felt like his head was about to explode with all this new information. Not to mention the heat.

"Then I'll cover it up myself," he said. "Show me where they are and I'll cover them all up. Fuck them and fuck you Barboza. You're not driving me out of this house."

He started kicking at the screw lens camera with the flat of his shoe.

"Fuck you!" he said.

With each kick, the walls of the house shook a little. It was a satisfying outburst, but it was too hot and Walker could feel himself running out of steam. He was breathing hard and his skin sizzling with an incandescent rage. His leg was sore and tingling.

"We don't have time for this Walker," Barboza said. "We have to get out of here. Don't you understand? Now that you know everything you're no longer safe here. You're going to have to leave this house and never come back. Not if you want to stay alive."

"No," Walker said, ending another violent outburst against the wall. "This is *my* home. If my parents come back..."

"Your parents are dead!" Barboza yelled. "You know that."

"I don't know anything," he said, turning to face her. "You could be full of shit for all I know. What if you're lying to me – again? I don't know you. I don't know anything about you."

"You saved my life man," Barboza said. "Now I'm trying to save yours. Listen to me Walker – you're going to have to leave this house and everything in it."

Walker pointed back towards the picture hook. "Are they watching us now?" he asked.

"The people who run the show are," Barboza said. "The top brass. Not the public. They cut us off the moment I started talking."

Walker closed his eyes. *Wake up. Wake up now.*

"We have to go Walker," Barboza said. Her voice was trembling and urgent.

Walker opened his eyes. It wasn't a dream. He could still feel the stinging sensation in his left arm. Real pain. This was real life after all.

"I can't leave this place," he said. "This is my home. You said it yourself – it's my sanctuary."

Barboza took a step forward and grabbed him by the wrist. He was taken aback at the strength of her grip and didn't even try to pull away.

"I just told you the most twisted little secret in the world," she said. "That makes me a traitor. And you in here, knowing what you know, that makes you a very dangerous individual. They're coming for us Walker. If we stay here – we die."

CHAPTER 23

TFL: Calling London! - Knife Bucket Challenge Special

Two SKAM Heli-Cams are filming from above:

One thousand students have gathered approximately twenty feet ahead of the M25's inner wall.

The students – sitting in plastic chairs that run in fifty rows of twenty – are taking selfies and enjoying the ongoing festival-like atmosphere. There is laughter and nervous energy in abundance. Loud rock music is playing on a constant loop. All this in anticipation of the record-breaking challenge that's about to be broadcast live across the world.

Most of the participants are under twenty-five. They grin and wave at the passing cameras, gesturing to both the audience at home and their friends and family who are gathered on the other side of the wall, watching on a large projection screen – twenty-three metres by ten – that has been erected in front of the outer wall.

A small military presence accompanies the one thousand participants. They have taken up position about fifty metres from the Knife Bucket Challenge area near the inner wall. Two armoured fighting vehicles are also on site, but remain stationary in the meantime. These eight-wheeled machines look like the product of some monstrous union between a tank and a truck. Both of them are drenched in traditional camouflage colours of dark green and tan. There is a single-piece circular hatch cover at the top rear of both AFVs, with a circular ring mounted around the hatch for attaching a machine gun to. A ramp door, which lies at the rear, and which gives access to the troop compartment, is open.

A small group of about thirty soldiers stands guard close to the AFVs. So far they appear relaxed and unconcerned by what is going on around them. History tells them that there's little to worry about. It's been a long time since any of the London natives dared to venture this close to the M25.

Georgia Perkins, Johnny Castle, and a small number of TFL crew, have joined the one thousand participants and are standing in front of the cameras at the inner wall.

GEORGIA PERKINS: We are live inside the M25!

JOHNNY CASTLE: *Inside* the M25. Can you believe it? We're standing on the outskirts of North London – that's right, London! Nine years later and we're back in what was once the greatest city in the world.

GEORGIA PERKINS: Guess we're not in Kansas anymore Johnny.

JOHNNY CASTLE: Coming up – the biggest Knife Bucket Challenge the world has ever seen. Are you lot ready to break the Internet?

The crowd watching on the big screen let out a tremendous roar.

Behind Johnny and Georgia, the remaining students who are still standing take to their seats. One thousand plastic buckets have been placed behind one thousand chairs. The buckets are filled almost to the brim with steel table knives. One thousand paper plates are on site, located in front of every chair on the grass. The grisly remains of an apple, dark red and mouldy brown, linger on the plate.

Volunteers take their positions behind each seat and as they do they give the thumbs up to the officials, indicating that they're ready. The main duties of these volunteers are to tip the bucket of knives over the student's head and to make sure that they don't throw up at the end. Each volunteer standing in front of a participant has a gold flag and this will be raised only when the challenge is successfully completed.

GEORGIA PERKINS: Okay everyone! You have two minutes to complete your Knife Bucket Challenge. Are you ready?

JOHNNY CASTLE: Set!

Georgia blows the whistle and a high-pitched squeal cuts through the morning air.

Family and friends watch on the big screen as a thousand buckets are tipped over at once. There is a tremendous noise – an avalanche of steel crashing onto human skulls. The camera skips back and forth between students, most of them laughing as they rub their sore heads. Some of them raise their thumbs to the camera, maintaining their optimism as they brace themselves for the second stage of the challenge.

Then the first scream is heard.

It is a high-pitched, god-awful shriek that cuts through the broadcast like a samurai sword through rice paper.

It's Georgia Perkins.

Moments later, everyone is screaming, both the crowd and participants. The laughter of moments ago has in a matter of seconds, transformed into a terrible cacophony of altogether different human sounds – crying, shouting, wailing – a chorus of fear that renders everything else insignificant.

Finally the cameras catch up with what everyone else has already seen.

About twenty or thirty students in the middle of the KBC area have stood up off their seats. They're moving in a slow deliberate manner, as if to encircle the other participants. At the same time, they've lifted up their shirts to reveal explosive devices attached around their waists in the form of a belt. They continue to split up, to spread themselves around the gathering of students like a human barrier.

The other students are aghast, looking on helplessly with their mouths hanging open. Many are sobbing. One young student, a teenage boy of about eighteen, tries to get up out of his seat and is ordered to sit down immediately. He does and buries his face in his hands, hiding his tears from the world.

JOHNNY CASTLE: Oh my God! What the hell? Are we still on air? Georgia? They've got bombs attached to their bodies. Ladies and gentlemen, we appear to have a terrorist situation here at the M25. A number of students, perhaps twenty or more, are wearing what look like explosive belts. I repeat – explosive belts and oh God, look Georgia...

One of the bomb-carrying teenagers walks towards the television crew. He is black with a distinctive blond goatee hanging from his chin. He points towards the big screen that's still playing on the other side of the wall.

YOUNG MAN: Keep filming! Keep broadcasting. You cut us off and we're going to blow up everyone. We ain't kidding. This is not a prank – keep filming if you want these people to live.

GEORGIA PERKINS: Jesus Christ Johnny. I know that kid. He was in the audience that day – the one who laid into us remember? Oh Jesus Christ. What the fuck are we supposed to do? Somebody help us.

JOHNNY CASTLE: Look. Somebody's coming.

One of the soldiers is approaching the young man. An older man in his mid-to-late fifties, he signals to the soldiers standing around the AFVs to lower their weapons.

SOLDIER: What are you doing son? You don't want to kill anyone. C'mon – there's no need for this. Whatever you want to talk about we can talk about it. Take the belts off please and stand down. We can do this the easy way and nobody gets hurt. C'mon – what do you say?

The young man laughs. It is a cold sound and the soldier is visibly taken aback by this unexpected response.

YOUNG MAN: We *will* kill these people. Do not think for a second that just because we're young that you're dealing with idiots. We'll kill them, you, all your soldiers and ourselves. You're not in charge anymore, so drop your weapons and step away from those armoured vehicles. Do it now please.

The soldier looks beyond the inner wall, his eyes searching for a signal – for some much needed guidance from afar. But he can't make eye contact with anyone there and he daren't touch his radio to try and communicate.

SOLDIER: Okay, okay. You're in charge son. What is it that you want? You don't look like a mass murderer to me.

The teenager's face is calm. Serene. At first he ignores the question and walks past the soldier, moving towards the AFVs. Some of the others with explosives attached to their bodies follow at a close distance. As they walk, they keep their eyes open for any sudden manoeuvres from the military or anyone else.

The young man turns back to the soldier.

YOUNG MAN: We want your vehicles. Now please.

SOLDIER: The AFVs? What do you want them for? You don't even know how to drive them, let alone operate them.

YOUNG MAN: Do you really believe I'm that stupid? Do you really think we'd come all the way out here, go through all of this, and then ask for your vehicles if we didn't know how to drive them?

The soldier hesitates.

SOLDIER: What are you going to do? Talk to me son because I'm not sure I can just give you those AFVs. You understand?

YOUNG MAN: We are The Good and Honest Citizens. My friends and I are going to take your AFVs and go on a little trip into the city. You on the other hand, will be waiting here with my other friends. And if you try anything while we're away, these friends of mine will detonate their explosive belts. That will make you responsible for a lot of deaths on live television. Although I suspect the ratings will be phenomenal, don't you Mr Rudyard Campbell?

SOLDIER: What do you want to go into London for? It's a wasteland. It's full of dangerous people who'll only try to hurt you.

YOUNG MAN: There are dangerous people everywhere. But don't worry about us – we'll be quite safe in your AFVs. We deem it a risk worth taking. There are people in London who deserve to know the truth about their situation. People who deserve to know why no one is coming to get them out. Yeah?

SOLDIER: You don't want to do this son.

The young man walks towards the soldier. He looks at the military man in a calm and clinical manner. His eyes are blank. He looks like he's sizing up an insect crawling over the floor, unsure of whether to kill it or let it go. The soldier knows this look only too well. And he knows that there's no bargaining with the person standing in front of him.

YOUNG MAN: Don't call me son. Now move your men away from the two vehicles please. I won't ask again.

The youth points to the big screen beyond the inner wall.

YOUNG MAN: There are millions of people watching us now. All over the world. Tell your men to step aside or they will see something that will haunt their dreams for the rest of their lives.

The soldier looks at the young man for a second. Then he turns and nods to the small crowd of men behind him. They lower their weapons and follow their leader as they gradually step away from the AFVs. At the same time, about ten young people wearing explosive belts move towards the vehicles, all the while keeping one hand in their pockets on the trigger device. Another ten to fifteen people wearing explosive belts have remained in place at the KBC area, surrounding the students and television crew.

The youth with the blond goatee approaches one of the AFVs. He climbs up, entering the vehicle through the circular hatch as if he's done this a hundred times. He looks back at the soldier and smiles while at the same time flipping him the finger. Then he's gone. The others follow, filling up both the first and second vehicle in a hurry.

About a minute later, a thick growling sound comes from both the AFVs.

The vehicles roll away at a steady pace, falling into a single line. They travel slowly towards the abandoned motorway – the original M25. Not far from there, the road will turn onto the old M1 and this is the road that they will take – the road that will lead them south towards the heart of London.

CHAPTER 24

"Walker," Barboza said. "We need to go."

But Walker didn't respond. He wasn't prepared to listen to Barboza's pleas or to entertain the possibility of leaving home. The red mist had taken hold and all he wanted to do was to fuck something up bad – kind of like they'd done during the riots of 2011.

He'd already managed to kick the living room door off its hinges – perhaps he wasn't so bad at capoeira after all. And with one strike, he'd knocked the old TV off its perch and sent it crashing onto the floor, cracking the screen in the process. Goodbye forever. It should have been a satisfying conclusion, but Walker wasn't satisfied.

The wrecking spree was about to continue with the furniture when Walker stopped.

It was Alba. She had hopped onto the front window ledge from the outside. The little cat pushed her ears back in confusion as she looked inside. She knew that something was wrong with her human.

Walker felt ashamed. He was like a drunk in a jail cell who'd just sobered up and realised his wasteful crime. He'd always believed that it was his calm nature that had attracted Alba to him in the first place. He'd heard somewhere that cats were drawn to people who radiated calm energy. But look at him now – a crazy man, out of control and laying waste to the place they both considered home. He saw himself through her icy blue eyes and swiftly the red mist vanished.

He took a couple of steps back, falling into the armchair with a soft thud. A dull throbbing gnawed at his head, not to mention his hands and feet where he'd pounded on half the living room.

"Walker," Barboza said. "We need to go. Do you understand?"

Walker looked up at Barboza. He saw the fear in her dark eyes and her bottom lip might have been trembling. But instead of responding, Walker got to his feet and hurried past her. He went into the kitchen and pulled the main window next to the sink open about halfway. Then he returned to the living room, walking past Barboza again, and opened the front window where Alba was still waiting. Alba slid through the gap, raising her bushy white tail at the sight of her favourite person, who seemed back to his old self.

He ran a hand over her, gently gripping the soft fur on her back and holding it there. The sensation triggered a surge of emotion. He turned fully towards the window, making sure to keep his back to Barboza so that she wouldn't see the solitary tear running down his cheek.

"This is your house now," Walker said. "Go easy on the birds and the mice, eh?"

He buried his face in her warm, soft coat and felt the cat purring underneath him. Perhaps she was soothing him, telling him that everything would be okay. Then Alba turned around, squeezed back through the gap in the window, leapt off the edge and made towards the road.

Walker watched her go. He'd just said goodbye to the only family he had left in the world.

"Walker?" Barboza said. "Please listen to me."

He turned around.

"We have to go," Barboza said.

"We?" Walker said.

"I'm dead to the world out there," Barboza said. "And it's because of my stupid fucking conscience. So whatever you're thinking of me right now, remember that okay?"

Walker ran a hand over the stubble on his chin. "But how can they touch us?" he said. "The public must have heard what you said before they cut the cameras. They know it's all bullshit. If something happens to us then they'll know who did it."

Barboza shook her head.

"I don't know how much got out before they pulled the plug," she said. "But it doesn't matter. They'll clean it up somehow. Sure, people will ask questions for a while. But the scandal will blow away – these things always do."

"What about the cameras on the street?" Walker asked. "Are they out too?"

"Everything," Barboza said. "The whole neighbourhood is off. They can't risk any more little revelations slipping out. And they can't risk letting us loose in London knowing what we know. You're a very dangerous person Walker. And so am I."

Walker sighed. "What a fucking day," he said.

"Please," Barboza asked. "Enough of this bullshit. We've stayed here too long as it is."

But Walker just shrugged his shoulders. "Fuck them. *Them.* Whoever *them* are. The people in the shadows who control everything – fuck them. Let them come and do what they want. If they enjoy watching me take a piss so much then I'll give them a live performance."

Barboza grabbed his arm. Once again, it felt like a steel vice had clamped its jaws around him.

"Stop it," she said. ""There won't be any negotiation with these people Walker. They're not going to send middle-aged men dressed in well-tailored suits and ties. They're not going to offer you a nice retirement package in the Costa del Sol for keeping your mouth shut. It's the fucking army – they're sending the troops here to kill us. We know too much. You understand?"

With that, Barboza turned and hurried out of the room. Walker heard her in the kitchen, slamming doors open and shut and piling things onto the counter. He heard heavy footsteps on the linoleum floor. Then she went upstairs. More footsteps. A few minutes later she came downstairs, storming back into the living room. She was holding two rucksacks in each hand by the strap. Walker recognised his dad's old sports bag. Archie Walker had once used it for squash games with his workmates in Edinburgh.

"It's as much as we can carry," she said. "Food, water, toothbrush, change of clothes – enough to get us started. Anything else you want?"

Walker looked at his father's sports bag. In that moment, everything became clear – as clear as it had been since the first day of September 2011 when civilisation had forsaken London in a blur of violence. He saw the path ahead. It opened up like the Biblical Red Sea before his eyes. The future. He knew exactly what he had to do. This was it. He had a purpose beyond Stanmore Road.

"Kill him," he said.

Barboza screwed up her face. "What?" she said.

But they were interrupted by a noise outside. Faint at first, and yet growing louder at an alarming speed. Growling engines. It was the sound of heavy wheels rolling across the hot concrete of Stanmore Road.

Barboza's face turned chalk white. She ran towards the window, pulled the curtains back and looked out.

"Oh fuck!" she yelled.

She ducked down underneath the window. "They're here! Oh shit, shit, shit. Jesus Christ, we're screwed."

Walker walked slowly towards the window. He pulled back the curtains, making little effort to conceal himself from the view of those outside. An army helicopter was setting down in the middle of the street. He recognised the shape – it looked like a Black Hawk, rugged, long and low-set, with four blades spinning in a blur. Looking to the left, he saw a large AFV making its way along Stanmore Road, crawling as if it had all the time in the world. The vehicle pulled up in the middle of the street, rolling to a gradual stop.

The hatch opened.

"Get down." Barboza hissed at him.

Walker didn't move. He continued to look outside as a squad of troops leapt out of the AFV, one after the other in quick succession. He watched as they took position at the outskirts of the garden, pointing their rifles towards the house. Towards him. At the same time, another AFV pulled up on the street, close behind the first.

Walker ducked down beneath the window at last. As he did so, Barboza squeezed beside him. He heard her breathing, fast and erratic, like she was having some kind of fit.

"Fucking hell!" Barboza said.

Walker looked at her. He knew so little about the woman sitting next to him – the real woman and not the character she'd been playing since they met.

"Do you have a family out there?" he said. "Husband, kids, parents...?"

Barboza wiped a tear from her eye.

"My parents," she said. "I've got a mum and dad in Leeds. I'm never going to see them again, am I? They won't know what's happened to me. Oh God what have I done?"

"I'm sorry," Walker said. It was all he could think to say.

They sat with their backs against the living room wall. They could hear the sound of the helicopter's engine outside. It was so loud that that Walker thought they'd landed the damn thing on the roof of his house. Any second now, he thought. An entire battalion of troopers would come crashing through the ceiling, trained assassins clinging to ropes with one hand, assault rifles outstretched in the other.

Bang. The end.

Walker heard the sound of voices on the street – fluid orders and commands being given in muted tones. This was an organised assassination. These were soldiers with years of instilled discipline behind them. What was the point in fighting back?

He heard footsteps creeping up the path.

Walker and Barboza sat quietly beneath the window. Nobody spoke. There was nothing else to say, nothing else to do but wait for it – to breathe in the last of that god-awful summer heat, to say their silent farewell to the world.

From somewhere in the garden, hushed voices and the crackle of a radio.

Walker closed his eyes. He wondered if he would see his parents soon.

CHAPTER 25

He could hear the soldiers breathing.

"On my count," a gruff voice said behind the front door. "On three."

Walker heard the crunch of footsteps wading through the long grass in the garden at the back of the house.

"They've gone around the back," he said.

"I'm sorry," Barboza whispered. Her eyes were closed. But she did something that surprised him – she reached over and took his hand in hers.

Walker squeezed her hand gently. It was warm and damp. He had long since made peace with the fact that he was probably going to die alone in his bed in London. At least there was enough time left for one last surprise in his life.

But nothing happened. Walker was convinced that the soldiers were stalling on purpose, prolonging the agony just for kicks. Perhaps they had been ordered not only to execute, but also to torture them, to punish them for their misdemeanours against entertainment. What sort of feathers had Barboza ruffled?

He heard random spurts of clipped speaking. The constant

crackle of walkie-talkies. The soldiers were still poised at the door but why hadn't they come in yet? This had to be the longest countdown in the history of the armed forces.

"Fuck sake," Walker whispered.

"What's going on?" Barboza asked. Her eyes were still closed. "Why are they just standing out there?"

"MOVE, MOVE, MOVE!"

Walker and Barboza nearly jumped out of their skins.

Here it comes.

There would be an almighty crash. Voices shouting. The door would come flying off the hinges and heavy footsteps would storm across the hallway. They would come charging through the living room door that Walker had half-destroyed, there would be a hail of bullets and that would be it. It would be the end. Nothingness. With any luck, it would be quick and painless.

But it didn't happen. Walker turned his ear towards the street. He pushed his head closer to the window so that he could hear what was going on. There was still a lot of noise going on out there, but it sounded like...

He didn't dare to hope but he was almost sure of it.

The footsteps were moving away from the door.

"MOVE, MOVE, MOVE!"

Walker heard the tone of the commanding officer's voice. It was a combination of someone doing their duty, trying to sound authoritative, but also trying to contain a flood of personal emotion that threatened to spill over.

Something had happened.

Thoughts raced back and forth in Walker's mind like a pinball flying around the table at ninety miles per hour. He clenched both fists, gritted his teeth and waited to see what would happen next. Was he going to die, or what?

He turned to Barboza. She had opened her eyes and was looking at Walker, furrowing her brow as if to say – *what the hell?* Walker shrugged. He pushed himself up a little further, so that he could turn around and sneak a look through the windscreen. But he needn't have been so subtle – the military seemed to have lost all interest in the occupants of the house in Stanmore Road. He saw a flock of soldiers running back to the AFVs. The measured discipline of just moments ago was shot to hell. They were bumping into one another like overexcited schoolchildren who'd just heard the bell to signal the start of the summer holidays, as they clambered back into the AFVs. At the same time, the helicopter blades were turning and the Black Hawk looked to be on the brink of taking off again.

"They're going," Walker said. "They're leaving."

Barboza looked outside, making sure to keep her head low.

Most of the troops had by now climbed back into the AFVs. But Walker noticed that it wasn't quite the end yet. Three men in uniform were standing in the middle of the road, their heads bowed in deep discussion. One of them – the overanxious commanding officer who had ordered the soldiers back to the AFVs – was barking orders at the two younger troopers.

Walker caught a little of the conversation over the sound of the helicopter and the AFVs.

"No choice...we have to intercept...you two...finish the job...we need the numbers at the superwalls...you know what has to be done...finish...finish the job."

"What are they saying?" Barboza asked.

Finish the job.

Walker turned away from the window and dropped back down onto the floor. He scratched absently at his forehead, trying to put the pieces of the puzzle together. What the hell was going on out there? Were they going or what? But no matter what way he looked at the problem, it all came down to the same conclusion. And that conclusion came in the form of two soldiers being left behind.

Finish the job.

"We're still in deep shit," he said. "Something's happened. They're pulling out but I think they're leaving two of them behind to finish it. They're not quite letting us off the hook. Sorry."

Barboza winced. "Then we're still dead?" she said, dropping down beside him.

Walker glanced at her. He could tell by the look in her eyes that Barboza was unwilling to relinquish the hope that she'd just recovered upon seeing the soldiers withdraw. And neither was he – he was no longer willing to lie on his back, expose his belly and let them do what they wanted.

"C'mon," he said to her. "Follow me."

"What?"

But Walker didn't answer. He was already down on his hands and knees, crawling towards the kitchen. Barboza didn't ask any more questions. He heard her dropping down on all fours, following close behind.

As they crawled across the hallway floor, they heard the rumble of the AFVs pulling away from Stanmore Road. The helicopter's mechanical hum was faint as it receded into the sky.

All that mattered now was staying alive. The odds were still against their survival but Walker felt like he'd just been handed a return ticket from the valley of death. A voice deep down told him that he was meant to survive this and travel beyond the limits of Stanmore Road. Something bigger was out there waiting for him.

They crawled into the kitchen. Walker looked through the stained glass panels on the back door but couldn't see anyone out there. Whoever had been traipsing through the back garden earlier had gone with the rest of them. With the coast clear, Walker leapt to his feet and grabbed the kitchen knife that Barboza had put back on the counter. The tip of the knife was still smeared with tiger blood.

At the same time, Walker reached over and pulled another two knives out of the rack – a bread knife and a carving knife. He handed the carving knife to Barboza and she took it without hesitation.

Footsteps.

Walker froze. They were coming from somewhere out back.

He hurried over to the kitchen window. The window was halfway open, just as he'd left it for Alba to come and go after he was gone. He listened for a second, wondering if he would hear the brief crack of a rifle shot. Would he have time to hear it before his brains were splattered all over the kitchen? But that's not what he heard. Footsteps. He heard the scraping of feet against a wooden fence, followed by a soft thud. Someone was close, but not in his garden. Not yet.

"They've split up," Walker said. "I think one of them has gone down to the end of the block. He's making his way through the other gardens, jumping fences. Has to be. He's coming here."

There was no easy path to Walker's back garden from the front. To reach it from the outside, the soldier would have had to walk down to the end of the row of terraced houses that Walker's house was adjoined to. Then, at the end of the row, he'd have to go around the back of the nearest house and cut through a number of other gardens, leaping six feet tall fences until he arrived at the rear of Walker's house. It was one of the advantages of living in the middle of a row of terraced houses. Previously, before 2011, it had been a limitation that the garden could only be accessed from the back door of the house and not from the outside, but not today. Today it bought Walker and Barboza a little time.

"We have to make a run for it," Barboza said, beating Walker to the punch.

Walker hesitated.

"Well?" Barboza said.

But the decision was taken out of their hands. At that moment, the front door began to rattle violently. From where he was standing, Walker could see the metal door handle moving up and down in a fast, jerky motion. Amidst everything else, Walker took a moment to appreciate how OCD he'd been about always locking the front door and teaching Barboza to do the same. Seems it had paid off at last.

But it wouldn't keep the soldier out for long. The door was under constant attack and a series of hard thuds followed. It sounded like three rapid-fire cannon shots in succession.

He was kicking the door down.

"Go!" Walker hissed.

They ran towards the back door, Barboza in the lead and Walker behind her. Barboza pulled the door open and they rushed out, the heat pouncing on them as they ran into the back garden.

Walker felt immediately exposed in the daylight. Vulnerable.

Behind them, the front door crashed open. Walker heard it land on the hallway floor like a crack of thunder. That was it – his sanctuary had been violated forever. He could hear the soldier running through the house. Just seconds away. Walker turned around and shut the back door behind him, pulling the lever up and locking it from the outside. It would buy them a few seconds, but every second counted.

Through the stained glass panel, he saw the blurry shape of the soldier rushing towards them.

"Go!" he said to Barboza.

They ran towards the wooden fence on their right hand side. Barboza scaled the six-foot barrier easily and Walker was right there behind her. They dropped down into the garden of the house next door and at the same time, heard somebody wrestling with the handle of the back door. Moments later, there was a volley of rapid gunfire followed by the sound of shattering glass.

Walker looked straight ahead, pondering the escape route in front of them. There were no more houses beyond this last one, no more gardens to take cover in – only the open space of Stanmore Road for them to run towards.

The obvious thing would be to keep going – to run and take their chances. But Walker knew that there wasn't enough time to get away from the two soldiers if they did that. It was too far and their pursuers were too close behind. Were they to keep running, the bullets would tear them to pieces sooner or later.

That left only one option left. They had to stand and fight. But that was suicide and yet it was their only real chance to live.

Walker looked up and down the garden that they had landed in. He was searching for something, anything that might give them a glimmer of hope and a fighting chance against the men who were hunting them down. This garden was the same as most of the other gardens in the neighbourhood – a short stretch of overgrown grass and little else besides a small garden shed tucked in at the bottom.

Walker ran over to the shed, signalling for Barboza to stay put by the fence. He doubled over as he ran, keeping his head down. When he reached the steel door, he pulled the sliding bolt lock open and went inside.

It was hot inside the shed. Unbearably so. But at least there weren't any corpses or piles of bones lying on the floor. It was small, little more than a six by four at most. There were a variety of garden tools lying abandoned on the floor – a rake, hoe, a decrepit lawn-mower that sat in several pieces, and a yard brush. There was also a small axe with a curved wooden handle lying amidst a pile of rotten wood that might once have been firewood. It was a no-brainer. Walker looked at the axe, grabbed it and then and ran back to the fence.

The soldiers had almost caught up with one another in Walker's garden. They were communicating and both voices sounded close, like they were within touching distance of each other. Walker was starting to regret not making a run for it. That would have been the smart option and now that the soldiers were upon them, assault rifles versus a knife and axe, the stupidity of his decision to make a stand was obvious.

Walker hurried back to the fence and saw Barboza clutching at the handle of the carving knife. There was a look of determination on her face that was worthy of the character she had come to play. He gave her a nod and they sat side by side, with their backs jammed up against the wooden fence.

Walker heard the soldier step through the shattered door and out into the garden. The sound of crunching glass was excruciating under the man's feet.

The footsteps came closer.

"Oh fuck," Barboza whispered.

Walker focused on the man's movement. At the same time, he pushed Barboza's head down, encouraging her to keep as low as she possibly could. Then Walker squatted silently against the wall, listening to the soldier's footsteps as he closed in on the fence. He concentrated intensely, trying to pick out exactly what section of the wooden structure that the soldier was moving towards.

Walker crept quietly to his left, pinning himself up against the fence. He could hear the other man breathing.

Back to the right a little.

Footsteps approached. Walker sensed hesitation in the man's movement.

He readied the axe.

The soldier was now standing directly on the other side of the fence from Walker. Nothing happened. Was the other man being cautious? Or perhaps he was waiting for his colleague to catch up with him. But then again, the longer he waited the more chance there was that the two targets would get away. And that couldn't happen. Walker was counting on the soldier thinking like that. The only real chance Walker and Barboza had was to take them on one at a time. The soldiers were young – he'd noticed that when the commanding officer had been barking out the orders. He'd seen their keen eyes, eager to please the man they admired so much. Glory seekers hopefully, which would make them impatient and reckless.

Walker held his breath. He looked up at the fence.

A pale hand appeared, gripping the top of the fence. The soldier was seconds away from vaulting over and landing in the garden beside them.

It was now or never.

Walker didn't hesitate. From a crouching position, he sprang upwards and swung the axe with everything he had – every ounce of speed and power went into that single blow. He brought the blade down precisely upon the knuckles of the soldier's hand.

There was a horrific scream that seemed to come from the sky. It wasn't a clean cut. All five fingers remained on the man's hand – at least for now. Walker had to pull the blade out of the shattered fingers to get the axe back and when he did so, the soldier fell back over the fence and landed in Walker's garden with a thud, screaming in agony.

Walker looked at Barboza. Her eyes were wide with horror, but she tightened her grip on the knife handle and gave him a nod. Despite looking like she needed to throw up, she seemed ready to make a stand.

"Billy!" the other soldier screamed from afar. "Are you alright? What's going on? Talk to me mate." He was close now – one or two gardens away at most.

Billy's gargled screaming, coming from Walker's garden, was the only answer.

"Jesus Christ! Billy! I'm coming."

Walker heard the other soldier jump over the last fence and land in the garden. He rushed over to his fallen comrade. As he ran, Walker heard him gasp with shock, intermingled with the sound of heavy breathing.

"You're alright mate. Look at me Billy!"

Walker and Barboza sat with their backs against the fence. They listened to the soldier trying desperately to comfort the other man. Walker caught onto the fact that the second soldier sounded even younger than he looked – no more than a boy. Younger than Walker, that was for sure. And they were both terrified. It was if the situation had been reversed. Walker and Barboza were no longer the hunted. It was becoming clear that these two boys, who had been left behind to finish the job that an entire platoon had turned up at first to do, were not up to the task.

"Billy," the young soldier said. "Are they in the house mate? I thought I heard something. They're in the house, yeah?"

Billy squealed in agony, unable to find the words.

"I've gotta go in and take 'em out," the soldier said. "Just hang on Billy, just hang on yeah? I'll get 'em for you mate and then I'll come straight back. I promise."

Walker listened as Billy tried to say something – no doubt trying to reveal the actual location of the two targets, which wasn't in the house as the other soldier presumed. But the wounded man was unable to form a coherent sentence. He was in agony and perhaps in shock too. All he could manage was one word:

'No!'

Walker and Barboza heard the other soldier get to his feet. They listened as urgent footsteps hurried towards the back door, stomping over the smashed glass that lingered around the doorstep.

"You motherfuckers!" he yelled.

The footsteps receded further into the house. All they could hear now was Billy over the fence, groaning in pain.

Walker leaned closer to Barboza. There was no time to lose and they had only one possible course of action if they wanted a clean getaway. But he knew that if he went through with it, his life would never be the same again. In the back of his mind, he heard a faint voice – the voice of his sixteen years old self, trying to talk him out of what he was considering. This was Mack's voice – little Mack Walker from Edinburgh, who back in 2011 had gone to Piccadilly Circus with so many other people in search of something better.

Walker ignored the voice of little Mack. He grabbed Barboza's forearm, which was burning hot to touch.

"I've got to go in there after him," he said. "We're not getting out of here unless they're both out of the picture. Do you understand?"

Barboza nodded. But the blank look in her eyes suggested otherwise.

"As soon as I jump over the fence and run towards the house the other one's going to start screaming to his friend," Walker said. He paused. "That's why I need you to take him out. Can you do that?"

Walker spoke in a cold, dispassionate tone. He might as well have been talking about removing an infestation of ants from the carpet.

Barboza's face turned grey. Now she understood for sure what he was asking her to do. He was asking her to commit murder, or at least that's what it would be considered by the people who lived beyond the two walls of London.

She closed her eyes and swallowed the cold reality of their situation. Kill or be killed.

"Are you with me?" he said.

"Walker," she whispered. "I'm with you. But I don't know if I can..."

"Think of it this way," he said. "I need the tough girl back. I need you to play the character for a little while longer. You're Barboza – the girl who fought off four rogues for two days and nights. Remember? The Brazilian ninja who can break through doors with capoeira kicks. Barboza. The badass. I need her back."

"It's just a part Walker," she said. "A fictional character."

"Sharon won't make it in London," Walker said. "This place will fuck you up bad. Hell it'll fuck you up anyway but it'll be a lot worse if you choose to be Sharon."

"I'm not like you Walker," she said.

She was about to say something else but stopped. Then she nodded slowly, as if accepting that there was no other way.

"Okay," she whispered.

"We need to move now," Walker said.

Barboza looked at him. "I'm with you."

Walker got back to his feet. Then he climbed the fence and peered over into the garden at the back of his house. Billy was lying on his stomach, his face buried in a large circle of grass that was stained red with blood. He was clutching onto his bloody hand with his good one, trying to hold the fingers in place. And although his screams had diminished, he was still writhing around in the tall grass like a wounded snake.

Walker felt a twinge of sympathy for the fallen man. But any thoughts of Billy's mother, father, or the possibility of a wife and children waiting at home were banished into the dark corners of his mind. There was only Billy the enemy who had come to kill him.

"Now," Walker said, signalling to Barboza.

He was worried that Barboza would freeze at the last minute. That she would be unable to go through with it. But it was quite the opposite. Upon his signal, she sprang into action, readying her knife with one hand as she climbed up and jumped over the other side of the fence. She landed on the grass as softly as a bird. Then, without stopping, she approached Billy with the knife cutstretched in her hand. His face was still buried in the dirt and he didn't see her coming.

She was like a machine, emotionless upon the surface, programmed to carry out a set of actions.

Barboza dropped to her knees, pulled Billy's head back and exposed his throat to the carving knife in her hand. There was time for one last gasp from the soldier. Then she ran the blade across his throat.

Walker turned away at that moment. Not because he couldn't bear to look, but rather he had his own grisly task to complete. He jumped down from the fence and landed in the garden, paying little attention to the gurgling sound coming from the dying man behind him. He was aware that Billy's assault rifle was back there, lying on the grass. But he didn't bother going back for it. The axe was all he would need.

He trod gently over a thousand fragments of broken glass. The tip of the axe was stained with fresh blood and it pointed forwards, hungry for more.

Walker stood perfectly still, a dark silhouette framed within the doorway of his former sanctuary. The heat of the afternoon sun came wafting in behind him.

From upstairs, he could hear the soldier moving violently from room to room. He heard doors slamming shut.

"Where are you?" the soldier said, yelling at the top of his voice. "I know you're in here. Just come out and I won't shoot. I'll take you both in, yeah? Come out and let's talk about this."

Walker smiled. The man upstairs was falling to pieces. Walker could hear it in his voice, even as the soldier tried to sound commanding. The soldier was upstairs, pleading with phantoms that weren't even there. Begging, not for the sake of Walker and Barboza's lives, but his own.

Walker crept quietly through the kitchen. He saw the living room door lying flat at the end of the hallway where Billy the soldier had caved it in.

"I hear you!" cried the soldier upstairs. "I hear you walking! I know you're in here!"

Walker stopped at the foot of the stairs. He lowered the axe and looked up, waiting for the soldier to come to him. He breathed slowly, in and out. He felt completely relaxed as the young soldier continued his rampage upstairs, knocking things off shelves, breaking mirrors in the bedrooms and bathroom. The soldier continued to call out to Walker and Barboza, assuring them that enough blood had been spilled already and that they could talk through this.

All the while, Walker waited at the bottom of the stairs.

Eventually, the soldier appeared on the upstairs hallway. At the sight of Walker, he shrieked and in a flash of instinctive movement, pointed the assault rifle downstairs. His arms were shaking. His aim wavered. His eyes darted back and forth between Walker's and the bloody tip of the axe, freshly coated with his comrade's blood.

Walker stood there. He might as well have been made of stone. His calm, silent demeanour was confusing the young man. Walker knew that this soldier was weak, that he was incapable of pulling the trigger. He was just a boy. He was a rabbit caught in the headlights of something much bigger than a car.

The young soldier stood at the top of the stairs. He looked up from the barrel of the rifle, lowering the weapon slightly as he did so.

"You're Mr Apocalypse," he said. His voice was shaking. "Ain't ya? You're Mr Apocalypse."

A manic grin appeared on the young man's face.

"Yeah," he said. "I've seen you on the telly. I watch you on the telly every day. Me and my girlfriend, eh? Bloody hell, it's really *you*. You're Mr Apocalypse."

Walker didn't answer.

There was an enthusiastic gleam in the man's eyes. He began to descend the staircase, with all the enthusiasm of a young child walking up to meet Mickey Mouse at Disneyland.

"You're Mr Apocalypse."

He said it again and again. All the while, grinning like a starstruck maniac.

The soldier stopped two stairs from the bottom. Almost within touching distance. He stared blankly at Walker, as if expecting the man he called Mr Apocalypse to do something, to entertain him, to launch into a song and dance routine or to blow a jaw-dropping fireworks display out of his arse.

After all, this was *the* Mr Apocalypse.

Both men stared into each other's eyes in complete silence. That silence was only interrupted by a sudden noise at the top of the stairs. Something moved in a hurry, a white blur, running downstairs to brush itself up against the legs of the soldier. The soldier yelped in terror. Then he snapped out of his daze, as if somebody had poked a large dose of smelling salts up his nose.

The soldier raised the rifle, but it was too late. Before his finger could reach the trigger, Walker came forward, raising the axe at speed and slamming the blade down into the young man's neck. The soldier didn't make a sound as the axe embedded itself into his white flesh. The rifle fell out of his hand and dropped onto the floor. The soldier kept his eyes on Walker. Then he dropped onto the staircase, his body toppling down the remaining stairs until he came to a halt on the hallway floor. Blood was streaming from a deep gash in his neck.

His eyes were open, still staring at Mr Apocalypse.

With one swift pull, Walker wrenched the axe out of the wound. Then he glanced behind him and saw what he was looking for. Alba was sitting on the hallway carpet, close to where the front door had been smashed in.

"Couldn't have timed it better," he said, throwing her a wink.

The little cat stared at him. Then in one fluid motion, Alba hopped over the fallen door and trotted out the open entrance towards the street. Walker watched her go, unable to tear his eyes away from the only thing he loved in the world. But Alba didn't look back. She made her way down the garden path, disappearing into the secret gaps in between the bright rays of sunshine and beyond.

Walker turned back to the house. Barboza was standing at the kitchen door. She was looking at the dead soldier sprawled out at the bottom of the stairs, next to Walker's feet.

"What have we done?" she whispered. "Walker?"

Walker looked at the fresh corpse at his feet. The young man's dead eyes continued to stare into the empty space where Mr Apocalypse had been.

"What we had to," he said. "Would you rather it was us?"

"But they were just boys," Barboza said. "They were just boys following orders, weren't they? And we killed them."

Walker took a step towards her.

"It gets easier," he said, putting a hand on her shoulder. "You know, about ten years ago I stabbed someone in Edinburgh. It was self-defence, but it used to haunt me every day and every night. What I did. I used to dream about it all the time. It's why my parents brought me to London in the first place – to escape the past. Now I don't think about it at all. If anything, I was right to do what I did back then – it was him or me. Just like this. You'll learn to live with it Barboza. I promise. This place, that's what it does to you."

She shook her head, not daring to believe him. "We need to go Walker," she said.

Walker nodded. This time there would be no argument.

CHAPTER 26

Transcript of a video uploaded to Immersion 9 - posted on _July 12th 2020_

She sits quietly for a moment.

She sits alone.

In silence.

Two black holes masquerade as eyes upon the mask that she's wearing. But upon closer inspection, her real eyes are visible too – a dual hint of blue or green – a speck of light buried deep beneath the dark netting that covers the eyeholes of the infamous skull hoodie.

She speaks:

'Do not grieve for those who are lost. Do not grieve especially for those who are innocent. The Good and Honest Citizens will light the way. We will always tell you the truth about what is going on in the world. When you hear them call us murderers tomorrow and you find yourself tempted to believe them, remember what am I about to show you. Remember that The Good and Honest Citizens told you the truth.'

The camera fades to black.

July 12th 2020. Location: M25, London.

The footage is shaky.

Someone is wearing a portable camera strapped to their head or upper body. Glimpses of the surroundings come thick and fast. The ground is covered in thousands of steel table knives and plastic buckets, many of which have been tipped on their side.

A large crowd of young people are sitting down, looking around in bewilderment, often directly at the camera. There is confusion in their eyes but above all, fear. Many of them are in tears. Others are rooted to the spot, unable to move. Their eyes are vacant and lost, as if unable to comprehend why no one has been able to help them. The occasional scream is heard, although this seems to be coming from somewhere else in the background, far away from the crowd.

The camera does a lap of the large seating area. People wearing explosive belts surround the KBC participants. They pay little attention to the camera as it passes by. The people wearing the belts encircle the multitude of young hostages and keep them on the inside. Amongst these hostages are several familiar faces from the TFL television crew, including Georgia Perkins and Johnny Castle. Johnny is weeping on his co-presenter's shoulder.

A voice yells out.

"How long have they been gone?"

"Nearly half an hour," someone replies.

"It's over!" a young man wearing an explosive belt yells at the camera as it passes him by. His face is distorted with anger and he brings it right up to the screen. "It's over! You sick fucking animals! No more TFL. No more human zoos. What a shame! I hope you..."

The young man stops talking. He steps back, looking over the shoulder of the person wearing the camera. His eyes are alert, as if he's seen something in the distance.

For a moment, nobody speaks – there are a few seconds of complete silence at the M25.

"What's that?" somebody says, breaking the silence. "Can you see it? Is that smoke in the distance?"

The camera turns in the opposite direction. The footage is still shaky but it's clear that there is a large plume of smoke rising in the distance. But what's even more apparent is that something is approaching the M25 on the green horizon. Multiple armoured vehicles are hurtling towards them. The sound of the engines grows louder with every passing second. At the same time, several helicopters can be seen in the sky, descending upon the hostage scene in what looks like slow motion.

"It's the army!" somebody yells. "The real fucking army!"

"Fuck! Fuck! Fuck!"

Gunshots. They're coming from behind the hostage scene – from the observation platforms on the outer wall. It's as if marksmen have been placed on all sides. Some of the people wearing explosive belts fall. They die quickly, without a sound. But it's not just The Good and Honest Citizens who are dying. The indiscriminate volley of bullets also strikes a number of students and television personnel.

The person wearing the camera runs, taking cover behind one of the seats that has fallen on its side.

Screams. The sound of gunfire.

"Bastards!" somebody shouts over the noise. "They're shooting us. They don't give a fuck. They're shooting all of us!"

The students, the television presenters and crewmembers – they all scream and dive for cover under the seats.

"Ready?" somebody yells. "Good and Honest Citizens. We do this now. Now! Detonate your belts on the count of three – show these bastards that we're for real."

A hand touches the lens of the camera. The fingers are swiping and touching the screen at a furious pace.

Heavy breathing.

Somebody shouts – "Good and Honest Citizens. Three..."

The cameraperson speaks. It's the voice of a young girl – a child-like voice, no more than a teenager at most. Her voice is trembling.

"I'm sending this footage into HQ," she says. "This will probably be the last thing I do."

The heavy gunfire continues unabated. It's coming from all sides now – from the M25, from the helicopter and the approaching AVFs. The bullets spray into the Good and Honest Citizens, the students and the television crew, all of them gathered in the Knife Bucket Challenge area.

"Two..."

Somebody screams.

"They're killing the hostages too," says the girl. "You must show this to the world. We are The Good and Honest and Citizens. We will free London or die. Goodbye Mum and Dad. I love you so much."

"One..."

Everything goes black.

CHAPTER 27

SkamNews.com

Headlines – July 12th 2020

Knife Bucket Tragedy – Brutal GHC Terrorist Attack Kills TV Celebs And Hundreds of Innocent People At M25!

It was supposed to be a joyful occasion.

The world's largest Knife Bucket Challenge was interrupted in devastating fashion this morning when approximately thirty participants stood up to reveal explosive devices wrapped around their waists.

The terrorists, affiliated with The Good and Honest Citizens, quickly made their demands to the military personnel on site. These demands included seizing control of two armoured vehicles and the terrorists also threatened to detonate their explosives if the live broadcast on TFL's *Calling London!* was cut, forcing the loved ones of KBC participants to witness the shocking events as they unfolded.

The stolen AFVs set off towards North London, intent on causing major disruption and emotional trauma to the people living in the city since 2011. The remaining terrorists stayed behind with the captives, including television crew members and beloved *Calling London!* presenters Georgia Perkins and Johnny Castle.

The government launched a massive intercept operation to halt the progress of the AFVs. Fortunately a squad of troops were positioned further south of the M25 at that time, and they were called in to block the route south. A brief skirmish followed between the soldiers and the terrorists. The terrorists, who opened fire upon the troops, were overpowered and about ten people were killed.

Military personnel report that the two stolen AFVs were recovered intact.

Following the skirmish, the soldiers returned to the M25 where approximately twenty of the remaining terrorists were holding over a thousand people hostage. The terrorists opened fire on the approaching troops and TFL were finally able to to cut the live broadcast at that point, sparing further distress to family members watching at home.

With no chance of escape, the callous terrorists set off their explosive belts. The resulting explosions killed hundreds of innocent people and seriously wounded many more. Georgia Perkins and Johnny Castle were amongst the dead.

Several hours after the tragedy, the GHC released a video on their I-9 page. The footage allegedly shows the army opening fire first and not the other way around. Experts have been quick to dismiss this clip as being doctored.

UPDATE: Police have arrested John Ballewa, 21, a student at the University of Leeds, this evening in connection with terrorist allegations. It's alleged that Ballewa and his younger brother Sam, who was killed leading the terrorists at the M25 yesterday, were in fact responsible for organising the record-breaking Knife Bucket Challenge, an intense campaign that was launched on social media last week. A spokesman for the police said that the Ballewa brothers' calculated actions, which claimed the lives of so many innocent people, reveal the 'chilling cold-bloodedness' of The Good and Honest Citizens. It is believed the Ballewa brothers, like all members of the GHC, are working directly for a mysterious woman who has appeared in recent broadcast clips on the GHC's I-9 page. This woman, known only as 'The Lady', is believed to be even more dangerous than her predecessor Chester George, in that she seems unfazed by the prospect of sacrificing her cohorts and committing mass murder to achieve her goals.

CHAPTER 28

Walker and Barboza stood in the middle of Stanmore Road. They were looking towards the northern horizon, at a large plume of smoke rising towards the stratosphere, seemingly in slow motion. They'd heard the explosions. One large blast, followed by several smaller ones. At first they'd feared that the soldiers were coming back to finish the job, to erase any signs that Mr Apocalypse and Cristiane Barboza had ever existed.

But it wasn't for them, at least not this time.

Walker pulled his dad's rucksack over his shoulder. The small bag felt heavier than it looked, especially while he was outside, his skin cooking under the intense heat of the sun. Their bags were crammed with essentials, which consisted primarily of large plastic bottles of water and enough food to last them at least a few days on the road. Walker had brought the axe with the curved handle along too, which felt reassuring in his grip. The blade of the axe was still smeared with a dark red coating.

Walker turned his face away from the rising smoke in the north. He began to consider the long road that lay ahead of them.

"Where will we go?" Barboza asked, standing beside him.

"South," he said. "There's nowhere else to go."

Barboza's eyes looked sore and heavy, like every last drop of energy had been squeezed out of her. Walker knew that it was going to take a long time for her to get over what she'd just done. Maybe she'd never get over it. He knew so little about her.

"South?" she said. "You know what's down there don't you?"

"The Hole," Walker said. "You were telling the truth about that?"

"Afraid so."

Walker squeezed the handle of the axe. The tendons in his arms stood out like taut cords. He'd come to a decision, or rather that decision had been forced upon him – he could no longer afford to be afraid of the world beyond Stanmore Road. Fear could no longer be the emotion that dictated his life. But what would he do? Where was he supposed to go? He had no desire to wander aimlessly across the city of London – at least not without a reason. Not without a purpose.

He turned back to the smoke plume in the north, still climbing above the outskirts of London. It reminded him of similar smoke plumes he'd seen during the 2011 riots.

"Hatchet," he said.

"What?" Barboza said.

"I wonder where he is now," Walker said. "I wonder *who* he is now."

Barboza shrugged. "The guy who killed Chester George?" she said. "He's probably dead. He could have been dead for nine years for all we know."

"True," Walker said. "But I know someone that can help us figure that out."

"Who?" Barboza said.

"Michael King."

"Michael King?"

"Aye," Walker said. He turned back to her, using the back of his hand to shield his eyes from the sun. "Didn't you say he was based in

Liverpool Street Station? That he was the top man in the north these days?"

"Yeah," Barboza said. She sounded a little out of it as she spoke – like someone trying to recall the details of something she once half-dreamed. "I think so."

Walker nodded slowly. "Michael King was the last person to see Hatchet at Piccadilly that day. At least that I know of. I figure he'd be able to tell me what happened next. Hell, he might have killed Hatchet there and then. But I'd like to know for sure."

Barboza sighed. "But why?" she said.

"I'd like to catch up with an old friend," Walker said.

"But you told me you didn't like each other," Barboza said. "Even back before he did what he did, right?"

Walker took a step closer to her. "Look," he said, putting a hand on her shoulder. "You proved yourself back there – in the garden I mean. All the lies you told me before don't mean a thing against what you did. But we got lucky – the army made a mistake and left two boys to kill us. Those boys weren't ready. But I don't think we're going to get that lucky in London. I don't know what's out there and neither do you. Maybe you should stick around, talk to them when they come back – tell them it was me. Tell them I killed both soldiers. You can still go home and see your family."

Barboza closed her eyes, as if the thought of her family was too much to bear.

"They already know I killed that soldier," she said. "They were watching. They *are* watching. I don't have a choice Walker. I'm coming with you."

Walker let his hand drop from her shoulder. Despite everything that had happened, he smiled.

"What do I call you?" he said. "Sharon?"

She shook her head.

"Barboza," she said. "In London, I'm Barboza. Besides, it sounds cooler than Sharon, don't you think?"

"Definitely," he said.

With that, Walker took one last look at Stanmore Road. He said a silent farewell to the house – to his sanctuary, the place that had protected him for nine long years. As he took the first step on the journey south, his eyes went back and forth across the old neighbourhood, still hoping for one last glimpse of Alba's white fur poking its way out of the tall grass.

THE END

GHOSTS OF LONDON
(BOOK 3)

CHAPTER 1

Walker felt like he was sinking into the hot surface of the road.

He hadn't walked that far yet, but the solid base underneath was now a sudden quicksand. It felt like the city had a mouth and that it was slowly devouring him.

He stopped in front of a road sign, thankful for the excuse to rest.

Walker's eyes scanned the details of the sign, looking up and down at yesteryear's place names and at the numbers beside them. Walker tried to make sense of it, to figure out where the hell they were and how they could get to somewhere else. As he did so, he heard Barboza catching up with him. She was walking in slow motion too, wading through the same quicksand.

Walker adjusted the black t-shirt that was wrapped around his shaved head to keep the sun off. He tightened the knot that he'd made using the two arms of the hot, soaking garment. And thank God for it. The early afternoon sunlight was vicious; it was pushing down on his head and elsewhere, his arms were getting red and prickly.

"So where are we?" Barboza asked, stopping beside him. "Any ideas?"

Walker shrugged.

"You know London better than I do," he said. "Does any of this make sense?"

"Not sure," she said.

As Barboza looked at the sign, she pulled at the blue sleeveless t-shirt that was sticking to her body. Walker looked at her and for the first time, noticed a small, dark stain at the waist of the shirt. It was a bloodstain – a grisly reminder of what had just happened back on Stanmore Road.

He wondered if she'd noticed yet.

"It says here we're on the A105," Barboza said. "So we're probably not much further than Harringay." She sighed. "We haven't made much progress have we? Feels like we've been walking for ages."

"It's hot," Walker said.

Barboza pushed several damp strands of black hair off her face, tucking it behind the ears on both sides.

"It's five miles to the city centre," she said. "So it's about the same to Liverpool Street Station. We're five miles away Walker, give or take a little."

Walker nodded. Five miles. It was a long way, and with the hot sun on their backs it would feel even longer. And that wasn't all they were carrying with them on the journey. They were still burdened by the weight of what had just happened on Stanmore Road.

Walker glanced at the bloodstain on Barboza's t-shirt. The killing of the two soldiers was fresh in his mind and it was coming with them, no matter how many miles they put between themselves and the place where it happened.

Barboza had been quiet since leaving Stanmore Road. Once or twice, Walker had tried to distract her by saying something – anything – but she wasn't interested.

Walker didn't mind the silence. He wasn't much of a talker anyway, having spent the last nine years living on his own without any interaction with other people. Besides, trivial conversation was a distraction they could ill afford. He wanted to keep his attention on the road because God knows what might be creeping up on them from behind. But he was surprised that – so far at least – the streets were empty. Where was everyone in this godforsaken city? He was experiencing that same desolate feeling that he'd felt on his regular excursions to the New River to pick up his Drop Parcel. It was the same but different. So many things, while clearly neglected, looked intact. There were the houses with their overgrown gardens, the abandoned cars sitting on the side of the road – there was still some hint of civilisation in these forgotten things.

But there were no people.

The birds were still singing. The bright chitter-chatter coming from the skies was as incessant as it had always been. It was ceaseless and thank God. What sort of world would it be without birdsong?

Walker and Barboza continued walking south along the A105.

"Are you okay?" Walker asked Barboza. He still felt the need to check in with her occasionally.

"I'm alright," she said. "You?"

"Aye," Walker said. "I'm boiling but you can't stop the sun being a cruel prick. And where the hell is everyone? I expected to see someone by now. Didn't you? I thought it'd be safer for people to move around the city by day."

"We haven't been walking that long," Barboza said. "And besides, we don't really want to bump into anyone, remember? Not in this place."

"But it's too quiet," Walker said. "Gives me the creeps."

Barboza shrugged. "Who knows?" she said. "Maybe they're sleeping through the heat."

"Aye," Walker said.

"I'll take the creepy silence," Barboza said. "We've still got a good two hours walk ahead of us. Let's just hope the rest of it is as uneventful."

Walker pulled the rucksack off his shoulder and unzipped it at the front.

"You want some water?" he asked.

"No I'm good."

Walker took out a small plastic bottle. He unscrewed the lid and tossed the cool liquid down his throat. A few drops dribbled down his chin and he wiped them off with the back of his hand. He was careful not to drink too much in case he put a serious dent in their water supply. That one bottle was supposed to be enough to get him to Liverpool Street Station. He didn't want to have to ask Barboza for any of her water, even though she wasn't drinking as much as she should have been.

As Walker drank, Barboza looked at the black t-shirt that he was wearing and at the other one wrapped around his head.

"You know black's not the best colour to wear in the sun, right?" she said.

"Aye," he said, screwing the lid back on the bottle. "I know that."

"What is it with you and black?" she said. "You've been wearing a black t-shirt ever since I met you."

"Not the same one," Walker said. As if that made a difference. "I have three. There's an extra one in the bag. I'll put the fresh one on when we get there. Hey, is it sad that I'm actually looking forward to that? To putting on dry clothes."

"A bit," she said, almost smiling. "But why black?"

"I don't have much choice," Walker said. His fingers probed at the knots on the improvised headgear, checking for any signs that it was coming loose. "My dad's taste in clothes was shocking to say the least. Come to think of it, I'm sure he had at least two bright orange shirts hanging in the wardrobe in their bedroom. When the other soldiers come back to the house, they're welcome to them."

Walker smiled, lost in the memory of his dad's wardrobe. And how he and his mum had cringed at some of the things the old man had come back with after a clothes-buying binge. It was like he was deliberately trying to shock them. Or maybe he was just trying to make them laugh.

Archie Walker.

"Jesus," he said. "Some of the clothes he bought. I wouldn't be seen dead wearing them, not even in a shithole like this. But you can't go wrong with a black t-shirt Barboza. Nice and..."

Barboza's arm landed on his chest with a thud.

"Walker," she said. As she spoke, she kept her hand pinned against his chest.

Her voice was trembling.

Walker looked at Barboza. Her eyes were focused on something on the road, something that had seemingly appeared out of nowhere.

There was a man. And he was watching them.

The man was standing on the faded white lines that divided the road into traffic lanes. Along with the shock of seeing the man, Walker couldn't believe how overdressed he was in this heat. The man was wearing a long, brown leather coat, over an elegant, matching suit that looked unwrinkled and brand new. The leather coat stretched far beyond the man's knees, down towards a pair of suede brown shoes. A dark fedora hat sat on his head, pulled low so that the eyes were as good as hidden. Walker couldn't see any hair spilling out of the hat onto the man's ivory white neck.

The stranger in the middle of the road stood perfectly still. From a distance, he was a human scarecrow, warning strangers about the dangers of travelling further south.

"You feel better now?" Barboza said. "We're not alone anymore."

Walker ran his index finger along the curved blade of the axe in his hand. The axe hadn't left his hand since they'd departed Stanmore Road. The tip was still coated in the young soldier's blood, although the stain was drying fast, turning into a dark red smear that would be hard to wash off.

"Who's that?" Walker asked. "And why's he just standing there in the middle of the road like that? It's like he's been expecting us."

Barboza shook her head. "I don't know," she said. "What do we do?"

"He obviously wants something." Walker said. "Let's go see what he wants."

They approached the man cautiously. Walker felt his axe hand trembling and he struggled to keep it under control. What were they walking into here? He had to be ready to explode into action if things went south quickly. Had they been so stupid as to think they could get away with murder? Of course it wasn't murder. It was self-defence, but who would care?

Certainly not the man in the hat.

As they got closer, Walker noticed that the man was smiling at them. He was probably about fifty years old, maybe even a little older. His teeth were a dazzling white. Walker could see two microscopic slits peering out at them from underneath a small pair of round lens glasses. Those tiny eyes didn't blink.

"Greetings my young assassins," the man said. He spoke in a high-pitched, nasally voice. If Walker had been talking to this guy on a phone, he would have sworn that the speaker was pinching his nose as he talked.

Walker and Barboza stopped about five metres away from the man.

"Well," said the man in the hat, rubbing his hands together. "Here we are."

"We?" Barboza asked. "Who's that then?"

"It's been quite a day," the man in the hat said. "So much has happened and it's barely even lunchtime."

He laughed, as if some private joke was contained within his words.

"Who are you?" Walker said.

"My young friends," the man said. "I represent the SKAM television network. And in particular – their flagship operation – the Future of London channel."

He looked at Walker and winked – a slow, repulsive manoeuvre.

"You know what I'm talking about," he said. "Don't you Mr Apocalypse?"

Walker shook his head. "Do I?" he said. "And what do you know? Sounds like you don't even know my real name."

The man in the hat kept grinning.

"I know that Sharon Freeman – the actress we employed to take part in a romantic narrative with you – has told you everything. I've seen the footage. The general public hasn't, but I have."

Barboza took a step closer to the man. Walker saw that both her hands were curled up into tightly clenched fists. "Fuck you," she said. "And fuck your Future of London friends. Bunch of evil bastards, that's what you are."

The stranger's grin slowly faded. "As you wish, Sharon. But you were the one who was supposed to be doing the fucking, remember?" The man in the hat pointed at Walker. "You were supposed to fuck him."

"I remember," Barboza said. "And I'm glad I didn't do it. I'm not the network's whore after all, eh?"

The stranger gave a curt nod.

"It doesn't matter anymore," he said. "You are both wanted for the murders of two corporals in His Majesty's Armed Forces. Two boys, twenty-one years old and nineteen years old – brutally murdered at your hands earlier today."

He pointed at Walker's axe. "I imagine you want to use that on me."

Walker didn't answer.

"Two boys?" Barboza said. Her voice was cracking with rage or fear, or both. "Boys that were there to kill us. Sent in by your people, right? Walker and I know the truth about this city and that's a very dangerous thing for you. Of course you want us dead."

"Justice must be done," the man in the hat said. "And that's why I'm here today. I'm here to escort you both into custody – if you'll come willingly of course."

Walker glanced up and down the road. Then he looked up at the streetlights, listening out for that familiar *whirring* and *clicking* noise that had been driving him crazy for the past six months.

"There are no cameras on you," the stranger said to Walker. "Not here, not now. This meeting is entirely between us."

"Bullshit," Barboza said. "You film everything, don't you? Bunch of voyeuristic motherfuckers. And if we're such heinous bloody murderers then I'm sure the viewing public will be queuing up to see us in a pair of handcuffs. That'd be pretty good for the ratings, no?"

"Think about it," the man in the hat said. "Think about what we're talking about here. Do you really think *this* is fit for public consumption? I can assure you that this conversation is private."

"Doesn't matter," Barboza said. "Because we're not coming with you. You can go fuck yourself mate."

"I would urge you to reconsider," the man in the hat said. "This will be a dignified exit for you, off camera. A route has been prepared that will take us to a nearby helicopter and there are no active cameras on that route. You will simply vanish from the Future of London set and..."

"And?" Walker said. "Then what?"

"A trial of course," the man in the hat said.

Walker glanced over the stranger's shoulder. "Are you really alone?" he asked.

"I am. Except for the helicopter pilot."

Walker caressed the blade of the axe with the tips of his fingers. He felt the faint, sticky sensation of dry blood.

"You think you'll be able to take us?" Walker said. "Just you?"

"I was hoping to be able to persuade you," the man in the hat said. "There is no need for anything else. No *taking*, as you put it. We are all civilised human beings and so much blood has been spilled already on this beautiful summer's morning. Wouldn't you agree?"

"You talk about civilised?" Barboza said. "Do you think it's civilised, what you do to the people in here? Filming them without them knowing."

The man in the hat was looking at Walker. He didn't appear to hear Barboza's question or he simply chose not to answer.

"What if we say no?" Walker said. "Then what?"

"You walk away," said the man in the hat. "I can't stop you. But you must know that if you choose to do so, we will come back. And we'll come back with something more forceful than just words. I can't guarantee either that your final moments in this world won't be captured on camera either. So you see, you have a choice to make. Choose a quiet, dignified exit now. Or face violent and exploitative consequences later. It's up to you."

"You make it sound so easy," Walker said.

Barboza shook her head. "No," she said. "We're not coming with you."

The man in the hat looked at her.

"Think very carefully my dear," the man in the hat said. "Think very clearly about what you're doing. *You* must think about your family."

Barboza hesitated.

"What did you say?" she said.

"You've put our organisation in a very difficult situation," the man said.

Walker thought that the man in the hat sounded like an adult scolding a naughty child, and one who enjoyed doing so.

"You were contracted by the casting director to perform a specific task here in London," the man said to Barboza. "You were paid money to play a part and you violated that contract by attempting to sabotage our broadcast this morning. Isn't that so?"

"Sabotage your broadcast?" Walker said. "She told me the truth."

The man in the hat ignored Walker.

"You don't get it," Barboza said. "You have no idea what it's like living in this city for real, day after day. And neither did I. There are real people in this city you bastard. A fucking tiger tried to kill me this morning in Tottenham. A tiger! I didn't hear the director yelling cut, did you? There was nobody there, waiting to escort me to my trailer. It was Walker who saved my life. And you expect me to keep lying to him? He was going crazy in here, you fucking creep."

The man in the hat shook his head.

"This is a problem Sharon," he said. "Your family and friends – don't you think they'll try to tell people that Sharon Freeman is a real person and that Cristiane Barboza is just a character? We're already trying to persuade the public otherwise but the people who know you are a problem. We chose you because you had few contacts and those contacts could be trusted to keep quiet while you worked in London. But now that things have gone wrong, these people might have the urge to say something to someone about your true identity. And that's bad for us."

"It's your problem," Barboza said. "Leave my family alone."

"It's your problem too," the man in the hat said. "Because of you, we've been very busy today, paying your loved ones a visit to ensure that nothing is said about your real identity. There are more visits to be made."

"I swear to God," she said. "If you touch my family or my friends, we'll tell every living soul in this city that they're being watched." She looked at Walker. "Right?"

Walker nodded. "Right," he said. "And that's why you're here today isn't it mister?"

The man in the hat turned to Walker. "What do you mean by that?"

"Your biggest fear isn't the people on the outside," Walker said. "You can always distract them with a fresh dollop of bullshit. But in here it's different. You don't have that sort of control over the people in here. If people here knew that their lives were being exploited for the sake of crass entertainment – the shit would hit the fan, right? I can't even imagine what would happen next."

Walker saw a flicker of uncertainty in the stranger's eyes.

"That wouldn't be wise," said the man in the hat.

"Have you got a gun by the way?" Walker said, taking a few steps closer to the man. Now they were almost within touching distance. As he spoke, Walker raised his axe up to about chest height, with the bloody blade pointing towards the man. "Because if you've got a gun, I'd pull it out and shoot us right now. That's your safest bet."

"I'm unarmed," said the man in the hat, lifting his hands in the air. "I'm only here to offer you a way out that doesn't involve violence. You will receive a fair trial and if you are pardoned, you will be free. I thought that would appeal to you but perhaps I overestimated your intelligence, Mr Apocalypse?"

"A fair trial?" Walker said. "By whose laws? We live in here – your rules don't apply. The soldiers died inside the M25 and in here, that's the end of it."

"Who's been feeding you for the last nine years Mr Apocalypse?" the man in the hat said. "Who provides electricity into this city? Clean water? You tell me you're no longer part of our society but if it weren't for that society you'd have died years ago. Isn't it so?"

The man in the hat smiled.

"Tell me," he said. "If you feel so aggrieved, then why haven't you said anything to the cameras so far? You've been out walking in London for some time now, passing many cameras on the way. Why haven't you told the viewers that Barboza is an actress? I can understand why your friend here wouldn't say anything – she has her family to think of. Or perhaps she's still too busy thinking about what she did to that poor young man this morning."

"Go fuck yourself," Barboza said.

"But what about you Mr Apocalypse?" the man in the hat said. "Why haven't you said anything yet?"

Walker looked at the man with cold contempt. "I have something to do," he said.

The other man's eyes lit up. "Oh? Is that so?"

"Aye," Walker said.

"And what is it you have to do?"

"None of your fucking business," Walker said.

"But it *is* my business," the man in the hat said. "The public have turned against you. Mr Apocalypse is no longer flavour of the month. The people want to see you brought in for the savage killing of these two young men. They want to see justice."

There was a wicked glint in the man's eye as he spoke.

"Did you know that one of those young men had a three-month old daughter?" he said, looking at Barboza. "I can't recall which one.

It might have been the same man whose throat you slit open earlier today."

Barboza lunged at the man. But Walker had sensed that it was coming, sooner or later. He was ready. He got his arm in the way of Barboza's progress, preventing her from getting her hands on the man.

"Fucking prick!" she yelled. She spat at his face, the gob missile falling short of its target.

Walker forced the enraged Barboza back with his left arm. With his other arm, he pointed the axe at the man in the hat.

"Get the fuck out of here," Walker said. "We're done."

The man in the hat nodded. "Very well," he said. "You've made your choice. You won't come willingly and I can't stop you leaving now. But I can make your life – whatever is left of it – extremely uncomfortable."

"You won't do anything," Walker said. "Because we're the ones with the upper hand. We've got your little TV show by the balls and if I see anything that looks weird, anything or anyone that reeks of your people then I'll make sure that – before you get me – everyone in this city knows what's going on. I swear to God, I'll spread the word faster than you can blink."

The stranger stared at Walker. Despite the heat of the day, the man's ivory white skin was bone dry.

"Assuming we let you go," the man said. "You truly have no intention of telling anyone?"

Walker lowered the axe – a little. "That's not on my agenda," he said. "And that's all you need to know."

"And when you have completed this task?" the man said. "What then?"

Walker shook his head. "I don't know," he said.

That was the truth.

The man looked back and forth between Walker and Barboza. Walker guessed that he was pondering his next move – that perhaps he was debating an alternate option that hadn't occurred to him until now.

"Very well," the man said after a lengthy silence. "Perhaps the easiest thing would be just to let you go about your business. That is, as long as you're sincere about saying nothing to anyone. But remember this Mr Apocalypse and Sharon Freeman – there are microphones everywhere in this city. You cannot speak of what we have spoken about here today."

"What about my family?" Barboza said.

The man in the hat reached into the side pocket of his jacket and pulled out a sleek, narrow-bodied mobile phone. Using his thumb, he swiped upwards on the black screen. Then he stepped forward and pointed the phone at Barboza.

"No one will be harmed," the man said, looking at the screen while adjusting the angle of the phone. "As long as they promise to keep quiet about your real identity. But if there are any leaks, I assure you my bosses will not be happy with those people."

"What are you doing?" Barboza said, scowling at the man.

"Taking a photograph for your family," said the man in the hat, slipping the phone back into his pocket. "And for your friends. With the time and date recorded on the phone, this will let them know that we have made contact and that we have spoken. I'll tell them about our little deal. If they agree to play ball, everyone goes about their business as usual."

The man in the hat looked at Walker.

"You do nothing, we do nothing," he said. "We'll call it a stalemate for now. Mr Apocalypse and Cristiane Barboza will be outlaws on the run in London. They will be wanted for murder but as long as you stay quiet, you will never be captured. That's the deal. The public will probably forget all about you but until they do, we're going to have to trust one another to keep silent."

"I'll never trust you," Barboza said. "And if anything happens to my family..."

"What choice do we have?" said the man in the hat. "But to trust?"

With that, he touched the tip of the fedora hat with his index finger and bowed without ever taking his eyes off the two fugitives. Then he turned his back to Walker and Barboza and casually strolled down the road, walking past a row of empty shops, a burned out solicitors office, towards a small road that cut off to the left.

Before he took that left turn, the stranger stopped and turned around. Now he was facing Walker and Barboza once again. He took off his hat, revealing a white, cue ball shaped head, completely devoid of hair. The sun beat down hard upon his face, turning it so white that he barely looked human.

"Oh I almost forgot," he said, that wicked grin back on his face. "Good luck tonight my young assassins. You're going to need it."

CHAPTER 2

The Future of London – A Special Announcement

July 12th 2020

VOICEOVER: Good afternoon ladies and gentlemen. We'd like to briefly interrupt all of our live streams across the Future of London network to bring you this special announcement from our CEO, Rudyard Campbell.

Cut to Campbell.

The Texan media mogul is standing in a TV studio, staring intently at the camera. There's a strained expression on his face that gives the seventy-seven year old Campbell the impression of being even older.

His grim countenance is at odds with the studio background; the bright, hip colours, the half-circle shaped couch, but above all, the large and still blinking map of London that dominates the set. This is the 'Calling London' studio and it's a particularly noteworthy location, considering that the hosts of that particular FOL companion show – Georgia Perkins and Johnny Castle – along with many others, were killed just hours earlier in an attack on the M25 by the Good and Honest Citizens.

Campbell straightens his tie as the camera slowly zooms in.

RUDYARD CAMPBELL:

My dear friends, tonight is the night. The Ghosts of London will climb out of the Hole and make their way north for the Big Chase.

To the people of North London, even though they can't hear us, we say this – our thoughts and prayers are with you.

And to you, the viewers, we understand that this isn't for everyone. In light of what has already happened today at the M25, who really wants to see any more bloodshed? We at the Future of London *will* broadcast what happens tonight, but only out of our ongoing commitment to showing you the truth. That is what we promised to do when we launched this channel earlier this year – to tell you the truth. It would be wrong only to show you certain things and omit others. To do this is to lie to our audience and we won't lie to you. We understand if you cannot watch tonight's events – but we will broadcast them.

I repeat. The Ghosts are coming north. To the people of London, I say this – hide, hope and pray for the sun to rise.

God Bless.

CHAPTER 3

Walker and Barboza continued along the A105.

The streets here were narrow and claustrophobic. On either side of the road, abandoned or destroyed shop fronts reminded Walker of the kind of things he'd forgotten had existed. He walked past all sorts of places, including a Chinese Medical Centre that – according to a poster that still barely clung to the wall – offered a variety of herbs and acupunctural treatments.

Walker caught himself looking over his shoulder more than once. He wasn't sure what he was expecting to see or hear behind them. Perhaps the muted growl of an armoured vehicle in the distance? Was that so far-fetched? Somebody had to be chasing them considering what they'd just done. Walker envisioned the pack of armoured vehicles hot on their heels, with the man in the hat poking his head out of the hatch of the leading car, that devilish grin lighting up his face.

"Walker!"

Barboza's voice came out of nowhere. It was distant, like someone calling him out of a dream.

He looked at her. "What?"

"Why do you keep looking over your shoulder?" she said. "You're making me nervous man. Even more nervous than I already am."

"Sorry," Walker said. "It's just..."

"What?"

"That guy in the hat," Walker said, fighting the urge to look behind him. "You don't think he's just going to back off and let us do our thing, do you? Knowing what we know?"

"Maybe," Barboza said. "Maybe not. Maybe his best choice is to hope we stay quiet like we say we will. What they should have done is killed us back there when they had the cameras switched off. I'll bet he only wanted us to go quietly so that they could have a public trial outside the M25 – more fucking headlines and sensationalism. The Mr Apocalypse trial! Dignified exit my arse. They'd probably hang us in a public square and sell tickets."

"Aye," Walker said.

"Yeah," Barboza said, glancing up at the tall, black streetlights that lined their route for the foreseeable future. "But we're not supposed to talk about it, remember?"

Walker nodded.

They walked in silence under the hot sun.

Walker looked up at the foreboding shape of the tall buildings in the distance – the concrete tower blocks that formed such an essential part of the skyline. Places that somebody had once called home. He was imagining what it was like to be inside the private dwellings within those gloomy monoliths – the corpses that were probably lying in the bedrooms up there, side by side, just like the ones he'd seen back on Stanmore Road.

He closed his eyes and tried to think of something else. Anything besides the smell of rotten corpses.

"Walker!"

He opened his eyes. "Eh?"

Barboza was staring at him, wide-eyed. Like he'd just sprouted a second head or something.

"What's going on with you man?"

"What? Did you say something?"

"Bloody right I did. I said there's someone down there. Look."

"Where?"

Barboza pointed towards the entrance of one of the abandoned shop fronts, located on the right hand side of the road. It was a place called Juice Stop, one of those trendy little pit stops where people would grab smoothies and fruit drinks on the go. A withered awning stretched from the front of the shop, extending over an area that might once have been full of tables and chairs.

Somebody was standing under the awning.

It was a man. He was watching them as they approached. Walker took a closer look and his first thought was that the guy looked like a stereotypical homeless tramp – the sort of down on his luck type that would rake the bins at night for scraps, all the while covered from head to toe in dirt. He had long filthy brown hair and a bushy beard that smothered most of his face, except for a pair of eager, fast blinking eyes that never stopped moving. He wore a faded black vest top, revealing a pair of wiry looking arms that at first glance, appeared to be badly sunburned. But as Walker got closer, he saw that it wasn't sunburn after all. The man's arms were covered in a plethora of red wounds. It looked as if an entire neighbourhood's worth of cats had ganged up on him and clawed him to pieces. The man had matching wounds on his legs, which were poking out of a flimsy pair of short black underpants. He was barefooted.

He watched them approach, jerking constantly like there was an electric shock going through him every five seconds.

"You think it's a rogue?" Walker whispered.

"I don't know," Barboza said. "If he is then why isn't he running at us?"

"Look," Walker said. "He's moving."

The man took several tentative steps towards them. As he did so, he placed his hands over his head. He looked like the last holdout, surrendering to an invading army after a long siege.

"Don't hurt me," he yelled. The man did a full spin as he

approached the side of the road, showing them that he wasn't carrying any weapons strapped to his back. "I'm unarmed, I swear."

He stopped a few metres away from them.

"What happened to you?" Walker said. "Did somebody cut you or something?"

"No," the man said, speaking in a rough, raspy voice. "Nobody cut me. Please, may I lower my arms?"

"Not yet," Walker said. He squeezed the handle of the axe, but kept it lowered at his side. "What happened to you?"

The man shook his head and looked off into the distance, as if distracted.

Walker and Barboza glanced at one another.

"It wasn't a tiger, was it?" Walker said to the man. He was thinking back to the encounter they'd had on the New River that morning. Walker still had three long scratches running along his left forearm. And they stung like a bitch. But his wounds were nothing compared to those of the man standing in front of him. The man's arms and legs were literally covered in sores and scratch marks. Walker had the feeling that if somebody pulled at all those wounds at once, there was a chance they could peel the man open like a piece of fruit.

"No," the man said. "No it wasn't a tiger."

"Your skin looks bad," Barboza said. "Can we help you?"

The man shook his head. His eyes darted back and forth between Walker, Barboza and their immediate surroundings. Whenever there was a hint of birdsong in the distance or from overhead, his eyes went after it, like a hunter getting his first whiff of prey.

"May I lower my hands?" he said.

Walker nodded. "Aye, I suppose."

"Thank you," the man said, sighing with relief. He dropped both arms and shook them out like he was loosening his limbs in preparation of a workout.

Then he immediately began scratching at the claw marks on his body. His long, dirty fingernails tore at the already tortured skin and to Walker's disgust, the man moaned with pleasure as he upped the ante, scratching ferociously at his wounds. In a matter of second, many of the fresh cuts were bleeding again.

"What the fuck?" Barboza said. "Walker?"

Walker didn't speak. What was he supposed to say?

The man looked at them as if he'd just remembered they were there. But he didn't stop scratching.

"No tigers," he said, grinning and showing off his long, yellowing teeth. And as he continued to scratch, his bright blue eyes danced with joy. "It's me. I can't stop. I just can't stop scratching."

He took a step closer, walking onto the road. Then he lifted up his vest top and Walker heard Barboza gasping out loud. Or maybe it was him. The man's body was splattered with countless wounds that made him look he was part of some post-mortem science experiment. The skin was torn and bleeding and there were chunks of thick, decaying flesh hanging off the self-inflicted wounds.

"I can't stop," the scratching man said. "Help me please."

Barboza tugged on Walker's arm. "I'm going to puke Walker. Or faint. Or something."

The scratching man's hands were working their way up towards his neck. Walker felt his stomach lurch as the man's fingers crawled up his body like two five-legged flesh spiders. Once they arrived on the lower neck, they tore ferociously at the damaged skin. The tips of the man's fingers were covered in fresh blood.

"I say, you couldn't do me a favour," the man said, calling out to them. He was glancing at the axe in Walker's right hand. "Any chance you could kill me please? It's just that I can't stop this bloody scratching and I don't think I'm ever going to stop until...it's such a terrible way to go. It's like there are things crawling all over me and it doesn't stop. It doesn't ever stop. Please just kill me."

He reached a hand out towards Walker and Barboza. There was fresh blood dripping off the tips of his fingers.

Barboza grabbed Walker by the forearm, almost yanking it clean off. Walker grimaced, but he understood the message.

They began to back away from the scratching man. Slowly at first, but increasing the pace with each step.

The scratching man stood there, close to Juice Stop. He was watching them as he scratched every inch of his body from top to bottom. Once or twice, he stopped for a moment and his body immediately jerked convulsively, like it was telling him to start all over again. Walker saw a tremendous sadness in the man's eyes and for a moment, he felt only pity that somebody could end up like that.

The scratching man looked at Walker and Barboza again. Then, without warning, he came running after them.

Walker's heart exploded like a bomb.

"Run!" he yelled in a voice that was loud enough for half the city to hear.

Walker and Barboza took off, both of them sprinting down the road with the fierce sun on their backs.

As Walker ran, he heard the scratching man's footsteps behind them. But worse than that, he could still hear that terrible slicing sound of the man's nails digging into his flesh.

Walker and Barboza ran down Harringay Road as fast as they cold. Walker felt as light as a feather, even though he was carrying a rucksack over his shoulder and he had the axe in his hand too. Fear was his fuel. Walker didn't want the scratching man to touch either one of them, in case he was carrying some sort of contagious disease. That was all either one of them needed.

Walker didn't think about slowing down for at least two or three minutes. When the adrenaline finally started to wear off, Walker looked behind them and the scratching man was gone. There was just a long, endless empty street leading back towards North London. Walker and Barboza slowed down further, content in the knowledge that their pursuer was no longer following them.

Walker and Barboza dropped their rucksacks onto the road. Two loud thuds, accompanied by the sound of heavy breathing. Now they were really sweating and it was time to take on some more water.

They didn't stop for long however. They were keen to press on towards Liverpool Street Station and what's more, they couldn't be sure the scratching man wasn't still coming after them at his own leisurely pace. They were still on the A105 but now they were closing in on the centre of London. As they travelled further south, Walker marvelled at the abundance of ruined shops – pound shops, travel agents, fast food places, hairdressers – all of them with their windows smashed in and with shelves and other pieces of debris lying visible inside. It took his mind back to the London riots of 2011, where it had all started.

"Are we close to the station?" he asked Barboza.

"Yeah," she said. "I think so."

They walked south onto Green Lane, which took them past a wildly neglected Finsbury Park. Occasionally, Walker and Barboza heard voices in the distance. Shouting or screaming – it was hard to tell.

Soon after, they reached Stoke Newington, about three or four miles north of the city centre. More quiet streets, abandoned houses, overgrown hedges and rotten shop fronts. They made a point of keeping to the middle of the road, their eyes and ears peeled for signs of anything unusual from the back, front and either side.

Eventually they found themselves entering the heart of the city. Everything was silent except for the sky, lit up by the constant music of the birds.

But not for long. Soon there was another noise.

Walker heard it first. He stopped in the middle of the road and Barboza did likewise. It was faint at first, but he was sure that he'd heard something. Or rather, he'd felt something. Like the road was trembling underneath him.

What the hell was that? An earthquake? In London?

He listened again.

Engines. They were coming straight towards them, travelling south to north. It sounded like a pack of motorbikes, and that was something that Walker hadn't heard for a long time. It was a terrifying, menacing growl that signalled danger.

And it was getting louder, closer by the second.

"Oh shit," Barboza said. "Whoever that is, we can't let them see us Walker. We're nearly there for God's sake."

"I know," Walker said.

He looked around, searching for a place to hide and get off the street fast. Where were they anyway? A street sign on one of the nearby buildings told him they were standing in Curtain Road. Where the hell was that? His eyes raced back and forth, looking for a sign of temporary shelter. Further down to their left, Walker noticed a pub called The Horse & Groom. Like everywhere else, the windows had long since been smashed in, as had the glass panel on the front door.

It was the best of a bad bunch.

"In there," Walker said, grabbing a hold of Barboza's arm and dragging her towards the ruined pub. He didn't have to pull hard – Barboza was in no mood to disagree with his choice of hiding place. There wasn't time to look for anything better anyway – if they couldn't hide from the bikers in the old pub then they couldn't hide at all.

Barboza led the way into the building, clambering through the gap at the front where a large window had once been. It was just a wide rectangular space now, that sat atop a wooden base on the lower part of the pub's exterior. It was easy enough for both of them to get through.

Inside, the building was a wreck – it was dark and devoid of furniture or anything that would have let someone know that it had once been a pub. Only the sign on the front gave it away now. The walls were black due to smoke and fire damage. There was a horrible smell of urine coming off the floor. Walker and Barboza positioned themselves belly down behind the large wooden panel underneath the window. Dust plumes floated around them. There was ash everywhere and the stale and musty odour of decay was intermingled with the potent, ever-present smell of piss.

Walker and Barboza scrunched their noses up in disgust.

Outside, the motorbikes arrived on Curtain Road. To Walker, it sounded like there was a small procession of them out there – a convoy coming after them with bad intent.

There was a low growl from the engines as the wheels of the bikes slowed to a stop.

Behind the window, Walker gripped the handle of the axe, bringing the weapon close to his body.

The motorbikes sounded like they were stationary now; they were purring in unison like a group of big cats gathered around a fresh kill. They sounded so close it was like every single one of the damn machines was parked on top of Walker's head.

Footsteps. They were coming towards the pub.

It sounded like one of the riders was standing directly outside, just a few feet from where Walker and Barboza were lying belly down on the pub floor. The footsteps went back and forth along the entrance, like whoever was out there was teasing them – letting them know that *they* knew they were in there.

"Little pigs," a man's voice called out. It was a deep, booming rumble of a voice – a voice that probably showed up on the Richter scale.

"Let me come in."

Walker put a hand on Barboza, instructing her to stay on the floor. Not that she showed any signs of moving.

"Or," the man's voice called out. "If you don't want me to come in, you could always come out here and say hi. Do that if it makes you feel better. I assure you little pigs that I'm not here to hurt anyone. On the contrary – my friends and I are trying to help the people around here. We have some news to share with you. Will you come out?"

Walker kept his face pinned to the hard floor. He grimaced as he was forced to inhale the gruesome combo of rotten wood and stale piss.

Outside, the riders turned their motorcycle engines off, one by one. The silence that followed felt more dangerous than the noise that had preceded it.

The rider outside the pub continued to move back and forth, from one end of the building to another. It sounded like he was a trooper standing guard outside a royal palace, stretching his legs. Walker cringed as he listened to the man's thick boots slapping against the concrete, each one of them like a baseball bat to the head.

"Little pigs," said the man with the deep voice. "Come on," he said. "Don't do this the hard way. Come out now, or we come in. Your choice."

Walker and Barboza looked at each other. Barboza nodded in resignation at Walker and he knew exactly what she was saying.

What choice do we have?

Walker nodded. He took a deep breath and pushed himself onto his feet. Then he grabbed Barboza by the hand, helping her up too.

There was a big man standing at the window. Behind him, were another four bikers – two men and two women, sitting on their motorbikes in the middle of Curtain Road. The man standing closest to them wasn't just big – he was huge. Not tall, but wide and barrel shaped – the sort of guy you'd want in your rugby team going into a life or death scrum. That's what he looked like – a rugby player dressed in biker leathers. Not somebody that Walker wanted to get into an argument with anytime soon.

The others were dressed in the same black biker leathers. The two men and women were sitting on their motorbikes, rigid like statues, and showed no signs of getting up anytime soon.

But they were all staring at Walker and Barboza. And there was a menacing look in every pair of eyes.

Except the big man – he was smiling. He was about thirty years old with a light brown complexion that hinted of Middle Eastern origins. Despite the man's exotic looks, his accent was all London. He wore his hair closely cropped with the exception of a long ponytail that dropped down to his back. The other two men in the mini-convoy were scrawny in comparison to their barrel shaped leader.

Both men sat on their bikes, looking at Walker and Barboza, and the look in their eyes was battle-hardened, as if they'd seen terrible things in their lives and lived to talk about it. One of the men had a wide, flesh-coloured scar of about six inches running down his cheek. The other was bald-headed, with a blond goatee sprouting from his chin that seemed to go on forever.

The two women meanwhile, were a little younger than their male companions – early to mid-twenties at most. One of them had milky white skin and flaming red hair that dropped to her shoulders. The other had short, spiky peroxide blonde hair. Out of all the bikers, she sported the meanest look and it was directed at both Walker and Barboza with an almost comical ferociousness.

"Wise decision," the big man said. He took a step back from the window, accompanied by the sound of squeaking leather.

"Now why don't you come outside?" he said. "All we're going to do is talk. And trust me, you'll be thankful for it."

Barboza was first to step through the empty window. Walker followed close behind her. Now they were lined up on the pavement, side by side, looking back at the five bikers who had them cornered on Curtain Road. Upon closer inspection, Walker noticed that the bikers were all riding Harley Davidsons. As a teenager, he'd had a thing for Harleys and had always envisaged himself owning one when he was older and richer. Of course he'd never gotten around to having that awkward conversation with his parents – the one about how he'd prefer to have motorbike lessons instead of driving lessons.

He was spared that at least.

The big man's bike was particularly impressive. It was a newer Road King model, although Walker wasn't exactly sure what year. But even so – the gleaming black bodywork, the old school Harley logo on the side of the fuel tank, the side covers and saddlebags – even in an uncomfortable situation like this one, Walker allowed himself a moment to glance in appreciation at such a perfect machine.

"You probably weren't expecting us," the big man said. "But

strange things happen in this city. You know how it is – sometimes it feels like you're walking down London as it was before Piccadilly. Before it all went tits up and kaboom. Everything looks normal, then you blink and when you open your eyes again you're standing in the middle of a nightmare. Right?"

Neither Walker nor Barboza said anything.

"You two got names?" the big man asked.

Walker nodded. "I'm Walker," he said, through gritted teeth. "This is Barboza. We're just passing through and not looking for any trouble. We're not trying to tread on anyone's turf either – we've never been down this far south and we don't know the rules."

The big man smiled. "A Scotsman, eh?"

"Aye."

"We've got a few Scots with us back at Station," the big man said. "Good people the Scots – hard workers, loyal – yeah, bet they wish they'd stayed up north, eh? Coming to London wasn't the best move they ever made."

Walker looked at him. "Station?"

The big man frowned. "Definitely not from around here, eh?"

"We've been living up north for the past nine years," Barboza said. "Close to the M25. But in the end rogues forced us out – there were too many of 'em. We don't know much about the rules, about what goes on down here so if we're stepping on your territory then we're sorry. We're just trying to get somewhere."

The big man raised his eyebrows. It looked like he wasn't expecting an apology.

"They call me Fat Joseph," he said. And then he gave his belly a few playful taps. "Can't imagine why, eh?"

Fat Joseph then pointed to Walker's axe. "Before we talk, I think you should give me that," he said. "At least until we get to know each other a little better."

Walker didn't move. He had no intention of handing the axe to over these strangers.

"Maybe you didn't hear me?" Fat Joseph said, leaning in a little closer. "Please, let's not be difficult."

"Kill him."

The voice came from the middle of Curtain Road. It belonged to the blonde haired woman – she was still sitting on her Harley-Davidson Street Glide, glaring at Walker like he'd just murdered her entire family in cold blood.

"You'll have to forgive Rhonda," Fat Joseph said. "She doesn't like strangers."

"I don't like anyone I don't know who's carrying a bloodstained axe," she said. "Especially with that cold, murderous look in his eyes. Take it off him Joseph."

"Why don't *you* try?" Walker said, looking at Rhonda over Fat Joseph's shoulder.

Rhonda smiled and it was a chilling, demonic grin. Was that what she'd been hoping to hear all along? At Walker's challenge, she reached a heavily tattooed hand into her jacket pocket and pulled something out in a blur. Walker heard a brief clicking sound and then watched as a gleaming blade unfolded itself from a sleek, silver handle several times over.

Walker almost gasped. It was easily the longest switchblade that he'd ever seen, more like a thin sword than a knife.

Rhonda swung a long leg over the side of the bike, not taking her eyes off Walker.

"Hold it Rhonda," Fat Joseph said. The big man was looking at Walker as he spoke to the young woman behind him. "I think you'd better give me that axe mate. I've seen what Rhonda can do to a man's private parts with that blade. It ain't pretty, especially if you're planning on having any children."

Rhonda stood in the middle of the road, glaring at Walker. The blade of the long knife was pointing at him, ready to poke a thousand holes into his skin on Fat Joseph's command.

"Look we don't have time for this," Barboza said. She pushed Walker's arm down, forcing him to lower the axe. "It's like we said – we're not looking for trouble. We're looking for Michael King. That's where we're going – to Liverpool Street Station to see him. We've come a long way and we're so close. Walker knows him – sort of."

Fat Joseph tilted his head.

"You know Michael King?" he said to Walker.

"I was at Piccadilly," Walker said. "Right up the front, just after Chester George was shot and killed. Michael King and I were both trying to get a hold of the same guy – the guy who killed Chester."

Fat Joseph smiled. "Tell me about the guy who killed Chester George."

"He lived on the same estate as Michael King and a couple of other kids I knew back then," Walker said. "Short, black, stocky. Sort of like a miniature Mike Tyson."

"His name?" Fat Joseph said.

"Michael King hasn't told you his name?" Walker asked.

"Michael King doesn't know his name," Fat Joseph said. "Or at least, he can't remember it. He knows that the kid lived on his estate back in 2011 but he never could pin down the name. It's been driving him crazy for a long time. And yeah, your description sounds just like our boy."

"I know his name," Walker said.

"You say you know," Fat Joseph said. "But if I take you to Michael King and you're lying then you've wasted our time. And if you waste our precious time, bad things are going to happen my friend. To you. To her. You get it? There's no playing around when it comes to the little twat who killed Chester. That's big time baby."

"I know him," Walker said. "And I'll tell Michael King his name."

Fat Joseph looked back and forth at Walker and Barboza. Slowly, the smile returned to the big man's face.

"Well then," he said. "Let's go see him."

CHAPTER 4

SKAM TV - The Lunchtime News Broadcast

July 12th 2020

The news begins by showing images of a once quiet suburban street in North London.

This is Stanmore Road.

Several armoured vehicles are parked alongside the kerb. Countless troops are spilling out of the AFVs, taking up position on both sides of the street. Others are searching the neighbourhood houses, scouring the overgrown gardens in search of something or someone. At the same time, a Black Hawk helicopter descends noisily from the sky, preparing to land in the middle of the road

The camera then cuts to the news desk where thirty-five year-old Gayle Campbell, is sitting behind a large caption with the main headline – 'MR APOCALYPSE MURDERS' – printed in bold, red letters.

GAYLE CAMPBELL: Good afternoon. I'm Gayle Campbell and welcome to SKAM's Lunchtime Broadcast. As reported earlier this morning, hundreds of lives were lost in a savage terrorist attack on the M25 by the Good and Honest Citizens. But there was a second event this morning, which is quickly being labelled on social media as the 'Mr Apocalypse Murders'. If you haven't heard, two young soldiers were brutally murdered today in North London and it's believed that two stars of the Future of London reality TV series – Mr Apocalypse, also known as Walker, and Cristiane Barboza – are responsible. Joining me now to discuss this is one of SKAM's resident Future of London analysts, Gordon Schultz.

The camera cuts to a thirty-nine year-old man sitting next to Gayle. Gordon Schultz, a professional sociologist at the University of Cambridge, is dressed in a three-button Yorkshire Tweed jacket and his face sports about a day's growth of dark stubble.

GORDON SCHULTZ: Thank you Gayle.

GAYLE CAMPBELL: What a terrible day it's been so far Gordon. Now we've got these Mr Apocalypse murders on top of what happened at the M25. It's just horrendous, isn't it? It's believed that the two young soldiers were assisting a routine maintenance task in North London when Mr Apocalypse and Barboza ambushed them.

The details so far are sketchy but grim. Apparently one of the soldiers had his throat cut and early reports also say that several fingers were hacked off one of his hands. The other soldier was apparently bludgeoned to death with an axe inside Mr Apocalypse's house. This really is shocking, isn't it Gordon?

GORDON SCHULTZ: Yes Gayle it is. It's particularly tragic when you consider that these two innocent young men were only in London in the first place trying to help these people. I believe at the time, they were assisting with a small electrical fire in the Stanmore Road area.

GAYLE CAMPBELL: Another important thing to consider Gordon – just before the electrical fire caused havoc with the Future of London's cameras, we witnessed Cristiane Barboza having a mental breakdown in Mr Apocalypse's house. She was hysterical and even claimed to be an actress at one point. Now a lot of people – quite rightly – jumped all over this but these initial concerns died down quickly as it became clear that Barboza was not literally claiming to be a professional actress. Is that correct?

GORDON SCHULTZ: That's correct Gayle. I believe that the stress of staying alive in such a harsh environment has caused Barboza to feel that she is playing a role. That is, she's playing the role of the survivor and that comes with a lot of pressure that people on the outside can't understand. It's also possible that Barboza has developed Dissociative Identity Disorder – that is she's created multiple personalities to help her cope with the stress of the situation she's in. That would certainly explain why we've heard her speaking with both a Brazilian and English accent.

GAYLE CAMPBELL: And perhaps something like Dissociative Identity Disorder, that would explain her ability to commit such horrific crimes like these murders. If the act of murder could be blamed on someone else – a different personality for example – then it's easier to live with. Yes?

GORDON SCHULTZ: Absolutely Gayle. It must be hard for people like Barboza who've lived in London for so long to understand what's real anymore. This is not to justify these brutal murders, but we must try and make some kind of effort to understand the minds of those who committed the act.

GAYLE CAMPBELL: This certainly addresses the ongoing debate about rehabilitation, doesn't it? The RELEASE versus PRESERVE argument.

GORDON SCHULTZ: Yes and as you know Gayle, I'm a long-standing advocate of PRESERVE – that is, to keep things as they are. What happened in Stanmore Road today should put all ideas of rehabilitation to bed once and for all. We cannot let these people back into our society.

GAYLE CAMPBELL: There's no hope for them?

GORDON SCHULTZ: They're no longer like us Gayle – it's that simple. They've been dehumanised through a tragic series of circumstances. It's terrible but we cannot trust these people around the rest of society – would you leave your children with one of them? Those who advocate RELEASE have to accept the hard facts – the people of London are not safe for us to be around.

GAYLE CAMPBELL: And to think, Mr Apocalypse had become such a hit with the viewers lately. For many of us who watched – myself included – it felt like we were watching a friend.

GORDON SCHULTZ: (*Nodding*) Sometimes we think we have a connection with an animal through the bars of a cage. We make eye contact. We feel something and believe that it's real. But there is no connection except the one we invent for ourselves. We cannot open the cage door because all of our lives are at risk around dangerous animals. Today's murders are another piece of sledgehammer evidence, showing us why we can't pull down the M25. These people are unstable – we saw that with the Lovebirds earlier this year and now with Mr Apocalypse and Barboza.

GAYLE CAMPBELL: Thank you Gordon Schultz. (*Turning back to camera*) Well, discussions are already underway between the military and police about how to bring the two murderers to justice. As of now however, both Mr Apocalypse and Barboza remain at large somewhere in the city.

CHAPTER 5

Immersion 9 – Live Chat Forums
#GhostsofLondon #MrApocalypseMurders

Ziggy Sawdust: LOL! Did you see Campbell's announcement today?

The Vegan Butcher: Yeah.

Ziggy Sawdust: The Ghosts are coming!!

The Vegan Butcher: How long since they were last out?

Mr Blue Sky: Not long enough. Don't think I can stomach

watching that all over again. Why are FOL broadcasting this vile shit to the public?

Ziggy Sawdust: People pay for 24/7 access. They can't cut it.

The Vegan Butcher: @MrBlueSky Oooooh! Too much for you is it mate? Look at these bloody savages we made, eh? LOL! Even Mr Apocalypse is a cold-blooded killer!!! Wow! What's up? Can't handle FOL anymore?

Mr Blue Sky: @TheVeganButcher Idiot! Mr A and Barboza were set up and everyone with half a brain knows it. Guess that excludes you though.

The Vegan Butcher: @MrBlueSky Cold-blooded killers mate, the pair of them. Him and the bitch should be strung up in public.

Mr Blue Sky: @TheVeganButcher How's that work then? The Londoners were shut out and yet you're still judging them by our laws? The soldiers were pissing about in their territory! Might as well put a shark on trial for killing a surfer.

The Vegan Butcher: @MrBlueSky I hope the Ghosts get 'em.

CHAPTER 6

The bikers led Walker and Barboza towards Liverpool Street Station.

Walker and Barboza travelled behind the small convoy on foot. Despite their heavy legs, they did their best to keep up with the steady, mechanical hum that beckoned them forwards to their meeting with Michael King.

From Shoreditch, the convoy travelled south onto a major road that was known as Bishopsgate. This massive road formed part of the A10, which in its time had been one of the main thoroughfares through the city of London.

Tall office buildings towered above them on either side of the street; abandoned places of commerce and enterprise that had in the last nine years, become five hundred foot tall gravestones growing out of cracks in the concrete.

About ten minutes later, they arrived at Liverpool Street Station.

Fat Joseph revved his motorcycle on the final approach, riding slightly ahead of the others. The others didn't let him get too far ahead. They quickly followed suit and broke ranks one at a time, riding towards the entrance of the station. Walker saw the bikes taking a sharp right turn off Bishopsgate, before pulling up next to the main entrance.

Walker and Barboza came up behind them, just as the bikers were dismounting from their motorcycles.

They'd made it. Liverpool Street Station.

Walker thought it looked more like a Gothic cathedral than a train station, with its soaring arches and two towers that flanked the main entrance. He'd heard a little about Liverpool Street Station during history lessons at school – World War Two lessons. He knew that it had been open since the late nineteenth century and in the intervening years had suffered significant wartime damage due to air raids. But what Walker remembered most of all was that the station had temporarily acted as a terminus for child refugees arriving in London prior to the Second World War. It was part of something known as the Kindertransport rescue mission. That was when Britain took in ten thousand predominantly Jewish children from Germany and surrounding countries that were threatened by Nazi persecution. And they'd arrived here, at Liverpool Street Station. Somewhere nearby, Walker knew there was a bronze memorial – a statue of five children, looking around wide-eyed at their surroundings. He'd seen pictures of it.

Walker wondered if it was still there. He hoped so.

He unwrapped the hot, damp T-shirt from his head. Then he wrung it out, watching the sweat fall onto the road in slow, steady drips. After putting it back into his rucksack, he wiped a thin layer of sweat from his forehead. He tried to dry his hand on the side of his jeans, which felt like they were stuck to his legs with hot glue. As he did this, Walker felt the scratches on his left forearm sting.

"What are we doing here Walker?" Barboza said. She was standing beside him, looking at the five bikers standing outside the station like a police line-up, waiting to escort the visitors inside. The bikers were in turn, looking back at Walker and Barboza, perhaps wondering why they were taking so long to come forward.

"Why didn't we just cross the river?" she asked.

"I need to know," Walker said. "I need to know what happened to Hatchet that day at Piccadilly, after he shot Chester George."

Walker approached the entrance, moving past a row of bollards, up a few concrete steps. He didn't even looking at the bikers as he passed them. There was an unexpected confidence in his stride now and as he walked, he heard Barboza catching up with him in a hurry.

"I have a bad feeling about this," she said.

"We get the information and come straight back out again," Walker said. "Okay?"

Barboza didn't answer.

Fat Joseph caught up with them. Then, with the rest of the bikers taking up the rear, he led Walker and Barboza through the main entrance of Liverpool Street Station. It was a massive place befitting of what had once been London's third busiest train station. It was everything Walker had hoped it would be. Walking down a set of stairs towards the concourse, he was struck by the old-fashioned beauty of the place, which effortlessly intermingled with the modern. The interior of the station was a stunning blend of contemporary and Victorian architecture. The roof was striking, built of iron and glass and it spanned multiple platforms, resulting in a Gothic feel that permeated the highest level of the building. Underneath the roof however, the station belonged firmly in the twenty-first century. On either side of the wide concourse, were dozens of spaces that had once housed a variety of retail units. There was also a selection of Ticket Xpress machines still scattered across the floor, designed for people who had needed to buy a ticket in a hurry.

The station's concourse was full of people, much as it would have been in 2011. But rather than being a busy transport hub, this was now a home. There were people everywhere, sitting at plastic chairs and tables, sitting on blankets or sleeping beds on the floor, Many of them were tucked into the old shop fronts that had once been part of the station – a card shop, clothes shop, flowers shop, a Burger King –

amongst others. Along the middle of the concourse, a narrow path ran through the station like a river through a city. The pathway was free of any obstacles, allowing access from one end of the building to the other.

The station was home to men, women and children of all ages and races. A lot of the younger men and women were dressed in black biker leathers, much like Fat Joseph and his accomplices. Walker guessed that it was some kind of uniform, even for those who didn't ride motorbikes. The elderly residents and the children were dressed differently – in more casual attire such as t-shirts, shorts and jeans – items that looked more comfortable, if a little tattered around the edges.

As he walked further inside, Walker had the feeling that he was intruding upon a massive community meeting taking place not in a town hall, but on the concourse of Liverpool Street Station.

All eyes fell upon the visitors.

Walker ignored the muted discussions going on around them as he and Barboza were led through the station.

Fat Joseph was looking into the crowds on either side, as if searching out a particular face. When Walker saw a smile creeping onto the fat man's face, he guessed that he'd found his man. Fat Joseph veered off the path, towards a small group of people gathered outside what had once been a newsagent.

Fat Joseph touched one of the men on the shoulder. The man, who was dressed in the ubiquitous biker uniform, turned around.

"Couple of people here to see you Michael." Fat Joseph said.

The man turned around and Walker recognised him immediately.

Michael King was a little heavier than Walker remembered. But that wouldn't have been hard because Michael King had been a stick insect of a young man in 2011, when he'd been in his early twenties at most. He was about thirty years old now, still lean but no longer boyish. Long black dreadlocks fell down his back. He had a thick, impenetrable beard and if not for this, Walker would have suggested there was a strong resemblance between Michael King and the great reggae singer-songwriter, Bob Marley.

Walker recalled watching the man talking on TV during the London riots. He'd been impressed by how sharp, intelligent and articulate Michael King had been. After Chester George, it was Michael King who'd been the spokesperson for the rioters. Now, nine years later, it seemed like he was the man who ruled North London.

"What do we have here?" Michael King said, approaching them.

"Special visitors," Fat Joseph said. "This young gentleman 'ere says he has some information that might interest you."

"Oh really?" Michael said, looking at Walker. "Have you got some information that might interest me?"

Walker nodded.

"Says he knows the name of the bastard that shot Chester George," Fat Joseph said.

There was an uncomfortable silence. At first Walker thought his information wasn't as valuable to Michael King as Fat Joseph had suggested it was. Maybe Michael King didn't care after all these years about who shot Chester George. Maybe he'd moved on and Walker had nothing of value to sell. Maybe he wouldn't get his information after all.

But then Michael King smiled. He ended that long silence with a loud greeting that almost everyone in the building could hear.

"Welcome to Liverpool Street Station," he said. As he spoke, he raised a hand into the air, gesturing to the building around them with an outstretched finger.

"Did you know this station was built upon the original site of Bethlem Royal Hospital?" he said. "It's quite the historical location, not that anybody cares about stuff like that anymore. Except me. As time passed, the hospital became better known as Bedlam. It was one of the oldest mental institutions in the world, built in 1247 by Christians to shelter and care for homeless people. As the years passed, its focus primarily turned to those who were considered mad. From there on, it became an infamous place, particularly for its harsh treatment of the mentally ill. What could be more appropriate?"

Fat Joseph smiled. "Now you folks know where you are," he said. "This is Bedlam."

"Bedlam?" Walker said. "I thought you called this place Station."

"*This* is Station," Michael King said. "Joseph is talking about the territory that you're standing in. The entire northern half of London, everything from the river up to the M25 – that is Bedlam. That's the name we've given it because this city belongs to the people now. There is no longer any east or west – only north of the river and south of the river. There's only Bedlam and the Hole. You didn't know?"

"We've been in hiding for a long time," Barboza said.

Michael King nodded. "A wise choice."

Walker looked at the hundreds of people who were scattered across the concourse. "Are these the Good and Honest Citizens?" he said. "From 2011?"

"We are the Bedlamites," Michael King said. "Some of us here were once part of the Good and Honest Citizens movement. But that's a name that we no longer use."

"Why not?" Barboza asked.

Michael King sighed. "That name died with Chester George. It's not 2011 anymore my friend."

Walker nodded. He was trying to concentrate but it was damn hot under the roof of the station. He felt a single, excruciating bead of sweat running down his back. There was sweat gathering on his brow too, something that probably made him look suspicious to Michael King and Fat Joseph, who were still sizing up the newcomers.

"So what are the Bedlamites?" he asked, trying to think of something to say.

Michael King looked at him, a slightly puzzled look on his face. "You really have been in hiding, haven't you?" he said.

"Aye," Walker said.

"The Bedlamites are the largest gang in the north," Michael King said. "Bedlam is our territory – everything that lives and breathes north of the river is ours – one way or another. Station is our base, our HQ. Some of us live here in the old train station itself, while others live out of the hotel next door. There are a couple of trains still on the platforms. Some people live in the carriages and there are even a few of us who like to sleep down in the underground with the spirits."

Walker looked around. "Did everyone come here after Piccadilly?"

"Far from everyone," Michael King said. "Most people with their wits still intact tried to get out the city when they heard about the super barriers that were being built. But those of us who were too late – who realised we were trapped, well we got organised. We founded this refuge on the site of the old hospital and over time it's become home to a lot of people. Not everyone, but a lot. We've grown to become a large, functioning family. I much prefer that word – family."

A little boy was standing behind Michael King, having crept up quietly while the Bedlamite was speaking to Walker and Barboza. He must have been about eight or nine years old at most and his wide eyes were almost buried beneath a mop of floppy brown hair that wasn't far from being a bowl cut. He was using Michael King's body as a barrier, tucking himself behind the man's legs, peering out at Walker and Barboza. His eyes were glued in particular, to the axe in Walker's hand.

"Charlie!" a woman's voice called out, from further down the station.

Walker looked behind the boy and saw a forty-something woman running down the pathway towards them. Her short brown hair, which was slightly greying at the sides, bounced gently at the sides as she ran. The woman – dressed in a dark t-shirt and black jeans – crept up behind the boy, glanced at Walker and Barboza shyly, then wrapped her arms around his waist and planted a kiss on his cheek.

The boy turned around and greeted her with a smile. Then he turned his attention back to Walker's axe.

“Don’t sneak up on people like that Charlie,” the woman said, speaking softly into his ear. “This conversation is between Michael and the visitors. It’s got nothing to do with us, okay? Eavesdropping is bad.”

Michael King turned around, greeting woman and child with an affectionate smile.

“It’s okay Carol,” he said. “Children are curious creatures. And who are we to interfere with the nature of a child?”

Carol smiled. She stood up straight, took Charlie by the hand and led him back down the path in the centre of the concourse. As they walked away, the boy turned his head back several times, looking at Walker and Barboza as if they were the most fascinating things he’d ever seen.

“I envy the children,” Michael King said, watching them go. “The ones who were born after Piccadilly. They have nothing else to remember.”

“Aye,” Walker said. “I can’t help but feel sorry for them myself.”

“Carol is Charlie’s guardian,” Michael King said. “Carol has been with us a long time, almost since the beginning. Charlie is a more recent addition, but he’s definitely part of the family now. Both their lives have been difficult – but they’re much better off having found each other.”

Michael King looked at Walker. “So you were at Piccadilly?” he asked.

Walker nodded. “Front row seats.”

Michael King took a slow, deep breath. It was like he was meditating standing up. “You know his name?”

“I do,” Walker said. “And I know that you caught up with him by the fountain that day. Right after he shot Chester George.”

“And how do you know that?”

“Because he was about to shoot me,” Walker said. “Don’t you remember? He was pointing a gun at my face just before you caught up with him. Lucky for me, that gun was empty or I wouldn’t be standing here today.”

Michael King closed his eyes for a second.

"Yes," he said. "I saw him pointing a gun at someone. You?"

"Aye," Walker said. "I knew him, just for a short while. He lived on your estate. But you don't remember his name?"

"Like you say," Michael King said. "He was a kid on our estate. I knew his face but that was all. Moody little man, built like an ox. Never could remember what they called him. God knows I've tried, especially in the first few years after it happened. But I never could remember."

"Hatchet," Walker said.

Michael King's face lit up, as if someone had just handed him a map to lost treasure.

"Of course," he said.

"I'm looking for him," Walker said. "That's another reason we came out of hiding. But I had to come here first. I had to make sure you didn't kill him that day."

"If Hatchet is dead," Michael King said. "It wasn't by my hand. More's the pity."

"What happened that day?" Walker said.

"We fought by the fountain," Michael King said. "I was going to kill him no matter the cost to myself. I didn't care about the crowds or the chaos. Killing him – that was going to be the last thing I ever did and it'd be the best thing I ever did. And I got a hold of him but the fight didn't last long. There were too many people – it was like we were lying in the middle of a stampede as the world lost its mind. We could have been – *should* have been – crushed to death. But it wasn't to be – he managed to wriggle out of my grasp. He was strong. I saw him disappearing into the crowd and tried to go after him but there were too many people blocking the way. It was only after I lost sight of him that my self-preservation instincts turned back on. Suddenly I didn't want to die so like everyone else, I tried to get out of there."

"I'm going to find him," Walker said. "I'm going to make him pay for it. For everything."

"You think he's in the Hole?" Michael King said.

Their conversation was interrupted by a child's voice.

"Anybody want a sandwich?"

Walker looked to his left. It was the little boy, Charlie. He'd returned and this time, he was carrying a plate of sandwiches in both hands – an assortment of white and brown bread cut diagonally – the same way that Walker's mother used to cut sandwiches. Just the way he liked them.

Carol was a few paces behind the boy. She was carrying a tray with two glasses of something that looked like orange juice.

Walker's body ached with thirst and hunger.

"Charlie," Michael King said. "Your timing is impeccable as always my boy. It looks like a late lunch is in order for our guests."

Charlie stood there, holding onto the plate of food with one hand. With the other, he tugged nervously at the Tottenham Hotspur football t-shirt he was wearing.

The boy was staring at Walker's axe again.

"You've travelled far enough for one day," Michael King said. "Stay here in Station tonight as our special guests. Take some food and rest. Then pick up your journey in the morning with my blessing. Find Hatchet and kill him – come back and tell me all about it."

Walker shook his head. As much as the offer appealed to him, he wasn't comfortable about the idea of hanging around in a place with so many people. He was already starting to feel dizzy. Too many faces, too much noise.

"Thanks for the offer," he said. "But I think we'd prefer to keep moving. Try and cross the river before..."

Michael King raised a hand in the air, like he was about to take a vow.

"Rest," he said. "I insist my friends. Staying here with us tonight is better than being out there on the streets. Nowhere is safe tonight, north or south."

"What do you mean?" Walker said.

"We can protect you in here," Michael King said. "This is

perhaps the one place in London where you are guaranteed to be safe tonight."

Walker gave the handle of his axe a gentle squeeze.

"I'd like to leave," he said.

Michael King shook his head. "No," he said. "You're going nowhere."

CHAPTER 7

"You won't let us go?" Walker asked.

His eyes darted back and forth across the station, searching for signs of an alternate exit. There had to be something – Liverpool Street Station had been a major transport hub back in the day. There had to be more than one way out of the building. But wherever they were, there was also the small matter of getting through all these people, finding the exit, and then not getting caught as they made their escape through the streets of London. Or Bedlam, or whatever it was called now.

Jesus Christ, it was so hot. Walker felt like his head was going to explode.

But Michael King shook his head, smiling at the two visitors as he did so.

"Please don't misunderstand my friends," he said. "Let me clarify. If you truly wish to go then nobody here will stop you. But I don't recommend it."

"No?" Walker said.

"Put it this way," Michael King said. "You've picked quite the day to go travelling my friends."

"What's so special about today?" Barboza said.

Michael King stretched out a small clump of beard hair between his forefinger and thumb. He looked at it thoughtfully for a moment. Walker got the feeling he was stalling for time, trying to think of the right thing to say.

"If I let you go," he said. "You'll both be dead by morning. And if you're not dead, you'll wish that you were."

Walker and Barboza glanced at one another.

"Why?" Walker asked him.

"The bad men are coming," Charlie said.

Walker had almost forgotten that Charlie was there.

"When the bad men come, we don't go outside."

"Charlie," Carol said, kneeling down beside the little boy, putting her hands on his shoulders. "Maybe you should let Michael explain."

Michael King looked at the boy and smiled. "Actually Carol," he said. "I think Charlie explained it rather well. You can always trust a child to tell the truth."

"I still don't get it," Walker said. "What's going on? Why shouldn't we leave?"

"Run along Charlie," Michael King said. "Why don't you and Carol go and help Joseph fill up the bikes with petrol?"

Fat Joseph bent down and lifted Charlie over his head like the boy was the FA Cup and he was the team captain holding the trophy aloft.

"We can't fill up the bikes without little Charlie, can we?" Fat Joseph said, walking away from the others. "Let's go get 'em boy. Give 'em a drink."

Fat Joseph – with Charlie now sitting on his shoulders – and Carol marched along the concourse. They went back up the stairs towards the front entrance and disappeared through the door that led onto Bishopsgate.

"Charlie's a good boy," Michael King said, after the others had left. "Very curious like all children of course. But while we believe it's important to be truthful with our children, we do keep some of the truth from them. The worst parts."

"Like what?" Walker asked.

"Like the precise details of what's happening tonight," Michael King said. "All Charlie and the other children know for sure is that the bad men are coming up from the south to do bad things. And that we stay out of their way."

"What's happening?" Walker asked. "What do the bad men do?"

Michael King looked back and forth between them. Clearly this wasn't a comfortable topic for him to discuss.

"First you must understand that certain allowances have been made in order to preserve peace between the people in the north and south," he said. "Nobody wants a war, not us and not them. So we do what we can in order to co-exist. Compromise. That's how it works – at least for now."

"I don't get it," Walker said. He looked at Barboza, who didn't look half as confused as he felt.

"Have you ever heard of the Big Chase?" Michael King said.

Walker looked at Michael King and shook his head. "No."

"The Big Chase – that's what's happening tonight. The Ghosts of London are coming north for their annual hunt here."

"Oh shit," Barboza said.

Michael King gave Barboza a curt nod. "So *you've* heard of them? You know what I'm talking about?"

Barboza glanced at Walker. She had guilty eyes, like she'd just been caught saying something she shouldn't.

"Sort of," she said quickly, turning back to Michael King. "That is, I met someone up north once who was trying to get as far way from the Hole as he could. He'd travelled across the city from top to bottom. He told me about the Ghosts of London. I didn't want to believe such things were real, but I guess they are, right?"

"They're real," Michael King said. "The Ghosts of London are the largest gang in the south. Along with the Bedlamites, they're one of the original gangs that sprang up after Piccadilly. We were the first to organise, to claim territory, to scavenge for the best of what the city had to offer. We were both smart but that's where the similarities between us end. We don't like them. They don't like us."

"You said they were coming here to hunt," Walker asked. "Hunt what?"

Michael King shook his head.

"The Bedlamites live off the Drop Parcels," he said. "We make it work – we are a large group of men, women and children, and because of this the Drops are of a high quality and volume around here. It's not ideal but it's enough to live on and..."

He hesitated.

"And what?" Walker asked.

"The Ghosts don't want any part of the Drops," Michael King said. "They get their own food – most of it they acquire during the Big Chase."

"People," Walker said.

"Yes," Michael King said. "The Ghosts have resorted to cannibalism. They nourish themselves on human flesh. It's how they choose to live."

"Jesus Christ," Walker said. "Like the rogues?"

Michael King shook his head.

"Not like the rogues," he said. "The Ghosts are far more dangerous and what's more they're completely sane. In fact, they would have us believe that *we're* the ones who are insane for living off Drop Parcels – for relying on the aid of our captors. And some part of me agrees with them, but not everyone is ready to stoop to the consumption of human flesh. That's not what I want for my people."

Walker looked at Michael King.

"But why do you let them do it?" he said. "Why do you let them come up here if this is your territory?"

"Like I said," Michael King said. "Compromise. We do it to preserve the peace. The Big Chase takes place three times a year. Two of those are down in the Hole but there's one in Bedlam every summer because that's what we agreed upon, a long time ago."

"You made a deal with them?" Walker said. "With people who eat...people?"

"If it wasn't for this deal," Michael King said, "then the Bedlamites and the Ghosts would have long since gone to war, fighting over each other's territory. It's this deal that preserves the peace. We let them come up here once a year and after that they stay away. No raids, nothing – we don't see them. They stay in the south, we stay in the north. And we always give warning to the people in the north when the Ghosts are coming. We get the word out and we invite them to come here to Station to spend the night. The Ghosts know that Station is out of bounds – it's part of the deal. They won't come near it. That means if you're in Station during the Big Chase, you're safe. That's guaranteed. That's what Fat Joseph and the others were doing when they found you today – they were warning the locals, inviting them here to take refuge. Many people will come soon. But of course not everyone in the north trusts us – so they'll do their own thing. They'll hide somewhere and hope for the best. But the best rarely comes."

"Bloody hell," Walker said. "I had no idea this was the sort of thing going on."

He longed to be back on Stanmore Road, back where he belonged. Let the rest of London keep its madness. He just wanted to go home – was that so much to ask?

"So you see, you're not safe out there tonight," Michael King said. "The Ghosts find everyone. Stay with us in Station and continue your journey south in the morning. There won't be another Big Chase until winter and they won't be back in Bedlam for another year."

Walker didn't want to stay. But what choice did he and Barboza have? After what he'd just been told – only an idiot would go back out there on the street. And even if they crossed the river early, who's to say the Ghosts wouldn't pick them up in the Hole on their way back from Bedlam?

It was exhausting. It was frightening. It was too damn hot as well.

"Will you stay?" Michael King asked.

"Yes," Barboza said without hesitation. "We'll stay. Won't we Walker?"

Walker saw the look in her eyes and knew there was no arguing with it.

He turned to Michael King.

"Sure," he said, sliding the padded shoulder strap of the rucksack down his arm. "We'll spend the night here."

CHAPTER 8

Immersion 9 – Live Chat Forums
#GhostsofLondon #BigChase

MaryG: Are they moving yet?

Rock Lobster: Yeah.

MaryG: And?

Rock Lobster: What? You ain't watching it?

MaryG: No, I can't stomach it darling. Going to the movies. Plan is to go and see three films in a row or something – anything that takes all night. Then straight home to bed, no FOL, no news, nothing. By the time I wake up it'll be over.

Rock Lobster: Yeah well, seeing as how you asked – they're on the move.

Immersion 9: (ADVERTISEMENT) Hi gang! Just checking in to see if you've purchased the official Future of London app yet? Yes YOU! C'mon! Keep up to date with all of the top stories coming out of Bedlam and the Hole. You won't miss a thing that goes on behind the M25 if you download the Future of London app TODAY. Comes with exclusive selfie filters for hours of fun. Turn on the FOL app in your camera and see yourself as a rogue, as Michael King, or even as one of the terrifying Ghosts of London. So what are you waiting for? Don't just watch the Future of London, be a part of it NOW! Download the app from the official FOL website and use FOLAPP Code to receive a 15% discount.

MaryG: OMG. Why don't the army just go in and shoot the sick bastards?

Rock Lobster: Dunno. Non-interference policy?

MaryG: They drop food parcels. What's non-interference about that?

Rock Lobster: Lol yeah. The army are shit scared too I suppose.

MaryG: Yeah well it's movie time for me. See ya later Rock darling – I won't be back on here tonight.

Rock Lobster: See ya love. Enjoy the flicks.

CHAPTER 9

Walker and Barboza were given a private space to themselves in Station.

At Michael King's request, they were put in one of the many retail units that ran down either side of the concourse – an old food place that according to the pictures on the wall – had once served hot and cold sandwiches, wraps and paninis. There was still a poster on display next to the counter, promoting a deal on toasted sandwiches, coffee or tea, which along with a donut or muffin of your choice, you could get for three pounds.

They settled into their makeshift hotel room for the night. Walker assumed that the café had been a trendy little pit stop for commuters back in the day, what with its chocolate brown walls and promotional signs that had been made out of old pallet wood.

They had been supplied with bedding – a large pile of multi-coloured blankets and pillows, enough for ten people. Walker and Barboza piled them up on the floor on the far side of the shop, furthest from the concourse and away from all the other people. Beside their bed, trays of food and drink had been supplied – water, tea, sandwiches and fruit. But there were other things too – hot chicken legs. That blew Walker's mind. He'd never seen anything like it in any of the Drop Parcels that he'd ever picked up along the New River. His parcels were nothing compared to what the Bedlamites were getting. While he'd been living off the basics for nine years – bread, fruit, water, a little cheese and thinly sliced meat – the Bedlamites were being provided with a banquet feast.

Walker didn't hold back. He ate as much food as he could, not knowing when or if he'd ever have another opportunity like this one. He didn't even realise how ravenous he was until he started shoving it down his throat, like a comic book character in a feeding frenzy. And when the people attending Walker and Barboza brought in two icy cold bottles of coke and put them down on the floor – Walker's jaw dropped. Coke? Here in London? More luxuries followed – crisps, chocolate, and there was even something that looked like a vanilla sponge cake.

Walker lifted one of the cold, plastic Coke bottles in both hands. He studied it like it was a priceless artefact, marvelling at the dark-brown, caramel coloured liquid that swirled around inside.

"I don't believe it," he said to Barboza. "Do you? All this stuff they get."

Barboza didn't respond at first. Walker noticed that she'd barely touched any of the things laid out for them. She'd only picked at a few items here and there.

"I guess he wants us to be comfortable," she said.

"A few biscuits," Walker said. "I considered that luxury for the past nine years."

"At least you weren't eating people," Barboza said.

"Even if I'd wanted to I would have had a hard time finding them," Walker said.

"Yeah."

"You knew about the Ghosts," Walker said. "Didn't you? I saw your face back there when you nearly gave it away."

"Yeah," she said. "I know about the Big Chase, but I didn't know it was happening tonight. I nearly blew it back there with Michael

King. It's hard pretending to be someone who's been trapped here for nine years."

"I don't think he noticed," Walker said.

"Hope not."

Walker unscrewed the lid of the Coke bottle and took a sip. As he did so, he screwed up his face in disgust.

"Oh Jesus!" he said. "Has Coke always tasted this bad? Or is it just me?"

"Probably both," Barboza said.

Out on the concourse, the Bedlamites were going about their everyday business. Walker thought that the scene was vaguely reminiscent of a busy city centre pedestrian zone – shops on either side of the concourse and human traffic flowing down the middle. Occasionally, people would stop and chat like old friends encountering one another on the street. Sometimes they'd even sit down at the plastic tables and chairs, continuing their conversation there. To Walker, it looked like they were sitting at a streetside café, waiting for someone to come and take their order.

In the shop unit directly opposite the one that Walker and Barboza were in, school lessons were taking place in what had once been Burger King. A group of kids of all ages were sitting on the floor with their legs crossed while a tall, elderly woman spoke to them about something that had them engrossed. As she spoke, the woman was gesturing wildly with both hands. Walker wondered if she was telling them a story – an old tale of myth and legend perhaps? Or something more contemporary? Whatever it was, the kids sat there, wide-eyed and hanging onto every word she was saying.

Walker saw the garage too. It was a unit with nothing but parked motorbikes scattered from one end to the other. There was an abundance of tools and spare parts lying around the cluttered floor. Fat Joseph and Rhonda were inside, as well as several other people dressed in dirty black leathers. They were all hard at work, performing routine maintenance duties. Walker looked at the ten bikes he counted in the garage. He wondered where the Bedlamites got the fuel to run their machines. Had they siphoned it from the abandoned cars that littered the streets of North London? That's what Walker would have done if he'd had a bike like one of those to run. After he'd raided all the petrol garages of course. That would have worked in 2011, just after Piccadilly. But now? It had to be getting harder to find the juice to run their bikes.

He turned back to Barboza.

"You're not eating," he said.

Barboza looked at the assortment of food in front of them. She might as well have been looking at a dried dog turd on a plate. "I'm not that hungry," she said.

"You're still thinking about it?" Walker said. "Aren't you?"

"Of course I am," she said. "It's only been a few hours. Are you telling me that you've forgotten about it already?"

"It was self-defence," Walker said. "Try to think of something else."

"Like what? The taste of Coke?"

Walker looked at her. "It was them or us," he said. "They were coming to kill us Barboza. You think they'd be that bothered if they were on their way back to the M25 now with our corpses in the back of the armoured vehicles?"

"No," she said. "But I'm not them. And I'm not you either."

Walker sighed. He watched as Barboza pulled several blankets over her body, stretching them all the way up to her chin.

"Aren't you hot?" he asked her.

"I'm freezing," she said.

Walker didn't say anything.

"You don't seem that bothered by it," she said, looking out towards the concourse. It was almost as if she was talking to herself.

"That's because I don't consider it murder," Walker said. "That's the difference between us – perspective."

Barboza closed her eyes. Walker saw her chest rising and falling quickly, in time with the shallow breaths she was taking.

"Even the one I killed?" she said. "Was that self-defence? He was wounded for God's sake, lying helpless on the grass in your back garden. He wasn't capable of hurting anyone and I crept up behind him and cut his throat."

"He was wounded because he was coming after us," Walker said. "Remember? Try to think of something else Barboza."

She opened her eyes. "Okay, like what?"

"Tell me about the Big Chase," Walker said. As he spoke, he glanced up towards the ceiling and along the length of the chocolate brown walls.

"We can talk in here," he said. "Can't we?"

Barboza lay her head down on one of the old pillows. "I think SKAM would have a hard time putting cameras in here."

"The Big Chase," Walker said. "They show that on TV too?"

"Yeah," she said. "It happened earlier this year. I didn't watch it but I heard all about it from other people and it was on the news. The Ghosts swept through the Hole – South London – gathering people up off the streets like they were rounding up lost cattle or something. Even by Future of London standards, it was sick man. Social media went crazy. Everyone on I-9 was talking about it.'

Barboza's head sank deeper into the pillow.

"Michael King's right," she said. "We can't be out on the streets tonight. Even if we crossed the river and got into the Hole in time, it doesn't mean we're safe. The Ghosts live down there in the Hole so they might pass us on their way up to Bedlam. Or on their way back after the Chase. And I doubt they'd hesitate to pick us up as a little bonus find. It's not safe anywhere tonight Walker, except here."

Walker put a hand over his stomach and groaned quietly.

"Too much food?" she said.

"Aye. Either that or it's all this Ghost shite giving me the ache."

Walker looked at her.

"What do they do with the people they catch?" he said. "Do they kill them on the spot? Do they drag them back down to the Hole alive? Or what?"

"They take them alive if possible," Barboza said. "They take them back to the Hole, to a barracks or base or whatever it is that the Ghosts call home. There are no cameras inside the base of course, but drone cameras have been used to fly overhead and record footage. Well some people have tried to zoom in on that footage with fancy surveillance equipment – in particular, some of the buildings out back – sheds, huts, whatever they are. Apparently they can see movement. Looks like there's people trapped inside. A lot of people."

Walker felt his blood run cold. "Are you telling me that the Ghosts *farm* people?"

"I don't know," Barboza said. "It's just what I read."

Walker laughed. But there was nothing remotely funny about the situation.

"I should have stayed in bed today," he said. "What a fucking day it's been. Worst ever."

"Walker."

"What?"

He looked over and saw that Barboza was sitting straight up in bed again. Like she'd moved in a hurry.

"Hi Charlie," she said.

Charlie was standing at the entrance. The way he was positioned, the little boy was standing halfway inside the shop and halfway on the concourse. Walker noticed that he was clutching onto a couple of pieces of A4-sized paper that were covered in indecipherable shapes – the chaotic scribbles of a child by the looks of it. Charlie was wearing the same clothes he'd been wearing earlier – an old Tottenham Hotspur t-shirt, light blue jeans that were a size too big, and black running shoes.

He stood at the entrance, a shy expression on his face. Like he wasn't really sure whether he wanted to come in or not.

"Alright Charlie?" Barboza said.

"Hi," Charlie said.

"Have you just come from school?" Barboza asked. She was pointing to the old Burger King directly opposite.

Charlie nodded. "Yeah."

"Do you wanna come in?" Barboza asked.

Charlie hesitated. He glanced at Walker, then looked at Barboza and nodded.

"C'mon then," Barboza said. Walker looked over at her – she was like a different person now. She seemed almost happy. He figured that if nothing else, the boy was a source of distraction, something to take her mind off what had happened on Stanmore Road.

Charlie walked inside. He went over to Barboza, putting a little distance between himself and Walker. And Walker's axe.

"Sit down," Barboza said, flattening out the pile of blankets and wiping off some of the crumbs that were the casualties of Walker's feeding frenzy. "Are you hungry?" she asked. "We've got lots of food in here and you're more than welcome to help us polish it off. What about a drink? Do you like Coke?"

Charlie smiled. "Yeah."

The boy unscrewed the lid and there was a brief hissing noise as the gas escaped from inside. Tipping the bottle back, Charlie poured the dark, sugary liquid down his throat, drinking it down fast like his life depended on it. When he was done, the boy put a hand over his mouth, as if battling the urge to burp.

"You want something to eat Charlie?" Barboza asked. "Help yourself."

Charlie looked down at the half-devoured feast that was scattered on the floor. His eyes scanned the meat, sandwiches and various snacks that had been brought in for Walker and Barboza. After some deliberation, he leaned over and picked up a bag of salt and vinegar crisps off the blankets. He tore open the bag and threw the potato snacks into his mouth, like he hadn't eaten for days.

The boy crunched on the crisps loudly. Walker grimaced.

"What have you been drawing?" Barboza said, pointing to the paper in his hand. "Something nice?"

Charlie shrugged, all the while shovelling crisps into his mouth.

"Can I look?" Barboza asked.

Charlie stared at her for a moment, like he wasn't sure he wanted to share his artwork with the two visitors. But slowly, he reached an arm out towards Barboza, offering her the paper in his hands.

Barboza took the two pieces of paper and looked carefully at both drawings.

"Wow," she said. "These are great Charlie. Look Walker."

She passed them over to Walker, who glanced at both images quickly. It was nothing special. It was a typical child's drawing – a mess of squiggly lines and bad colouring in. Both pictures featured – as far as Walker could tell – two people standing side by side, one a giant and the other a midget. They were standing on what looked like a sea of long, green grass underneath a giant orangey-yellow orb that was spitting out heat like it was rain falling from a cloud.

He handed the drawings back to Barboza.

"Great," he said.

"Is this you?" Barboza asked Charlie, pointing to the smaller of the two figures.

"Yeah," Charlie said. "Can I have one of the sandwiches?"

"Sure honey," Barboza said.

Charlie reached over and grabbed the nearest sandwich off the plate. He tore into the crumbly white bread and the cheesy filling, and to Walker's horror, the boy's lips made a horrendous smacking sound as he ate. Walker had always hated that noise.

"So if you're the little person," Barboza asked. "Who's the big one?"

The boy slowed his chewing down. And thank God, the lip smacking noises stopped with it.

"It's my Mum," Charlie said, looking at the drawing.

"Oh," Barboza said. "Do you mean Carol?"

Charlie shook his head. "Nah."

"It's your real mum?"

Charlie reached over and grabbed the two pieces of paper out of Barboza's hand. He put them down at his side, face down so that the drawings were hidden.

"Are you okay?" Barboza asked.

He didn't answer.

"Is it something to do with your mum?" Barboza said. "You can tell us Charlie – we're your friends."

The little boy looked up. Once more, he stole a nervous glance at Walker.

"Charlie?" Barboza said. "Did something bad happen to your real mum? Is that why you ended up here in Station?"

"I suppose so," the boy said, mumbling quietly. "She never showed up."

Barboza moved closer to the boy, pushing herself further along the pile of bedding until their arms were almost touching.

"What does that mean?" Barboza said. "She never showed up for what?"

"She told me to wait at the station," Charlie said, looking at Barboza. The boy spoke quietly now, almost in a whisper. Walker had to lean forward in order to hear what he was saying.

"Said she'd be back to get me but she never showed up," Charlie said. "Told me to wait at the station."

"What station?" Barboza said.

"Old Street Station," he said.

"You were supposed to meet her?" Barboza said. "When was this?"

"Couple of years ago," Charlie said. "We were staying in a flat up there – it's not far from here. One day, we were going out to pick up our Drop Parcel – to get our food bag and..."

The little boy's face darkened.

"It's okay Charlie," Barboza said, putting a hand on his shoulder. "You don't have to tell us if you don't want to."

"There was a rogue on the street," Charlie said. "A madman – that's what Mum called them before we knew that other people called them rogues. It came after us, screaming and hissing. Mum tried to run away with me in her arms – she had to drop the parcel 'cos she couldn't carry that and me at the same time. So she dropped the parcel, but I was too heavy anyway. She put me down and then she screamed at me."

"She screamed at you?" Barboza said. "Why?"

Charlie nodded. "She was screaming at me, telling me to go to Old Street," he said. "The station. Said she'd come back and meet me there later. I was crying because I didn't want to leave her with that monster chasing her. But she was yelling and screaming, like she was angry with me. She ran off, making a lot of noise, so that the rogue went after her and not me."

"And what did you do?" Barboza said.

"I did what she told me to," Charlie said. "I went to Old Street and I waited until it got dark but she didn't come back."

Walker and Barboza exchanged a quick glance, as if neither one of them were quite sure of what to say.

"You know Charlie," Barboza said. "Just because she didn't get back to Old Street...it doesn't mean that she's dead."

"She's dead," Charlie said. "The rogue got her."

Barboza slid an arm around the boy's back.

"No," she said. "You mustn't give up hope Charlie. That's all we've got after all isn't it? Hope. We've met quite a few rogues in our time and they're pretty stupid you know? And they can't run very fast either because they're in such bad physical shape. Was your mum a good runner Charlie?"

Charlie nodded. "Yeah. She was."

"Well then," Barboza said. "I'd say there's a good chance that your mum got away from that rogue. Yeah? Wouldn't you agree Walker? Don't you think that there's a good chance that Charlie's mum got away?"

Walker glared at Barboza. He could fell the boy's eyes upon him, probing him for some further assurance of hope.

"Maybe," Walker said.

"Then why didn't she meet me?" Charlie said. "I was there at the station. Why didn't she show up?"

Barboza looked at Walker. Walker shook his head at her, trying to let her know that it was dangerous to feed the boy false hope. And that it was cruel too.

But Barboza didn't seem to understand.

"There could be lots of reasons she didn't make it," Barboza said. "She might have gotten delayed. I don't know – maybe she fell and bumped her head. Amnesia? I don't know Charlie but all I'm trying to say is that the rogue might not have got to her. You know? It's not an absolute certainty that things ended up that way."

Walker saw hope in the boy's eyes, flickering like candlelight in the dark. It was painful. Yes, some madman had probably devoured her and it was a terrible thing.

But it was the truth.

"Who knows Charlie?" Barboza said. "Just don't look so sad, please."

"But if she's not dead," Charlie said. "Then she's out there with the bad men tonight. Isn't she? What if she's alive? What if she's out there looking for me with the bad men running about?"

Walker heard panic leaking into the boy's voice.

"Shouldn't you be in school or something?" he said to Charlie.

Charlie looked at Walker, wide-eyed, like he'd just snapped out of a daydream.

"It's finished for the day," Charlie said. "I'm going to meet Carol and then we're going for a walk around the block. We do it every day and we have to to get out early today because of the bad men. Do you want to come with us?"

Walker shook his head.

"Nah," he said. "We've done enough walking for one day. Off you go mate. Take the Coke and takes some food with you if you want."

"Yeah?"

"Aye, on you go."

Charlie knelt down and scooped up the half-empty bottle of Coke. Then he gathered a few items from the leftover trays of food on the floor. He jumped back to his feet and Walker noticed that the boy's step was lighter now.

Just before he ran off, Charlie turned around and gave them both a quick wave. Then he hurried out the entrance, back into the concourse.

Walker looked at Barboza, shaking his head.

"What the hell were you thinking?" Walker said. "His mum's dead. What's the point in giving him false hope like that? He's probably spent the last couple of years trying to come to terms with it and you've just set him back."

"I know," Barboza said. She looked pissed off with herself. "It just spiralled out of control. I didn't even see it happening until it was too late. I couldn't help it – I'm just sick of all this death and sorrow Walker. I just wanted to say something to make him feel better. To make a little boy smile, you know? Is it really that bad? So he thinks there's a chance that the rogue didn't kill his mum. Who wants that image in their head when it comes to their mother and how she died?"

"Sometimes it's better to say nothing," Walker said. "That way he'll accept the hard truth early."

"And is that what you did Walker?" Barboza said. "Accepted the hard truth early on?"

"What do you mean?"

Barboza looked at him.

"Nine years you stayed in Stanmore Road," she said. "Nine years living in that house alone, waiting for them to come back. All that time passed and you still didn't give up hope that they might be alive somewhere. Yeah? And despite everything, you still haven't given up hope. Deep down, you think there's a chance that your parents are still alive and you're clinging to that. Is it so bad that little Charlie's got something to cling to now?"

CHAPTER 10

Walker's eyelids felt heavy.

He found himself sinking deeper into the pile of warm blankets. And yet a part of his mind resisted the need for sleep. Here he was, trapped by circumstances beyond his control, surrounded by people that he knew nothing about.

What would happen if he closed their eyes? Sleep? Something else?

But he was losing the fight. He was tired and it didn't help that Barboza had already drifted off beside him. She was lying a few feet away in a crumpled heap on top of the blankets, curled up into a tight ball, her head submerged in a dirty white pillow.

Walker's eyes shut slowly, regardless of his concern. He kept his fingers wrapped around the handle of the axe as his back slid down the wall. His head landed on one of the battered pillows and it felt like warm and gentle fingers running down his cheek.

Then everything went black.

When he opened his eyes, somebody was screaming.

Panic flooded his mind. He reached for the handle of the axe, which his fingers had let go of at some point while he was asleep. As soon as he grabbed the axe, he jumped off the makeshift bed. But for a moment he had no idea where he was. He was in a strange place, acting on instinct. His head was swimming and all the pieces hadn't come back together yet.

He was in Liverpool Street Station.

A woman was screaming – she was somewhere out there on the concourse. It sounded like it was coming from the front entrance of Station, the one near Bishopsgate. Why was she screaming? What was happening? There didn't seem to be anything unusual going on outside the little shop space that they were staying in.

Barboza was standing at the entrance, looking further along the concourse.

"What's happening?" Walker asked. His voice sounded thick and groggy, like an old punch-drunk prizefighter.

"Dunno," she said, not taking her eyes off the concourse. "There's a crowd gathering down at the front of the station. Somebody's hysterical but I can't see who it is."

Walker glanced up at the arched windows. He squinted his eyes as sunlight poured into the station through the elegant windowpanes. So it was still daylight outside, but then again it was summer and the days were long.

"How long were we asleep?" Walker asked.

"Not that long," she said. "It's late afternoon or early evening at most.

"Aye," Walker said. "It's not as warm as it was."

"I think we should go down there," she said. "Whatever's going on, maybe we can help."

Walker shook his head. "It's none of our business Barboza," he said. "We're just passing through, remember?"

"Yeah I remember," Barboza said. "But they've given us a place to stay for the night. They've also given us food and drink. I think we ought to show a little concern."

But Walker had already dropped back down onto the blankets.

"Or we'd just be getting in the way," he said.

But Barboza didn't move. Walker looked at her, shaking his head. He felt a genuine concern for Barboza and her prospects inside the M25. She had a sensitive heart and somewhere down the road it was going to choke the life out of her. Or rather the city would be the one doing the choking and her heart wouldn't be able to stand up to it. She'd already blown her cover as an actress because she couldn't stand to deceive Walker. Now she was telling him that defending her life against the soldiers that morning was murder. Bullshit. Walker considered it an act of self-preservation.

Walker looked at her. She was wearing clean clothes now, which had been provided for her after their arrival at Station. That meant at least she'd been able to get rid of the bloodstain on the other t-shirt. Now she was dressed in a simple white t-shirt and a pair of tattered, bell-bottom blue jeans that fit perfectly. Her long black hair was bone dry and hung loose over her back.

"Get up Walker," she said. "Oh shit, you need to get over here. Fast."

Walker heard the panic in her voice. He threw the blankets off and rushed back to his feet.

"What?" he said. "What's going on?"

"Look," Barboza said, pointing towards the stairs near the station entrance.

Walker looked down the concourse. A large group of people – perhaps fifty or sixty were huddled close together. Elsewhere, the other Bedlamites were nearby, standing at shop fronts or further back on the pathway. Like Walker and Barboza, they were all watching the drama unfolding before their eyes with some concern. Walker noticed too that there were more people in Station now than when they'd first arrived – like it had been filling up while he'd slept.

"What is it?" Walker said. "What's everyone looking at down there?"

"It's Carol," Barboza said. Her voice was shaking. "Don't you see Carol? She's standing in the middle of that crowd down there. She's the one who's been crying."

Walker saw Michael King, standing in the thick of the crowd. He had an arm around Carol, who was standing next to him. She had her face buried in her hands, like she'd just been given the worst news of her life. Michael King was talking to the people in the crowd, trying to deal with the situation – whatever it was. Fat Joseph was there too, doing likewise. It was hard to hear anything that was being said clearly. It was just a bunch of loud voices, all talking over one another.

Barboza grabbed hold of Walker's arm and dragged him towards the concourse.

"What are you doing?" Walker said.

"We're going down there," she said.

He didn't resist.

"Charlie's foster mum is crying her eyes out," Barboza said. "Do you see Charlie anywhere? They were going out for a walk, remember?"

They hurried by a flock of onlookers, none of who paid them any attention as they moved towards the front of the station. Walker saw the large group of people down there getting bigger and he had the feeling that he was walking towards the scene of a tragedy. Like he was closing in on the site of a plane crash, one still freshly ablaze.

They hovered on the outskirts of the large crowd. It was hard to breathe because the air was still a little muggy in the station. But Barboza wasn't satisfied waiting there on the fringes of the crowd. Walker groaned as he watched her squeezing her way through the crowds, battling towards the centre. She no longer seemed to care whether he was following her or not.

Walker groaned. Then he started squeezing his way through the crowd too, working towards the eye of the storm.

Michael King still had an arm locked around Carol's shoulder. Walker took a closer look at the woman who'd been introduced to them earlier as Charlie's guardian. Her eyes were sore and red and it looked like she'd been crying for a long time. Michael King whispered something into her ear. Walker saw Carol shake her head, her chest rising and falling as she took quick, shallow gulps of air.

"What is it?" Barboza asked. She was yelling through the crowd, as if demanding to be heard above all the others. "Has something happened to Charlie?"

Carol looked at Barboza and then buried her face in her hands again. Michael King pulled her close, allowing her to rest her head on his neck.

"It's okay," he said to Carol. "It's okay."

"What's happened?" Barboza said. "Please tell me."

"It's Charlie," Michael King said looking at Barboza. As the Bedlamite spoke, Walker came up slowly behind them, creeping through the crowd and stopping only when he was standing next to Barboza.

"What about Charlie?" Barboza asked.

The crowd around them quietened a little, as if curious to find out why the two visitors were so concerned about the situation.

"He's run off somewhere," Michael King said.

Barboza gasped. "Run off?" she said. "Why? Where?"

Carol lifted her head off Michael King's neck. She wiped both of her eyes with the back of her hand and took a deep breath. Then she looked at Barboza, her eyes tortured and glistening.

"The little bugger," she said, her voice cracking. "Just gave me the slip. I can't believe it. I can't believe he'd do that to me – today of all days."

"Why?" Barboza said. "Do you know why?"

Carol shrugged. "It was just a normal walk," she said. "We didn't stray too far. We went up Bishopsgate and then onto Curtain Road. Nothing out of the ordinary. When we reached Curtain Road, I wanted to turn back like we always do. But this time, Charlie wanted to go further."

"Further?" Barboza said.

Carol nodded. "Further north."

"Why?" asked an elderly man, standing behind Walker. "Did he say anything? What the bloody hell was the boy thinking?"

"He was talking about his mum a lot," Carol said. "But he does that sometimes. They lived up that way didn't they? Before we found him. But he's never wanted to go back up there, not really."

Walker looked at Barboza. He saw the terror spreading in her eyes, raging like a forest fire. He knew exactly what she was thinking in that moment.

He was thinking the same thing.

"I went after him," Carol said. "But there's no sign of him anywhere. I've been running around the streets for the past two hours, looking for him, calling his name over and over again."

"We've been out on the bikes," Michael King said. "The boy's vanished."

"He's been taken," Carol said. "I know it. A rogue or the Ghosts – something got him."

"Still too early for the Ghosts," Michael King said.

"Well it's a rogue then," Carol said. "Or another gang has picked him up. I mean, a little boy wandering them streets all alone. What chance has he got?"

Michael King put both hands on Carol's shoulders. He turned her towards him so that they were standing face to face.

"We're going to find him," he said. "We're going back out now and this time we're going to find the little man. I promise."

He nodded at Fat Joseph, who was standing nearby.

"Ready when you are Michael," Fat Joseph said. "The bikes are out front, engines running."

"No," somebody yelled in the crowd. "You can't do that."

Michael King looked into the swarm of bodies. His dark brow creased in confusion.

"What?" he said.

"Those murderous bastards will be here soon," the voice yelled. It was a woman's voice. "The sun will be going down soon," she said. "You can't go out there on the streets Michael. We can't risk you getting caught on the hop by the Ghosts."

"What do you expect us to do?" Michael King said to the woman. "Leave Charlie out there on the streets by himself?"

Barboza jumped in.

"Where did you search?" she asked. "What areas did you search?"

Michael King looked at her. "Bishopsgate. Kingsland Road. Curtain Road. Then we went up into his old neighbourhood – every corner of every street..."

Barboza shook her head. "I don't think you're going to find him standing in the middle of the street," she said.

"Of course," Michael said. "I understand that. But we have to start somewhere..."

Barboza nodded. "I know where he is," she said. "At least I think I do."

Everything went silent after that.

Walker stood behind Barboza, feeling more than a little nervous. He knew what was coming and it wasn't going to be pretty. It was that good heart of Barboza again, coming back to haunt them both.

Carol was staring at the younger woman with a puzzled expression on her face.

"Where?" Carol said. "How would *you* know where he is?"

Barboza hesitated. "Because it's my fault," she said. "I think Charlie ran off because of something I said to him earlier today."

Carol screwed up her face. The wrinkles there dug deep grooves on her forehead as rage and bewilderment battled to seize control of her.

"What?" she said. "What did you say?"

It sounded like the entire population of Station was quiet now.

"He came to see us earlier," Barboza said. "We ended up talking about his mum. He told us about what happened to her and I...I didn't mean it. I just wanted to give him some hope but I didn't think..."

Carol walked towards Barboza. Walker saw a furious, manic glint in the older woman's eye and in that moment, he placed a hand on Barboza's back, a supportive gesture to remind her she wasn't alone.

"What did you do?" Carol said, stopping a few feet away. "What the hell did you do?"

"I told him there was a chance," Barboza said. She sounded like she was on the brink of tears as she spoke. "Just a chance – that his mum might still be alive somewhere."

Carol's jaw dropped in disbelief.

"Sweet Jesus," she said. "Oh you stupid bitch."

And then she lunged at Barboza, swinging with wild punches that were well out of range.

There were a few shrieks in the crowd as Michael King rushed over and grabbed a hold of Carol's arms. He pulled her back towards him, wrapping an arm around her waist and pinning her close to him. Carol struggled, but couldn't break free.

Walker also put an arm around Barboza, gently guiding her back a couple of steps. A little space between the two women was clearly required.

"You fucking bitch!" Carol screamed at Barboza. "You've killed him! Why? You better tell me."

Barboza struggled to speak, like the words were caught in the back of her throat. "I'm sorry," she said. "I didn't mean for that to happen."

"You bitch!" Carol yelled at her.

"Quiet," Michael King said in a firm voice. He pulled Carol back, keeping his arm locked around her. "This doesn't solve the immediate problem of finding Charlie. The more we talk, the more time we waste. Now the bottom line is this – the Ghosts are coming soon and Charlie is still out there."

He looked at Barboza.

"You know where he is?" Michael King said. "Tell me. We'll go and get him right now."

"Old Street Station," Barboza said. "I'm sure of it. Didn't anyone check in there?"

Michael King shook his head. "We passed it several times," he said. "But we didn't go all the way inside the station. There was simply too much ground to cover and not enough time. But if he was in there, he would have heard us calling out to him. I'm sure of it."

"You're assuming he wants to be found," Walker said.

"Yeah." Michael King said. "Exactly."

"His mum's been dead for two years!" Carol screamed. She was staring at Barboza with cold hate in her eyes. "Two fucking years! And now thanks to you, he thinks she's still out there. We don't lie to our children about things like that."

Michael King let go of Carol. He then took a short step forward, placing himself in between her and Barboza, like a boxing referee at the pre-fight instructions. "Enough of this," he said. "It's not the time for blame. Let's go Joseph. We know where we need to be."

But when Michael King turned around, another voice called out after him, stopping the Bedlamite in his tracks.

"No," said a man in the crowd.

Walker looked over his shoulder and saw an old man wading through the crowd. He was probably in his seventies, and he was wearing black shorts and an old denim shirt that was unbuttoned all the way down, exposing a shrivelled body with the ribs poking out of the pink skin.

He was walking towards Michael King.

"No Michael," he said. "It's like Deidre said, you can't go out there."

The old man turned pointed to the windows. Outside, the bright sunlight was dimming fast. Now a dull, threatening grey was taking root in the skies; it was a hint of the impending darkness to come.

"It's too late," the old man said. "We don't know where they're coming from. You know how tricky those bastards are – they don't just come up straight from the south every year. Sometimes they drive around the city and attack our streets from the north. So who knows where they're coming from tonight? And when. They could be here earlier this year and that means they might catch you on the way back if you're out there. It's already early evening. We can't risk losing you Michael. There shouldn't be any Bedlamites out there on the street anyway – the Ghosts might interpret that as hostility on our part."

"What do you expect me to do?" Michael King said to the old man. "Leave the boy out there to die? Or worse?"

"I'm not leaving him," Carol said. "I don't give a damn about the Ghosts or where they're coming from. I'm going after him and I'm bringing him back."

"We'll go," Barboza said.

She turned to look at Walker. Without hesitation, he nodded his agreement.

"It's not that far to Old Street," Barboza said, turning back to Michael King. "And it'll be quieter if we go out there on foot rather than you doing it on a pack of motorbikes. He's up there in Old Street Station right now – I saw the look in his eye earlier and I'll bet you anything he's looking for his mum. Or waiting for her. We'll find him and bring him back before the Ghosts get here. I promise. We won't come back without him. And besides, we're not Bedlamites so if the Ghosts do see us, they wouldn't have any reason to think it's hostility on your part. We're just two people on the street."

Michael King sighed. He looked at the crowd, looking back at him. Then he turned to Walker and Barboza.

"You must be quick," he said. "It's true. We don't know exactly when they're coming. But you're not safe the moment you step out that door. Understand?"

Barboza nodded.

"I'm coming with you," Carol said. She was looking at Walker and Barboza defiantly, daring them to challenge her. "I'm his guardian and that means he's my responsibility."

Walker decided against arguing with her, even though he would have preferred going after Charlie with just Barboza.

"Okay," he said.

"Yeah," Barboza said.

Just as they were about to get moving, one of the younger women in Station – no more than nineteen or twenty years old – stepped up behind Barboza. The young woman gently wrapped a black, suede jacket over Barboza's shoulders.

"You want to be invisible out there," the young woman said. "No bright colours."

Barboza nodded in thanks to the woman. Then she took the jacket off her shoulders, threading her arms through the sleeves and pulling the zip up to her neck.

Michael King took a step back. He held an arm out, gesturing for the crowds to move away from the entrance, to make room for the small search party.

"My friends," he said to them. "Good luck. And whatever else you do, be quick."

CHAPTER 11

It was getting dark in London.

The bright summer sky was gone, leaving behind only a pack of grey clouds that moved tentatively across the roof of the world, like a scout party travelling ahead of the night.

The heat of the day refused to yield, although it was much cooler than it had been earlier on.

Walker, Barboza, and Carol travelled north along Bishopsgate. The two women had been at each other's throats since leaving Station, but Walker knew that whatever they had to say would have to wait. They didn't have time to get into any further arguments about who was to blame for Charlie's disappearance. At first, Barboza had been quite willing to accept responsibility, but as Carol continued to insult her on their way out of Station, Barboza snapped back and left a few choice remarks about how Carol could have allowed Charlie to give her the slip so easily.

That's when Walker had slipped in between the two of them.

The only thing that mattered was finding the boy and bringing him back to Station. And doing it before the Ghosts arrived in Bedlam. But as the sun slowly dipped behind the high-rise buildings, they knew their odds of doing so were getting slimmer. They might find the boy, but would they get back to Station safely? Or they might get back safely, but would they find the boy?

The whole thing was a giant shot in the dark.

At Carol's lead, they increased the pace. Anxious footsteps pounded off the concrete, accompanied by the sound of their shallow breathing. Walker occasionally heard the whirring and clicking from the streetlights above. But he told himself to forget it. There was nothing he could do about that – the people on the outside were watching, so be it.

"How long will it take us to get there?" he asked Carol.

"Ten minutes if we get a move on," she said.

Considering that he'd been living alone for the past nine years, Walker wasn't one for unnecessary conversations. He enjoyed silence. But even the most banal small talk was better than the lingering tension he felt simmering between these two women.

"Have you lived in Station long?" he asked Carol.

The older woman sighed. At first, Walker thought she wasn't interested in talking and if so, he would suck it up and let it go without another word.

"Yeah," she said after a moment. "I've been there since the beginning, pretty much."

"Since Piccadilly?"

"Almost to the day," she said. "My original escape plan didn't quite work out. But it could have been a lot worse if Michael King, Fat Joseph, and some of the others hadn't found me and took me in."

"Escape plan?" Walker said. "You tried to get out of London?"

"Oh yeah," she said. "Didn't everyone? Damn right I tried. Anybody who didn't try needs their head read."

"What happened?" Walker asked. "If you don't mind my asking."

"I don't mind," Carol said, keeping her eyes on the road. "As long as we don't slow down that is. We'd been watching it on the telly at home – Piccadilly and the aftermath and all that crazy shit. But when it got real bad – scary bad – that's when we decided to get out of the city for a while. We'd lay low and then come back when everything had calmed down. So a group of us – my family and some people on our street – drove north in one of them people carriers. There was no plan, not really. We were just trying to get as far away from London as possible. It was me, my husband Tom, Sarah – my eleven-year-old daughter, and a few good neighbours who we'd rounded up."

"Where were you coming from?" Walker asked.

"Stoke Newington," she said. "About five miles from Piccadilly Circus. We travelled north and with the car we had, we could have been clear of London in about forty-five minutes. Well that's depending on traffic 'cos everyone was doing the same thing. That's what it looked like anyway."

"So you knew? About the M25?"

"We heard the rumours," Carol said. "You couldn't help but hear 'em. There was somebody running down our street – literally just sprinting down the middle of the road like he was in the hundred metres final of the Olympics. God he was screaming so loud. He was yelling about barriers being built around the city to keep the trouble in. It sounded crazy but I believed him. So yeah, we drove up. Figured north was probably the safest route to take."

"Were the barriers already up?" Walker asked. "By the time you got there?"

"Don't know," Carol said. "We never made it. Our car got attacked just outside Tottenham."

Walker scratched at a small growth of stubble on his chin. Elsewhere, his face was a little sunburned and as his fingers strayed outside the realm of the itch, he felt a hot, tingling sensation that was mildly painful.

"You got attacked?" he said.

Carol nodded. "Yeah," she said. "A big group of kids – well teenagers I suppose. They came for us. Swinging baseball bats, cricket bats – all sorts of bats. They ambushed us on the road – on the A10 travelling north. God there must have been about thirty or forty of them at least. They just ran onto the road like they didn't care about anything. Tom was driving and you know what? If he'd have kept going, if he'd just driven through 'em, ploughed through the little bastards, then we might have made it. My life would be a lot different today. But Tom wasn't that sort of man. He wasn't ready to accept the idea that civilisation had collapsed in the great city of London."

Walker felt like he'd invaded her privacy enough. But curiosity got the better of him and he couldn't resist asking further questions. Fortunately Carol didn't seem to mind continuing with her story.

"What happened?" he asked.

"We fought them as best we could," Carol said. "And that was the second mistake we made after not ploughing through the bloody lot of them. We fought because we needed our car and we assumed that's what they wanted. But if we'd just gotten out of the car and let them have it – held our hands up – they probably would have left us alone. I don't know. I think they just wanted to smash it up, to burn it, or drive it down to Piccadilly, into the eye of the shit-storm."

"Aye," Walker said. "They didn't take kindly to you trying to fight back then?"

"Tom and the other men thought they could scare them off," Carol said. "Well, those kids – they weren't backing down to anyone. Not anymore. They weren't afraid to use their weapons either, bloody little savages. So there I was, sat in the car, holding my daughter tight, and watching them beat my husband to a bloody pulp. All the children in the car watched their fathers die. Yeah well, there's only so much you can take, right? I got out the car and ran at them. Screaming, telling them to stop. He was the love of my life. You know? I couldn't just let him go like that."

"I'm sorry," Walker said.

Carol nodded, drawing her lips tight together.

"And that was mistake number three," she said. "I should have tried to make a run for it with the kids. I didn't think about driving away at the time because it meant leaving Tom behind. And gut instinct would never allow me to do that. Yet it was the most obvious solution. Instead I charged and fat lot of good it did. They hit me on the head with a baseball bat and there was a crunching noise in my head. I went down and I heard some of them cheering like they'd just scored a home run. Little pricks. But just before I blacked out, I heard her – I heard my daughter Sarah screaming. Everything went blurry; I saw the faint shape of her running over to my side and then lots of hands grabbing her and pulling her away from me. White hands. Black hands. They had my daughter. After that I blacked out."

"Jesus," Walker said.

"I don't know if they meant to kill her or not," Carol said. "But when I woke up, everybody was dead. I was the only one left alive – they must have thought I was already dead. I don't think they were doing me any favours. But I was alive anyway. Does that make me lucky? I didn't feel lucky. My family and friends were dead, and I was stuck in this shithole."

Walker felt a chill go through him. "Sorry," he said. "You must have told that story more than a few times. Didn't mean to put you through it again."

"Yeah," she said. "But to tell you the truth, it's starting to feel like someone else's story. Like it happened to someone else I knew once. Know what I mean?"

Walker understood. He sure as hell wasn't the same person anymore and if he'd been asked to recount the story of the teenage boy, Mack Walker, and what he did on the first day of September 2011, then maybe it would have felt like he was talking about someone else too. Maybe that's how people coped with it.

"So how did you end up at Station?" Walker asked.

Carol shrugged. She was walking faster now, trying to keep up with Barboza who'd edged a little ahead of them.

Walker hurried along with her, trying to keep his place in between of the two women.

"They found me a few days later," she said. "Michael King, Fat Joseph and some of the others who were the first Bedlamites. I was still on that same stretch of road, lying amongst all those corpses. I guess I was waiting to die. I was delirious, dehydrated and beaten up.

They picked me up took me to Station – it wasn't called Station then – and slowly brought me back to life. We went back later and buried the bodies. But after that, it took a long time to heal, mentally more than physically. I'll be the first to admit that I haven't been easy to deal with sometimes. Nightmares, things like that. The tiniest little thing can set me off. But then a couple of years back, something happened that brought a bit of light back into my existence. A little boy came to us off the streets. And you know what? He needed a mother."

She was smiling. But then a dark cloud passed across her features, as if their grim purpose was recalled.

"We'll get him back," Walker said.

"We'd better," she said. "I'm not going back until we do."

During this conversation, Carol had taken them on the quickest route from Liverpool Street to Old Street. After a short walk north on Bishopsgate, they'd travelled west onto Pindar Street. They'd continued in that direction, walking past Finsbury Square Garden, and eventually coming onto City Road, which would lead them north towards Old Street.

Walker was beginning to tire of the scenery – the gruesome left-overs of a lifetime ago. There was an old Travelodge without a front door. They walked past an off-licence and an electrical store, standing side by side. Both shops looked like a bomb had tore through them many years ago. Rubble spilled out of the building and onto the street. Outside the off-licence, the burned out skeleton of a car was parked halfway up the pavement.

They passed Bunhill Fields burial ground. Walker glanced to his left, peering over the steel fence that ran along the perimeter of the ancient graveyard. He saw the ancient headstones, peeking back at him over a sea of wildly overgrown grass. It was a city of the dead, much like the rest of London.

At last, they came to Old Street.

At first Walker, couldn't see the underground station that they were looking for. The only thing he could see was a massive roundabout, an urban island that was surrounded by road and concrete buildings as far as the eye could see.

"Where is it?" he asked Carol. "Where's the station?"

"There's no street level building to Old Street," she said. "You access it down the ramp or stairs." She pointed to the other side of the roundabout. "Over there."

Carol didn't hang about. She took off towards the station in a hurry and Walker and Barboza followed close behind. They crossed over the roundabout, hopping over a small concrete island that was located in the middle. A few moments later, they were standing at the top of a set of stairs that led down into Old Street Station.

"Ready?" Carol said, looking at them both.

Barboza nodded. "Yeah," she said.

"C'mon," Walker said. He looked up towards the sky and felt his heart sinking. It was now a mixture of dark blue and grey up there. Whatever little light was left, it wasn't going to last much longer.

They walked down the stairs. Despite the eeriness of what they were walking into, Walker felt a sense of relief at getting off the streets. At the very least, he felt a little less exposed to the millions of eyes that inhabited the city. But despite this, it was going to be hard to see anything in Old Street Station. It was almost pitch black in there.

Charlie was alone in there?

But the darkness didn't seem to bother Barboza and Carol. They were already rushing ahead of Walker, moving into the station. He wasn't certain, but he got the sense they were trying to outdo one another – that whoever found Charlie first would be the winner of their ongoing feud.

They hurried past an old ticket sales window on their left. Walker was a few feet behind them, stepping tentatively onto the narrow concourse, which was much smaller and narrower than the one at Liverpool Street Station. That narrowness only made it feel more dangerous and claustrophobic, walking around the station in the dark. What else came creeping around in here after the sun went down? To his surprise, Walker found himself thinking back to a scene in *An American Werewolf in London*, where the American werewolf was chasing some English guy in a suit around the London underground.

Of course, the lights had been on in the movie.

But despite the lack of light, they hurried through the station as fast as they could, checking every nook and cranny. Their footsteps in the darkness made them sound like giants. The noise reverberated off the walls and ceilings and it felt like there was no way they could sneak through this place unheard, unnoticed.

Walker searched through a few empty shops and abandoned units that ran alongside the concourse. He heard the others calling out from nearby.

"Charlie!" Carol yelled. "Where are you?"

"Charlie!" It was Barboza. "Are you here? Please talk to us."

Walker found nothing of interest in the old retail units. He tried the bathrooms too but all he found in there was the rancid smell of ancient piss and shit. It was enough to send him running back outside, vowing never to set foot in there again.

After that, Walker hurried down the escalator that led towards the platforms. The platforms themselves were terrifying – everything was black and it was like something out of the climactic scene in a horror film. It had been creepy enough standing in the London underground when the lights were on. But in the dark, it was terrifying. It was like being dropped into a massive underground tunnel. Anyone or anything could have been in there with him.

A sudden noise made Walker jump.

He looked left and right. As his eyes adjusted to the darkness, he saw the shape of someone or something hurrying along the platform. Whoever it was, they were running away from Walker, heading towards the tunnel on the far side of the tracks.

"Charlie!" Walker yelled. "Is that you? It's Walker, and Carol's here too. We've come to take you home."

No answer.

"Fuck."

Heavy breathing. High-pitched and frantic. It was almost certainly a child down there and whoever it was, they were getting away.

Walker ran along the narrow platform, spitting out his breath in short, sharp bursts. There was no time to worry about frightening Charlie – he had to grab the little shit and they had to get out of this godforsaken place. Where did the boy think he was going anyway? Into the tunnel? That's exactly what it looked like he was doing. Up ahead, Walker saw the dark outline of Charlie stopping dead at the platform's end, as if bracing himself to jump onto the train tracks.

And then? Into the tunnel. Where anything could be waiting.

"Charlie! Stop!" he yelled. "Please. Don't jump onto the tracks."

"Charlie!"

It was Barboza's voice. She was behind them on the platform, running towards the tunnel.

"Charlie!" Carol yelled from further back. "Is that you? Are you down here?"

"He's here," Walker yelled back. "He's trying to run."

The boy hesitated at the edge of the platform for too long – it was just long enough for Walker to catch up with him and grab a hold of him. As Walker reached an arm around the boy, he dragged him back onto the platform.

"No!" Charlie screamed. "Let me go!"

"Shut up kid," Walker said, breathing heavily. "You really want to jump off the edge? You want to go into that dark tunnel by yourself?"

Carol and Barboza caught up with them at the edge of the platform. Carol rushed over and grabbed Charlie by the arm, pulling him out of Walker's grip. She knelt down and lifted the boy into a tight embrace, nearly squeezing him to death. The boy's legs dangled helplessly, a few inches off the ground. Then she put him down again.

Tears were streaming down Carol's face. But Charlie looked gutted, like he was horrified to see them.

"Why did you run off like that Charlie?" she said. "How could you do that to me?"

Charlie wriggled free of her vice-like grip. Carol stood up and took an uneasy step backwards, trying to disguise the expression of deep hurt in her eyes with a smile. But Walker saw it, even in the darkness.

"Leave me alone," Charlie said. "What if she's here somewhere and you scared her off with all that noise? What if she's waiting in the tunnels? What if she came looking for me and got hurt? I'm not going back without her."

Barboza stepped forward. She did so gently, so as not to spook the boy. Then she knelt down in front of him and smiled sadly.

"Charlie," she said. "I'm so sorry. This is my fault. I should never have said anything about your mum today. I just wanted to make you feel better – that's all. But you must know yourself that she's not coming back. Not today, not ever."

Charlie was blinking hard, like she'd just shone a beam of torch-light into his eyes. "But you said she was alive," he said.

The hurt in his voice was palpable.

"I'm sorry Charlie," Barboza said. "We don't lie to the children, I know that now."

"We've got to go," Walker said, looking around the black void that surrounded them. "If we wait any longer, there'll be something worse than this waiting for us outside."

Carol pulled Charlie towards her. Then she lifted him up and this time he didn't resist. Instead he buried his head in her chest and Walker heard the boy sobbing quietly.

"Can you manage okay?" Walker asked.

"Yeah," she said. "Let's just get the bloody hell out of here. I want to go home."

Walker led the way back through Old Street Station. He moved as quickly and quietly as possible, keeping the axe in front of him. Keeping it ready.

Fortunately they made it back to the entrance without any interruption. Walker breathed a sigh of relief as the warm evening air touched his face. It felt like a caress from the gods, a pat on the back for finding the boy. Now all they had to do was get back to Station.

Ten minutes. That was all it would take to get them home.

Walker reached the foot of the stairs that led back up to the Old Street. Just as he was about to climb the first step, he stopped dead.

There was a noise.

It took Walker a moment to figure out what he was listening to. But when he did, he was certain of it – it was a drum. It was a single drum beating in a steady, monotonous and powerful rhythm – *one-two-three-four*. It was a primordial sound, out of place in that gritty, urban environment. The drumbeat made Walker think of sailors arriving on uncharted islands in the South Pacific, hundreds of years ago. He imagined those old merchant vessels, like HMS *Bounty*, approaching the unknown, black and shadowy land on the horizon. Listening to the drums in the distance.

Walker looked up the concrete stairs towards the sky. The last of the sunlight had disappeared while they'd been in the station – a cruel joke on the part of Mother Nature.

Walker turned back to the others who were still standing at the entrance. Three horrified faces were looking back at him.

"Please no," Carol whispered.

Before anyone else could speak, something growled in the distance. Walker thought he felt tremors underneath his feet, something rumbling, like the earth was having a seizure and was about to give way.

It was the sound of an engine – lots of engines. Walker thought he heard cars and trucks up there. They were roaring and bearing down upon the Old Street roundabout at a tremendous speed.

One-two-three-four.

Then the drums stopped.

There was an explosion of noise. This time, it was a noise that drowned out everything else – the car engines, the rumbling of the earth, and even the screaming, irrational voice in Walker's mind that told him he needed to get out of there.

It was music. It sounded like an entire nightclub was on the move, with speakers as big as skyscrapers. The pulsing bass was powerful enough to make Walker's senses scramble.

Walker knew the song they were playing. He knew it well.

It was called 'Ghost Town'.

CHAPTER 12

CBC 1: The Weekly Debate (with Joe Antony)

July 12th 2020.

The CBC stage lights up, accompanied by lukewarm applause from the studio audience.

Three men are sitting around a circular shaped wooden table on the stage, facing the cameras and the audience.

The man in the middle is Joe Antony, presenter of The Weekly Debate. Forty-five year old Antony is a former political journalist, well known for tackling the most controversial topics on his weekly TV show.

Sitting on the presenter's right is Billy March, lead guitarist from popular seventies rock band, Flaccid Cactus. Billy is dressed in a Black Sabbath t-shirt and tight black jeans that smother his long, spindly legs. His shoulder-length, grey hair falls well past his shoulders.

On Joe's left is Cedric De Vere, the twenty-first Earl of Oxford. De Vere is fifty-five, with sharp, angular features, thin lips and a nose that curves outwards forming something of a hook shape. He's immaculately dressed – wearing a navy suit over a salmon pink shirt and tight blue jeans.

JOE ANTONY: Good evening and welcome to The Weekly Debate. Now in a change to tonight's scheduled topic, we're going to be looking at events in London. Not today's tragedy at the M25, but what's happening tonight. As you'll all know by now, the Ghosts of London are back and this time, they're travelling north of the river. Of course we all remember the horrible images we saw in March when the last Big Chase took place. Utterly shocking, I think you'll all agree. Well it's happening again and as you no doubt know by now, SKAM *are* broadcasting the Big Chase on their Future of London channel. It's certainly a controversial decision by Rudyard Campbell and his team, and joining me tonight to discuss this, we have Billy March of the great Flaccid Cactus, and the Earl of Oxford, Cedric De Vere. Thank you gentlemen for joining me tonight.

BILLY MARCH: No problem Joe.

CEDRIC DE VERE: Pleasure.

JOE ANTONY: Now Billy, let's start with you. You consider yourself an evolved man – not only are you an accomplished musician in one of the great rock 'n' roll bands, but you're actively pursuing a PhD in astrophysics at Cambridge University. As a man of both science and the arts, you see no place for this sort of thing in modern society. Am I right?

BILLY MARCH: (*Nodding*) Yes Joe. There's no excuse for continuing this cruel exploitation of the people of London. It's obscene to let them go on suffering like this. And what's even more obscene is the decision to broadcast something like the Big Chase – the absolute worst of what's happening in there. And then Campbell has the cheek to call it a learning process for the rest of us, like it has some sort of educational value instead of just being the crass entertainment that it is.

JOE ANTONY: Cedric, do you disagree?

CEDRIC DE VERE: I disagree entirely. The whole RELEASE campaign is an overemotional farce, incapable of objective and rational thought. And in regards to what's going on tonight with the Ghosts, well here's what I think. As human beings we have an in inherent fascination with the hunt. I'm sorry but we do. The idea of one creature pitting its wits against the other is thrilling. You may not want to admit it Billy, but it's true. We as a species are fascinated with the superiority of the strong – why is man destined to outwit the fox? And now in London, we have the twenty-first century equivalent of the old hunting sports – men hunting men. What will happen? Who will survive? These are questions that teach us a lot about ourselves.

BILLY MARCH: That's a complete load of bollocks. I'm sorry Joe but it's fucking bollocks mate.

JOE ANTONY: (*Smiling to the camera*) Please excuse the colourful language. Of course, this is a very passionate subject.

BILLY MARCH: The Big Chase is a blood sport of the most heinous kind. We should not be broadcasting this torture porn and pretending that there's some educational benefit to be gained. It's an absolute scam – a front for people like Cedric and Rudyard Campbell who simply enjoy watching people suffer from the comfort of their living rooms. It's time we broke down those bloody walls and showed a little compassion to the people that we've kept prisoner behind the M25 for nine long years. There are children in there for God's sake!

CEDRIC DE VERE: If I may, I think that Rudyard Campbell and Aileen Ure, the Prime Minister have laid down some perfectly valid reasons as to why the M25 must stay intact. And let's be honest here –the Big Chase, as horrific as it may be to some, does actually serve as a means of population control within the city. That might sound cold but there are simply too many people in London. We don't know what the population or the birth rate is, but it's not sustainable to have so many people claiming Drop Parcels at the British taxpayer's expense. Not to mention there are no medical facilities in the city, so a larger population means a greater risk of disease.

BILLY MARCH: (*Laughing and shaking his head*) Are you serious Cedric? These people are being chased around the city by a gang of cannibals. Does that sound humane to you? Women and children are run to the point of exhaustion before being captured and bundled off to the human farm in the Hole. And God knows what happens to them before they're slaughtered – they could be force-fed for weeks or months for all we know to fatten them up. Does that sound humane to you?

CEDRIC DE VERE: I believe a quick death at the hands of the Ghosts is preferable to wasting away in a back alley to disease or starvation, don't you?

BILLY MARCH: (*Gasps*) A quick death? Didn't you just hear what I said? How can you come on this show tonight and not know what the bloody hell you're talking about Cedric? These people aren't killed quickly. I've just mentioned the human farm that's down there in the Hole. They're kept alive and they live the rest of their short lives in terror – men, women and children – knowing that they're going to be butchered for meat.

CEDRIC DE VERE: Rumours my boy. And if it is true, the Ghosts are stocking up on food because they choose not to accept charity in the form of Drop Parcels. That's their decision and given the circumstances they live in, it's one we must respect. In a way, we do the exact same thing here although most of us don't hunt our own meat. We go to the shop, take it home and put it in the freezer until we're ready to eat it. It's not all that dissimilar and we'd be hypocrites to slam the Ghosts for doing something that we do ourselves.

BILLY MARCH: Cedric, do you even consider the people living in London as human anymore?

CEDRIC DE VERE: (*Laughs briefly*) We can no longer measure their society alongside ours Billy. Mother, father, brother, sister – are these terms even relevant anymore? That is the sociological fascination with London as it is now – it's a brand new society in its infancy, completely unique and like nothing we've ever seen before. I for one, shall be watching the Big Chase with interest tonight in the hope that I can learn something about human nature.

BILLY MARCH: You really are a posh twat aren't you Cedric? You're a nasty piece of work. You're a horrible little bastard who doesn't understand suffering because you were born with a silver spoon shoved up your fat arse. You've never had to work a day in your life, have you mate? Go fuck yourself.

De Vere smirks.

JOE ANTONY: (*Laughing nervously*) Well apologies again for the language. We're going to take a quick break now but it's been a fascinating debate so far. We'll be right back with more chat after this commercial break. And by the way, if you're watching CBC on split screen with the Future of London, you'll already know that the Ghosts have arrived in the north. Now if you choose to watch the Big Chase, remember that what you're about to see is graphic and extremely disturbing. Viewer caution is advised.

CHAPTER 13

"This town is coming like a ghost town."

The music was blaring through the speakers, getting louder with each second. 'Ghost Town' by The Specials was a song that Walker knew well. He'd gone through a phase back in Edinburgh in late 2010 where he listened to nothing but ska music for about two months. Thinking back, he recalled how he'd strutted his stuff around the city dressed in a pork pie hat, polo shirt, turned-up jeans, and Doc Martens. That is, until enough people told him he looked like a dick.

The song had brought him joy once. Not now.

Walker crept slowly up the concrete stairs that led back towards street level. As he did so, the fat bassline rumbled like thunder in his bones. The hypnotic vocal repeated the chorus line over and over again.

"This town is coming like a ghost town."

Walker kept his arm outstretched behind him – a signal for Barboza, Carol, and Charlie to stay back at the entrance to the station.

When he was near the top of the stairs, he looked through the steel bars that ran alongside the staircase. There was nothing there, not yet.

But they were close.

A hand touched Walker on the shoulder. He gasped.

Carol was standing behind him on the stairs. She was looking over his shoulder, staring through the bars at the empty street, towards the roundabout.

"Nothing?" she said.

"No," Walker said, turning back to the street. "I can't see them yet."

Carol nodded. "It's okay," she said. "They won't be stopping here, at least not yet. They're playing the music to taunt people, to let them know they've arrived. It's when the music stops, that's when we need to worry. Silence, that's what you fear. Let them move on, then we run. Okay?"

"Aye."

Walker glanced behind Carol towards Barboza. She was standing on the path with one arm around Charlie's shoulder. The boy looked pale, like he was about to be sick.

"Alright," Walker said. "We wait."

They hurried back down the steps together. The four of them gathered at the entrance of the station, where the wall on either side of the steps kept them out of sight from anybody on street level.

Walker saw a chunk of dark, cloudy sky overhead. There would be no stars tonight.

The music was louder now. It was so loud that they could have been standing in the front row at a major rock festival. Walker wondered how the Ghosts had conjured up such a powerful sound system, but then he reminded himself that in the aftermath of Piccadilly, the fruits of London would have been a looter's paradise. Most of the shops had been plundered in the London riots, but the Ghosts had probably helped themselves to whatever they could find in professional music studios or private houses that had been abandoned. Clearly they'd done something right in the early days, considering how much sway they held over the city.

Now they'd arrived.

Walker looked up the stairs towards street level. His heart was pounding.

The convoy was up there now, circling the roundabout. Walker couldn't see it, but he could hear it – the thumping music and angry engines.

"They're just passing through," Carol said. She'd pulled Charlie towards her and was stroking his light brown hair, soothing him and whispering reassurances into his ear.

But Charlie didn't look like he was listening to the words of his guardian. His frightened eyes were looking up towards the street.

The throbbing bass. The growling of the engines. It seemed to go on forever.

In reality, the Ghosts' convoy couldn't have been up there for much longer than a minute. Gradually, the music and the cars faded out of earshot. The arrival parade had moved on. At first, nobody standing outside the entrance dared to move. But after a couple more minutes, there was only silence up there on street level.

"Time to move," Carol said.

"Didn't you just tell me to fear silence?" Walker said. "Are you sure they're gone?"

"Yeah," she said. "For now at least. But you have to fear the real silence that comes later. When they turn that music off after their little parade is over. Because that's when they go to work."

"Let's get out of here," Barboza said. "We don't have time to talk about this."

No one argued with her. They climbed the stairs back towards the street. It was completely deserted. Walker looked across the roundabout and saw the sleek and modern office blocks in the distance, as ghoulish and haunted house-like as ever. The silence was eerie, like an icy cold finger running down Walker's back. It was like that brief visit from the Ghosts had never happened.

"The cars will split up soon," Carol said. "It's what they do. They'll start spreading themselves out and some of them will be back here. Guaranteed. We don't have long."

"We need to get back to Station," Walker said. "Now."

"We can't go back," Carol said. "It's too risky. It's too far to travel on foot without running the risk of being seen."

"Shit," Walker said. He'd dared to hope they were through the worst of it. "So what do we do?" he asked.

"Why don't we hide in the station?" Barboza said, pointing back towards the underground. "Charlie did alright. We could climb into the tunnel or something like that. We're hardly going to get hit by a train."

Walker didn't like that. He didn't like the idea of going back into Old Street Station. He certainly didn't like the idea of climbing into that tunnel. That endless black abyss, resembling an open mouth.

"The tunnel is no guarantee of safety," Carol said. "These maniacs are thorough and that's exactly the sort of place they're going to be checking out later. You want to get trapped in there with the Ghosts?"

Barboza raised her eyebrows. "Have you got a better idea Carol?" she said. "Seeing as how you know everything an' all."

"We've got no choice," Walker said, jumping in before another argument could break out. "We've got to get back to Liverpool Street Station. If that's the one place we're guaranteed to be safe then it's the one place we have to go."

"Yeah," Barboza agreed.

"We won't make it," Carol said. As she spoke, she glanced over her shoulder, as if expecting the Ghosts to come back at any minute. "I'm pretty sure they took off down City Road just now. It's ten minutes back to Station that way if we stay on the main road. And if we're on the main road they'll see us. If we come off the main road and take another route, we're just as likely to get trapped with nowhere to run."

Walker sighed. "Fuck sake," he said. "We can't hang about the streets all night."

"So what do we do?" Barboza said. She was staring at Carol, her eyes flashing with anger. "If you know so much about what *they're* going to do, why not tell us what we're supposed to do to get the bloody hell out of this mess."

Carol took a hold of Charlie's shoulders, like she was leaning on him.

"We've got to lay low," she said. "Find a place to hide. Somewhere they're not going to look for us."

The three adults stared at one another, knowing that they didn't have much time to discuss the matter in depth.

"Where?" Walker said. "I don't know anything about this neck of the woods."

"What about that big cemetery we passed on the way here," Barboza said. "The park with all the old tombstones. What was it called?"

"Bunhill Fields," Carol said.

"You want to hide from Ghosts in a cemetery?" Walker asked. "Is that supposed to be a joke?"

"Yeah 'cos I'm in the mood for a joke right now Walker," Barboza said, glaring at him.

Walker backed off.

"Or what about the church on the other side of the road?" Barboza said. "Opposite Bunhill Fields or whatever it was called. We could hide in there if Walker's too scared to go into a cemetery at night."

"Wesley's Chapel," Carol said.

"Yeah it was tucked in off the road a little," Barboza said. "It'd be more comfortable than the cemetery too."

"Won't the Ghosts check in there too?" Walker said.

"Probably," Carol said. "And if we get caught in there, we're trapped."

"Well what about the graveyard then?" Barboza said, sighing in exasperation.

Carol looked at Barboza. Walker thought the older woman was about to shoot down the idea but to his surprise, she nodded at Barboza.

"It's a good idea," she said. "Bunhill is probably the only place around here that's big enough for us to hide in. The Ghosts might give it a miss. And even if they do come in, it's big enough to give us a chance of being invisible."

Barboza smiled. "What choice have we got, eh?"

Walker looked at Charlie, then gave him a playful tap on the shoulder. "What do you say wee man?" he asked. "Will you look after me if I let these two women drag us into a graveyard?"

Charlie looked at Walker and smiled. "Yeah alright," he said.

Having made the decision to hide in Bunhill Fields, the quartet hurried back over the roundabout and onto City Road. A road sign informed them that they were on the A501, which was a section of the London Inner Ring Road.

They followed the road south. The heavy tip-tap of their feet hitting the concrete was the only sound that Walker could hear.

It took them about two minutes to reach Bunhill Fields. On the other side of the street, Walker noticed Wesley's Chapel for the first time. The chapel was indeed a little further back from the main road – it was an attractive, two-storeyed Georgian building located at the end of a short, cobbled courtyard. It appeared to have been built mostly out of brown brick and had round-arched windows, five running along the top floor and two on either side of the lower floor entrance. Walker noticed a couple of Greek columns on either side of the main door. In the middle of the courtyard, the statue of a man in a robe extended its arms outwards, beckoning them towards shelter.

"Are you sure we can't hide in there?" Walker said. "What is that place?"

"It's a Methodist church," Carol said. "*Was*. Built by John Wesley – that's the bloke in the statue out front."

"It looks like a safe place," Barboza said.

"It's not worth the risk," Carol said. "If we get cornered in there, we're finished."

Walker was about to respond but he was cut off by a noise in the distance. He looked over his shoulder, back towards the Old Street roundabout. There was no music this time, no drums – just the sound of vehicles approaching.

"Oh shit," Carol said, grabbing Charlie by the arm. "We need to move, get out of sight."

Barboza looked towards the roundabout. "That was bloody quick," she said.

"Alright," Walker said. "No more arguments. Bunhill it is then."

They ran over towards the entrance of Bunhill Fields. The black steel gate was located in between two stone pillars and it was lying wide open. It too was inviting them in, but it was a less reassuring welcome than the open arms of John Wesley.

Instead of rushing into the old graveyard, Walker and the others tucked themselves in at the edge of one of the stone pillars. They turned back and watched as two vehicles in the distance pulled onto City Road from the Old Street roundabout.

Two sets of bright yellow headlights came closer. One of the vehicles was a dark coloured, black pickup truck. The other was a long white van, possibly a Mercedes Sprinter van, judging by the sheer length of the body, which stretched back about six metres.

There was a fierce skidding sound from further down the road. The tires of the pickup screeched to a sudden halt against the warm road surface. Then slowly, it pulled into the side of the road, parking next to one of the old restaurants that Walker and the others had passed a few minutes ago on their way down City Road.

The Mercedes van pulled in behind the pickup. Both vehicles kept their engines running and their lights on.

"What's going on?" Barboza said. "Why have they stopped there?"

"They're onto something," Carol whispered. "Either they know something we don't or they're just taking a punt that someone's in there."

A moment later, there was a loud clicking noise as the doors of the Sprinter and the pickup opened at the same time. Countless dark figures spilled out of both vehicles, stepping onto the road.

From afar, Walker saw the Ghosts of London for the first time.

CHAPTER 14

Immersion 9 – Live Chat Forums
#GhostsofLondon #BigChase

Harry Krishna: Anybody watching FOL 10? Is that Mr Apocalypse and Barboza I see shitting themselves on the City Road?

WelcomeTo1984: Yeah lad.

Harry Krishna: Who else is with them?

WelcomeTo1984: Woman and boy? They're from Station. Weren't you watching earlier?

Harry Krishna: Nah I'm just sitting down with my GF and a take-away to watch ***#GhostsofLondon*** There was a Big Chase meal deal on at McDonalds. Fast food! Guess that's what the Ghosts are getting in as well. What else do you call it when your dinner runs away at a hundred miles per hour? LOL!

Ajax: LOL! Mr A and B are in deep shit. Look at all 'em Ghosts standing outside that restaurant. Fucking hell. Something big's about to go down here.

WelcomeTo1984: Fuck Mr A and B! Instant karma baby!! It's what they deserve after what they did to them two soldiers today. Good men killed by those bloody London animals. Come on the Ghosts – knock 'em out and put 'em in the van. You're going to the farm! LOL!

Ajax: **@WelcomeTo1984** You stupid twat! You don't actually believe those troops were doing maintenance work? For real bro? Troops were sent there to kill them. It was self-defence. Don't be such a gullible fucking moron!!

WelcomeTo1984: @Ajax LOL! It's Mr Conspiracy Theory! Calm down sunshine. Don't knock that tinfoil hat off your head on the way out.

Ajax: **@WelcomeTo1984** Fucking sheep!! You're everything that's wrong with the world. Too lazy to think and form your own opinion.

WelcomeTo1984: @Ajax HA-HA-HA-HA-HA-HA-HA!!

Harry Krishna: Calm down ladies! Keep your eyes on the ***#BigChase*** Something's happening on FOL 10. It's not Mr A or B though. Looks like the Ghosts have found something in that building.

WelcomeTo1984: Or someone.

CHAPTER 15

Walker and the others hid by the entrance to Bunhill Fields.

He knew they should have been deep into the cemetery by now. But his feet were like giant concrete blocks that had taken root in the ground. Something was holding him back. The others were making no signs of moving either. It was as if they were all hypnotised by what was happening further down the street. It was terrifying and yet, they couldn't tear their eyes away.

Carol had a hand pinned over Charlie's mouth. Walker guessed she was making sure the boy didn't scream.

The Ghosts of London, or at least some of them, were standing on City Road. There were about fifteen to twenty of them that Walker could see. They were all dressed in a similar outfit – casual, street clothes for the most part – jeans, vest tops and what looked like a chunky pair of Doc Martens boots on their feet. Walker noticed that most of their arms were heavily tattooed, displaying an array of striking designs, the precise details of which he couldn't make out from afar.

But that wasn't the half of it.

Gas masks. The Ghosts were wearing gas masks over their faces. And on top of these gas masks, white or grey judges' wigs had been attached, adding a uniquely old-fashioned air to this most striking of twenty-first century uniforms. Several short dark horns sprouted from atop the wigs, like a demonic cherry on the cake.

The gas masks weren't the usual type that Walker envisioned – he always pictured the darker coloured ones, maybe black or brown or green – the kind that he'd seen featured in the old World War Two highlight reels. He knew about the later British S6 or S10 models too, with a smaller filter canister positioned over the mouth. But the Ghosts were wearing something different. The face piece of their masks were made out of white rubber and it wasn't just strapped onto the front of the face like with some gas masks – this one fit entirely over the head like a helmet and it obscured the wearer's features entirely. At the front, two large lenses acted as eyeholes and most notable of all, an extra-large filter canister protruded from the mouth of the mask. The canister grew out of the rubber like a long tumour, providing the Ghosts with a bizarre, extra-terrestrial look.

"Jesus Christ," Walker said. "What's with the fancy dress?"

"I've seen those masks before," Barboza whispered. "On a film set. They're Russian civilian gas masks. Creepy as hell man."

Walker and the others remained perfectly still, huddled around the entrance of Bunhill Fields.

Further down the street, the Ghosts were sizing up the building they'd just parked beside. One Ghost was standing on the back of the pickup truck, handing out steel or wooden baseball bats like he was a politician handing out campaign leaflets. Walker noticed too that along with the baseball bats, many of the Ghosts had daggers tucked into a small scabbard that was hanging off a leather belt at their waist.

Walker heard the engines of both the pickup and the Sprinter van still running. Considering that fuel had to be scarce, he figured that the Ghosts weren't planning on a long stop here.

The hunters moved towards the building. Two of the Ghosts started kicking at the front door with the soles of their Doc Martens.

There was a harsh, thudding sound that travelled down to where Walker and the others were hiding. At the same time, the sound of smashing glass exploded in Walker's ears. He saw that several other Ghosts were attacking the large window at the front of the restaurant, going at it with their baseball bats.

Walker noticed a few of the Ghosts standing behind the attackers, carrying what looked like large cuts of netting.

That was when he heard a voice in his head.

Run. Why are you still here? Why are you watching this?

It didn't take long for the Ghosts to break into the restaurant. They charged through the door and into the building, a squad of post-apocalyptic stormtroopers tracking some unseen bounty within. Immediately, Walker heard loud thumping noises coming from inside. It sounded like the furniture was being thrown up against the walls.

Screaming. Both men and women, terrified for their lives.

There was a sudden explosion of noise. Shattering glass. Walker looked towards the upper floor and saw a figure crashing headfirst through one of the windows. The figure plummeted down towards the street, a thousand shards of broken glass falling with him.

It was a man.

He fell swiftly with his body folded up into a tight ball, as if somehow by doing this, it might protect him from the impact below. Walker guessed that it was about twenty feet to the ground from the upper floor window. The man could make it – he would survive the jump, but what about the aftermath?

The man landed on the road with a sickening thud. As he did so, he rolled over several times on the broken glass, shrieking in pain with each turn of his body. Walker felt like he was standing on the edge of a film set, watching a stunt man doing a take for an action movie.

The man – who couldn't have been older than twenty-five – leapt back to his feet and started running down City Road, trying to get away from the building and the Ghosts. He was running towards where Walker and the others were standing, tucked in behind the stone pillars at the entrance of Bunhill Fields.

But the Ghosts weren't about to let him get away. Two of the masked men came charging out of the front door of the restaurant, chasing after their prey. The man took off, sprinting at full speed down the middle of the road. Walker looked on in horror. He listened to the man, who was making a weird, animalistic grunting noise as he fled for his life. His face was covered in fresh cuts along the nose, cheeks, mouth and even the eyes, which made it look like he was crying blood.

The man looked back over his shoulder. The hunters in the white masks and judges wigs were closing in on him. The Ghosts were fast too. Walker noticed that all the ones he he'd seen so far were in impressive physical shape – lean and muscular. Not the type of people who were going to be outrun by just anyone.

The young man let out a pitiful shriek. His body was betraying him. He was slowing down.

One of the Ghosts caught up with him, and reached for the young man. He wrapped a sinewy arm around his victim's neck like it was a hook, and then yanked him backwards at tremendous force. There was a wheezing sound as the man was knocked off his feet and down onto the road. Now he was lying flat on his back and the two Ghosts were standing over him. Several other Ghosts arrived on the scene, but they weren't running. They were walking at a casual pace, content in the knowledge that they'd won. One of them was carrying a large sheet of netting and when he got closer to the man, he tossed it over him in a scene that reminded Walker of the gladiators in Ancient Rome, the sort of warriors who'd used nets and tridents to get the better of their opponents.

The young man had no more fight left in him. He remained perfectly still underneath the netting, as if he'd resigned himself to his fate. Two of the Ghosts then dragged their fresh victim back to his feet and led him back along City Road towards where the pickup and the Sprinter van were still waiting with their engines running. The young man was taken around the to back of the Sprinter van and Walker heard the sharp click of the back door opening. Although he couldn't see what was going on, he imagined they were dumping the man inside.

Another one for the farm.

"We have to go," Barboza said.

Nobody was about to argue. But just as they were turning around they saw more Ghosts coming out of the restaurant. Walker paused, trying to get a better look and his heart sank at the sight that greeted him. He saw the masked hunters leading out a small group of five or six people, all buried underneath a large net.

"Oh no," Carol said.

At that moment, the sound of screeching tyres exploded from the other end of City Road. Walker's heart was pounding with fright as he looked over his shoulders to see what was going on behind them.

He saw a car pulling up at the side of a zebra crossing. It was at most, about forty or fifty metres away from the entrance of Bunhill Fields. Walker thought it looked like a black Audi Saloon, or something similar.

Just as the car pulled up, a lone figure came running across the street. Whoever it was, they were about ten metres away from the car at most. The Audi's headlights were pointing at the runner, showering them in two tunnels of white light.

It was a young woman. With the headlights pointing at her, Walker saw that she wasn't entirely alone after all. She was clutching something tight to her chest – or rather someone. It was a young girl, no more than two or three years of age.

The woman ran harder. Walker didn't know how long this game of cat and mouse had been going on, but she must have known how close her pursuer was. The child in her arms began to scream as she was carried across the street in her desperate mother's arms. Walker saw the blonde hair of the little girl bouncing up and down along to the chaotic rhythm of their escape.

The car door opened and a lone Ghost stepped out of the driver's side. Like the other gang members, he was wearing a Russian gas mask and a judges' wig. Walker noticed that this Ghost also had a police badge hanging over his chest, like it was a medallion. His mask was darker than the others too – a sort of rusty brown colour that contrasted with the whiteness of the wig. He was an impressive physical specimen, even by Ghost standards. He was tall, almost freakishly so, like a thicker, muscular version of an NBA basketball player. His skin was dark brown and unlike the other Ghosts, there were no tattoos on his arms. And while the others Ghosts had knives hanging from their belts, this guy had a full-length sword sitting in a lean scabbard that was positioned on the left hand side of his waist.

The tall Ghost went after the woman and child. He ran along City Road, covering ground like a world-class sprinter in the Olympic hundred metres final. His arms and legs were a lightning fast blur, the muscles pumping back and forth, generating tremendous speed.

It was a foregone conclusion. It only took the tall Ghost a few seconds to catch up with the woman as she tried to exit City Road. The woman stopped running and turned to face her pursuer. There was a fierce look in her eyes and for a moment, she no longer looked like a prey animal. Walker believed it too; he believed that she would stand there and fight to the death in order to save her child. But although she did struggle, the Ghost was too strong for her. He didn't even look like he was close to breaking a sweat as he dragged them back to the car.

"Oh fuck," Barboza said. "Walker, can't we do something?"

"There's nothing we can do for them," Carol said. She and Charlie were now standing a few feet inside the gate, having entered Bunhill Fields ahead of Walker and Barboza.

"Don't even think about being a hero tonight," Carol said. "Either one of you. No matter what you see, stay out of sight or join the rest of the victims in the farm. That woman should have been in Station tonight. She failed her daughter by taking her chances on the street."

Walker looked back towards City Road. The tall Ghost had by now tied the woman's arms behind her back with heavy tape. He then did the same with the little girl and to finish, he put the tape over their mouths to gag them. Finally they were bundled into the backseat and pushed down so they were lying on their sides.

Walker felt sick. He could only imagine the fate that awaited them. But he knew that Carol was right too – if they tried to play heroes hey would end up as victims instead, joining the others in the back of the Sprinter van en route to the farm.

"Okay," Walker said. "Time to..."

He was cut off in mid-sentence by a series of short, sharp beeps coming from either the pickup or the Sprinter van, still parked outside the restaurant. Walker and the others looked down that way. The Ghosts had by now bundled their captives into the back of the van. But instead of getting back into their vehicles and moving on, they were standing huddled outside on the street, grouped together in one giant pack.

They were standing stiff and alert, like they'd seen something.

It didn't take Walker long to realise what it was. And when he did, his blood ran cold.

The Ghosts were looking at them.

Somebody shouted a command and all hell broke loose. The Ghosts hurried back into their vehicles, moving as if it was their lives that depended on it. Seconds later, both vehicle engines roared, like a great god growling in the bowels of the earth. The pickup truck came speeding along City Road towards Bunhill Fields, followed close behind by the Sprinter van.

"Move!" Walker yelled to the others.

They ran into the old burial ground – Carol and Charlie at the front, Barboza in the middle, and Walker at the rear. Everything was black and the warm night air grasped at their skin as they rushed forward. The faint outline of tall trees and large headstones surrounded them, dark spectres standing watch over the dead.

Walker heard the sound of screeching brakes on City Road. The pickup truck and the Sprinter van were pulling up outside the gate of the old graveyard. He heard the doors being flung open, the sound of Doc Marten boots jumping onto the concrete.

Walker and the others ran deeper into the vast darkness of Bunhill Fields. Walker was slightly ahead of the group, searching for anything that resembled a good place to hide.

His eyes worked frantically but although there was enough visibility to avoid bumping into things, it was too dark to see anything clearly. There were too many clouds that night to allow any moonlight from the heavens to seep through into Bunhill Fields. It was just Walker's luck – almost every other night that summer had seen clear skies.

He veered off the public path, running onto a stretch of long, dry grass. All around, the tall trees bent over them like villainous giants out of a fairy tale. The footsteps of Barboza, Carol and Charlie were close behind him. Walker figured that their best option was probably to seek shelter behind the trees or the headstones and bury themselves in the long grass as best they could. There was no way they could outrun the Ghosts, not with a little boy in their midst. That meant darkness was their new best friend. So too was the vastness of Bunhill Fields, the long grass and the decaying headstones.

The Ghosts must have been confident about catching their prey. So confident that they felt no need to bother with the silent and subtle approach. To Walker, it sounded like a herd of buffalo were closing in on them.

He glanced over his shoulder. Several narrow beams of torchlight were darting back and forth amongst the trees.

Walker felt his heart pounding. There had to be somewhere they could lay low. He saw several rows of old headstones situated on the grass off the main path. They were ancient and had been ravaged over time by the English elements. There were probably hundreds of thousands of people buried in these grounds, dating back many centuries. Some of the more notable monuments had been fenced off to protect them from being damaged by the public.

He led the others towards a crowd of smaller headstones. These were located on a rectangular stretch of grass, off the main path. The headstones in this section of the graveyard probably belonged to the deceased commoners of long ago, people who had been considered less important than those who'd been given the monuments. But Walker would forever be in debt to these commoners if they offered them shelter from the murderous rain.

And that was a big if.

The grass was long and it intermingled with an endless supply of tall wildflowers. Walker and the other adults ducked behind a stone each, sinking down into the grass, burying themselves so deep that they became part of their surroundings.

Carol kept Charlie close to her, both of them ducking behind the same headstone. She pulled the boy tight to her chest, all the while forcing herself deeper into the long grass. Walker looked over and saw the mute terror in the boy's face. Charlie looked as if he was in a trance, his eyes vacant, not blinking.

Walker and Barboza lay silent in the tall grass. If they didn't move or breathe – if they could remain as quiet as the hundreds of rotten corpses underneath them, then Walker figured they had a chance.

The Ghosts' footsteps were fading. Walker could still hear them somewhere in the graveyard, but they weren't any closer. But he didn't dare to hope. He just lay there, burrowing as far into the dry earth as best he could. After a few moments, Barboza's face peered at him through the grass. He nodded, letting her know that they were okay.

For now.

A few seconds later, she wriggled through the grass towards him.

"You think they're gone?" she whispered.

Walker shrugged. "Maybe."

Soon there was no sound. There were no voices calling out to one another in the distance. No Doc Martens slapping off the concrete paths. But Walker remained cautious. His best guess was that the Ghosts were searching for them in another part of the cemetery – it was a huge place after all and there was a lot of ground to cover. With any luck, the Ghosts would realise that Bunhill Fields was too big. And maybe they weren't willing to spend all night searching from one end to another for four people. Not when there was an entire city to plunder.

Walker looked over at Barboza.

"You know something?" he asked.

She scrunched up her face in confusion. "What?"

"My life wasn't so bad up there on Stanmore Road," he said. "Was it?"

Barboza shook her head. "I'm sorry Walker," she said.

"I know."

To Walker's left, Carol and Charlie were sitting up a little, poking their head out of the grassy hiding place. Carol looked over at Walker and Barboza.

"Are you two okay?" Walker asked.

Carol nodded. "We got lucky," she said. "I think we've given them the slip."

Walker looked at Charlie. The boy was coming out of his daze a little. He was looking around at his surroundings, his eyes bright and curious. Walker recalled that Charlie still didn't know exactly what the 'bad men' were doing out there on the streets tonight. He just knew that they were 'bad men' doing bad things.

"You alright wee man?" Walker asked.

Walker was expecting a nod or grunt at most. But to his surprise, Charlie spoke back to him.

"I'm sorry," he said, looking first at Carol, then at Walker and Barboza.

Carol squeezed him tight, burying her face in his bowl-cut hair. Her eyes were closed but Walker knew that she was crying.

"It's okay," Walker said. He kept his axe buried underneath the grass so that Charlie didn't have to see it. "You wanted to see your mum. I get it. I waited nine years in the same house, waiting for my mum and dad to come back."

Charlie's eyes were wide open. "Did you lose them?"

Walker smiled. "Aye, I lost them."

The little boy stared at Walker.

"Are they going to grab us?" he said. "Like they did with that man on the street?"

"No," Walker said. "But listen up. I'm going to tell you what to do just in case they do, alright? If somebody grabs you like they did that man on the street, you do whatever you have to do to get them off you, okay? Don't be shy. Be nasty. Poke them in the eye, bite them – bite them as hard as you can okay? Get your teeth right into the skin and make them bleed. They deserve it 'cos they're bad men Charlie. Aye? Do what you have to do."

Charlie nodded. "Do what you have to do," he said.

Walker winked at the boy. "Right."

Carol lifted her head up and smiled at Walker. To Walker's surprise, she even smiled at Barboza too.

Barboza returned the gesture, ending their feud silently.

"My mum's dead," Charlie said, looking at Walker. "The rogue got her."

"Probably," Walker said. "It makes sense, but you know what? You don't have to believe it. I think my mum and dad are still out there somewhere."

Barboza reached over and gave Charlie a playful tap on the arm. She was about to say something but was cut off by a sudden noise.

Voices. Footsteps.

The Ghosts were coming back.

Walker and the others dove back down into their hiding places. Nothing to worry about, Walker thought, immersing himself in the dry, dirty surroundings. The Ghosts were just passing through after an unsuccessful search elsewhere in Bunhill Fields. Now they were on their way back to the City Road entrance, having given up the chase. Soon they'd all be back in the pickup and Sprinter van. They'd drive the hell out of there and it would be over.

They were getting closer. The voices, although muffled through the masks, were louder than ever.

"Four of 'em," a gruff voice said. "They're still in 'ere. I know it."

"Split up," another man's voice said. "Look in those little square bits of grass over there, just off the path. Spread yourselves about and use the torches. They can't hide from all of us."

Walker's heart sank. He felt like screaming with fear and frustration.

He lay there in the dirt, listening to several of them approaching the narrow pathway. Now they were walking alongside the stretch of grass where Walker and the others were hiding. They were on the path and it was too damn close. He looked up and saw a thin beam of torchlight moving back and forth amongst the scattering of headstones, just a short distance away.

Walker didn't dare breathe. He didn't dare blink. He wished that he could bury himself deeper in the grass but there was only so far he could go without bumping into the original occupant of the gravesite.

He heard two of them talking on the pathway. Somebody was shining a torch into the grass, searching both areas on either side of the concrete walkway. The light was coming closer.

"They're in 'ere somewhere," a muffled voice said.

Walker took slow, deep breaths. He fought the urge to panic, to get up and make a run for it. He turned to his left and saw the faint outline of Barboza, buried deep within the grass. But behind her, Walker saw something that almost made his heart stop.

Carol was sitting up. And Charlie was sitting up with her. She hand her hands under his armpits, like she'd dragged him out of their hiding place.

The light was closer still.

Walker signalled towards her, screaming with his eyes, pleading with her to lie back down again. But Carol was looking straight through him. She just sat there, shaking her head back and forth like she'd reached her breaking point. Like she'd succumbed to the same panic that Walker had been fighting off.

She looked at Charlie, her eyes all apologies.

Torchlight landed on nearby headstones.

Walker didn't know what he was supposed to do. It was too late to rush over there and drag her down into the dirt against her will. Has she really lost hope? Did she love Charlie so much that she couldn't bear the thought of what they'd do to him?

Carol looked at Walker, her eyes gleaming in the darkness. She whispered the words – "I must save him."

Then she turned back to Charlie.

Carol pulled the boy towards her – a fierce embrace that lasted a second or two. She then whispered something to him and began to crawl away from their hiding place on her hands and knees. Looking back at Charlie with a tortured smile, she encouraged him to do the same. Charlie turned back, looking at Walker and Barboza for guidance. Barboza knew better than to make any sudden movement, but Walker saw the horror in her eyes as she watched events unfolding.

Carol reached over and lifted Charlie into her arms. With one last look at Walker and Barboza, she leapt to her feet and ran off into the night, carrying the bewildered boy through the darkness.

A single beam of torchlight went after them.

"There!" a man's voice said. "I see one of 'em. She's taking off!"

There was a loud crunching noise. Heavy footsteps trampled through the dry grass, going after Carol and Charlie.

Walker and Barboza kept still, lying down in the dirt. Walker listened to the frantic, gruesome breathing of the two men underneath the gas masks.

Soon the footsteps and torchlight receded into the distance. Walker and Barboza sat upright at the same time. They looked at one another – Barboza looked like she was going to throw up. Walker felt the same.

"What the fuck?" Barboza said. "Why did she do that?"

"She got spooked," Walker said, checking to see if the coast was clear.

Before Barboza could say anything else, they heard a scream. It was nearby, somewhere within the burial grounds. It was a woman's scream – a bloodcurdling shriek that made Walker jump out of his skin.

"Charlie!" Carol yelled. She sounded a long way off now. Walker barely recognised her voice, so twisted and distorted with panic as it was.

"Run Charlie!" Carol screamed.

CHAPTER 16

Barboza jerked forwards, like she was about to run after Carol and Charlie.

To her credit, this was her first instinct – to play the part of the hero. But Walker knew that playing the hero meant losing. Carol had already told them that. It meant both of them ending up in the back of the Sprinter van, taped up and sitting alongside all the other fresh produce on its way to the farm.

And he didn't want that for either of them.

When Barboza moved, Walker reached out and grabbed her by the forearm. He yanked her back down into a sitting position, ignoring the hurt and confusion in her dark brown eyes.

When she didn't resist, Walker guessed she understood why he was doing it. Anything was better than a kamikaze rescue mission.

They heard Carol screaming again, a little further away this time. It sounded like they were taking her towards the City Road exit.

"She's fighting them," Barboza said. "Oh fuck Walker. They've got Carol and Charlie. We can't leave them. What are we going to do?"

Walker didn't know what to say. There wasn't any clear-cut solution that was going to result in a happy ending for everyone. That much was clear. It all looked so easy in the movies, being a hero. But if he was to charge across Bunhill Fields gung-ho like a white knight he was certain that the bad guys weren't going to roll over like they were following a script.

But doing nothing wasn't an option either. Sure, it was their best chance of staying alive. But how was Walker going to live with himself if he left Carol and Charlie to their fate? It was bad enough that he'd already left so many strangers to the same fate – the people in the restaurant, the woman and child on City Road. How could he do the same to Carol and Charlie?

Walker looked back and forth, making sure there were no more Ghosts in the area. He got back to his feet, helping Barboza up at the same time.

"I think they're shipping out," Walker said. "They're taking them to the vans."

"We've got to do something Walker," Barboza said.

"I know," he said. "Look let's get down to the front, okay? Take a look before we do something stupid."

"Yeah."

They crept down towards the front gate, staying on the grass in order to avoid the main path. Whenever they heard anything they'd take cover behind the nearest tree and wait for about thirty seconds. Only when they were certain the coast was clear, did they come out and continue towards the gate.

Walker could feel the sweat running down his back. Trudging through Bunhill Fields was like walking through the corridors of a stifling, claustrophobic nightmare.

Up ahead, they saw the bright lights of the vehicles parked at the entrance of the graveyard. Walker thought he could see three sets of headlights this time – the pickup and the Sprinter van he knew about but the other one? Was it the Audi with the woman and child in the back?

He thought about the tall Ghost, the one with the sword at his waist. Walker didn't want to see him again.

Staying off the path, they ducked behind the trunk of a large tree. Now they were just a short distance from the City Road exit, but still safely tucked out of sight.

Walker looked down towards the gate. There were about ten to fifteen Ghosts down there.

Carol was there too.

One of the Ghosts – a thickset man with pale white skin and tribal tattoos plastered over his arms and chest – had his arm locked around Carol's waist. He was pulling her towards the Sprinter van on the main road. Carol resisted, punching and kicking at his body and legs. The Ghost clamped a hand around her throat. As he squeezed, Carol gasped and closed her eyes. Her hands immediately went to her neck, trying to prise open the Ghost's fingers.

Walker felt sick to his stomach.

"Fuck," he said.

"Where's Charlie?" Barboza said. "I can't see him."

Walker looked into the huddle of Ghosts gathered at the entrance. Most of the masked figures were standing on the sidelines, watching Carol as she was led towards the back of the van. Much to Walker's dismay, the tall Ghost was there too. With the aid of torchlight and the car headlights coming into the graveyard from the road, Walker got a better look at the sword the tall Ghost was carrying. Walker was certain that he was looking at the graceful curved shape of a samurai sword.

"See him?" Barboza asked.

"I don't see Charlie," Walker said.

"Where the hell is he?" Barboza said. "What happened to him?"

They'd heard Carol yelling at Charlie to run. By the looks of it, that's exactly what the boy had done and not only that, he'd given the Ghosts the slip too. At least that's what they were hoping had happened. But how far could a little boy, alone and scared out his wits, go in this place?

The pale Ghost had by now dragged Carol to the back of the Sprinter van. She didn't stop fighting him but it was no use. He opened the door and Walker and Barboza watched as she was thrown inside. The Ghost slammed the van doors shut and walked back to the others.

"Shit," Barboza said. "She's in the van. How do we help her?"

But Walker didn't answer. He was trying to listen in on a conversation that was taking place between the tall Ghost with the police badge, and one of the others. They were speaking just loud enough for Walker to overhear if he strained his ears.

"The kid's still in here Captain," the other Ghost said. "And the other two, but they might be long gone by now. I think the boy's close though. Want me to take another look?"

The tall Ghost didn't answer at first. He seemed to be looking over the shoulder of the speaker. Although Walker couldn't see the man's eyes behind the mask, he knew they were moving back and forth across the burial ground. For a second, the tall Ghost looked at the tree that was shielding Walker and Barboza.

They both ducked their heads behind the trunk.

Walker didn't dare breathe. There was a moment's silence that seemed to last forever. Then finally, Walker heard the tall Ghost replying to the other one.

"We don't have time to waste in here," the Ghost said.

Walker poked his head out from behind the tree again. The tall Ghost was no longer staring in their direction, thank God. He had his back turned to Walker and Barboza, and he was talking to his men, speaking in a loud, deep voice that commanded their attention.

"Forget the other two," he said. "We might stumble across them somewhere else. But the boy's still in here and we'll get him now. You lot ship out, I'll grab him. I'll put him in the boot and meet you at the next stop. Got it?"

"You sure Captain?" the other Ghost said.

The tall Ghost nodded. "You lot move on – go on, get out of here. We've got a lot of stops to make tonight."

The rest of the Ghosts did what they were told. They filed out of Bunhill Fields and hurried back towards the pickup and Sprinter van parked out front.

"They're taking Carol away," Barboza said. She grabbed a hold of Walker's arm. "Shit Walker, if we don't do something now we've lost her for good. Are we going to help her or not?"

Deep down, Walker knew the answer. It wasn't pretty. It wasn't heroic either.

"What?" he said looking at Barboza. "You tell me what to do. What do you suggest? All my ideas for saving Carol end up with us getting thrown in the back of that van. Carol's gone. You think she'd come after us? No, and she'd be right to stay put. What was it she told us earlier Barboza? Don't try to be a hero. And what about Charlie? He's alone in here somewhere and that big fucker with the sword is about to go looking for him."

Barboza's brown eyes glistened in the darkness. Walker felt her pain, but he knew he was right. And she probably did too.

"I know," Walker said. "It sucks. I hate myself for saying it but the truth is we've lost Carol. But we *can* help Charlie. That's what she'd want us to do."

Outside the gate, the pickup and the Sprinter van pulled away from the kerb. They took off down City Road, travelling south to the next destination.

The Audi remained parked outside the gate The tall Ghost was now standing alone near the stone pillars at the entrance. Walker and Barboza watched from afar as he shone a torch into Bunhill Fields. The narrow strip of white light went back and forth, returning briefly to the tree where Walker and Barboza were hiding. Fortunately they saw it coming and ducked out of sight in time.

The torchlight lingered nearby for a second or two. Then it moved on.

Walker then heard the sound of footsteps, crunching over the dry grass. Looking out, he saw the Ghost walking off towards his right, off the main path.

"Are you ready?" Walker said. "We need to find Charlie before he does."

She nodded. "Ready?"

They stepped out from behind the tree, cutting along the grass that led towards the main path. From there, they followed the Ghost's route, moving deeper into the burial grounds. Deeper into the darkness.

After that, it was a guessing game.

They climbed over a short steel fence that led into a small plot of land, yet another one spilling over with ancient, broken headstones and long grass. They climbed over another fence, which brought them onto yet another path. They might as well have been walking through a labyrinth blindfolded.

Walker looked back and forth for any sign of movement. He was listening for the slightest sound to alert them to the Ghost's presence. But there was no sound, just an eerie silence permeating through the graveyard.

After a while, Walker was about to suggest to Barboza that they turn around and retrace their steps. He thought it wise to go back to the gate, to make sure the Ghost hadn't given them the slip. Just as he was about to say this, they heard a noise behind them, off the main path.

Heavy footsteps. Somebody was running, and it sounded like they were going back towards the City Road exit.

A child screamed.

"Charlie!" Barboza yelled. She took off, running in the direction of the noise.

Walker went after her. They were running through the dark graveyard, guided only by that lone scream and the sound of the tall Ghost thundering along the path. The Ghost must have known he was being followed. He must have waited for them to go past before trying to make a run for it.

Walker and Barboza threw all caution to the wind. They ran as hard as they could and to hell with the risk of running into a trap, toppling over gravestones, or running face first into one of the trees. They couldn't lose Charlie. To make matters worse, Walker had seen the tall Ghost running earlier and he knew how fast the man could move.

Against all odds however, they were gaining on him. Perhaps Charlie was fighting back and making it difficult for the Ghost to run fast enough. Maybe the boy was heavier than he looked. Whatever it was, the footsteps up ahead were getting louder. Seconds later, Walker could see the freakishly tall Ghost running at full speed over a stretch of long grass. He was taking giant strides, with Charlie scooped under his arm like the boy was a folded up rug.

The Ghost stormed onto the main path, about ten or fifteen metres ahead of Walker and Barboza. Now that he was back on the concrete, he took off, moving with the speed of a gazelle.

He was close to the gate. To the car.

"Walker!" Barboza yelled.

"I know," he said.

Walker's legs felt like lead poles weighing him down. He cursed himself for eating all that sugary crap earlier on. Now it was floating around his body, slowing him down. But he pushed through the urge to stop, drop onto his knees and puke all over the path. He could do that later. For now, he tightened his grip on the handle of the axe, which had never felt so heavy. He kept running, knowing that they didn't have to catch the Ghost in the cemetery – they just had to be close enough so he didn't have time to get in his car and drive away with Charlie.

They had to keep this chase on foot. Otherwise they'd lose the boy.

As Walker and Barboza ran down the path, they saw the Ghost standing at the entrance of Bunhill Fields. The man in the mask was looking at them. Walker could almost hear the debate raging in the Ghost's mind at that second. Did he have enough time to bundle the boy into the back of his car? Did he have enough time to get away before the two pursuers reached him?

Or should he stand and fight?

With Charlie tucked under his arm, the Ghost turned around and fled across the street, running away from the parked Audi and towards Wesley's Chapel.

Walker and Barboza didn't stop running. They charged down the path and with Bunhill Fields now at their back, they crossed over City Road, just as the unmistakeable figure of the tall Ghost could be seen hurtling past the open steel gate that led down the courtyard towards the chapel.

Walker's legs were almost completely numb. But somehow they kept moving – they carried him towards the chapel gate, just as a shrill explosion that sounded like smashing glass could be heard up ahead.

Walker and Barboza hurried past the gate, running down the cobbled courtyard that led towards the old Methodist building. The statue of John Wesley was nothing more than a passing blur.

As they approached the chapel, Walker noticed that one of the lower floor arched windows had been smashed. Glass fragments lay scattered on the ground, and jagged edges remained stuck in place around the frame itself – a warning to anyone who would dare enter.

"Careful," Barboza said, pointing at the window. "Don't cut yourself."

Walker nodded. Then he stepped over the fallen glass pieces and peered through the shattered window. It was dark inside but for a second, Walker thought he could see the faint glow of torchlight up ahead. He heard footsteps echoing along a hard surface.

Doing his best to avoid being pierced by the broken glass, Walker squeezed through the window and set foot into yet another blackness. As he went forwards, his axe was extended in front of him at all times, ready.

He heard Barboza climbing through the window frame.

"Oww!" she hissed.

"You okay?" he asked.

"Yep," she said. "Didn't take my own advice that's all."

"Let's go," Walker said. "Stay close to me."

Using their hands to guide them, they fumbled their way forwards into the chapel. Walker and his axe took the lead. Barboza stayed close behind him.

They continued into a large open space. Although Walker's eyes hadn't fully adjusted to the dark, he assumed they'd wandered into the main part of the chapel.

The only sound was their footsteps echoing off the walls.

"Sod this," Barboza whispered. "We need to find a light switch Walker. We could be walking into anything in here."

"I thought we were looking for Charlie," Walker said.

"Fat chance of finding him in here," Barboza said. "You never know, some of the lights might still work. I can see the stained glass windows up the front of the chapel. You see it? I think I see the pulpit too. C'mon, there's probably something down there on the walls. Look for a switch."

Walker grunted in agreement.

They continued down the aisle of the chapel, pressing their hands up against the wall, sliding them back and forth in search of some kind of light switch.

Walker heard a noise behind them – it sounded like someone groaning in pain on the other side of the chapel.

"Did you hear that?" he whispered.

"Yeah," Barboza said. "What was it?"

"Don't know," he said. "But I don't like the sound of it. C'mon, let's find that light switch fast."

They moved down the aisle, a little more urgency in their step. There were wooden pews on their right hand side, each row with a pull-out seat at the end, designed to provide extra seating. Walker put a hand out, touching each bench, letting them guide him on his way towards the pulpit area.

Walker knew he was supposed to be looking for a light switch. Truthfully however, he was thinking about the whooshing sound that samurai sword would make as it sliced through the darkness.

Fortunately, Barboza was committed to the task of bringing light. He heard her hands running up and down the walls, searching frantically for that elusive switch.

Finally, her efforts were rewarded.

"Found something," she said.

As she spoke, Walker heard that strange groaning sound, coming from further back in the chapel.

"What the hell is that?" Walker asked.

"It's the Ghost," she said. "What else can it be?"

"Hit the switch," Walker said. "Let's hope to God it works."

Walker heard a series of sharp clicking sounds as Barboza flicked several switches all at once. At first nothing happened but after a short delay, a white electric glow stuttered overhead. A single beam of light trickled down from one of several hanging light fixtures attached to the ceiling.

It was better than nothing.

Walker glanced at the interior of the chapel. There was a stunning single-tiered pulpit at the head of the room, in front of three massive stained glass windows with various displays of biblical imagery imprinted upon them. A small winding staircase led up to the pulpit and Walker could envision the ministers of old standing up there, delivering sermons to the worshippers with gusto. The upper level of the chapel was an oval shaped gallery that ran across the top of the room, several rows of raked seating offering spectators a view of the pulpit.

"Walker," Barboza said.

She was looking towards the back of the room.

Walker spun around.

The Ghost was standing at the back of the chapel. He had squeezed into the last row of pews, like a lone worshipper, waiting for the service to begin. Except that he wasn't entirely alone. Charlie was right there beside him, his big, frightened eyes staring at Walker and Barboza. The Ghost held the tip of the samurai sword against the boy's throat, the deadly steel pressed up tight on the soft skin. The

Ghost's arms, black, lean and muscular, were flexed and ready. With his free hand, the masked man covered Charlie's mouth.

It looked like the Ghost had been trying to slip away while Walker and Barboza searched the other side of the chapel.

Walker took a step towards them.

"Stay where you are," the Ghost said. The deep voice was calm and it reverberated off the walls and ceiling of Wesley's Chapel. "I'll cut his throat and do the same to both of you. But that's not what I want. Nobody has to die here, not if you play smart."

"Bullshit," Barboza said. "You fucking animal. You want us alive so you can put us in your farm."

Walker didn't think it was smart of Barboza to antagonise the Ghost. But he didn't say anything.

"That's not true," the Ghost said. "He doesn't have..."

The Ghost stopped in mid-sentence. He looked to his right, towards the side of the chapel that was still cloaked in darkness.

It was that noise again. That moaning sound, and they all heard it this time. It was spilling into the rest of the chapel, coming out of that dark corner.

There was something else too. It was the sound of clumsy movement.

There was a man coming out of the shadows. He staggered at first but when he saw the Ghost and Charlie, he picked up the pace. Next thing, he was running past one of the marble pillars that supported the upper floor gallery. He was so damaged and dishevelled that it was hard to tell his age but Walker guessed that he was about fifty years old. Maybe. The man didn't have any trousers or underwear on. He was completely naked except for a tattered denim shirt, unbuttoned from top to bottom, that clung to his blistered skin.

Walker had seen that crazed look in a man's eyes before. It was the same look he'd seen at the New River barely a week ago.

It was the look of a madman. A rogue.

It charged at the Ghost, groaning pitifully with hunger. It

reached its sunburned arms out, grasping for the tall man and the boy. There was a yearning look in its eyes.

The Ghost turned to face the rogue. With one arm, he removed the sword from Charlie's neck and pointed it towards the thing coming towards him. With his free hand, the Ghost kept a strong grip on the collar of Charlie's football shirt.

Walker saw his chance. He crept forwards, keeping his eyes on what was happening with the Ghost and the rogue.

The rogue screamed with excitement as it charged towards the Ghost. The Ghost finally let go of Charlie's collar and sidestepped to his right along the wooden pew, his samurai sword still pointing at the rogue. The Ghost was quick to get out of that enclosed space and the two cannibals met in the far aisle.

The rogue flung himself at the tall Ghost, like the sword wasn't there. The Ghost took a backwards step, sliding out of range of the rogue's outstretched arms. After that, it was no contest. The Ghost leapt forwards in a flash, his footwork exquisite, and the sword extended like a part of his arm. And even though the samurai sword is primarily a slashing and cutting weapon, the Ghost stabbed it straight through the rogue's heart with ease, like the madman was built of melting butter.

The rogue made a pitiful hacking sound as the Ghost twisted his sword deep into its heart. The Ghost then pulled his sword out and the rogue's body shuddered violently, before dropping to the ground.

During this short-lived fight, Walker had made good ground on the Ghost. He'd jumped over the third to last row of pews and squeezed along the wooden bench towards the opposite aisle where the action was taking place. As he came within range, Walker brought the axe crashing down on the Ghost's sword hand. He was aiming for the wrist but instead the axe landed hard on the handle of the sword, sending the blade flying out of the Ghost's hand. It landed several feet away, close to the body of the dead rogue, underneath which a small trail of blood was spreading across the chapel floor.

Walker brought the axe up again, aiming for the Ghost's chest.

But the Ghost was too quick. He leapt onto the back pew, jumping out of range so that Walker missed with his wild swing easily. Then the Ghost came forward and threw a hard punch that landed on Walker's shoulder. It was enough to jar Walker's rhythm and send him crashing backwards onto the hard floor.

Walker looked up. The Ghost was running over to his sword on the floor. Walker pushed himself upright, charging towards the Ghost, trying to intercept the masked man before he could pick up his bloodstained weapon. At the same time, Walker heard Barboza behind him, screaming at Charlie to make a run for it.

"Charlie!" she yelled. "Run! Come to me now."

The boy didn't move. Fear had paralysed him.

Walker bounded across the aisle, intercepting the Ghost before he could grab the sword. The Ghost, seeing that he'd been cut off, reached for Walker instead, using his long arms to seize control of Walker's right wrist – the one holding the axe. The Ghost proceeded to twist Walker's arm behind him, pushing it upwards towards his neck in an effort to either break his arm or make Walker surrender the axe.

Walker couldn't match the Ghost for strength. As his arm was being twisted backwards, he felt like a kids doll being tortured by a merciless child.

The Ghost leaned towards him, and another option opened up.

Walker stood tall, then slammed his forehead into the Ghost's face, *one-two-three* times. Each one of these 'Glasgow kisses' landed with a crack on the rubber surface of the mask, just above the canister. They were hard blows that sent the Ghost reeling backwards, groaning in pain. He let go of Walker's arm immediately and brought his hands to his face.

Walker went after him. But instead of hitting the Ghost with his axe and finishing him, something made Walker reach a hand towards the Ghost's face. Everything happened so fast. It felt like Walker was outside his body, watching somebody else's hand moving towards the Ghost in slow motion. Walker reached out, slid his fingers underneath the rubber, and grabbed the back of the mask. Then he pulled it off with as much force as he could muster.

The judges' wig came off with it. Walker tossed the wig and mask combo onto the floor. He wanted to see how frightening the man was, the ordinary man underneath the Halloween costume.

He took a step backwards and looked at the man's face.

Walker almost screamed.

He knew the face of the young black man standing in front of him – it was immediately familiar. It was so familiar that he didn't have to think or question it; this was a face he'd never forgotten over the past nine years.

It was the face of his old friend. It was Sumo Dave.

CHAPTER 17

Walker staggered backwards down the aisle.

His mind was racing, but he couldn't find the right words.

As he slowly backed off, he saw the confusion on the Ghost's face. He had to be wondering why Walker hadn't finished him off. Walker had the axe. The Ghost had nothing. But it was Walker on the retreat, looking like a man who'd just seen the Devil over the Ghost's shoulder.

The Ghost had to be wondering if it was some sort of trap.

But when nothing happened, the Ghost scrambled, dropping onto his hands and knees and crawling like a spider towards the sword on the floor. Grabbing the weapon, the Ghost leapt back to his feet and rushed along to the centre of the wooden pew where Charlie was still frozen to the spot. The Ghost grabbed Charlie and once again, put the sword to his neck.

They were back to where they started.

"Walker!" Barboza screamed at him. "Have you lost your mind?"

But Walker didn't answer. His eyes were fixed upon the sword. Upon the dark shadow of the blade reflecting onto the boy's pale skin. But he saw something else in that shadow – it was the face of his old friend, the man wielding that sword.

Walker halted his retreat. "I know you," he said.

The Ghost's dark eyes locked onto the man with the axe. "Do you?"

Walker stared back at the Ghost. Nothing else existed, nothing. He lowered his axe, dropping the weapon to his side.

"Sumo Dave," he said. "That's what we used to call you."

At last, Walker saw the human being in those black eyes. With two words, he'd reached deep into the man's soul and shook him violently there.

Walker could still see something of the boy he remembered. But there were more differences than similarities. Sumo Dave's hair was shaved down to the bone, much shorter than Walker recalled. The lankiness of his old friend was still evident, although now he wasn't skin and bones – he'd added lean muscle to his frame and it made him a formidable, athletic looking man. He must have been about 6'5 or 6'6 at least. He looked like a giant standing next to Charlie.

"Is this a trick?" the Ghost said. He was moving away from Walker, sidestepping towards the other aisle where Barboza was. He was taking Charlie with him.

Walker shook his head. "The last time we saw each other was at Piccadilly," he said. "We went there together, the four of us. You, me, Tegz and Hatchet."

The Ghost let out a quiet gasp. It was barely there, but Walker heard it.

"Mack?" Sumo Dave said. "Mack Walker, is that you?"

Walker nodded. "Aye."

With that, Sumo Dave's face broke into the most astonishing smile. The cool hatred, the vicious intensity – it evaporated, leaving a new man looking back at them.

"God help us," Sumo Dave said. Even his voice sounded different now, more like the boy Walker had once known. "I thought you were dead."

Walker shook his head. "I thought the same of you."

"Yeah?" Sumo Dave said. "I made it out of Piccadilly, only just mind."

"Tegz?" Walker asked.

Sumo Dave pressed his lips tightly together. He broke off eye contact with Walker. "No," he said. "He didn't make it."

Walker sighed heavily. "What happened?"

"He got trapped in the crowd," Sumo Dave said. "There were people running into us like it was the end of the world. It was hard staying on your feet, let alone figuring out an escape route. And if you fell, you weren't ever getting back up again. Well, Tegz was only a little bloke wasn't he? I saw him go down, just a few feet away from where I was. He called my name. Screamed it, like I'd never heard anyone scream before. Those people trampled over him like he wasn't there. Poor little sod."

"He was a good lad," Walker said. "I liked him."

"Yeah."

"What about you?" Walker asked. "How'd you get out?"

"I stayed on my feet," Sumo Dave said. "That was the key to staying alive that day – stay on your feet and keep moving. But I guess you know that as well as I do Mack."

Sumo Dave looked at Walker.

"I'll tell you something Mack," he said. "I had to do terrible things to survive that day. Like pushing other people out the way to make a path through the crowd. I'm sure some of those people must have died because of what I did. I'm talking about women and children too. But I don't regret it – I wasn't ready to die in 2011. Sixteen years old, both of us, eh? I was scared out of my bloody mind. Anyway, I got away from Piccadilly Circus. Somehow. I found an old office block nearby with the door smashed in. I ran inside, went all the way up to the top floor. Didn't stop until I couldn't get any higher. And I stayed there, me and a few others. Waiting for it to pass."

"I'm glad," Walker said. "I'm glad you made it."

"Thought you were dead for sure," Sumo Dave said. "You and Hatchet."

"I don't think Hatchet's dead," Walker said.

Sumo Dave lowered his sword. A little distance opened up between the blade and Charlie's throat. They'd reached the other aisle by now. They were standing directly opposite Walker, who was still on the other side of the pews. Barboza was in the same aisle as Sumo Dave and Charlie, standing about ten or fifteen feet away at most.

"Do you know where he is?" Sumo Dave asked Walker.

"Not yet," Walker said.

"Were you with him when it happened?" he said.

Walker nodded. "Sort of," he said. "Look, there's something you need to know about Hatchet."

"What?"

Walker hesitated. This was a conversation he thought he'd never have. Why did it feel like all the dark secrets of the city were his burden?

"Hatchet killed Chester George," Walker said.

Sumo Dave's face creased up into puzzled smile. "What?" he said.

"Hatchet killed him," Walker said. "I saw him do it. He got past the bodyguards and he was sitting on the steps of that fountain. Do you remember the gun? The one he used to always carry around with him?"

Sumo Dave nodded. "Yeah."

"He took it to Piccadilly," Walker said. "And he used it to shoot Chester George."

"No way," Sumo Dave said. "Why would Hatchet want to kill Chester George? Chester George was the man who was going to save us from our shitty lives."

"Phase Two," Walker said. "Do you remember that? The riots were Phase One. After the riots came civil disobedience – Phase Two. Chester George was trying to calm things down. He encouraged civil disobedience over looting and running wild. Hatchet hated that – I think he felt betrayed by Chester George. Hatchet wanted the chaos to last forever. And look what happened. He got his wish."

"I can't believe that," Sumo Dave said. "I won't."

"It's true," Walker said. "Everything that's happened since, it's all Hatchet's fault."

"Walker!"

Barboza was yelling at him from the other side of the chapel. "What the hell is going on here?" she said. "You know *him*?"

"Aye," Walker said, nodding. "I do."

He turned back to Sumo Dave, pointing a finger at Charlie.

"Will you let him go Sumo?" Walker said. "I don't know what the fuck happened to you man. I'm sure as hell not judging you, but Charlie, he's just a little boy. He doesn't deserve what you've got waiting for him down there in the Hole."

"Please," Barboza said, pleading with Sumo Dave. "Let him go."

Sumo Dave glanced down the aisle at Barboza. Walker didn't like what he saw in that brief exchange – in the dark eyes of his old friend. He watched as Sumo Dave brought the sword back up to Charlie's throat. The boy let out a quiet shriek as the cold steel pressed up against his neck.

"I'm sorry Mack," Sumo Dave said. "But that's not how it works. Not tonight."

Walker squeezed down on the axe handle. It felt like the knuckles on his right hand were about to burst through the skin. Was this really going to happen? Was he supposed to kill or be killed by Sumo Dave here tonight?

What other cruel tricks did the city have waiting for him?

Walker heard Charlie sobbing on the other side of the chapel, as if on cue. And to think, Charlie didn't know the worst of it – he didn't know what the bad men did to the people they threw into the back of their vans.

People like Carol.

Walker had the germ of an idea forming in his head. But for it to have any chance of working, he needed Charlie to be frightened.

Even more frightened.

"Sumo," Walker said, raising his voice. He pointed a finger at Charlie as he spoke. "Are you really going to do it? You're going to cut that little boy open and eat him?"

Charlie's eyes opened wide. The boy's mouth hung open, like he couldn't believe what Walker had just said.

"Walker," Barboza said, calling out to him. "Don't."

But Walker shook his head. "I'm sorry Charlie," he said, looking at the boy. "But you need to know what happens. This is what the bad men do – they take people away down to the Hole and they cut them open and eat them. Ain't that right Sumo?"

Sumo Dave glared at Walker. "You don't know much about it do you Mack?" he said.

"No?" Walker said. "You're not going to eat them? All those people you're putting in the back of the vans tonight?"

"Some of them *will* be used that way," Sumo Dave said. "You see we value our independence Mack. We don't kneel to our captors outside the walls like Michael King and his Bedlamites. Better to be ruthless than relying on the once a week scraps that you call Drop Parcels. Do you like being locked up mate? Do you like being somebody's pet dog? The Ghosts of London are as free as anyone in this shithole can hope to be. We take nothing that we can't take ourselves."

"What the fuck Sumo?" Walker said. "I saw you grab that woman and her little girl earlier. I saw you tying them up and throwing them into the back of your car. You're going to eat them? Because you're so free?"

"Don't mistake us for rogues," Sumo Dave said. "Not everyone ends up that way."

"What do you mean?" Walker said. "What do you do with the rest of them if you don't eat them all?"

"We build things," Sumo Dave said.

"You build things?" Walker said. "Like what?"

"Power," Sumo Dave said. "To put it simply, we build power. We establish control."

"What are you talking about?" Walker asked.

"There's no money in this city anymore Mack," Sumo Dave said. "But some form of currency is still required in order to buy and sell things. "

"Buy and sell what?" Barboza said, taking a step towards Sumo Dave and Charlie.

"Loyalty," Sumo Dave said. "Respect. Fear. The Ghosts are the most powerful gang in this city for a good reason. You know Mack, when I hid in that office building during Piccadilly – I met someone. There was this man, this great man, and he had a vision. It was like he knew what was going to happen to this city. He was already building the future in his mind. After we got out, I stuck with him and so did a lot of other people who recognised his genius. We didn't just wait around, hoping for the best. We didn't go begging for scraps or asking for our freedom at the M25. We knew that once the walls went up they wouldn't come back down. For us, it was all about moving forward. So we started to build."

"What are you talking about?" Walker said.

"We've built many relationships over the years," Sumo Dave said. "But it took a few years to realise that we needed some form of currency to properly take a hold of this city. And unfortunately, people are the only currency we have. People are food – yeah we don't deny it. The Ghosts can provide the rest of the gangs in the Hole with enough meat to keep them healthy and fed. We take care of all the dirty work – the hunting, the preparation, and they pay us with loyalty. And if they stay loyal, we can provide them with other things too – servants, women, men – whatever it is they want. You understand Mack? People are money. People are power."

"Slaves," Walker said. "You're talking about slaves."

"There are hard rules to surviving in this city Mack," Sumo Dave. "The rules are even harder if you want to *thrive*."

Walker pointed his axe at Sumo Dave. "Enough of this empire-building bullshit," he said.

He squeezed his way through the pews, walking towards the other aisle. Towards Sumo Dave and Charlie.

"Give me the boy Sumo," he said. "You think I'm okay with him being given to some gang in the Hole? Even if you don't turn him into meat, you think I'm okay with letting him become a slave or some twisted pervert's sex toy?"

"You're too soft Mack," Sumo Dave said. "It's a wonder you're still alive."

Sumo Dave pulled Charlie's head back, exposing the boy's pale white neck. He pushed harder with the sword – so hard that Walker expected to see a trickle of blood running down the boy's neck.

"Don't!" Barboza yelled at him. "Leave him alone."

"Don't make me kill him," Sumo Dave said, looking at Walker and Barboza. He kept one hand pinned over Charlie's chest while the other one gripped the handle of the sword. "I don't want to do it Mack, but I will. I didn't become a Captain in the Ghosts by having a weak stomach."

Walker stopped. He was standing in the middle of the pews.

As he stood there, Walker noticed where Sumo Dave's hand was positioned – the one without the sword. It was high up on the boy's chest, keeping Charlie locked in a tight grip. Walker thought about the plan that had come to him earlier. It was still a long shot, but it was all he had.

And it all depended on Charlie. Was he frightened? Was he brave enough?

Walker looked at the boy, trying to make eye contact with him. Charlie was opening and closing his eyes intermittently, like he was drifting in and out of consciousness.

"Charlie," Walker said.

At last, the boy looked at him. It was now or never.

"Remember what I told you in the graveyard?" Walker said.

Charlie didn't answer.

"Do what you have to do," Walker said.

There was a blank expression on Charlie's face.

"Charlie," Walker said. He barked out the boy's name like he was a Sergeant Major bawling at a hapless new recruit. "Remember what I said in the graveyard about the bad men. Do what you have to do."

Walker opened and closed his mouth in a snapping motion.

At last there was a glimmer of understanding in Charlie's eyes. He nodded briefly, then leaned forward, pushing back the tip of the sword with his neck.

It left just enough room.

Charlie bit down on the fingers of Sumo Dave's hand.

Sumo Dave didn't see it coming, not until it was too late. It was probably the surprise, rather than the pain itself, that forced him to release his grip on Charlie. And this time, Charlie wasn't hanging around. He took off, hurrying back down the aisle towards an ecstatic looking Barboza.

Walker was already racing towards the aisle where Sumo Dave was standing, shaking the pain out of his hand. When he was close enough, Walker swung his axe at the samurai sword. The axe came down upon the centre of the blade, making a loud clanging noise as it knocked the weapon out of Sumo Dave's hand for a second time.

Sumo Dave's face was a mask of incandescent rage. He was about to say something but Walker wasn't in the mood to talk. He charged forwards and kicked at Sumo Dave's midsection with the flat of his shoe. The kick landed on Sumo Dave's waist with enough force to knock him off his feet. He doubled over as he landed on the hard floor with a booming thud.

Walker didn't stop there. He hurried over to where Sumo Dave was still rolling about on the ground. The Ghost was grounded, possibly winded. He was helpless, and now Walker stood over him with his axe raised high, ready to finish the job. Sumo Dave looked up at Walker, knowing it was too late to fight back. Walker saw the humiliation and anger in the other man's eyes. But there was no plea for mercy.

Walker stood over him, the axe held aloft.

The two men stared into one another's eyes, communicating without words.

Walker took a step back and dropped the axe. Again, it was like someone or something bigger had taken over, stopping him from doing what had to be done. The axe fell to the ground with a thud and it sounded like the walls of the chapel were coming down.

Walker screamed with rage. He leapt at Sumo Dave, landing on top of the Ghost. He threw a volley of hard punches down on the man's head. Sumo Dave, still dazed from the fall, covered up at first. But it didn't take long before he began to fight back. He threw a series of long punches from the bottom. After that, he thrust his hips upwards, throwing Walker off him.

Walker fell backwards. From the ground, he heard Sumo Dave coming after him.

"Walker!" Barboza yelled. "Look out!"

He looked up and saw Sumo Dave rushing towards him. Walker jumped back to his feet. Immediately he felt a battering ram of a right hand slamming into his face.

Next thing he knew, he was the ground.

Something inside told him to get back to his feet again. To fight back. Walker got up and he charged at Sumo Dave, trying to wrap his arms around the bigger man's waist and wrestle him to the floor. But Sumo Dave was too big and strong and Walker realised too late that he wasn't going to have much success grappling with the bigger man. Sumo Dave stuffed the attempted takedown with ease and to make matters worse, he threw a barrage of slashing elbows to the top of Walker's head while Walker was doubled over and trying to tip him off balance. After several hard elbows, Walker dropped to the floor, his legs folding underneath him.

For a moment, the chapel was spinning around. It felt like the building had been lifted into the air by a violent tornado.

Walker was sitting on the ground. He looked up.

There was a blurry giant standing over him. Someone was

breathing heavily, like they were about to die. Was it the giant? Or was it him?

"Had enough?" Sumo Dave said.

But Walker wasn't done yet. He lunged at the bigger man, swinging with a whirlwind of wild punches, aiming at the blurry shape in front of him. The three blurry shapes in front of him. But he couldn't seem to hit the giant – not once. Still, Walker came forwards and continued to punch, connecting with nothing but air.

Sumo Dave countered with punches of his own, one to the head and one to the body. Walker felt like a wrecking ball was having its way with him.

"Walker!" Barboza yelled.

Her voice sounded distant.

Walker dropped onto one knee, like a prizefighter taking a ten-count. A voice in his head urged him back onto his feet, but he couldn't do it. His head was throbbing. His body felt broken. And damn it, he was thirsty.

"Why'd you give up the axe?" Sumo Dave said, standing over him. "To give me a chance? That's weakness Mack. Weakness is what will get you killed in London. A wise man once said that to me."

Walker heard someone rushing over beside him. He looked up and saw Barboza standing in front of him, her arms spread out, blocking Sumo Dave from getting any nearer.

"Get out the way Barboza," Walker said. "I'm going to break this lanky cannibal fucker's jaw if it's the last thing I do. It probably will be, but I'm going to do it anyway."

Barboza didn't move.

"Barboza," Walker said. "I said get out the..."

A noise outside the chapel cut Walker off in mid-sentence.

He turned his head towards the door. He listened to the noise and his heart sank as he realised what was happening.

There were cars on City Road. Several of them, and at that moment they were pulling up somewhere close to the chapel.

"Oh fuck," Barboza said, looking towards the door. She sounded like someone defeated. "Oh God, no."

Walker tried to get back to his feet, but his body was shutting down. Telling him to give it a break. There was no way around it – he wasn't going to be able to stop the Ghosts coming in. Neither was Barboza, neither was Charlie.

Why'd you give up the axe?

He heard voices on the street outside. Loud footsteps, making their way towards the chapel.

"Captain!" somebody yelled. "You in there Captain?"

Walker looked up. Sumo Dave was standing over him, staring down at Walker, like a giant standing over a mortal man.

Walker saw nothing comforting in those dark brown eyes.

"You shouldn't have come out tonight Mack," Sumo Dave said. "You should have gone to Station."

Outside, the Ghosts were getting closer.

Sumo Dave sighed. Then he glanced over his shoulder towards the door. After a long pause, he turned back to Walker. With a smile on his lips, he shook his head, much like a disapproving adult scolding a naughty child.

"Stay here," he said. "All of you. Don't go back out until the sun comes up."

Sumo Dave walked away without another word. He hurried over to where his sword was lying on the floor and picked it up, putting it back into the brown leather scabbard that hung from the belt around his waist.

After that, he hurried back down the aisle of the chapel, his Doc Martens slamming off the floor. Sumo Dave sidestepped along a row of wooden pews, stopping to pick up the mask and judges' wig on the floor of the other aisle. He put the mask on quickly, burying his face underneath the disguise.

Then he grabbed the dead rogue by the hair and dragged the fresh corpse behind him like it was a suitcase on wheels.

He walked towards the chapel exit.

"Sumo!" Walker called out to him.

Sumo Dave stopped and turned around. He tilted his head, like a confused dog.

But Walker didn't know what to say. He only knew that he should say something, but no words came out.

"Stay here," the Ghost Captain said. "Don't move. Don't talk until we've gone."

Sumo Dave disappeared out of sight, still dragging the dead rogue behind him, leaving a trail of smeared blood on the floor.

Walker heard the Ghosts gathering on the cobbled courtyard outside. It sounded like there was an entire platoon of them.

"Captain!" someone said. "Everything alright? We saw your car outside the graveyard but we couldn't find you anywhere. Thought something might have happened when you didn't show up at the next stop. Did you find the boy? Is he in there?"

"Little bastard gave me the slip," the Captain said. "I underestimated him. He must have met up with the other two somewhere. Did you find them?"

"Not yet," said the other Ghost. "One of the other units has probably grabbed them by now."

"Yeah," the Captain said.

"What about in there?" someone said. "Thought we heard something."

"Rogues," the Captain said. "Dirty bastards, riddled with disease just like this one. I took care of 'em. Chapel's clear except for a few stinking corpses."

"Want us to go in for another look?" one of the Ghosts said. "It's a big place, yeah? The boy might be hiding somewhere."

"Chapel's clear," the Captain said. "We've wasted enough time here as it is tonight. C'mon let's clear out."

"Yes Captain."

The footsteps receded, moving further away from Wesley's Chapel.

Inside the building, Walker, Barboza, and Charlie kept perfectly still.

CHAPTER 18

FreakySkandal.com – The Hottest Celebrity Gossip!

July 12th 2020

Excerpt from a clip posted to the FreakySkandal website at 10.59pm.

Rudyard Campbell, CEO of SKAM Media, is walking out of the front door of the exclusive Prime Craft Steakhouse in Birmingham's trendy South Side. Even amongst seasoned restaurant-goers, Prime Craft is notorious for its outrageous prices – a bone-in ribeye for example, will set customers back at least two hundred pounds.

Campbell steps onto the pavement, accompanied by several family members including his wife, three of his five grown up children, and a scattering of grandchildren aged between five and fourteen. The

Campbells are surrounded by several large bodyguards who are swiftly ushering them towards a black Rolls Royce Phantom 2020, which is waiting on the street with the engine still running.

At this point, one of Freaky Skandal's roving reporters – with his camera phone pointing towards the Campbell group – moves in.

FS REPORTER: Mr Campbell sir, a quick word please?

One of the bodyguards puts a hand out, blocking the reporter's path.

BODYGUARD: Make room please.

FS REPORTER: Just a quick word sir – we're broadcasting live to millions of people on the Freaky Skandal website. Also on our I-9 page, which has over three million followers.

Campbell looks over the bodyguard's shoulder at the reporter. The old man's leathery face looks uninterested.

RUDYARD CAMPBELL: Who did you say you're with?

FS REPORTER: Freaky Skandal sir. Home of the hottest celebrity gossip – we get millions of visitors to our website every day of the week.

RUDYARD CAMPBELL: Okay. What can I do for you?

FS REPORTER: Just wanted to get your thoughts on tonight's Big Chase sir? Have you been watching? Early indications suggest that SKAM are receiving even more complaints than last time.

RUDYARD CAMPBELL: Well I haven't really been watching – as you can see I've been out for a meal with my family tonight.

FS REPORTER: What do you say to the people who are complaining about tonight's Future of London broadcast? To those who call it sick exploitation?

RUDYARD CAMPBELL: (*Edging towards the parked car*) Well they've been saying that since the day we launched, haven't they?

FS REPORTER: But the Big Chase takes it to a whole new level. Don't you think sir?

RUDYARD CAMPBELL: (*Stops walking towards the car and turns to face the reporter*) No I don't. In fact, I would disagree strongly with anyone who thinks this is sick exploitation on our part. There is great importance in showing these events and specifically it's in regards to the ongoing RELEASE versus PRESERVE debate. Watching these people at their worst, this is crucial evidence for the PRESERVE campaign, don't you think? Can you imagine trying to rehabilitate these people into our society? People who have tasted flesh, who live in an environment devoid of law and order. We have no choice but to contain them. We have no choice but to watch and learn something new about ourselves, about the human condition – no matter how awful it is. That's the gift the people of London give to us every day.

FS REPORTER: I also wanted to ask about the recent rumours sir. The word is that mobile phones are going to be added to the Drop Parcels sometime soon. That some sort of contact is going to be made between people on either side of the M25. Is that true?

RUDYARD CAMPBELL: This is something that's being discussed right now. Certainly we're not monsters. We don't want to abandon these people entirely just because we can't rehabilitate them back into society. The phone drop idea has been mentioned but it's not like a regular cell phone where people make calls and texts back and forth. We're not going to be able to talk to these people. The idea is that we get them to send something back to us. We drop the phones, provide a number for them to send messages or photographs to their loved ones. To tell us *their* story. We're hoping to introduce this before the end of the year.

FS REPORTER: Do you think that will please the extremists sir? What do you think The Good and Honest Citizens will have to say about that?

Rudyard Campbell turns away from the reporter. He walks towards the open door of the waiting Rolls Royce Phantom and climbs inside. One of the bodyguards uses his massive bulk to block the reporter from getting any closer.

FS REPORTER: (*Yelling to Campbell*) Enjoy the rest of your evening sir.

CHAPTER 19

Walker felt like he'd been sitting on the chapel floor for hours. But it was probably no more than five minutes after he'd heard the Ghosts leave that Barboza came up behind him and threaded her arms under his armpits.

"What are you doing?" Walker said. His voice was groggy.

"Getting you back to your feet," she said. "What does it look like?"

Walker looked down and saw Barboza's hands clasped tightly together in the middle of his chest. She was pulling at him, encouraging him to get up off the floor. Tough love, they call it. Painful too. As Barboza tried to get him back into a standing position, sharp jolts of pain shot up and down Walker's body.

"Go easy will you?" he said.

Barboza stopped pulling. Gently, she sat him back down again.

"Sorry Walker," she said. "Just trying to keep you upright and awake. I don't want you to black out or anything like that."

Walker flopped back down into a seating position on the floor. The pain was bad but it felt superficial – cuts and bruises mostly. It didn't feel like anything had been broken and fingers crossed, there was no long-term damage. Sumo Dave had for the most part, landed his blows on Walker's arms and legs.

"I'm not going to black out," Walker said.

He got back to his feet by himself, refusing any assistance from Barboza. As he got up though, she stood beside him, her arm outstretched and on stand-by in case he needed it.

Walker stood in the aisle, his head swimming. It was going to take a few minutes for all the pieces to fit back together again.

"Bloody hell Walker," Barboza said. "He's your friend?"

"Aye," Walker said. "Well, sort of."

Barboza shook her head in disbelief. "With friends like that who needs enemies, eh?" she said.

Walker looked at her. "Are you kidding?" he said. "If he wasn't my friend, we'd be tied up in the back of one of those meat wagons right now. Destined to be food or slaves or God knows."

"Like Carol?" a voice said behind them.

Walker turned around.

Charlie was standing further down the aisle. The boy's skin was still a sickly pale colour, which only seemed to highlight the red welt on his neck where Sumo Dave had pressed the sword against his skin.

"What was that?" Walker asked.

"Carol's gone isn't she?" Charlie said. It was a question, but it sounded like he was telling them something.

"Aye," Walker said.

"I'm sorry Charlie," Barboza said. "But *you're* safe and that's what Carol wanted, more than anything else in the world I think."

Walker glanced up at the ceiling of the chapel. He scanned the edges and corners of the large room, the hanging lights – everything, searching for signs of anything unusual.

"Any cameras in here?" he said, whispering in Barboza's ear.

Barboza shook her head. "I doubt it," she said. "If there is, we just put on one hell of a show."

"What are we going to do?" Charlie said, cutting in. He seemed irritated that they were excluding him from the conversation.

"We stay here until sunrise," Walker said. "We get our heads down, turn off the lights and keep quiet. And when we wake up, it'll all be over."

"Yeah," Barboza said. She walked down the aisle towards Charlie and put an arm around his shoulder. Then gently, she guided him to the nearest bench.

"We're going to sleep here tonight," Barboza said, sitting down beside Charlie. "Then tomorrow morning we'll take you back to Station. We'll get you home, yeah? Just like we said we were going to do."

The boy nodded.

Walker stood in the aisle, watching them for a moment. He was thankful that Barboza was there because Walker wouldn't have known what to do with the kid. He'd had no experience whatsoever with children and up until he'd walked into Station earlier that day, he hadn't seen one of them in nine years.

"Let's find somewhere to sleep," he said, casting an eye around the chapel.

"Can we do something first?" Barboza said.

"What?"

For a second, Walker thought she was going to ask if they could pray.

"Check the front door's locked. Or at least that it's shut and wasn't left hanging open by your mate. That's a surefire way to tempt someone in off the street, and I don't want to see anyone else tonight."

"Aye, okay."

Walker limped slightly on his left leg as he made his way towards the door. The front door was locked – it didn't look like it had been touched. To his left, he saw a smear of dark liquid on the floor leading towards the broken window. Walker guessed that Sumo Dave had found the door locked and climbed back through the same window he'd used to enter the chapel. He must have pushed the corpse out ahead of him.

Walker peered through the broken window. The dark outline of Wesley's statue was visible in the middle of the courtyard. It was quiet out there now. Almost peaceful.

That's when it hit him – the realisation of what had happened. Sumo Dave, his old friend – he was alive. Walker should have been ecstatic. So why did it feel like he'd just discovered Sumo's corpse rotting up a London back alley?

Maybe it's because his friend was dead after all.

Walker stayed there for a while, looking out of the broken window and standing in the darkness. Time passed, but he wasn't counting.

When he eventually returned into the chapel, Barboza and Charlie had already found somewhere to sleep. They'd made their way upstairs to the oval gallery, out of reach of the horrors that had just taken place on the lower level. Walker found the wooden stairs that led up to the gallery and when he got there, he found Barboza setting down a couple of light brown tablecloths on the hard, narrow space in between the pews. Charlie was standing next to her, watching her do it.

"All good?" she asked, noticing Walker at the top of the stairs.

"The door's shut," Walker said. "Locked. Sumo Dave climbed out through the window."

"What about that rogue?" Barboza asked.

"I think he's still dead."

Barboza laughed. "Very funny smart arse," she said. "I mean, how do you think he got in? He was already in here before your mate smashed the window. Know what I mean?"

Walker sighed. "I don't know," he said. "Maybe he smashed a window round the back. Look, if anyone else was in here we'd have seen them by now. Right? We're only going to be here for a short while so let's try and get some sleep."

He looked at Barboza's handiwork on the floor. "Are we using tablecloths as bed sheets?"

"Got a problem with that?"

"Nope."

"Found 'em downstairs," Barboza said. "Had to take Charlie for a pee and I didn't want to take him outside. So he ended up using an old glass bottle that was sitting on the table downstairs. There were two tablecloths on it and one of 'em just happens to your bed for the night sir. Best we're going to get. Did you find any water?"

Walker shook his head. "Didn't even look. I'm too tired to drink."

"That's alright," Barboza said. "I think we can wait till morning, eh Charlie?"

"Yeah," the boy said.

Charlie walked over and dropped onto the floor where Barboza had laid the tablecloth down. Barboza lay down beside him, keeping one arm on the boy's shoulder.

"Sleep well," Walker said.

"Better get these lights out quick," Barboza said. "We've left them on too long as it is."

"Aye I know. I'll take care of it."

Walker limped back downstairs as quickly as he could and turned off the light switch next to the pulpit. The chapel was plunged into darkness. Apart from some minor bumps and a slight trip on the stairs, he got back up to the gallery without any major incidents.

Walker found the narrow space on the floor that was his bed for the night. With an exhausted groan, he lay down on the cool tablecloth and wriggled around on the hard surface, trying to get comfortable.

Fat chance. But it was better than being out there on the streets.

He heard Barboza breathing softly in the next row down. It sounded like she'd already drifted off into a deep sleep. The boy was snoring too – a soft whistling sound that Walker found oddly soothing and irritating at the same time.

For Walker, it was going to be a long night. He was sure of it.

How could he be expected to sleep with everything that had happened?

And yet it didn't take long until his eyelids grew heavy. He felt his head rolling back and forth on the thin strip of tablecloth that lay in between him and the floor.

The room was spinning again.

Walker fell into a deep sleep and thank God, he didn't dream.

CHAPTER 20

Daylight poured into the chapel. It came hard like a flood, gushing through the large stained glass windows that towered above the pulpit.

Walker put a hand to his face, shielding his eyes from the light. He lifted his head off the floor and looked to his right. There was no sign of Barboza and Charlie in the next row along. Their crude table-cloth bed was wrinkled and empty.

He sat up, trying to shake the sleep out of his head. Immediately, he felt a dull pain in his arms and legs but it wasn't as bad as it had been the night before. Looking down, he noticed some light yellowy-brown bruising scattered upon both arms. Along with the scratches the tiger had given him at the New River, his arms were marking up noticeably.

The aches and pains he could handle. His thirst was more of an immediate concern. Walker hadn't had a drink of water since they'd left Station yesterday evening and by now that felt like a lifetime ago.

He pushed himself onto his feet, dusting down his black t-shirt and jeans. His clothes stank of stale sweat and they were covered in dried dirt stains, a reminder of their time in Burnhill Fields. Walker tried to brush some of the dirt off with his hands but just like the memories, the dirt was imprinted upon him.

With a sigh, he walked downstairs. His movement was slow and laboured, like that of a man fifty years his senior. He trudged down the aisle, trying to avoid looking at the bloodstained floor where the rogue had dropped dead. But as he approached the door, Walker saw the thick trail of dark red smeared across the aisle where Sumo Dave had dragged the corpse towards the window.

The front door of the chapel was lying wide open. Walker could see Barboza and Charlie sitting on the front step outside, in between the double Greek-style columns on the building's exterior. Barboza and Charlie had their backs to Walker as he approached but he could tell they were soaking their faces in the morning sun.

Barboza must have heard his footsteps. She turned around and smiled at him.

"Morning," she said.

"Morning," Walker replied.

All things considering, Barboza and Charlie looked refreshed. Like it was just another day in the city of London and they couldn't wait to get started on whatever the world had planned for them. Last night was in the rear-view mirror; the terrible things that had happened still felt like a dream.

For now.

Walker sat down beside them, putting Charlie in the middle of the two adults. He closed his eyes and felt the heat touching his skin – a strange, almost cleansing sensation. From somewhere nearby, he could hear the birds chattering away to one another in the trees.

"It's a beautiful morning," Barboza said.

Walker nodded, then he looked at Charlie. "How's it going wee man?" he said. "Did you get any sleep?"

Charlie shrugged. "I had a dream about Carol," he said.

"Aye?" Walker said. He didn't want to hear about that dream. And upon closer inspection, he noticed that the boy's eyes were red and swollen, like he'd been crying for days.

Barboza pulled Charlie closer to her.

"So now what?" she asked, looking at Walker.

"We take him back to Station," Walker said.

"Back to the good guys," Charlie said.

"Back to the good guys," Walker repeated.

"And then what do we do?" Barboza said. "You and me."

Walker shrugged. "We go south," he said. "The plan remains the same."

There was a moment's silence.

"But that's where *they* came from," Barboza said. "You still want to go down there? After everything you saw last night?"

Walker scratched his chin, his fingernails working through the coarse stubble.

"Nothing's changed," he said.

Barboza looked at him. Occasional pockets of bronze skin shone through the dirt that clung to her face.

"Yeah," she said.

"Hatchet did this," Walker said. "He did all of it. He made the Ghosts, the rogues, the M25 and everything else in this city. He killed Charlie's mum, he locked you up in here with us, and he stole my parents from me. He destroyed Sumo Dave too – the person I knew. He has to pay for it all. He has to."

Walker looked at her.

"It's not your fight though," he said. "You can stay here, you know that. In Bedlam."

"Sure I can," Barboza whispered. "I'm the one who ruined your life. You were forced out of your home because of what I pretended to be. What kind of person would I be if I ditched you on the side of the road?"

"The smart kind," Walker said. "It wasn't you who forced me out of my home."

"Maybe," Barboza said. "Maybe not."

"Is there any water?" Walker asked.

"Yeah," she said. "There's a sink in that little house on the left."

Barboza pointed towards a small Georgian style house that was neatly tucked into the side of the large courtyard.

"We ran the tap and the water's still good," she said. "I think people have been stopping here, you know? Using this place like a hotel."

"Aye," Walker said. "Just like us."

"How you feeling anyway?" she asked. "No broken bones?"

Walker slowly got back to his feet.

"No broken bones," he said, starting towards the house.

Charlie stood up at the same time as Walker. Just as Walker felt older than his years that morning, Charlie looked like he'd abandoned the last pretence of childhood overnight. Walker saw a hardness forming in the boy's eyes. It would be the same for all other children behind the M25, who would be forced into premature adulthood.

"I want to go home," he said.

Charlie walked towards the gate. He didn't bother to check if Walker or Barboza were following.

They travelled south, towards Station.

Throughout the short journey, they kept to a steady if sluggish pace. All around them, the city was asleep and they were creeping past, trying not to wake her.

There was no one lingering on the street corners, no scratching man, and no man in the hat. The screeching tires and revving engines of the meat wagons were gone.

It was about fifteen minutes before they were back on Bishopsgate.

Just before they arrived at Station, a small convoy of five leather-clad riders rode out on Harley Davidsons to greet them. The motorbikes came roaring down the road in single file and as they came closer, the leader of the pack lifted his hand in the air, signalling something to the riders behind him.

The leader pulled into the side of the road. Upon seeing the signal, the bikers did likewise.

The leader – instantly recognisable as Fat Joseph – dismounted his bike and hurried over to the returning trio. There was a huge grin on his face. Behind Fat Joseph, Rhonda and some of the others remained sitting on their bikes at kerbside, but watching events with interest. Walker even thought he saw a glimmer of relief in Rhonda's eyes.

"What the bloody hell?" Fat Joseph called over to them. "You're alive?"

But when he got closer, Fat Joseph looked over their shoulders. He was quite clearly searching for the other person who'd been due to return with Charlie last night. Walker saw dismay creeping into the big man's eyes.

"Carol?" Fat Joseph said.

For a moment, nobody spoke. It was Charlie who broke the silence in the end.

"She's gone," he said. That was all he had to say.

Fat Joseph looked at the boy. His bottom lip trembled slightly and although he looked like he wanted to speak, he couldn't get the words out.

"We were trapped in Bunhill Fields," Barboza said. "We got split up from one another trying to get away from them, but the Ghosts caught up with Carol and Charlie. She gave herself up so that Charlie would have a chance of getting away. Walker and I found him and after that, we took refuge in Wesley's Chapel across the street. But it was too late to do anything for Carol. They were already gone."

Fat Joseph lifted a massive, chubby-fingered hand and he put it on Charlie's shoulder.

"C'mon," he said quietly. "Let's get you lot back to Station."

It was only a few minutes walk back to the old Liverpool Street Station. The bikes led the way, cruising down the middle of a road. Walker, Barboza and Charlie followed at the rear. Upon arrival, Fat

Joseph and the others parked their bikes on Bishopsgate. Then they led Walker, Barboza and Charlie through the entrance of Station and downstairs onto the concourse.

Station was packed with people, more so than the day before. These were the north Londoners who had taken up Michael King's offer of refuge. There were people everywhere – lying on mats, sleeping bags, coats and anything else that might have passed for a bed. He saw entire families huddled up together, and others sitting at the plastic tables and chairs, talking in small groups over light refreshments. It reminded Walker of photographs that he'd seen years ago in school – black and white images of people sitting on the platform of the London underground, which had been turned into temporary air raid shelters during World War Two.

Fat Joseph walked along the pathway that cut through the middle of Station. Many of the Bedlamites saw Charlie and cried out in delight. Others rushed over and embraced the boy as if he'd been gone for weeks. Walker saw them – every one of them – looking for Carol and he saw the heartbreak in their eyes, just like he'd seen it with Fat Joseph.

But nobody said anything.

There were smiles and handshakes aplenty for Walker and Barboza. But Walker knew and no doubt Barboza did too, that they'd failed in their task. They'd brought Charlie back safely but at the cost of another life. Walker felt dizzy with all the attention. Despite being exhausted, all he wanted to do was get out of Station and get back on the road.

By now, Fat Joseph had caught up with Michael King. After a brief discussion further along the path, Michael King approached Walker and the others.

"Thank God," he said, grabbing Walker by the hand and shaking it warmly. He did the same with Barboza. "You're okay."

"Carol's dead," Charlie said, looking up at the Bedlamite leader.

"Yes," Michael King said, kneeling down beside the boy. "Joseph told me she died saving your life. As your guardian, Carol would take great pride in knowing that she'd kept you from harm. Nobody will ever forget her Charlie. I promise."

"We're sorry," Barboza said. "There was nothing we could do."

Michael King gave Charlie a playful tap on the arm. Then he stood up straight, his leather trousers squeaking as they stretched.

"There's no need to apologise my friends," he said to Barboza. "I know what it's like out there when the Ghosts pay us a visit. You did what you have to do to survive. Carol would have understood that better than most and she knew the risks when she decided to accompany you to Old Street. Isn't that right Joseph?"

Fat Joseph sighed. "Yeah," he said.

"Did you get any sleep last night?" Michael King asked.

"A little," Walker said.

"The hotel next door is at your disposal. Sleep, eat, recover. We'll bring you food, drink – whatever you need. You brought Charlie back to us and we're in your debt."

"Thanks," Walker said. "We'll take you up on the offer of some food. But we should be heading south while it's still quiet out there."

"Are you sure?" Michael King said. "You're more than welcome to stay here in Station for as long as you want. Both of you. I mean it, we're in your debt."

"But it was my fault Charlie ran off," Barboza said.

"You were only trying to be kind to a broken-hearted little boy," Michael King said. "Nobody should be punished for that. Right Charlie?"

Charlie nodded. By now, the boy's eyes were almost shut. It looked like he was he was dead on his feet.

"Come on little man," Fat Joseph said, putting his shovel-like hands on Charlie's shoulders. "Let's get you cleaned up and get some food into you, yeah? Then you can sleep all day in the hotel." He looked at Walker and Barboza. "We'll be down there in the old chemist. Right hand side off the path. Come down if you change your mind about leaving. We'll get you some food and a room next door like Michael says."

Walker nodded. "Thanks Joseph."

"Cheers," Barboza said.

They watched as Fat Joseph led Charlie away. A moment later however, Charlie stopped and turned around. He looked back towards his new companions.

"Barboza?" he called out. "Walker. Are you coming with me?"

Barboza smiled, giving him a brief thumbs-up.

"See you in a bit," she said. "Go with Joseph."

The boy seemed satisfied. He grinned before being led away again by Fat Joseph.

Michael King watched them go.

"I hope Carol *is* dead," he said. There was no emotion in his voice. "The other possibilities don't bear thinking about. Tell me something my friends – was she alive when they took her?"

Barboza nodded. "She was."

Michael King cursed quietly to himself. Then he shook his head and smiled.

"I cannot thank you enough for bringing Charlie back to us," he said. "He's a good boy."

"You're welcome," Barboza said. "It was the least we could do."

Barboza looked at Walker. There was a strained look in her eyes, and he had the feeling she wanted to tell him something.

"Can you give us a moment please?" she said, turning to Michael King. "I just want to have a quick word with Walker."

Michael King nodded. "Of course," he said.

The Bedlamite retreated to an old shop space about ten feet back. No sooner had he arrived there than at least six or seven asylum seekers rushed over, eager to talk with him about something.

Barboza turned back to Walker. He was surprised and a little embarrassed when she lifted his hand into her own.

"I'm going to stay here," she said. "I'm going to stay with Charlie – I think he needs me more than you do."

Walker's heart sank a little at the news, even though deep down he'd been expecting it. And regardless of his feelings, it was the right thing to do. He'd seen the close bond that had developed between Barboza and Charlie in such a short space of time. Carol was gone, and there was an important role that needed to be filled.

It would get her off the streets too, away from the killing. Maybe she needed that most of all.

"Aye," Walker said, looking her straight in the eye. "I thought you might say that, sooner or later."

"I'm sorry Walker," she said. "I'm letting you down aren't I? I'm bailing out on you to stay here with the good guys. To stay safe. Guess that makes me a coward and disloyal, doesn't it?"

"You're a good soul Barboza," Walker said. "You don't belong out there."

"It's too real," Barboza said. "Soldiers and gangs trying to kill me. I'm just an actress for God's sake – not even that good an actress, not really. I came here to work, not to die."

"Not that good an actress?" Walker said. "You could have fooled me. You *did* fool me."

She smiled.

"When you're outside the M25," she said. "When you see London on TV every day and you know it's horrible, but it's okay 'cos it's not your problem. It's okay because you can switch the TV off if it all gets a little too real. You can close the laptop and put your phone in your pocket and forget about it. Until next time. And if you do that, London goes away. But it's not going away, not now. Not ever. I killed a man yesterday Walker."

Walker gave her hand a gentle squeeze. "You'll be fine here," he said. "Stay."

"But I owe you," Barboza said.

"You don't owe me anything," Walker said. "Remember? Hatchet owes me – he's the only one who does."

He let go of her hand. Then he looked over towards Michael King, who was being hounded by the asylum seekers. Walker caught his eye immediately. The Bedlamite winked at him, then said a few words, excusing himself to the people around him.

"Everything okay?" he asked.

"Aye," Walker said. "I could ask you the same thing."

"Oh," Michael King said, smiling. "My fan club? They just want to say thank you for letting them stay here last night. So they say it, over and over again."

He turned around and waved at the asylum seekers, all of who waved back.

"Look if it's still okay," Barboza said. "I'd like to take you up on your offer of staying here. I'd like to help Charlie, now that...well you know? He needs a guardian and we get on really well."

Michael King smiled as he offered an outstretched hand.

Barboza shook it.

"Charlie's very fond of you," Michael King said. "I can see it in his eyes. But what about your trip to the Hole? What about Hatchet?"

"I'll go on alone," Walker said.

"Supplies are being prepared for you my friend," Michael King said, turning to Walker. "Food, water, clean clothes and other things you might find useful."

"Thanks," Walker said. "I'll be heading off then."

"Yes of course," Michael King said. "But it'll take a short while to get these things together and to bring them down onto the concourse. We have ten minutes to spare at least. And that's good. Because there's something that I'd like you to see before you go. Something that you deserve to see, considering what you've been through."

Michael King looked at Barboza. "You should see this too, especially if you're going to be living here with us. "

Walker and Barboza exchanged confused glances.

"What is it?" Walker said. "What's this thing?"

Michael King smiled and it left Walker feeling uneasy.

"Come this way," Michael King said, gesturing towards the other end of the station. "Trust me, you'll be glad you did."

CHAPTER 21

Michael King led them down the concourse.

They walked past hundreds of people, lying or sitting scattered around the old shops on either side of the station. At the end of the concourse, Michael King took a sharp right, passing an old WH Smith that temporarily housed about fifty people, half of them sitting on the floor playing cards, using marbles instead of money prizes.

They travelled down a set of stairs, underneath a large sign that said 'Way Out'. At the bottom of the stairs, a long corridor led them to one of the station's other exits.

They stepped into the morning sunlight.

Walker saw they were on a small side street, about a minute's walk off Bishopsgate.

Michael King hadn't spoken during their short journey through Station. Now he led them back towards the main road, specifically to a massive red brick Victorian building that stood next to the train station. The lower section of the building was notably different than the rest of its red exterior – it was pale, stucco and stone with a design that looked classically inspired.

"Is this the hotel?" Walker asked. "*Your* hotel?"

"The same," Michael King said. It was a relief to hear him speak again after such a long silence. "This my friends, is casa de Bedlamites. If you like, think of Station as the office and this old place as home. Well, that's how I see it. C'mon, follow me."

They walked inside the building. Walker was immediately struck by the elegance of the interior and how well it had been preserved despite the passage of time. It was like stepping into a hip temple of serenity – something apart from the disaster that had befallen the rest of the city. It was clean and everything looked to be in order – so much so that Walker might very well have been setting foot inside a functional hotel beyond the M25. The lobby itself was quirky and stylish. There didn't seem to be any reception desk located in the foyer, just a variety of different items of trendy furniture – brown leather sofas, multi-coloured tables with stools. It looked like the perfect place for lounging.

But Michael King was in a hurry. He marched straight through the lobby, leading Walker and Barboza towards an elevator further inside the building.

"This was originally the Great Eastern Hotel," he said. "It opened back in 1884 and it was also built over the old Bethlem madhouse. In more recent times, the hotel was known as the Andaz – this was just a few years before the London riots took place. There are exactly 267 rooms in our hotel. We fit several people into most rooms although some of us – myself included – have a room to ourselves. A little reward we allow ourselves for the extra responsibilities we take on."

"And the lift still works?" Walker said. He was looking at the silver elevator doors up ahead.

"Yeah it does," Michael King said. "The Bedlamites are fortunate enough to have a lot of skilled people in our midst. We still have a few of 'em who understand things like electrical motors, braking system, cables – and who can ensure our safety in using such old-school technological wonders. Nothing to be afraid of here."

Michael King pushed the round button on the wall with the

arrow pointing upwards. Then he turned back to look at Walker and Barboza, a wicked smile on his lips. Moments later, the elevator pinged and the doors slid silently open. Walker felt increasingly uncomfortable but he followed Barboza, who stepped inside the lift behind Michael King.

Walker kept the axe ready at his side.

Michael King pressed the button for the first floor. Then he stepped away from the panel and nobody spoke as the elevator hummed upwards.

It was a short ride to the first floor.

The elevator doors slid open and Michael King led them out into a carpeted hallway. Walker and Barboza followed him down a narrow corridor, past the doors of numerous hotel rooms. About a minute later, they stopped outside a large pair of double doors at the end of another corridor. It looked like someone had used a catapult to launch a barrage of white paint cans at the doors. The paint had run down the wall, creating a chaotic, splattered effect that reached the floor. The Bedlamites had at some point, painted something over this sloppy white background – three words printed in bold letters, using red paint:

'THE SPOILS OF BATTLE'

Walker and Barboza kept their distance.

"What's going on?" Walker said. He pointed his axe towards the doors. "What's in there?"

Michael King turned around.

"Don't worry my friends," he said. "I assure you, you are in no danger here. There is something behind these doors that you should see – something you deserve to see as friends of Chester George. This is my favourite room in the entire hotel – my favourite room in the world. This is the Masonic Temple, otherwise known as the Grecian Temple when the hotel was up and running. This room is special. For years nobody knew it existed and it was only discovered by accident during a restoration when engineers noticed a few discrepancies with the blueprints. They found a forgotten chamber – a Masonic Temple, built in 1912. Isn't that remarkable?"

"How do you know all that stuff?" Barboza asked.

Michael King laughed. "Travel books mostly," he said. "Hotel guidebooks that I found in the remains of book shops and newsagents. I was curious about our new home and wanted to find out more about where we'd be living. Like if the hotel was haunted or not."

He laughed again, and still Walker felt uneasy.

"It's not important now," he said. "Are you ready to go inside?"

Michael King didn't wait for an answer. He turned around and with both hands, pulled the double doors open.

Walker and Barboza came forward, stepping inside the old Masonic Temple. Upon first glance, the room itself took Walker's breath away. It was indeed something special – a jewel of neoclassical luxury. It must have been an incredible moment when it was discovered again. The room looked like something out of a fantasy novel; the sort of place where a king or queen might easily be sitting on a golden throne and not look out of place. The checkerboard floor and pale walls were constructed of marble, as were the numerous columns that ran along the circumference of the room. There was a long, rectangular shaped space in the middle where Walker imagined the old Mason's table had once been. There were all sorts of other remarkable things: an organ, hand-carved chairs, and silver and bronze candelabras with clawed feet at the base. One of the most striking things of all was a blue and gold dome on the ceiling, displaying a five-pointed 'blazed star'.

But as lavish and eye-catching as it was, the Temple's fancy decor wasn't the most remarkable thing on display. Walker looked up at the ceiling and at last, he saw what they had been brought there to see.

He almost dropped his axe on the marble floor.

Barboza gasped.

"What the hell?" Walker said, looking up at the ceiling.

There was a wooden cage. It was suspended from the ceiling,

hanging on by a bronze chain that was connected to a steel hook fastened onto the centre of the blue and gold dome. It was like a giant birdcage, no more than six feet tall and three feet in width.

There was a woman inside the cage.

She was an older woman, perhaps in her fifties or early sixties, but it was hard to tell from so far away. Her hair was lank and long, falling all the way down her back. It was so dirty and dull that it was almost colourless. The woman's skin was greasy and covered in black grime; it looked like she'd been there, unwashed and untended for a long time.

The woman didn't acknowledge their entrance. She was sitting down with her back pressed up against the bars of the cage. Walker saw the thousand-yard stare on her face – her eyes blank and unfocused, pointing at the wall or something else on the other side of the room.

A thickset Bedlamite stood guard at the back of the room. He was dressed in black biker leathers and as the visitors entered the Masonic Temple, Walker spotted his eyes briefly looking their way and then returning back out front.

"What the fuck is this?" Walker said.

"The spoils of battle," Michael King said, looking up towards the cage.

"Who is she?" Barboza said, her voice little more than a whisper. Her eyes were wide open, puzzled and frightened.

"She's the grand prize," Michael King said. "Look Walker. Don't you recognise her?"

Michael King was grinning, but his eyes were ablaze with contempt.

"You must remember Sadie Hobbs," he said.

Walker looked up at the dishevelled shape that was trapped behind the wooden bars. He felt his jaw drop open.

"I remember," he said.

Sadie Hobbs. The woman who'd fought against Chester George and The Good and Honest Citizens in 2011. At the height of the

London riots, she'd written anti-Chester George articles in newspapers, rallied against him on social media, and appeared several times on television speaking out against him.

And she'd been there that day. Piccadilly. Sadie Hobbs had marched into Central London with thousands of followers, gathering on the outskirts of Piccadilly Circus. She'd stood at the head of her people, who were being contained by the armed forces and police. That was the last Walker had ever heard of Sadie Hobbs.

Until now.

"How did you find her?" Walker said.

"It took a while," Michael King said. "She was a real slippery little snake. But I was always looking for her. *Always*. Somehow I knew that she'd survived the sinking ship – I just knew it. Eventually I pinned her down in the old West End. We got word out and she was flushed out of a lovely little house in Chelsea with some of her friends."

"How long has she been here?" Barboza asked.

"Five years now," Michael said. "My Sadie. She's my most treasured possession in the entire world. This is Hell for her you know – living alone in a cage like that. Nobody sees her, nobody hears her but us. Her thoughts and opinions don't mean shit anymore. All that attention and everything she used to feed off? She gets none of it. She's my little pet, and she only ever gets out to eat, piss and shit on my say-so. And that's how it's going to be right up until the day she drops off her perch for good."

Barboza's hand was cupped over her mouth.

"How can you do this to someone?" she said. "To anyone? Put them in a cage for five or six years!"

"It's beautiful isn't it?" Michael King said. "And it sends out a message to all the other gangs in Bedlam. To all the people who would try and hurt me or take what I have. It shows them that there's nothing I won't do to hurt my enemy."

"I've seen enough," Walker said, tearing his eyes away from the cage. "It's time to go."

"Your supplies should be ready by now," Michael King said. He didn't even look at Walker as he spoke. He was still staring up at the cage, his eyes gleaming with twisted joy. "They'll be waiting for you at the main entrance."

Michael King raised his hand, like he was waving goodbye.

"You guys take off," he said. "I'm going to stay here for a little longer. You'll come back Walker, I hope. And tell me about Hatchet's slow and painful death."

At last, Michael King turned to Walker.

"Of course," he said. "You could always bring him to me alive. Let me take care of him for you. And for Chester."

But Walker didn't respond. He turned around, as did Barboza, and they both hurried out the door of the Temple, back out into the hallway. But they didn't stop or slow down there. They kept going until they'd reached the elevator further down the corridor. Walker – who was finding it hard to breathe – hit the button but when it didn't ping right away, he decided to take the stairs instead.

They ran down the stairs, rushing through the lobby. Nobody looked over their shoulder on the way out.

Barboza eventually stopped outside the hotel door. She turned around and stared at Walker, leaning onto the wall for support. She looked like she was about to throw up all over the pavement.

"Jesus," she said, gasping for breath. "What *was* that?"

Walker seized her gently by the arm. "Are you okay?"

"Was he deliberately trying to frighten us?" Barboza said, ignoring Walker's question. "Or was he actually bragging to us about having a woman trapped in a cage, hanging from the roof of his hotel?"

"Listen Barboza," Walker said. Now it was his turn to ignore a question. "Maybe you shouldn't stay here after all. You know?"

But there was a defiant look in Barboza's eye.

"I'm staying," she said. "But I'm staying for Charlie, not Michael King or the fucking Bedlamites. I don't give a shit about any of them, not if they know what he's got up there in that hotel. His *prize*."

"Are you sure?" Walker said.

"Maybe I can help her," Barboza said, glancing towards the upper floors of the hotel. "It's worth a try."

Walker shook his head. "You saw the look in his eyes," he said. "The best thing you can do for Sadie Hobbs is to put her out of her misery. But if you do that, you might be the one taking her place. Leave it alone Barboza."

"No Walker," she said, still with that defiant look in her eyes. "I don't think I can."

Ten minutes later, Walker and Barboza were standing on Bishopsgate. After coming out of the hotel and going back into Station to pick up his supplies, Walker had come out with a change of clothes, consisting of a fresh black t-shirt and a pair of khaki hiking trousers that were a lot more comfortable to walk in than his dad's old jeans. A large sports bag was draped over his shoulder, carrying enough supplies to get him over the Thames and into the Hole.

His axe was hanging by his side, as always.

Barboza was standing in front of him. She was smiling, but Walker thought he saw a hint of sadness in her dark brown eyes.

"You're going to make me a promise Walker," she said.

"Am I?" he said.

"Yeah. You're going to promise to come back to me. Can you do that?"

Walker tried to think of the right thing to say. Something reassuring, that wasn't an outright lie. "I'll try," he said. "I promise that much."

He extended his hand towards her. He'd thought about pulling her into an embrace – that's what he wanted to do – but something inside was holding him back. How long had he known Barboza? Had it even been a week yet? The weird thing was that after Alba, his feline companion on Stanmore Road, Barboza was the closest thing to family he'd had over the past nine years.

It was a sobering thought.

She took his hand and they shook.

"You be careful," he said to her. "I'm not so sure you're staying with the good guys after all. Know what I mean?"

"Yeah," she said. "Hey, what if you're the only good guy left in London?"

Walker broke off the handshake.

"I killed a rogue last week Barboza," she said. "And I can't even remember what the filthy bastard looked like. Yesterday I killed a soldier in my mum and dad's house – I stuck the axe in him like he was a chunk of firewood. Like he was nothing. His face is disappearing too. Does that sound like a good guy to you?"

Barboza looked away. "I'll never forget the face of the one I killed," she said.

"I know," Walker said. "And that's why you're staying here."

Barboza smiled. She leaned forward and stole a kiss on Walker's cheek. Like her handshake, the kiss was warm and soft against his skin. Then she turned back towards Station and walked over to the entrance like she was in a hurry to be gone.

"Remember your promise Walker," she called back to him. "Come back to me."

He watched her disappear through the entrance of the old Liverpool Street Station, leaving him standing alone on the sun-drenched road.

"Aye," he said.

THE END

DEAR READER,

Dear Reader,

Mack Walker is closer than ever to his revenge…

But where is Hatchet?

If things are bad in North London, how will Walker survive in the South, aka The Hole?

Sleeping Giants (Book 4) is 'a darker shade of madness than the first three.'

Blood must be spilled.

How far is Walker willing to go for revenge?

If you've enjoyed The Future of London series so far, don't miss out on **Sleeping Giants**.

'This dystopian story keeps getting better.'

Get it now!

ALSO BY MARK GILLESPIE

Sleeping Giants (Future of London #4)

Kojiro vs. The Vampire People (Future of London #5)

Black Storm

(The Exterminators Trilogy #1)

Black Fever

(The Exterminators Trilogy #2)

Black Earth

(The Exterminators Trilogy #3)

For more info on the books (plus mailing list details - No Spam Guaranteed!) visit:

www.markgillespieauthor.com/books

30420039R00404

Printed in Poland
by Amazon Fulfillment
Poland Sp. z o.o., Wrocław